# Dragon Fate

# DRAGON FATE

## WAR OF THE BLADES: BOOK ONE

J.D. Hallowell

SMITHCRAFT PRESS

Smithcraft Press
1921 Michels Drive NE
Palm Bay, FL 32905

SmithcraftPress.com

ISBN 978-0-9793935-9-4

# DEDICATION

DRAGON FATE is dedicated to my family, especially my wife, Jennie, my son, Connor, and my daughter, Rashel, for giving me the motivation to write this in the first place, and the encouragement to continue once I'd started.

# Acknowledgements

I WOULD LIKE TO thank everyone who has been involved in the process of bringing this to publication, particularly Craig R. Smith of Smithcraft Press for his incredible design work and his saintly patience; my son, Connor, and my wife, Jennie, for their discussions, critiques, and assistance with editing and proofing; and my brother Jim and my niece Kimberly for their comments and encouragement through the process.

# CONTENTS

# PROLOGUE

THE OLD MAN knelt by the sticks he had arranged for his fire. His hair had once been black: now even the gray had gone, and it was entirely white. He looked to be in his mid-seventies, but in fact, he was far older. He carried no flint, but he didn't need it. He concentrated on the sticks. At first they smoked a little, and then a small flame burst into view. Soon the little fire was crackling merrily, and he placed the petite kettle close enough to heat the water inside.

Suddenly there was a voice in his head that was nearly a scream: *"You're surrounded, Love; I don't know how they got so close, but I am coming!"*

The old man stood and drew his saber. The blade looked like it was made of some type of ceramic, and gleamed dully in the late afternoon sun. He heard the noise of a bowstring behind him and started to turn to face the threat while trying to get a magical shield up, but he was too late. He felt a searing pain in his low back as a small, wicked, rough-fletched arrow pierced him just above the hip, and he fell to his knees. He could feel the poison on the arrow already beginning to work its way through his body.

At the same instant four Roracks, or beast-men, charged out from the trees. Their hide ranged in color from black to dark brown, and looked rough, like tree bark. They blended with their surroundings well. Their faces were vaguely man-like but distorted. Their noses were broad, flat, and crooked. Their thin lips were pulled back in fierce snarls showing jagged teeth. Two of them carried swords, but those were old, worn, and rusted almost beyond use. The others simply carried clubs. The one who had shot him stepped into view and made some noises in a strange, guttural language. They all looked to that one and answered with a quick sort of bark without breaking their stride.

As all of that was happening, there was a deafening roar, and a huge dragon landed, crushing two of the beast-men outright. The dragon turned quickly and killed the beast-man closest to the old man and then turned on the one with the small bow still clutched in its hands. The leader of the Roracks tried to fire an arrow at the dragon, but never got the chance; she simply grabbed him by the head and squeezed so hard that the skull breaking was clearly audible. The last of them tried to run, but the dragon jumped and closed the distance before he got three steps.

She turned to the old man and said, "Quickly, Love, there are more of them coming. We must go. Now!"

The old man shook his head weakly, "I'm too far gone already, Love. So cold . . . that arrow was poisoned . . . can't feel my hands or feet."

"You have to get up. We can't stay. There are a score of these foul creatures coming. They will be here very soon, and we won't have the element of surprise this time. Please, Love, come with me!" The dragon was crying and the tears were falling on her Bond-mate's face.

He simply shook his head sadly, "We both knew this would happen eventually, one way or the other. We can't live forever."

"No!" she roared as if she could use the sheer volume of her voice to stop the inevitable. "I won't leave you!"

"You have to. You carry hope. Everything we do is for the next generation. You have to go . . . protect the eggs you are carrying."

His breath was rapid and shallow, and he couldn't last. The dragon wanted to deny that he would actually die, but knew it was happening, and there was nothing she could do. She tried to call enough magic to stop the poison, but it had spread so fast that it was no use.

"Your kind . . . believe we come back again . . . always wanted to believe that, too . . . maybe . . . see you again. . . ." He closed his eyes and was quiet so long she thought that perhaps he had passed, but he opened his eyes again and said, "Go . . . now . . . before more come . . . you must live for the young . . . always love you. . . ."

He closed his eyes for the last time. She knew he was gone and that she could do nothing for him. Just as more beast-men broke into the clearing, she launched herself skyward and roared so loud that the creatures in the lead fell on the ground holding their ears. She flew high, and then, unable to think past her grief, she headed north over the mountains with no clear destination in mind, instinctively heading for more familiar territory.

# CHAPTER 1

DELNO STOOD OVERLOOKING a waterfall several miles from his home in the city of Larimar, the capital of Corice. After escaping the city, it had taken him all morning to get to the base of the small cliff over which the river that was the life's blood of Larimar flowed. He hated that he had to run away like this, but given his circumstances, he saw no choice.

It had taken him most of the afternoon to climb to this vantage point, where he was certain no one could find him. He was good at climbing, even though he was afraid of heights. In fact, climbing was one of the few things he seemed to be really good at: that, and finding things. He wasn't sure how he found things. It was a talent, like knowing instinctively where to find hand and foot holds while climbing. Perhaps, he thought, the two were related talents. Of course, if that were the case, he reasoned, then he really couldn't even lay claim to being a good climber.

He hated it when his thoughts turned so morose, but, like the rest of his life, he seemed to have no control over such things. He was twenty-seven and should be a journeyman at a career by now. Instead, he had never been good enough at any of the things he tried to become better than an advanced apprentice. He'd tried many different jobs. His father had attempted to make a carpenter out of him. He wasn't bad at it, but it didn't hold his interest. He liked the wood well enough; the look of it, the feel of it, and he could appreciate a well-finished project. He just preferred to appreciate it after someone else had finished it.

His mother was a baker and cook. She had taught him her skills as well. He could certainly cook better than most people, and he enjoyed preparing a good meal for friends now and again, but slaving away in a hot kitchen all day was not something he wanted to spend the rest of his life doing.

He'd even tried being a musician. Oh, his voice wasn't bad at all, ranging from a quite passable baritone to a rather pleasant tenor, and he could control it fairly well. However, while he could certainly entertain a group at a gathering or party, the music didn't stir him to the point of wanting to spend the hours every day it took to practice to become good enough to be a court entertainer. That would mean that he would be relegated to being a traveling troubadour. While traveling wouldn't necessarily be a bad thing, singing every night in taverns for tips and meals didn't exactly appeal to him, though it was beginning to look as though that might be the position he would be forced into.

He had even tried soldiering. He had been twenty-three when he enlisted, and while that didn't seem like such an advanced age to him, most of the young men in town who had reached their twenty-third birthdays were at least advanced apprentices if not journeymen in their chosen endeavors. So, since he was being pressured by both family and friends to do something, and Corice was at peace, he had joined the army. The physical training was difficult, but he rather enjoyed the activity. It left him little time at the end of each day to do much more than clean his gear and fall exhausted into his bunk. That was fine for the first six months. He'd even done so well that he had been promoted to corporal; quite a feat in the peacetime army. His sergeant had said he had leadership abilities and would do well with a military career.

The problem came when a neighboring kingdom decided to expand into Corice's territory. Bourne, the kingdom to the north, attacked an outpost without warning. Corice had no choice other than to retake the outpost. Delno's company was moved north to the fighting.

It was a bitter war that had lasted nearly two years. In the end, both kingdoms had depleted their resources and the lines on the map had remained as before. A treaty was signed and the fighting stopped. The only ones who had seemed to reap any real benefit were the vultures, both human and avian. The avian variety couldn't be blamed for only doing what nature had designed them to do; the human versions were detestable.

During the war Delno had distinguished himself many times in combat. What he was especially known for had been the Battle of Stone Bridge. It got its name because it was a natural stone bridge that spanned a chasm on the border between Bourne and Corice, and was a narrow point on the main route for troops and supplies heading south. Recognizing that taking possession of that bridge would greatly hamper Bourne's ability to re-supply their troops on this side of the border, the Corisian commanding general ordered the bridge to be captured and held. The problem was he had only sent one company of two hundred men to do it.

Delno's company had been given the job. What they didn't know was that Bourne had dispatched a large number of new recruits to cross the bridge and join the Bournese troops already in Corice. It was simple chance that put the two forces in the same place at the same time.

The Bournese weren't stupid; their archers had targeted the officers and senior non-commissioned officers first. In the end, Delno, by then a sergeant, had ended up holding the bridge with less then fifty seasoned veterans against a force of over six hundred untested recruits. The only reason they weren't all killed was that once the Bournese had run out of arrows they had been reduced to charging the Corisians, but they couldn't do so in overwhelming numbers because of the narrowness of the bridge itself. Experience and the Corisian training regimen, which was big on stamina, won out; the Corisians simply cut them down as the Bournese came on six at a time. Eventually, their force nearly destroyed, those Bournese who remained alive, less than two hundred, retreated back to their side of the bridge. The battle had started midmorning; by late afternoon over six hundred men total from both sides lay dead or dying.

Fortunately, the first reinforcements to arrive were Corisian. It had been a pivotal battle and so disrupted the Bournese supply lines that it was the main reason that Bourne agreed to cease hostilities and work out a treaty.

By the time war was over, Delno had been promoted to lieutenant for his leadership abilities and his bravery. That left him with little prospect of further promotion, though, since he wasn't of noble birth, which meant he had no real future in the army. The other officers, all nobles themselves, wouldn't accept him, even with his rank and a Corisian medal of valor (the highest award for bravery the Corisian army could bestow on any soldier). Because of his common birth, he wasn't really considered one of them, but because of his rank, he wasn't accepted by the common soldiers, either. Alone in the midst of hundreds of men, he did his best to complete his duties until his four-year term of enlistment ended.

While his medal had earned him a small pension, he was loath to try and live on that alone. He would eventually like to consider settling down and having a family, but the pension certainly wasn't enough to support a wife and raise children on: thus his need to climb the cliff and find a good place to sit and think away from other distractions.

His best friend, Nassari, who was two years older than he, had done quite well for himself in Larimar in the field of politics. Nassari had offered to help him work his own way into the political system, saying that with his war record and the right political advisor, he could do well. When Delno pointed out that he was no politician, Nassari simply said that he could easily learn.

In Corice there were two ways to earn the right to vote and participate in politics. Even being born a noble didn't guarantee that privilege. The first way, since the kingdom always needed money, was to pay enough tribute to the crown to be considered worthy of the honor, and since most business men and women wanted a say in how the capital city was run and what taxes were levied, they found the funds to do so. The second way of earning a say in politics was through service, either in the military or some other government work. While he had only served four years instead of the required eight, his promotion to lieutenant and earning the Medal of Valor entitled Delno to that right also since it could be awarded for some special, one time service to the kingdom: such an award was rare, though, because often such spectacular acts were dangerous enough that the person doing them was given his or her award posthumously.

Nassari had assured him that with Nassari's help and the fact that many men who had acquired political rights through military service would vote for him, he would be a sure winner for the next seat on city council to come open. It all sounded good: in fact, it sounded much too good. Just because Nassari was Delno's best friend, and a good man for the most part, didn't mean that he could be trusted in this matter. Delno had no doubt that Nassari could be trusted as long as Nassari's own interests didn't conflict with his: if a conflict arose, Nassari could be trusted only to do what was best for himself and everyone else could swing in the wind.

While trying to look at the different angles of his situation, Delno slowly became aware of a sound that seemed, at first, to be more felt than heard. He tried to ignore it and go back to his own thoughts, but the sound wouldn't go away. There was something familiar about it. It took a few more moments to realize it was the low moaning of someone who was in obvious distress.

As puzzling as it was to find another person way up here, he had never been one to ignore the sufferings of others, so he rose and began moving toward the source of the sound. As he stepped into a clearing, he found himself face to face with a huge, somewhat reptilian-looking head. The head, bigger than his whole torso, was snarling and showing a large number of very impressive teeth. Then he noticed that the head was attached to a longish sinewy neck which joined to the rest of a body of a . . . DRAGON!!!

# CHAPTER 2

THE FIRST THOUGHT to flash into Delno's mind was that the dragon would be the last thing he ever saw. It was obviously in pain and, from the snarl, dangerous. His second thought was that he wouldn't have to make a decision and possibly alienate his friend Nassari. He stood motionless, waiting for the dragon to strike. "*At least,*" he thought, "*with those teeth, it will be quick.*"

The dragon seemed to be considering its next move carefully. While Delno was sure that only a few scant seconds had actually elapsed, it seemed as though he had been standing in that gaze for hours.

Finally, the dragon said in a snarling voice, "What do you want here, human?"

Delno was taken aback: he had heard tales of dragons actually talking to people, but he had never believed them. In fact, until just a few seconds ago, he hadn't been sure if he actually believed in dragons at all. Tales told of dragon riders in the southern lands, and a few people claimed that there were actually some wild dragons in the east, but no one he had ever met had actually seen one.

The dragon made a low growling noise and said, "Well, human, I'm waiting for your answer. What do you want here?"

Without thinking, Delno stated his most fervent desire "Merely to live through this encounter, if you please . . . my lady." He added the title as almost an after thought, but it seemed appropriate, as he realized from the way her voice resonated that she was indeed female.

"If you wish to live, then why did you intrude on my solitude?" the dragon asked.

"I didn't mean to intrude," he said, hoping the dragon would accept his apology, "I thought I heard someone in distress and came to offer what assistance I could."

The dragon considered his words for a moment, then, after looking him over as if she recognized him from some former meeting, she said, "Since you meant no harm and have been polite, I will give you what you said it is that you want and not kill you. Go quickly."

Delno, although confused by the dragon's reaction to him, was so relieved that he almost fell as he released the tension from his legs. As he turned to leave, the dragon moaned again, in obvious pain. He spun back around to her and said, "You *are* in distress; is there something I can do to help? I could run and fetch a healer, though it will take time to find one and return."

The dragon eyed him curiously. Then he felt something on the edge of his consciousness. It wasn't physically discomforting, but he felt as though he were being watched through a window while naked. After a moment, the dragon actually smiled and said, "You really are offering aid as a simple act of kindness." Then another spasm wracked her, and it was a moment before she could continue. "Even if you could find a healer willing to come, it would be too late by the time you could return." Then, in a much gentler voice, she added, "You are very kind to offer though; most of your species would simply have run away when the opportunity presented itself."

While he didn't fully understand why, he pressed the point, "There must be something I can do to help you." If he happened on a dying beast, he would put it out of its misery. The dragon, however, was not just a beast. "You are obviously an intelligent being with feelings. It would be criminal, or at least immoral, to just leave you to your fate without trying to help."

Again the dragon smiled. "If we are not careful, human," she said, "I might grow to like you. I don't think there is much that can be done for me now; you should go."

Delno stood there unwilling to leave. "If nothing else, you deserve to have someone to comfort you until the end; I will stay if you will permit it." On impulse he reached out a hand and touched the dragon tenderly on the snout.

The dragon was moved to tears by his simple kindness. "A rider would do as much, but most humans fear dragons, and it is not uncommon for humans to hate what they fear. Perhaps I can tell you my story, so that someone will remember me and who I was, and I do take some comfort in your presence." Then, more to herself than to him, she said almost in a whisper, "There is something about you. . . ."

"Then I will listen and give what comfort I can," he responded gently.

"I am a riderless dragon," she said. "My rider was killed by a Rorack who shot him in the back with a poisoned arrow. I slew the Rorack, and his four companions, but there was nothing I could do to save my Bondmate." Seeing his puzzled look, she said, "The Roracks are a foul race of humanoids who pledge themselves to no one. They are vile creatures much like small trolls, but about the size of a large man. Unlike trolls however, who are stupid and only kill to eat, the Roracks are cunning and kill for their own pleasure."

"Know this," she continued, "a dragon will give up her life if her rider dies. The only thing that will stop a dragon from giving herself over to shadow in such an instance is if a stronger urge holds her to this world. The only urge stronger is the urge to bring forth new life."

Delno considered her words carefully, then said, "So, you are pregnant." It was a statement, not a question.

She nodded and continued her narrative. "I carried two eggs when the Roracks attacked. After slaying them, it was my intention to lay those eggs far away from the Rorack's territory and then die peacefully."

"But why must you die?" asked Delno. Though he had known this dragon/person for only a few minutes, he felt that the world would be a sadder place if she weren't part of it. "Were you wounded by these Roracks?"

The dragon smiled. "No, I was not wounded; it is merely the way of things," she said. "The bond between dragon and rider runs soul deep and the pair are magically linked. When that bond is severed by death, it is as though half your soul is ripped away. The remaining partner's will to live diminishes to the point that we give ourselves over to death, so that we may be reborn whole again."

He began to form a question and she said, "Hush now, I must finish my tale and then perhaps you *can* help me."

Delno said, "Though I fear that you will ask me to end your suffering, which I will find not only difficult but distasteful, I will keep silent and allow you to continue. Know this, however: I will do everything I can to persuade you not to die, for I feel the world is a better place with creatures such as yourself in it."

She smiled, and drawing a breath, resumed her narrative. "I flew for many days and nights until I felt the time was near to lay the two eggs I carried. One was male and the other is female."

Speaking of the male in the past tense wasn't lost on Delno, and it must have shown on his face because she said, "You are quick-minded human; as you surmise, the little male is dead."

Though the sadness for the loss of the male was apparent on his face, he didn't interrupt her with questions.

"Perhaps," she continued, "I was too old to have mated again, perhaps it was the attack, perhaps it is just the way of things, but his egg was not hard enough to withstand the laying, and it has broken and his half formed body was crushed by the second egg. Unfortunately, while his body slid out easily, the shards from that shell did not, and *are* hard enough to prevent his sister's egg from being laid. I am egg bound."

Delno could hold his silence no longer, "There must be something we can do!" he nearly shouted at her. "To lose one of you is bad enough, to lose two a tragedy beyond measure; we must prevent the loss of a third." He didn't quite understand why, but he was near to tears. Though it had only been a few moments since he had stumbled upon this elegant creature, he was extremely distressed at the prospect of losing one of her kind and felt he must do whatever he could to prevent it.

The dragon was taken aback. She had felt that this human was compassionate and worth telling her story to, so that her tale would be remembered, but for him to care for her and her kind as he did could only be expected from Riders. She put her snout against his chest. A lesser man might have been terrified by the action, but Delno merely thought the dragon was reaching out for comfort and placed his hands on her face compassionately. She breathed easily for a moment, then she drew a deep breath so hard that he could actually feel it pulling his shirt almost into her nostrils.

After a moment of consideration she said, "Quickly, time grows short, tell me your lineage."

"What?!" he responded. "My lineage, why?"

"Lineage is very important to dragons. Tell me yours, I must know!"

"Well, my father's people settled in the north when men first moved here as far I know. My mother is an orphan and I don't know who her parents were."

"Just the names of your parents will be enough," she said impatiently.

"My father's name is John Okonan. My mother is Laura Okonan," he replied.

"Laura," the dragon drew her head up sharply and looked at him. "What was her name before she took that of your father?"

"Well, like I said, she was an orphan, but the name she bore was Warden."

She looked at him through half closed eyelids for a moment before saying, "Very well, son of Laura Warden. Dragons measure their lineage matrilineally." She paused for a moment as another spasm made her shudder. "There might be something we can do, but it will be difficult."

"I will do what must be done!" He spoke those words with more conviction than any oath he had ever before given.

The dragon, realizing that fate had stepped in to deal with what she herself could not, smiled and said, "Then prepare yourself, young rider, for the task before you is difficult."

It was Delno's turn to be taken aback. "Why," he said, "did you call me 'young rider'?"

"Because fate has decided that you will help bring my last egg into this world. She will hatch under your care and you will become her rider," she answered, as if this should be completely obvious and he was being thick headed.

"But, I, we, you can't mean. . . ." he stammered.

"Enough!" her exclamation was close enough to a growl that any difference was a moot point. Seeing that she now had his full attention, she went on as if instructing a young pupil in his math lessons, "The whole egg must be pushed back and the broken shards shifted and removed so that it can then continue through the passage. You will have to reach inside the passage and do this. It won't be easily accomplished, but you look strong and capable."

# CHAPTER 3

D ELNO MOVED BACK along the length of the dragon toward the rear legs, assuming that the egg duct was in that direction. As he moved rearward, she shifted over on her right side and exposed her underside to him. Between her back legs he found an opening that looked like a slit about four feet long.

"All right," he said, "what now?"

"You will have to reach inside of the opening and then further into the egg passage," she told him.

As he reached into the slit, she continued, "You will find two openings. The rearmost is for the elimination of waste, the foremost is the egg passage."

It was so warm inside of the dragon as to be almost uncomfortable. Delno quickly found the foremost passage. "Good," she said "now reach inside that opening with both hands. Good, keep pressing your hands in until you feel the shards and the whole egg."

He quickly found the remains of the male's egg, and there, pressed tightly up against the debris, he felt the unharmed egg. "Now what?" he asked.

"Now," she said, "you must push the egg back with one hand and pull the shards free with the other. As you work, I will try to relax enough to allow you to complete the task."

Partly to instruct him and partly to distract herself from the urge to push down, and therefore allow the unharmed shell to be moved away from the now restricted sphincter of the egg duct, she began telling him about dragons. "Only female dragons choose to accept riders" she began. "Males are solitary and don't even commune with other dragons except to mate. That is the way it has always been and that is the way it shall remain."

While she was talking, Delno pushed with all of his strength on the egg. At first nothing happened, but then, as she relaxed, it inched backwards. It took several moments to move it far enough that he could feel the tension release on one of the shards. He took hold of the first shard and realized that it had been driven into the tissue by the pressure bearing down on it. "I'll have to work this free," he said, "it might hurt."

"Of course it will hurt," she said, sounding a bit irritated. She then continued to talk. "A female dragon reaches mating age somewhere in her third to fourth year. The mating urge may be ignored for the first several years, but eventually she will have to answer the call. When that happens, she must fly to the east and find the territory of a male and court him. When they reach the territory of a likely male, her rider must wait on the edge of that territory, otherwise the male will reject her outright and there could be violence: she will not be the only female present courting the drake. The courtship could last several days and sometimes as long as several weeks. Once the courtship is successful, the mating flight itself is brief, lasting only a few hours. After that, the male returns to his dwellings and the females leave the territory." The pain of moving the shard was only slightly apparent in her voice.

The shard came out and Delno threw it aside and reached in for another. "You don't have to remove every piece," she said, "only the ones blocking the egg."

"You said you may have been too old to mate," he said. "How old are you?" While he was curious about the answer, he also wanted to continue to distract her, because the next piece he found was larger and sharper.

"I am old for a bonded dragon" she said, "but not really beyond the age that many other bonded dragons have attained." "I was over half a millennium old when these lands were settled by the exiled nobility of the south."

Delno almost forgot his task as he considered this. There were legends of "the Exiled Kings" who had founded the kingdoms of the north, but for her to have seen the exodus. . . . "This kingdom was founded a little over two thousand years ago," he stated. "That would make you over two thousand six hundred years old." As he was pondering this, the large shard came loose and he pulled it free.

"Yes," she said, "I am older than that. You sound surprised. Don't be: it is not that unusual for a bonded female dragon to watch this world change for three millennia before passing to shadow."

He reached back into the opening and found one last shard barring the passage. "This last piece should do it," he said. "There is something I don't understand then. . . ." An exclamation escaped him as a sharp pain lanced through his right hand and he realized he had cut himself on the shard.

"How can we choose a rider if we live so long and humans don't?" she asked, anticipating his question. "That's easily answered. When a human and dragon become linked, they each receive certain side effects. One of the side effects is an alteration to their life spans. The human's life is extended, while the dragon's normal life span is shortened by about half."

"That sounds very well for the human," he said trying to distract himself from the pain in his hand, "however, the benefit sounds a bit one-sided."

"Yes," she sighed, whether in exasperation or pain he wasn't sure, "we die younger than we would otherwise, but all things die eventually. We, however, become much stronger magically, and we are no longer alone."

She grimaced in pain and was unable to continue while Delno pulled the shard free. As he pulled the shard out of the dragon's body, he could see that he had cut himself much more extensively than he had at first thought. The cut ran from the base of his index finger diagonally across his palm all the way to his wrist, and he had apparently bled quite a bit. He told the dragon that the last shard was free, and at her instruction, he pulled his other hand out and allowed the egg to proceed. After being constrained for so long, the egg came quickly.

# CHAPTER 4

EVERYTHING HAPPENED SO fast there was no time to react. The egg, for all intents and purposes, popped out so rapidly that Delno was hit in the chest by it and knocked down. As he fell, there was a brief but blinding flash of light during which he seemed to lose his hold on reality for a few seconds. When he came to himself again, he had the strangest sensation of having been in two places at once, and a flash of memory of being confined in a small dark place. He felt as though had been burned in the hollow of his right shoulder just below his collarbone. As he surveyed his surroundings, he realized he had landed on his backside, and the egg, nearly as big as himself, was lying in his lap.

"Well," gasped the dragon, "it is done."

He was suddenly afraid she would leave him with the egg and no further instructions. "I don't know how to care for a dragon," he said. "What do I do?" The question was more a plea for help than a query for more information.

Though still in some discomfort, she chuckled. "Don't worry, I won't simply die and leave you to raise a young dragon without first giving you the basics you will need. Though my time is short, now that I am no longer egg bound, the immediate mortal danger has passed, and my daughter needs the best start in life she can get. After all, she will be my namesake and therefore will be the one to continue my family's honor."

"Your namesake?" he said.

"Yes, my namesake. It is the custom of female dragons to entrust their own name to their last female offspring," she said.

"What is her name to be then?" he asked.

"I'll get to that," she said, "in my own time." Her tone was that of a teacher who had heard enough questions and wanted to continue on to the rest of the lesson.

"First, you are hurt." He started to protest that he was fine, but she continued without allowing him to give voice to his objections. "Show me your injury."

He held his hand out, palm up for her to examine. "The cut is deep, but no tendons were severed," she said.

"I've had worse," he said, "it should heal all right."

"Of course it will heal all right," again she sounded a bit annoyed, "but it will heal much faster if you stop interrupting and allow me to work."

Saying that, she then concentrated for a moment on the cut before she breathed a word that Delno didn't quite hear directly onto his out-stretched palm. There was an odd sensation in his hand, and as he drew it back and looked, he realized that the flesh was healing so fast that he could actually watch the process. Within a moment, the wound was completely closed, and only the faintest line of a scar remained. He scratched his hand, more from reflex than from any itch, and thought about what he had just witnessed. In this part of the world, magic was mostly feared. Though Delno had never really held such beliefs himself, even those who could do the simplest healings were suspect, if not out-right shunned.

"That's amazing," he said, "are all dragons able to work such magic?"

Again she was amused by his question. "That," she said, "is some of the simpler magic of which bonded dragons are capable. All dragons, and their riders, can work magic to varying degrees."

"But, but. . . ." he stammered. "You have named me dragon rider, and I can't work any magic."

"Hmmmph," the dragon snorted, "did I not tell you that there are advantages to being a rider? All riders gain magical powers through their bond with their draconic partner." Then, after a moment's consideration, she asked, "Are you quite certain, though, that you possess no magical abilities? All riders have some connection to magic or they would have no connection to dragons. The two, dragons and magic, are inseparable entities."

"I have never worked magic in my life, that I know of. Magic isn't something one pursues in these parts," he stated.

"That you know of . . . ?" she queried. "Perhaps there is something of which you aren't fully aware?"

"Well . . . ," he said thoughtfully.

"There is something then. . . ."

"Well, I'm not sure it qualifies as *magic*," he said. When he hesitated she prompted him to continue. "I can find things. It isn't much, but when something has been lost and I concentrate on it, I just seem to know where to look for it. It's not something I use too often, though. As I've said, people who have some type of magical talent aren't exactly looked on favorably around here."

"Well, I would say that that does qualify as magic. So, I suppose that it's a good thing you won't be staying around here for much longer, isn't it?"

"What?!" Delno was a bit shocked by the dragon's matter-of-fact observation. "Why would I leave my home? Everyone and everything I know is here."

"You can't very well raise a dragon in the city below us, can you?" she asked.

"If you knew that," he asked incredulously, "why did you decide to lay your eggs here?"

"Because," she stated flatly, "I had intended that my last clutch would be born free and the female would not be linked."

They sat staring at one another for several moments, each considering the other, before she continued. "As I told you, there are advantages to being linked to another being. The two biggest advantages are never again being alone, and the fact that the two together are stronger than either of them would ever be singly. There are disadvantages as well. The two biggest disadvantages are never again being able to be completely alone, and sharing everything. When I say everything I mean everything, joy, sorrow, sensations of both pleasure and pain: affecting each other's moods, even each other's life cycles. It can be quite distracting if the two aren't careful, but even with all of that, the advantages outweigh the disadvantages."

Again they stared openly at each other. Delno finally broke the silence between them by saying, "I merely wished to help you in your difficulty; I didn't ask for this."

"No," she said flatly. "You didn't ask for this, but it has been thrust upon you. I didn't ask for this for my last daughter, either. Fate has forced this on us regardless of our original intentions."

"And if I refuse to accept this?" he asked.

The response from the dragon startled him. He had expected out-rage, perhaps threats, possibly even to be physically bullied. What he didn't expect was the dragon's dry laughter. "What's so funny?" he asked, perturbed.

"If you are serious about refusing this, perhaps you should leave quickly," she responded, still chuckling.

"Well, that does it," he said, "After everything else that has happened to me in this life, I am not going to tolerate the condescending laughter of a suicidal female dragon. You are obviously suffering some mental fatigue from your ordeal, and I will leave you to it. I've done more than most would have anyway, so, by your leave, I will go on my way."

The dragon merely nodded.

The first thing he realized as he decided he had had enough of drag-ons to last several lifetimes was that he was sitting there holding that enormous egg in his lap. In fact, he hadn't noticed until now, but his legs were nearly numb from the weight. He started to roll the egg off of his lap, but as he did, he realized that he was exceedingly reluctant to do so. In fact, the very idea of being separated from the tiny, relatively speaking, creature inside the egg seemed almost foreign and unnatural to him. He tried several more times to push the egg aside, without success. Finally, with cold sweat breaking out on his brow, he recognized that the very effort of trying to rid himself of the egg was not only exhausting him, even though he had not actually expended any energy in the attempt, but the very thought of being separated from it was somehow frighten-ing. Finally, he gave up and sat there, looking up dumbfounded at the dragon.

"Having trouble?" she said in a cloyingly sweet, mock-innocent tone.

"What have you done to me?" he hissed.

"I have done nothing," she said. "You have bonded with the young dragon in that egg. The only way to break that bond is if one of you dies, and if that happens, the other will surely want to die also."

Delno sat for several moments contemplating the implications of all the dragon had told him so far. The more he thought about it, the more natural it felt to him that he should be bonded to the young dragon curled up in the egg. He noticed that when he really concentrated on her, he could feel her presence. Not quite fully conscious yet, but aware on a deeper level, and she was especially aware of him. When he concentrated even more, he realized that she felt a deep affection for him, and he was surprised to find that he shared that affection. He slowly pulled back from the contact, not wanting to separate completely from it.

He realized that he was rubbing the burn the on his chest and it still smarted. Finally, he looked up at his dragon's mother and said, "You could at least heal this burn like you did for my hand."

Again the dragon chuckled, "I wouldn't even if I could."

"What?" he said. "Why not?"

"Because," she told him, "that is no burn. It is the mark of a rider. It is placed upon a rider when he is bonded to his dragon. It is where the dragon energy first touched you."

He pondered this for a moment. "Why then," he asked, "didn't it mark my hand instead of my chest?" "After all," he continued, "I first touched the egg with my left hand while she was still stuck inside of you."

"Because a dragon cannot bond until she is born. While she was still inside my body, my energy prevented the bonding. Usually a dragon doesn't bond until after she has actually escaped her shell: to do so before hatching indicates a very strong connection indeed," she said thoughtfully before continuing. "Then, normally, she will choose from among candidates presented to her. The candidates stand still in a circle around the hatchling, and she chooses one of them. Where she first touches that person, usually on the leg or thigh, is where that rider will be marked. When a bond is unusually strong, the dragon's energy can pass through the shell after the egg is laid and place the mark on the human she is bonded to. Usually the hand is marked in such a case as it often happens when the candidate reaches out to touch the vessel. As her egg was expelled from my body, her head must have been positioned forward, and the energy passed between the two of you when you were struck on the chest."

"Is it a scar?" Although he had never considered himself vain, he didn't want a large scar on his body, either.

"No," she laughed, "it feels like a burn for a couple of days or so, but it will soften and look like a birth mark. As time passes and the bond strengthens, it will eventually take the shape of a dragon and assume the color of the one to whom you are bonded."

"Great, I'm going to have to walk around for the rest of my life (unnaturally prolonged) with a dragon-shaped birthmark on my chest," he said.

Again the dragon chuckled. "Mind sharing the joke with me?" he said, "I could stand to hear something funny about now."

"Your mark could have been worse," she answered in that annoyingly amused tone.

"Really? I'm going to have to be careful about who is around every time I wish to remove my shirt to wash for the rest of my life." He knew his annoyance came through in his voice, but he no longer cared. "How could it have been worse?"

"Well," she said, almost giggling, "my older sister's chosen rider was so sure that she was unworthy of the honor of being bonded to a dragon that she had just turned to leave the circle when my sister moved to touch her. The girl couldn't sit comfortably for three days, and she carried the mark on her rump for nearly three millennia." Then she started to laugh outright, finally controlling herself enough to say, "Of course, only a very select few ever saw that one."

"At least," he grumbled, "it's normal for a person to not remove his trousers on a hot day."

"Well," she quipped, still chortling, "at least you didn't try to duck and end up with the mark on your forehead."

Realizing he couldn't win this one, Delno changed the subject. "How long until it takes its final shape, and what color will it be?" he asked, looking inside his shirt to see the mark.

"As to how long it takes, that is dependent upon your bond with her: the stronger the bond, the sooner it will happen. The color will match hers, but until she hatches, even I can't know that for certain," she explained.

"You know so much about her, but you don't know her color?" Delno was not quite ready to accept that answer.

"A dragon's color is mostly dependent upon her parents," she said. "However, since her father was red and I am green, she could be either color or a combination of both, or neither of them."

"Neither of them?" He was more confused than before she had spoken.

"You see," she went on, "a dragon's color is mostly dependent on heredity, but not entirely. There is some choice while she is still in the egg. If she wills it, she could be any color she chooses, though usually she will contain some of the color of at least one of her parents. Also, both her sire and I have the traits for the colors of our parents in us, which could give her an entirely different hue."

"So," he asked, "what does all of that mean?"

"In what way?" she answered.

He thought for a moment to clarify his question, "You are green, what abilities do green dragons have that, oh, say, red dragons don't?"

"Ahhh," she said. "I see what you are asking. Color has nothing to do with abilities. All dragons have the same abilities to one degree or another. We can fly, we can use magic, and we can breathe fire. Color has nothing to do with anything really, except that some dragons do prefer some colors over others, though it makes no difference during mating as that is controlled by instincts that supersede such pettiness."

There was a moment of silence between them. During this time Delno looked down at himself and started to laugh. At first it was just a small chuckle, but it quickly grew into a near fit. The dragon looked at him with some concern in her eyes. "What is it?" she said.

He managed to control himself long enough to say, "I must look completely ridiculous sitting here with this egg in my lap," he said, looking up at her with laugh tears blurring his vision.

"Yes, you do," she said in a dry monotone.

That simple observation brought on a huge fit of laughter from both of them. When they again had control of themselves, Delno gently rolled the egg off of his lap, though he kept it near in a protective manner. As he rose to relieve his cramped legs, he bade the dragon to continue her instructions.

# CHAPTER 5

"**T**HE FIRST THING you need to understand is that a growing dragon needs meat, lots of it," she said. "She will eat more than any animal of her size you have ever seen. A hatchling can eat one-third her weight each day. Fresh is best, but she will eagerly devour any meat you can provide."

Delno calculated the young dragon's weight by subtracting what he figured the shell would weigh from the weight he had shifted out of his lap and was suddenly daunted by the enormity of this: she already weighed as much as a full-grown man. Meat was expensive, and while he was a passable hunter at need, being able to supply such quantities was beyond his capabilities. His savings would be exhausted in the first few days if he tried to buy that much, not to mention having to leave the young dragon alone to get into mischief while he made daily trips to procure fresh provender.

Noticing the look of worry on his face, the dragon said, "Do not be overly alarmed. She will be able to hunt for herself by the end of her first month, though she will quickly deplete an area of game if you stay in one place too long."

"I suggest," she continued, "that you begin working your way south as soon as she begins to hunt. There are several passes through the mountains. Choose one that is not heavily traveled. If you have training in map reading, you should get one, as those who would guide you on your journey may not be reliable."

"Know this, too," she said after a brief pause. "That mark you bear will betray what you are more and more as you move southward. Many in the south will revere you and help you along your path. Some will hold great enmity toward you for slights, real or imagined, that they feel they, or their ancestors, have suffered under the wings of the riders.

"Suffered under the wings of riders?" he asked. "What kind of suffering?"

"You must understand this, young rider: not all riders are noble, and not all dragons are kindly disposed to those of your kind to whom they are not bonded. There are, and probably always will be, those riders who feel that they have the right to take what they want, and allow their draconic partners to feed indiscriminately on other people's herds without paying for what they take. Even in lands where the ruling nobility welcomes the dragon and rider, because their friendship provides a measure of protection, there may be many farmers and tradesmen who don't share their lords' opinion of the situation due to the greed and arrogance of such riders. Often such enmity is projected onto other riders even when they have done no wrong."

While Delno didn't tend to project his emotions in this manner, and tried to judge all individuals by their own merit, he knew that many people did. The example that sprung readily to mind in this land was the use of magic. To many of the people in Corice, the use of magic, whether it was used to commit a crime or heal the sick and injured, was, at the very least, suspect, and any who used magic were simply not to be trusted. He said as much to the dragon.

"Ah, then you have some understanding in this matter," she said. "That is good; it may save you trouble in the future. Now, let us continue about dragon hatchlings and their growth, for I am weary and would like to finish some of my instruction before we sleep tonight."

Delno quieted himself and waited patiently while the dragon collected her thoughts.

Finally, she continued. "I have told you how much a dragon eats. Do not be worried about over feeding her. While she will, at first, eat herself into a stupor, she will not over eat. A newly hatched dragon grows at a prodigious rate and needs a great deal of food to supply the energy for that growth. She will more than triple in size in her first month. By the end of her third month, she will be more than twice as large as any draft animal you have seen here in the north. By her sixth month, she will be nearly as large as any adult female dragon and larger than an adult male."

Delno looked at the egg with an expression that was a mixture of awe, horror, and wonder. He calculated that the adult female had wings that were twenty yards long each. Added to the distance between the wings, that would give her a wingspan of nearly one hundred and thirty feet, and a body length of about ninety feet from nose to tail. Then a thought occurred to him, and he asked, "When will she start to fly?"

The dragon chuckled a bit before answering. "She will start flying within days of her hatching. Her first flights will be short, and she will be ungainly. Don't let this alarm you; all dragons have to find their wings in this way. By the end of her first month, she will be proficient enough that she will be able to swoop down and take even the swiftest boar or similar-sized beast. Her wings won't be strong enough to take the strain of bearing you as a rider until about her sixth month when she has attained most of her growth."

And so the rest of the evening passed, with the dragon giving instruction and Delno occasionally asking questions. He learned about flight, about how and where to sit, with and without a saddle. He even learned the basics of constructing a saddle.

She spoke at length about how to judge the weather and the wind, explaining that such a large wingspan meant that high winds and strong sudden crosswinds could be dangerous. She told him about how to watch the clouds and the smaller flying creatures to help watch for such things as well as other possible airborne hazards. The young dragon, she said, would know instinctively about much of the way of flying, and they would have to learn the rest for themselves by actually experiencing it. For his part most of what she passed on was simply explanation of the mechanics involved to satisfy his curiosity since he would have little say in the matter once he and his partner were in the air. The role of the rider, as far as just flying was concerned, would be as a passenger with little real say in process other than direction of travel.

Finally, the dragon said, "I am weary, from my long flight and from the laborious birthing process I have gone through. Mostly, though, I am weary of talking. My grief for my rider is once again coming to the surface, and I fear my parental duties will not hold me to this world much longer. Tomorrow I will fly both you and the egg down from this cliff. For now, though, let us get what rest we can."

After saying that, the dragon simply laid her head down, curled her tail protectively around both the egg and its rider, and appeared to go to sleep. During the night, Delno was awakened by a curious sound. It sounded something like a cat mewling, but also a bit like a child whim-pering. He looked at the dragon and realized that she was awake and crying. Huge tears rolled down from her eyes to be absorbed by the grass and soil of the clearing. He sensed that now that she had nearly fulfilled her parental duties, she was finally able to fully grieve for the loss of her rider, her soul-mate. The term, soul-mate, startled him and he began at last to understand the deep connection he and his draconic partner had made to each other even though she was not yet hatched. He knew that there were no words of condolence that he could offer the dragon for her loss. Instead, he settled for moving closer to her head, and wrapped one arm as far under her neck as he could and placed his other hand higher up while he pillowed his head on her front foot. Then, keeping her in that somewhat clumsy embrace, he softly hummed to her while she slowly returned to a light slumber.

# CHAPTER 6

D ELNO WOKE TO the sound of birds singing their morning songs; however, it seemed strange that the birds would be
singing when it still appeared to be dark. He was only more
puzzled when he found that the reason for the darkness was due to the
large leathery cover over his entire body. Then, as memory of the previous afternoon and evening returned, he realized that the cover over him
was the dragon's wing. She must have covered him and the egg to keep
them warm during the night.

As he stirred, the dragon lifted her wing and asked, "Did you sleep
well, young rider?"

"Quite well," he replied. Then, noticing that he was slightly wet with
sweat under his arms, he added, "In fact, if I'd been any warmer I would
most likely have been uncomfortable." He added a hearty thank you for
her thoughtfulness as he bent to check the egg. It was doing fine as well,
and the mental contact with the little dragon inside was just as strong as
yesterday. After ensuring that everything was all right, he moved off to
the bushes to answer nature's call.

As he stepped back into the clearing, he saw that the dragon was
now lying with the egg between her front legs. When he asked why, she
stated, "Now is the time for you to get your first taste of what it is like
to ride a dragon."

"What do you mean?" he asked.

"Well," she said, "it is one thing for a wild dragon to live up here on
this small plateau, but you can't be expected to climb it everyday to feed

her now that she has bonded with you. Therefore, I will fly both you and the egg to a more suitable place in that valley closer to your town.

"Closer to town?" he said. "Won't that be more dangerous?"

"A little," she replied. "However, unless you plan on growing your own wings in the next fortnight, I don't see that we have any choice. Once she hatches, my daughter will need you almost constantly to feed her and keep her safe until she is about a month old. Now climb onto my back, and let's get going."

With a little coaching from the dragon, Delno found that it was quite easy to climb using her front leg as a step and that, even without a saddle, the space formed where the neck ridges stopped and her neck joined her body made a niche that fitted as though it was designed for the purpose of carrying a rider, and was even big enough to accommodate a passenger as well. He mentioned this to the dragon.

"Yes," she said, "that space is sufficient to keep a rider safe and comfortable in normal flight, though you would do well to wear leather britches and long underpants, as the scales can abrade your legs on a longer flight. Of course, when you are going to do more acrobatic flying, you will need the security of a saddle and leg straps."

The flight, all too short by Delno's way of thinking, was smooth, and they were soon back on the ground. While he would have loved to have spent much more time flying, there was a sense that the flight caused great sadness for the dragon. In fact, all of her movements and speech had seemed subdued today. He reasoned that, now that she had ensured her daughter's safety and care, she was feeling the loss of her rider more and more. He didn't mention his thoughts to her. Like the incident of finding her crying in the night, it was a subject they didn't discuss by unspoken mutual agreement.

The dragon had chosen the location well. The clearing, not much more than a thin space in the trees, was near a small creek and accessible only by a couple of game trails. While it was closer to town, it was still about three miles to the nearest human dwellings. This part of the forest spent a portion of the year underwater when the spring thaws swelled the river, which accounted for the lack of development, but it was nearly high summer now, and they would be long gone by the time the river again turned the area into little more than a swamp.

"You will have to go to your town and make what arrangements you can concerning the care of your partner," she said. "The egg will hatch sometime within the next two weeks. You must be here when that happens. If she cannot immediately find you when she hatches, she will go looking for you. A newly hatched dragon is vulnerable to predation. Get what you need and return. I will watch over the egg while you are gone."

Sensing that the dragon would appreciate the solitude, he gathered himself up and started off to town.

The trip to town was uneventful. He met no one on the way, which was to his liking, as he enjoyed the opportunity to think about his current situation. In many respects, becoming bonded with the dragon had solved his problems, even though it would undoubtedly create more. His future was certainly decided. He had no choice but to head south with his *partner*—he was really beginning to like the sound of that very much—and try to find someone to help him become the best dragon rider he could become, whatever that meant. The old female had been a bit vague on that issue. She had said that many riders did good works for folks. However, she had also hinted that some riders simply indulged themselves as they saw fit, even when those indulgences where at the expense of others. "I won't misuse my position," he said out loud, as if it were an oath.

Thus his morning went, musing on how to be the best dragon rider he could, until he found himself at the northern gate of Larimar.

# CHAPTER 7

ENTERING THE CITY felt almost surreal. He had been born and raised here, and though he and Nassari had often spoken together as children about leaving Larimar to go adventuring, he had never really expected to do so. He walked more slowly than he otherwise would have, realizing that this would be one of his last opportunities to look around the city of his birth. He was already beginning to feel a bit homesick, and he hadn't even left yet. He also hadn't decided how he would explain to his parents that he must leave.

The only sure course of action he had decided on was to visit the military pension offices and convert his five crowns per month, barely enough for one person to live on, into a lump sum. He was entitled to collect that pension for up to thirty years. He could, however, at any time within the first year of becoming eligible for the pension, opt to take a lump sum that amounted to ten years worth of pay all at once. He had initially thought that doing so was a very bad idea, since he had planned on settling into a career and remaining right here in Larimar. Now it looked as though one large payment would be necessary. Also, if he moved out of the kingdom, he couldn't very well collect on the pension anyway.

Eventually his path led to the city's official buildings. Well, one building really, but divided into several sections that had been added after the original construction as the city grew and its government's headquarters required more space. The additions looked more like out buildings that butted up against the original structure and vied for dominance of the space rather than part of an integrated whole. Of course, that seemed only fitting since the different sections of the government often didn't work well together and frequently found themselves at odds over policy.

As he entered, he heard one of the things he had most wanted to avoid for the time being: the sound of Nassari's voice calling his name.

"Delno," Nassari said as he approached him at a swift walk, "I had wondered where you had gotten off to. When I stopped in at your parents' home last night and they said you hadn't returned from your hike, I had worried that something had happened to you."

"*He has no idea*," thought Delno. Out loud he said, "I'm fine, I just have some business to. . . ."

Nassari cut in before he could finish his thought. "Your parents were worried also. You have told them you're all right, haven't you?"

"I was going to see them as soon as I. . . ."

"Well, never mind that now," Nassari said. "We have much to discuss, and big plans to make, and little time to do it all. We have to get your name on the special ballot."

"I have to go into the pension office, Nassari. I have to. . . ."

Again Nassari cut him off before he could complete his thought, "There's damn little time right now, Del. We have our work cut out for us at the city council office. Councilwoman Oran's husband has died. Seems he retired early yesterday eve with a headache and died in his sleep. She sent her resignation over this morning, saying that she could not bring it in person because she had funeral arrangements to make. She resigned because she feels that she can no longer give her full attention to the council with no one to help her raise her children."

"Well," Delno began, "I'm very sorry to hear about the Councilwoman's troubles. Please convey my sympathies. However, I must get to the pension office; I have important business of my own."

"Del," Nassari looked at him like a parent who intends to scold an errant child, "Whatever business you have can wait. The council was in session when Councilwoman Oran's resignation arrived. They immediately voted that since it will be over eight months until her seat is to be put up for election, and her district will still need a voice in the council, a special election will be held within a fortnight to fill the vacancy. We have to get you on the ballot now if you hope to stand a chance of winning that seat."

He grabbed Delno by the arm and began to physically pull him along. Delno planted his feet and refused to move, saying, "Enough! I have no intention of going anywhere besides the pension office."

Nassari was startled and opened his mouth to begin some argument, but Delno was quicker. Before Nassari could utter a syllable he said, "If you will allow me to get a few words into this conversation, I will explain."

Nassari looked as though he would like to argue, but he had known Delno long enough to realize that it would do no good. He released Delno's arm and bowed by way of apology, indicating with a wave of his hand that he would listen.

"Good," said Delno, "now that I have your attention, I will explain my business here today. I have come to cash in my pension." He paused to let that sink in.

Delno had expected Nassari to be shocked; however, the look on his face was one of sheer delight. "Wonderful," he said, "I was going to suggest that you do just that."

Delno was the one who was shocked, "You were?" he said. "I thought you wanted me to run for that seat on the city council."

"I do," Nassari went on as though there had been no real break in his train of thought, "I was going to talk you into cashing in your pension as soon as we had you registered as a candidate. How did you think we would finance your campaign?"

"Ah, well, that," said Delno, "I have also decided not to enter into politics."

Delno realized by the look on his friend's face that he couldn't have given him worse news if he had told him that a favorite pet had died. In a way, he supposed, he had done just that.

"Del," he said, "we've talked about this. You are sure to win. Right now, the war is still fresh enough in everyone's mind that a veteran, and a war hero to boot, will find his path to a council seat paved with rose petals. If you wait, even until the normal election in eight months, you run the risk of people forgetting that you are the Hero of the Battle of Stone Bridge. Not to mention that those who would like to run for that seat have geared all of their machinations to running for it after the New Year: they have their campaign money tied up now for the next few months. If you run now, you will be virtually unopposed."

"Nassari, my dear friend," Delno said, "Though I hate to disappoint you, I have decided not to pursue a life in politics."

Nassari looked at Delno as if he had just grown horns and started speaking blasphemy. "Not pursue a life in politics?" he said. "What, then, do you plan on doing with your life?" After a pause he went on. "Let's face it, Del, your other career choices haven't exactly worked out for the best. What do think you are going to do? Cooking? Wood working? Perhaps you've decided to become a traveling entertainer?"

Being taunted like this was infuriating and Delno had had enough. "I will do as I please," he said. "What pleases me at this point in my life is not running around licking the boots of politicians hoping to be thrown a few scraps like some mongrel. I never told you that I would buy into your plans for my future. In fact, if you recall, that was why I left yesterday, to think this whole issue through thoroughly. While I may not know precisely what it is that I am, I do know that I am not a politician."

They stood there glaring at each other, staring each other down exactly the way that they had when they had fought as children.

Then they both began to see how ridiculous the argument was. It was Nassari who cracked first. He smiled and said "I guess I have been pushing you rather hard. I suppose I've been quite a pain in the arse, huh?"

Delno chuckled before answering good-naturedly. "Only enough to drive me from my home to spend the night in the wilderness."

"Well, then," Nassari continued, "you've obviously made a decision about what to do with your life, so tell me what it is."

"It's only a partial decision, my friend," he said. "I am going to cash in my pension and leave Larimar."

"Leave Larimar?!" Nassari was shocked. "Larimar is your home. You've never been anywhere else."

"You forget, my dear Nassari," he replied, "I spent more than two years away from this city. I've seen more of the wide world than you have, old friend."

"That's different," he retorted, "you were a soldier then, marching when and where you were told."

"Not so different. As an officer, I was often the one doing the telling. However, I don't intend to go north this time. I have decided to go south, probably all the way to the southern kingdoms." Delno hoped that this sounded well thought out. He was making it up as he went along to avoid telling his friend the truth about where he was going and why he had to leave.

"South?" Nassari was more astounded with each new revelation, "The southern kingdoms are a very long way from here. Only a few traders dare the trip. The southerners are a strange lot with even stranger customs." Then he whispered, "I've heard that everyone practices some magic in the southern kingdoms," as though this was confirmation that all people from the south were insane. "Of course," he went on, more as if thinking out loud than actually talking to Delno, "I've also heard that women are known to bathe naked in the rivers down there, too."

In response to the last statement, Delno laughed and playfully punched his friend on the shoulder, saying, "There's the lecherous sixteen-year-old I've always known and loved." Then he said, "Seriously though, I intend to travel to the port city of Idor and hire on as a guard with a caravan heading to the southern kingdoms. Along the way, I will learn as much as I can from the merchants. Then, once I get to the southern kingdoms, who knows?" He hadn't outright lied, but he still felt a bit ashamed about misleading his friend.

"Delno the trader," Nassari laughed. "Well, at least it's almost honest work."

"Yes, just slightly more honest than politics," said Delno, returning the barb.

The two friends laughed for a moment, and then Nassari said, "Look, Del, I have to be about my business. I wasn't kidding about needing to get a candidate registered. Since you aren't going to do it, I have to find my back up man and get him to the council before noon."

"Back up candidate? Didn't take long for you to get over my decision, did it?" Delno said, though he was smiling, happy that he hadn't truly left his friend with no options.

Nassari returned the smile, "Never bet all your money on just one horse in any race."

There was a moment of awkward silence as they were reluctant to part company. Then Nassari laid his hand on his friend's arm and said, "Del, I'm going to be extremely busy over the next two weeks. However, don't leave the city without at least finding me and saying goodbye."

"I'll find you," he said, "and we'll have a dinner fit for royalty before I go."

Nassari looked as though he had more to say, however, he just stared into Delno's eyes for a moment, then, squeezing his friend's arm, he turned without a word and strode away.

# CHAPTER 8

THE REMAINDER OF his day in town had gone much more easily than he could have hoped. He had had no problem collecting the lump sum for his pension. Then he had gone to his parents' home and told them of his plans to go south. They took the news even better than Nassari had. Since he had served honorably in the army, they considered him to be a grown man capable of making his own decisions. In fact, since his younger brother showed the aptitude for carpentry that he never did, his leaving solved the problem of which one of them would inherit his father's business. They didn't even object when he told them he intended to move out that afternoon, ostensibly in order to take quarters closer to the traders with whom he intended to travel. They made no argument. He hated lying to them, but, he reasoned, they wouldn't want to know the truth anyway. Also, he rationalized, he had never in his life been able to lie to them successfully, so if they believed him this time, it was because they wanted to. Besides, his father's business was doing so well that he was taking on another apprentice, and he would be expected to provide quarters for the new boy. Delno's bed was all but occupied by the time he left his parents' house.

As he stepped out the front door, he met his younger brother, Will. Will was tall like Delno, and since their father was short, as were his paternal grandparents, Delno figured they got their height from their mother's side. Their height was where the similarities ended. Will was blonde like their father, while Delno had black hair, unlike either parent. Neither parent had dark eyes, but his were a rich dark brown, while Will's were light blue: the exact shade of his sire's. Delno was definitely the better looking of the two: Will, though not ugly, had inherited the roughly handsome look of the mountain folk.

The brothers didn't dislike each other, but they had never been friends. They exchanged greetings, and then Delno explained that he was going south to seek his fortune. Will simply shrugged and wished him good luck, and they shook hands and parted company.

The next item on his agenda, procuring food for the hatchling, was such a stroke of luck as to be nearly unbelievable. When he went to the stockyard, he found a man with a small flock of sheep, and a few pigs all for sale. Further inquiry led to the rental of a small, somewhat isolated patch of pasture land less than two miles from the clearing where the egg would hatch. While the loss of a few animals to other predators could be foreseen, there was a low, stone wall around much of the pasture, and dense brush closed off the rest, so the animals shouldn't stray. All in all, it couldn't have worked out better, so, after hiring two boys to herd the beasts to their new home, and procuring a tent and some other basic supplies for himself, he left the city somewhat lighter of coin but brighter of spirit.

Returning to the clearing, he was startled to find the dragon gone and no trace of the egg. He was just beginning to panic when a huge shadow blotted out the sun. It was, of course, the dragon returning from wherever she had been.

Delno smiled and waved in greeting to her as she quickly circled and landed.

"There you are," she said. "I was beginning to wonder if you had gotten into some trouble."

"It took some time to convert my pension into usable funds and then make provisions for enough herd animals to feed a baby dragon for a month," he said somewhat defensively.

"How did you accomplish all of that in one day?" she asked.

Delno started to answer her, but then, realizing that she wasn't carrying the egg as he had expected, asked nervously, "Where is the egg?" Panic was again surging to the forefront of his thoughts.

"Relax," she chuckled, "I buried it under a pile of leaves and brush. It is well hidden and the rotting vegetation kept it warm while I went above the falls to bathe where I wouldn't be seen." Then she added, "Now then, tell me what happened in town today."

Delno started his tale of his day's adventure with how he had procured the food and where it was stored, which brought an appreciative response from the dragon. Then he told her everything else, including his fabrications to Nassari, and to his parents. He added, "I don't like lying to them. Even as a small boy I never lied to my parents, and Nassari and I have always been completely honest with each other, but I could think of no other way, short of slipping out of town under cover of darkness, and risking that someone might come looking for me."

"You have done the right thing," she said. "You told them the truth about your destination. The lie of omission you told about your purpose couldn't be helped. Don't let it worry you."

As if by mutual agreement, they both stopped talking. They sat that way for nearly an hour, as the sun moved down until it could no longer be seen through the trees, and the clearing was washed in twilight.

Almost unconsciously, Delno reached out with his mind to touch the not quite conscious mind of his dragon partner. While they were never completely separated, he had allowed the awareness of the contact to recede while he was about his errands and while he spoke with his partner's mother. The awareness he had felt before rushed to meet him, elated to have the link fully restored. Even still inside the egg and not fully conscious, the little dragon possessed a powerful mind. He realized that if she decided to turn that mind on him in a more aggressive manner, he would be hard pressed to protect himself. As that thought occurred to him, one word surfaced from the semi-consciousness of the dragon: NEVER! The word was wrapped in layers of deep and unrestricted affection. As all this was happening, Delno felt a crawling sensation on his face, and when he reached up to wipe away the bug that he was sure was there, all he found was a single tear rolling down his cheek. At that moment, though he had suspected it, he knew for sure that whatever else this bond was, love was the very core of it.

"You are in contact with her now, aren't you?" the dragon's question startled him as it interrupted the silence that had permeated the clearing.

"How can you tell?" he responded.

"Besides the far off look you get when you reach out to her," she replied, "I can feel the connection between the two of you. To be bonded so strongly this early on is rare and beautiful."

"Rare?" he asked.

"Yes, indeed," she said, "normally dragon and rider can do little more than feel each other's presence for the first week or so after hatching. They actually don't convey much emotion until the hatchling begins to hunt for herself."

"Then what she and I are doing is a good thing," he mused almost dreamily, unwilling to pull back from the contact enough to carry on a real conversation and feeling proud of his connection to his partner.

"Yes," she said in that tone he had already come to recognize as her teacher voice, "good," then, after a dramatic pause for effect, she added, "And dangerous."

# CHAPTER 9

"**D**ANGEROUS?!" HE SHOUTED, as the word sank into his mind and he became more fully centered on the conversation. "How can a bond which brings both her and me so much joy be dangerous?" He was suddenly terribly afraid he would somehow injure the little dragon. "How can such contact possibly harm her?" he asked, full of concern.

Again the dragon gave one of those annoying chuckles before answering. "It's not her I'm worried about, young rider." She let that sink in for just a few seconds, then spoke again quickly before he could interrupt her with questions. "It is still early, so I believe that we have enough time tonight to further your education about dragons. Are you ready to listen?"

He was suddenly brimming over with questions, but, even though he had only known the dragon a little more than a day, he realized it would be best to hold his tongue and let the dragon tutor him in her own way. So, at his nod, she continued. "As I have told you, a hatchling has a voracious appetite. While she will be large by human standards, she must eat enough to support a growth rate that most humans can't comprehend."

"Yes," he said, "you've already explained that to me."

Before he could further interrupt her with questions, she looked at him sternly and said, "Hush now, I am not finished, and you are not seeing my point. Let me continue and all will be clear."

Again he held his tongue and bowed his head in acquiescence.

"Good," she snorted, "let us move on." "Look at things this way. You are large for a human, a little over two yards tall and weigh about fifteen stone, am I correct?" He started to open his mouth to respond, but, seeing the stern look she gave him, nodded his head. "When you were born, you were most likely about a half a yard long and weighed less than half a stone, correct?" At his nod, she smiled and continued. "During your life you have had to eat to grow. It most likely took you the better part of two decades to grow from small babe to large man, correct?" Again he nodded. "It took you nearly two decades to quadruple your height and increase your weight by a factor of thirty or more, correct?"

By now Delno's eyes were beginning to widen, and the realization of what the dragon was getting at was just starting to sink in. Wanting to be sure he fully understood, she said it anyway. "Your partner is nearly as big as you are now and must grow to be as large as I am. She will do in six months what it took you two decades to do, and she will need to eat accordingly." She again paused for effect. "Do you begin to see what a monumental task that is?" she asked.

Delno could only stare slack jawed and nod his head mutely as the full understanding hit him. "Good, now that you understand, we can continue.

"Do you remember me telling you that one of the drawbacks to the bond between dragon and rider is that they share everything, joy, fear, pain, everything?" she asked. At his nod, she went on, "Usually, the rider is spared from the hatchling's ravenous hunger pangs because it takes about a month for the bond to get that strong. By the end of the first month, young riders have been taught by a mentor to blunt such feelings so that they can concentrate on their tasks. Also, the hatchling is usually hunting on her own, and her concentration on catching prey further buffers her rider from the sensation."

He could keep silent no longer. "What am I going to do?" he asked. "I will have no mentor, and if I am incapacitated by her hunger, I will be unable to care for her."

"What you are going to do," she replied in her stern teacher's voice, "is pay attention, and I will teach you techniques that will keep her thoughts from overwhelming you."

Realizing that he might not get a second chance at this lesson, Delno sat patiently, paying very close attention to his tutor.

"There are techniques," she went on, "that dampen the connection between you and your partner. You will find these techniques very useful in her early growth periods to avoid being besieged by her needs, but you will both find them useful in the future when you need to think without the distraction of having another's mind intruding. You will especially find these techniques useful when you take a lover or she participates in mating flights."

While the prospect of either of them taking a lover hadn't occurred to him until the dragon mentioned it, he could certainly see that these techniques might prevent awkward moments in their relationship. Although—the thought of dragons mating did seem like an interesting subject in an academic sort of way—having some knowledge of the draconic anatomy on the female's side, he couldn't quite suppress his curiosity at the mechanics involved.

The dragon cleared her throat irritably and he snapped back to the task at hand, realizing the she had been speaking, and he hadn't heard a word she had said.

"If you are going to daydream," she said, "we won't get anywhere with this."

He flushed and stammered a quick apology, after which she continued the lesson. "The first thing you must learn is that thoughts are nothing more than a form of energy. Energy can be controlled. This is not only the basis of mental training, but magical training as well. In fact, without learning mental discipline, you won't be able to control the magic."

Delno had nearly forgotten what the dragon had told him about riders being able to use magic. His attention on the lesson increased.

"Ah, I see I now have your full attention" she said. "Think of your mind as a container, like a glass ball, or box. Within this container there is energy. Some of this energy is always flowing, controlling the unconscious actions of your body like breathing, heartbeat, digestion, and so on. Some of the energy is dormant, or potential energy, not being used. The more consciousness a being has, the more potential energy there is available for things like conscious thought. Most of those creatures we consider to be conscious convert this energy into conscious thought and then express that thought in the form of physical action."

She paused for a moment, letting him ponder this, then continued. "The physical action that we convert the thought into can take many forms; often these forms are so automatic that we perform them without thinking. The thought—I want to walk to the door—results in you getting out of a chair and walking to the door without further conscious attention on your part: though the thoughts for each footstep are there, you aren't consciously aware of them, otherwise it would take you a quarter of an hour to walk across a room."

Delno began shifting in his seat. While this lesson was interesting, he didn't see what walking across a room had to do with telepathy, and said so to the dragon.

"Humans," she snorted, "I think it's the short life span that makes your species so impatient."

Again he flushed and resigned himself to letting the dragon teach in her own time.

"Now then, as I was saying. Thought becomes action. The action that many thoughts are converted into, especially among your kind," she added sarcastically, "is speech. You think about what you want to say and then you say it." She quickly amended, "At least, you sometimes think about it first."

Delno chuckled, realizing that he certainly couldn't disagree with her last observation.

"What you and your partner do," she continued, "is really not much different than the way you have been conversing with others all of your life. The only difference is that there is a channel of energy that connects the two of you, and you are able to project your thoughts directly along this to each other."

Delno couldn't hold his next question; "If that is the case, can I do this with others as well?"

Rather than being annoyed, as he had expected, the dragon seemed to be anticipating this question and was ready with a reply. "As your power grows, and you practice consciously moving energy, you will be able to do this with others. Most will be unable to project their thoughts back, but you will be able to hear what they are thinking. The stronger you get, the deeper into their minds you can see."

The prospect was fascinating, but Delno began to wonder if such eavesdropping was not a serious trespass, and said as much to the dragon.

"That it is," she replied. "To enter the mind of another is a serious invasion of that person's privacy and should never be done unless there is real need. Scanning the surface thoughts of someone you are dealing with to ensure that he isn't trying to betray you is one thing. Becoming a psychic voyeur is something else again."

Delno deliberated on that for a moment, and then said, "I've seen enough of humans at their best and their worst to know that I don't want to randomly read other people's thoughts."

"Good," she said, "because there are many ways that could be danger-ous. You could find something that you didn't want to know and then be compelled to act on the information and get yourself into no end of trouble. But the biggest danger is in delving into the thoughts of those who can detect what you're doing. They could use the channel you open to get into your mind and work their own mischief. Two evenly matched opponents in such a contest could exhaust themselves quickly, and the result could be physical damage ranging from a simple headache up to death. In a mismatched contest of this type, the stronger of the two, once the channel was established, could do worse than kill the weaker one."

"Worse than kill?" He hadn't meant to speak the question out loud, but the dragon wasn't perturbed by it.

"There are worse things than death, young rider," she said. "Imagine someone having his mind obliterated, all memory wiped clean with no more wit than that of a newborn babe. That person could be kept as a mindless slave, or re-educated in a manner that suited the whims of the one who wiped his mind."

"That sounds too fantastic to believe; is such a thing possible?" he asked.

"Oh, yes," she replied, "It's possible. How do you think the nobility of your lands were forced to move to the less hospitable north? There was a blood feud among the ruling clans of the south. The wars had gone on for several generations; even many of the dragon riders became ensnarled in the political machinations of the time. Eventually, two of the families put aside their own differences and banded together. They were very powerful by themselves, but together they were invincible. One of the lesser families felt they had no choice but to resort to dras-tic magical means. A son of this lesser family was a sorcerer, especially skilled at the use of mental telepathy."

"You're saying . . . ?" Delno let the question trail off.

"Yes," she said, "his family managed to capture a son from each of the two powerful houses, and he obliterated their minds. Then, using his magical abilities, he replaced what he had destroyed with his own con-structs. His foul act turned each of the young men into assassins who were able to walk right through the defenses of the two noble houses and murder many of their own elders before the plot was discovered and the assassins could be stopped. In the end, the two great houses were so badly devastated by the loss of their leaders, and so terribly demoral-ized, that they felt that they could fight no more and their only choice was to flee from their enemies. They took whatever they could carry and went north. They were "The Exiled Kings" who founded the northern kingdoms over two millennia ago. After that, the feuds in the south continued for almost three decades before the families realized that their resources and their people were exhausted and continued fighting would destroy them all. When the full truth of how the two great families had been defeated, and how that defeat had then paved the way for the most devastating fighting of the feuds came to light, a council of kings declared such practices to be the foulest of magic and decreed that any who did similar acts in the future would forfeit their lives."

The dragon paused, allowing Delno to absorb this before she went on. "So you see; the skills I am trying to teach you are powerful indeed. These skills have been used to commit foul acts that have destroyed kingdoms, and, despite being outlawed, such skills are still practiced by some to this day."

"How can I hope to keep myself and my partner safe from such dishonorable magicians?" he asked.

"Do not underestimate your own power, young rider," she chided, "and never underestimate the power your dragon brings to this partnership. As I have told you, there are advantages to being linked to a dragon. One of the advantages is that you share each other's strength. When you have both gained more experience, the two of you together will be more powerful than any single being ever could. Even the elves, who practice magic as powerful as that of the dragons, can't produce a sorcerer who is the equal of a dragon and rider together."

"Elves," he said thoughtfully, "I thought the stories of elves were tales told to children at bedtime, not real beings."

"Oh, they are real enough," she said. "They don't much concern themselves with the affairs of humans or dragons. They live in their own realm, which is off to the southeast, and avoid getting involved in the affairs of others. Occasionally one of their kind will develop a wanderlust and travel for a time in the southern kingdoms, and a very select few choose to travel north each year to hunt down and destroy as many Roracks as they can find, but most elves simply keep to themselves, gardening and practicing their own magic. I have seen a few over the many years when I have rested near their lands after mating, but they are more interested in talking with trees than with dragons."

Delno thought about this for a few moments and was brought out of his reverie when the dragon mentioned that if they didn't get back to the lesson, they would not make much progress. They continued the session long into the night. At first, he mainly learned not to project his thoughts and to shield himself from those who would try to invade his mind. It was well into the wee hours of the morning, when he had begun to develop the art of skimming the surface thoughts of others that the dragon called for a break, and they both retired.

# CHAPTER 10

**D**ESPITE HOW LATE he got to bed the previous night, Delno woke early. Sunrise was just a hint on the horizon. He crawled from his tent, which had been hastily pitched by fire light after many hours of lessons. His camp was on the side of the clearing away from the stream. There was just enough room for his belongings and the old female dragon in the clearing.

As he crawled from the shelter, intent on relieving his distended bladder, he felt the strong presence of the baby dragon in his mind. He noticed that she felt more *awake* than ever. Not wishing to share his bodily functions with her, and wanting to practice his mental skill, he damped down the contact, not completely shutting it out, but preventing the link from carrying complete emotion and sensation. The young dragon seemed a bit unsettled at being blocked and tried to reassert the full connection. Using more of his own energy, he gently but firmly reinforced the block. There was a brief struggle of wills before the little dragon resigned herself to the fact that the contact could be controlled from his end.

When he had finished washing in the stream, he decided he would reopen the full contact. He was surprised to find that it was now blocked from the other side. When he tried to assert himself, he found that he was barred by the iron will of his partner.

*"There's no need to be that way,"* he told her through the link.

He had expected no answer, and was a bit startled when he received one. *"There was no reason for you to block the contact either,"* she retorted, sounding somewhat hurt.

"*I didn't want to hurt your feelings,*" he replied. "*I thought that I would practice my skill while not imposing my bodily functions on you. It wasn't a slight in any way.*"

"*I understand your bodily needs and they do not bother me,*" she said. "*It is terribly boring being stuck in this small space. It makes me much lonelier than I would be if I were free to move around.*"

He was amazed at how coherent she had become. In just the last few hours, she had come to full consciousness.

"*If that is the case,*" he said, "*why don't you come out?*"

She hesitated for a moment, considering her answer then said, "*It is nearly time, but not quite yet.*" Then she paused again, considering her words before continuing. "*Also, there is another with you. I will not come out while she is here.*"

At this, Delno was taken aback. "*But she is your mother!*" he exclaimed.

"*That does not matter,*" she told him vehemently. "*I know who she is, and I sense that her presence is necessary for now, but I don't have to like it. I don't like sharing you.*"

The flood of affection and jealousy as she then allowed the link to *open* fully on her end nearly overwhelmed him. Realizing that he couldn't reason with such sentiment, he simply allowed his feeling of affection for her to flow back along the link. His response seemed to sooth her better than any words could have, and soon they were basking in each other's presence as he fed himself, while waiting for the mother dragon to decide to get up and moving for the day.

The first thing the mother dragon did when she rose was fly off to bathe. When she returned, Delno recounted his conversation with her daughter.

The old dragon was completely speechless for many minutes when he finished his oration. She sat silent and motionless considering the implications of what he had told her. Finally, she asked, "So she spoke to you through the link as though the two of you were having a normal conversation?" At his confirmation, she went on, "And she is completely aware of herself and her surroundings?" Again he nodded affirmatively. "And she said she will not come out while I am here?" When he nodded to that, she chuckled, and then again became silent for some time.

Nearly half an hour had passed, and Delno wondered if the dragon had put the incident out of her mind when she turned to him and said, "We must continue your lessons on magic today." It was apparent by the tone of her voice that she was worried and eager to continue.

"Why the sudden rush?" he asked. "After all, we've known for some time that she would hatch."

The dragon started to give him a look that made it clear that he was being thick headed again, but then her demeanor softened and she said, "I suppose it isn't your fault. I keep forgetting that you are not taught about dragons here in the north."

She regarded him for a moment before going on, "You see, it is unusual for a dragon to become so aware before hatching. It speaks of high intelligence and an extremely strong bond with her rider. She will hatch very soon, and I must prepare you as best I can before I have to leave. It would not be good for me to be here when she emerges from her shell."

"Why?" he asked, puzzled. "It seems strange to me that she would be so jealous of you. Is that normal among dragons?"

"Yes," she answered, "I'm afraid it is. You see, dragons are very large predators. Even though an adult dragon only eats two to four times a year depending her activity level, perhaps a bit more if she will rise to compete for a mate that year, she can quickly deplete an area of suitable game. Fortunately, going so long between meals allows the game time to forget the hunt and recover their numbers. That is why dragons don't congregate. It's in our make up to live away from other dragons so that we don't compete for resources."

"But that doesn't explain the jealousy," he said.

"I'm getting to that," she said, annoyance once again creeping into her voice. "As I've told you, a young dragon eats a great deal of food. It's all a female can do in the wild to provide for her hatchlings until they are ready to hunt for themselves. That is why a non-bonded female never lays her eggs in her own territory. By the time the hatchlings are old enough to hunt for themselves, they are usually moving toward establishing their own territories which they will guard even from their own mothers."

"But," he blurted out, "I'm not her food, I'm her partner. Why the jealousy?"

"If you will be patient," she pronounced each syllable with great care as if speaking to a dullard, "I will explain."

Delno closed his open mouth with an almost audible snap. She continued, "The jealousy is a projection of the territorial instinct. You see, while the male dragon is a solitary creature who disdains any company, even the company of females unless both are ready to mate, the female dragon craves companionship. If the male dragons shared the female's craving, the world might become over populated with dragons. Even if dragons allowed other females in their territory, they would soon deplete an area of game. If dragons congregated and propagated the way you humans do, they would eat themselves to extinction. That is why female dragons first began bonding to humans. It fills a large empty void that we feel when we are alone. The jealousy my daughter feels is an extension of her territorial instinct projected onto you."

Delno was shocked; he had seen the results of unbridled jealousy among soldiers when they had drunk enough to remove their inhibitions in the presence of willing "ladies." He didn't think this was a good thing, and said so to the dragon.

"Don't worry," she replied, "right now she is still very young and immature. This will soften in a short time as she grows. By the end of her first month, she will even be willing to tolerate the presence of another dragon, providing the other dragon's rider is there also. By the time she is three months old, she will be relatively civil to another dragon even if the rider isn't there." Then she added, with a mischievous grin, "By the time she is ready to bear you as rider, she will most likely even tolerate you sharing the affections of a human female, provided, of course, that you don't get too emotionally involved."

As Delno was about to make a comment about the last tidbit of information, the dragon said, "Now then, we have spoken of this enough; we must get on with your lesson. It may be your last, and I have much to teach you."

While he had known that the young dragon would eventually hatch, and most likely sooner than later, it had not loomed so large until the dragon's last statement. He was startled into silence.

# CHAPTER 11

H E SAT QUIETLY while the dragon composed her thoughts. Finally, she began the lesson.

"Magic is, when applied correctly, quite simply, the movement of energy in a controlled method that brings about a desired result. Force of will, though certainly important, is not enough by itself. Intent and focus are vital to success. When I wanted to heal you and focused my mind, through the use of a word, on the cut on your hand, the cut healed."

"I have always believed that there was a magical language that was used when casting spells," he said, then quickly closed his mouth and flushed, mentally chastising himself for speaking out of turn.

The dragon, however, appeared unperturbed by the interruption. "There are many who believe this, and, for them, it is true."

As often happened, Delno was more confused than enlightened by the dragon's statement. It must have shown on his face, so she explained her comment. "You see, there are two things that affect magic and how well, or how badly, it works: intent and focus."

She paused and looked at him to be sure she had his undivided attention. "Think of it this way. If I were to look at a cut on your hand and say the same words I spoke two days ago, but not really intend to heal you, nothing would happen. By the same token, if I intended to heal you, but my attention was focused elsewhere, the result would still be nothing. I first must decide what to do and decide to do it: intent. Then I apply my thoughts to directing the energy to accomplish the action: focus."

"That makes sense. I have thought a little about how I can find lost items. I first want to find it, then I clear my mind and focus on the lost object, then I simply let the impulse move me to where it can be found."

"Yes," she said, pleased by his observation. "You have the force of will to work magic, or you would not be able to bond with a dragon, and now you begin to understand how intent and focus work. Very good."

Seeing his pride swell at the compliment, she went on quickly, "Don't get too full of yourself just yet, though. There is still much for you to learn. Tell me, have you ever found something, anything, that would be better off lost?"

He started to laugh at the question, then realized the dragon was being completely serious. After considering the question for several moments, he said, "There was one time."

When he seemed unwilling to go on, she pressed the point, "Tell me about it."

He paused and collected his thoughts. "I was quite young and had told several people about my talent. A young man came to me and said that he had been told that I could help him find something. He seemed to be in great distress, and begged me to find his wife. I was afraid that she might have wandered off and been injured, and knew that if that were the case, she might need help, so I agreed. I asked him for something of hers, and he gave me her scarf. I concentrated on the scarf for a while, and then I knew I could find her, so I led him to her."

He stopped, unwilling to proceed, but the dragon insisted, so he continued. "When he found her, a change came over him. He went from concerned, caring husband to enraged tyrant in the blink of an eye. He began swearing at her, telling her how she had humiliated him by running away, and calling her the foulest of names. Then he began beating her with his fists. I tried to stop him, but I was only a boy. He struck me down so hard that I was unable to get back up. Then he dragged her off by her hair. She never said a word, but the terrified look she gave me as he threw her through the door of the shed she had been hiding in haunts me to this day. I have never again used my gift to look for a person."

The dragon nodded, "Then you understand that even with the best of intentions, magic can cause harm. Good, you should remember that always so that you don't inadvertently harm the innocent in an effort to help.

"Now," she intoned, "we will deal with *magic words*. Remember, all words have power. All words can be used to work magic. It is how you perceive that word that gives it its specific power. Therefore, one word may have different powers for different people. My intent is to heal a wound. I focus that intent by putting my mind to the task, and release the energy I am using through my focus word: heal. To me, that means that the wound will heal completely. If you look at your hand, you will be hard pressed to find even a faint trace of scar."

Delno quickly looked and was surprised to see that she was right: there was no longer even a scar were the deep gash had been.

She smiled at him, "If 'heal' meant 'stop the bleeding and keep out infection' to me, then you would now have a thick scab, and you would be favoring that hand until a scar formed."

After allowing him to consider this for a time, she went on. "So, you see, you must first decide what you intend to do, then focus the intent. Words help, but you must make sure that you use words that mean, to you, exactly what you intend."

"What would happen if I chose a word that has more than one meaning and I'm not exactly sure of it? Can it cause harm?" he asked.

"Oh, yes," she replied. "It can cause great harm. You must understand that the energy used to work magic doesn't care how it is used. It is completely neutral. Once released to do the work, it will accomplish that task in the easiest way possible.

"Look at it this way. You decide you want to become a farmer like your favorite uncle, Ben. You decide to use magic to get yourself set up. You work the magic, saying, "I want a farm just like Uncle Ben's," then release the energy. Your favorite uncle drops dead, leaving you his farm."

"That's horrible," he said.

"That's magic," she replied. "In the example, you simply said you wanted a farm just like Uncle Ben's. You didn't stipulate that you didn't want Uncle Ben's farm, or that you didn't want any harm to come to him. The energy has no interest in whether or not he lives, so it accomplishes the task in the simplest way possible."

She allowed that to sink in for a few moments. "There are those who believe that you can add a simple catch phrase like, 'for the best interest of all concerned,' but they are merely deluding themselves to avoid their own responsibility in not thinking it through thoroughly.

"Here's another example using a favorite uncle, and older sister. You need money, so you work magic to become wealthy. You are your favorite uncle's heir. You are also your sister's heir after her husband and her three children. Now, realizing that someone could die if you aren't careful, you add "for the greatest good of all concerned" when you cast the magic. Favorite uncle dies in his sleep, leaving you wealthy."

He looked as though he wanted to say something but thought better of it, so she continued. "Why did favorite uncle die when you added the phrase that should have kept him alive? Very simple; the energy will still use the simplest method of achieving the desired results. The choices for the easiest course were favorite uncle or sister and her family. The greatest good for all concerned, and for you to get your money, was for one to die instead of five."

"It sounds like magic is something to be avoided," he said.

"Magic," she said in her sternest voice, "is something to be used with utmost care and not frivolously dallied with for personal gain. Those who are selfish enough to use magic for their own gain without regard for the ripple effects they set in motion do so at great expense to those around them.

"Now then, we will start your practical lesson with simple healing." Her abrupt change of subject caught him off guard, so she pushed ahead before he had a chance to ask further questions. "I managed to cut my foot slightly on a very sharp rock during my bath. While it is really nothing, healing it will be a good first lesson for you."

Despite years of conditioning against magic and his own bad experience with his talent, he was eager to proceed. "Tell me what to do first."

"Very well," she said, "last night I taught you to project your thoughts and shield your mind using your own personal energy. Today I will teach you to work this magic using the energy around you."

"Do you remember me telling you that the energy used in working magic is neutral?" At his nod, she said, "Good. You also need to know that everything has energy that can be drawn upon when working magic. All living things draw energy from the world. The world draws energy from the sun. Energy cannot be destroyed, it can only be altered. When a living thing dies, it gives up its energy and that energy returns to the world. Once you understand this, you can begin to feel the energy around you. You can draw on that energy and bend it to your will."

"But," he interrupted, "doesn't drawing the energy of other living creatures harm them?"

"It can," she replied, "if you drain them too much. However, you don't have to draw the energy from living creatures. The stream running by this clearing releases a great deal of energy as it flows over the rocks. The campfire releases much energy as it consumes the wood. Even a candle can give off enough energy to work a simple healing."

Delno was intrigued by her explanation. He began to reach out with his feelings to connect with the energy around him. At first, he felt nothing, but then, just on the edge of his senses, he felt the energy of the campfire. As he expanded his awareness he felt the stream. He began to feel the trees, the small animals in the brush; he even found that he could easily locate the little dragon within her egg. She was delighted at the touch and started to mentally laugh until her mother interrupted.

"Good, I see that you can feel the energy around you. Now concentrate on a word that will bring the results." While saying this, the old dragon showed him the small wound on her forefoot. It looked very small on her foot, but Delno realized that it was easily as severe as the wound on his hand had been. He concentrated on what the word heal meant in this instance. Heal to him meant that the wound should close and the skin knit so well as to leave no scar. As he was concentrating, she continued her instruction, "Now, do not draw on your own energy. Imagine that you are a hollow tube and the energy, whether you draw from the stream or from the fire, is like water that will flow through the tube. Then, as you keep all of this in mind, reach out for the energy and direct it by speaking your word of power."

He could feel the energy he was about to draw, he was pulling it from the stream, and he released it by speaking "HEAL" while directing it to the dragon's wounded foot.

The dragon let out a sharp exclamation and shook her foot as if she had been stung.

He quickly let the energy go and asked, "What's happened? Did I do something wrong? Have I injured you further?"

She hushed his rapid-fire questions and said, "No, it is I who erred. I hadn't expected that you could move the energy so well. I should have explained that you didn't need to draw the full energy of the stream."

She showed him her foot. The wound was gone without a trace, but as he examined it he realized that there was a burn where the excess had had nowhere else to go.

"I'm sorry," he said, feeling terrible that he had hurt her when he had intended to help. "Should I try and heal the burn that I caused?"

Her response was much kinder than he felt he deserved. "It is all right; I should have expected that you could move the energy more easily than most and anticipated such a result."

"How could such a thing have happened?" he implored.

"When you moved the energy, you called as much energy as you could from the stream and allowed it to flow unchecked. There was a great deal more energy than was needed to accomplish the task. The amount of power you used could easily have killed a human. Fortunately, I am larger and much more resistant to magic than one of your kind, but learn from this mistake. It would be bad to accidentally kill an ally while trying to heal him."

"This time," she continued, "you will heal the burn, but you will direct the energy more conservatively. Examine the burn to see how much energy was spent causing it: that will give you an idea of how much to channel to heal it."

Once again, he opened his mind to the energy, this time concentrating on the burn. He realized that he could actually get a feel for how much force he needed to mend the injury. He bent his will to the task, drawing a small amount of power from the dying fire, just enough to counter what he felt from the burn. As he released the energy, the dragon sighed in relief. When she showed him her foot, it was completely unmarked.

"Very good, young rider," she exclaimed. "You have learned an important lesson and started down your own magical path today."

Delno thought about the men he had seen who had died of camp fever during the war and asked, "Can I heal sickness in this same way?"

The dragon considered his question carefully before answering, "Yes, and no. You see, sickness has many causes. Some sickness is caused by something external entering the body and disturbing the body's natural balance. Some sickness is caused by weakness in the body. Some sickness is caused by weakness of the spirit. Some sickness can even be caused by magic."

She allowed him to reflect on that while she further composed her thoughts. "Sickness can be treated with magic, but the cause must be determined. If the sickness is caused by external forces, such as fever or festering, then you must draw out the sickness. When this is done, it is especially important to remember to not take the sickness into yourself, but to convert it to energy and allow it to pass through you and into the ground; otherwise, you may contract the sickness yourself; though you will soon be protected from disease by your bond with your partner."

"Send it to the ground?" he said, "Doesn't that intentionally cause harm to the world itself?"

"Do you not remember me telling you about energy?" she chided. When he nodded, she went on, "As I have told you, all things in this world get their energy from the sun, or directly from the world itself. Energy is energy, neither good nor bad. When you direct energy that is causing disharmony away from the body and into the ground, the world absorbs that energy and returns it to the source so that it is cleansed and can be used again. No harm comes to the world."

He then thought more about the wounded men he'd seen who had lived, especially those who had been maimed and still carried the scars, both physically and mentally. "What about old injuries? Can you heal someone who was crippled by an injury? Is it possible to undo the crippling effects of such a wound and make the person whole again?"

She considered his question for several moments before finally answering. "The healing you have practiced is moving energy to enhance a natural process that is already occurring; it requires no special knowledge on your part. It just requires that you provide the extra energy needed to speed up the process so that it happens in seconds or minutes instead of days or weeks, not that it isn't a very useful skill that can save a life in the event of a serious wound." She paused and drew a deep breath before continuing. "It might be possible to rearrange the living body to mend the crippling caused by an old injury, though it is currently well beyond your skill to do so. At this point, you lack both the magical skill and the medical training. There are mages who have the power, but most of them don't possess the knowledge of anatomy required to do it either."

She paused, gathering her thoughts, "Remember what I told you about intent?" When he nodded, she continued, "If someone is crippled by an injury, you would need to know about the physical structures within the body to heal them, otherwise your efforts would simply be hit or miss. You might get lucky, but you might cause even more harm. The same would hold true for a fresh wound such as a severed limb. You could use magic to reattach the limb, but if you know nothing about the structures, you might end up with a reattached limb that has an inadequate blood supply. That would then result in the limb becoming septic and infecting the rest of the body. You could kill the person trying to save his arm or leg." Before he could ask, she added, "As for healing a cripple, or re-growing a limb, that takes a very high degree of skill with magic, and an uncommonly complete knowledge of anatomy."

After a moment, she said, "Also, remember that not everyone wants to be healed."

"Why wouldn't someone want to be healed of a crippling injury?"

"Well," she told him, "some people become comfortable with their infirmities." Before he could object to her statement, she went on, "I'm sure you've seen instances where a person with a moderate to severe physical impairment finds a way to function at some meaningful task." Again, he nodded. "I'm also sure that you've seen people no more disabled who either let others take care of them or end up as beggars, seemingly unable to do anything else."

"Yes," he said thoughtfully, "I have."

"While not all who are crippled in some way have the ability, or the opportunity, to rise above their infirmities, there are those who let their disabilities rule their lives because it gives them an excuse not to try. They define themselves by their disability rather than by their abilities. Removing that disability, if you are able to do so safely, could cause them to lose the one hold they have on life. Once they are no longer disabled, they then have no reason other than their own inadequacy for failing, and they can easily become suicidal."

They were both silent for a long time before she spoke again. "You have been given a great opportunity. The thing you need to remember in everything you do, but especially when magic is concerned, is that you must be sure of the situation before you act, because a careless act of kindness could easily go awry and cause great harm. Unless your life, or the life of someone else, is in immediate danger, you must learn to think things through thoroughly before acting. It is always easier to not make a careless mistake than it is to remedy the act once it's been done."

He started to ask another question, but was silenced by a sharp hiss from the dragon. "Hush now, our time is short, and I must tell you several things before we part."

At her words, Delno became acutely aware of his contact with the young dragon. She had grown anxious, and he felt she was in some need. He started to go to her when the old female called him back. "She will be fine. You must listen to what I have to say."

He was momentarily torn between his perceived need to help his partner directly and his need for the training the old female wanted to impart. He decided that her words were important and that he had best listen.

"You have felt the magic, and you have some degree of control over it," she said. "You must understand that the same energy that you use to heal can be used for defense or attack. That knowledge can save your life if you keep your wits about you when a crisis arises. You summoned enough energy today to kill several of your kind. That is great power and should only be used at great need, but don't hesitate to use it if the need is great. There is no dishonor in using magic to kill when you are out-numbered or outmatched."

"Killing is not honorable, but is sometimes necessary," he stated flatly.

The dragon was stopped short at his comment. She considered him for a moment, and said, more to herself than to him, "Yes, I believe you were the right choice."

Then she drew herself up and said, "I have taught you only the very basics of one type of magic. I haven't the time to teach you more and you need the training. There is an old conjurer in the southern kingdom of Palamore. You must seek him out and learn from him. His name is Jhren."

"Will he be willing to instruct me?" he asked.

"I doubt it," she responded, "but when he refuses, you must tell him your dragon's name and say to him that teaching you will fulfill his debt to Corolan."

The name she spoke was almost a whisper and brought such sadness to the old dragon that Delno realized at once that Corolan could only have been her rider. He bowed his head and said, "I will do as you have bidden me, but can't you tell me my dragon's name?"

"No," she stated in a way that invited no rebuttal. "Have you not noticed that I have never asked your name? Haven't you noticed that we have not referred to each other by names at all?"

At his nod, she continued, "As I have told you, words have power, and names have great power. By knowing each other's names, we make a much stronger connection. I like you, human, but I have no desire to strengthen that connection by exchanging names. If we did, I would have one more thing to tie me to this world that I am desperate to leave. Your partner will know her name, and she will tell you."

They stared at each other for several moments. Finally, he nodded once, and with tears coursing unchecked down his cheeks, he placed his hand on the old dragon's snout said, "I understand, and I would not hold you to this world longer than you wish, but know this; you have touched me deeply, and you will never be forgotten."

The old dragon reached out to the pile of forest debris and uncovered the egg. She bent forward and spoke to the egg for several moments.

Delno couldn't catch the words, but he understood that the mother was somehow passing on her daughter's legacy.

Then, with her own tears flowing, she said, "I have but one gift left to give you in payment for saving my life and the life of my daughter. It is a small thing, but it is all I have." She again leaned her head over her daughter's egg and breathed a small gout of flame on the shell. The fire was so hot that it was uncomfortable from several feet away.

He was initially alarmed that the little dragon would be harmed. At the look on his face, she said, "Do not worry, she has taken no hurt. What I have done is mark the shell so that when it breaks, one shard will form a blade. It will need to have a handle fashioned, but it will be impervious to harm and never dull. I hope it serves you well."

Then, with one last backward glance, she gathered herself up and leapt to the sky. In just a few moments she was lost to sight, though Delno stood and watched the sky where she had vanished for nearly a quarter of an hour, until the sound of the little dragon breaking through her shell brought him back to where he was and what was at hand.

# CHAPTER 12

W HILE HE WATCHED the egg, it rocked frantically as the young dragon fought to escape her tiny prison. At first, it looked as though the shell was just too hard for the creature to break, then a small crack appeared near one end. The egg rocked even faster, and the crack widened. More cracks began to line the surface. Then a small piece of shell broke loose, and the little dragon's nose poked out, and she began working at the shell around the hole. Soon, her whole head was sticking out, and she was pushing, almost angrily, at the rest of the tough casing in which she was trapped.

Delno started to move to help but she hissed and told him in no uncertain terms that she could and would manage this herself.

She gave a last shudder, and then the shell seemed to almost explode, and she was left standing, spreading her small wings. Her posture looked exactly like her mother's posture just before she leaped in the air to fly. The only word he could think of to describe her was majestic.

Delno's second thought was how wonderfully gorgeous she was with the sun shining on her. She was a beautiful bronze color, and, as the sun glinted off her scales and hide when she flexed her muscles, he could see hints of both green and red iridescence.

The next thing he noticed was that now that the immediacy of freeing herself from her egg had passed, her hunger was rapidly moving to the forefront. He cast around for something to feed her and realized that all he had in camp was a slab of bacon and some jerky. He had no sooner thought of these then she made an awkward, but ferocious attack on the pack that held the provisions. She tore through the tough canvas bag as easily as if it had been nothing but a layer of butcher's paper. Realizing that this would not hold her long, he reached out and told her that he would have to leave her to get meat.

"*Why must you go?*" she said. She seemed afraid of the prospect of being alone.

"*If I take you with me we might be seen,*" he replied, "*that would be bad. It isn't that far, I won't be gone long. Just wait here and I will bring you back enough for the next couple of days.*"

"*I don't want to be alone,*" she whined petulantly.

"*If you had given me a bit more warning before breaking out of your shell, I would have had the meat here,*" he told her. "*As it is, I have no choice but to go and fetch it.*" Then he added, "*Unless you would rather go hungry?*"

His question convinced her. "*You will hurry?*" she implored.

"*I'll run as fast as my legs will carry me,*" he assured her. "*You stay here and stay out of sight. There are most likely no people about, but I don't want to take any chances.*"

She wasn't happy about staying, but she controlled her hunger, which was considerable despite the fact that she had just devoured enough bacon and jerky to fill the stomachs of three men, and found a comfortable place under a large bush to hide while he went for more food.

As he turned to leave, he noticed the shards of the dragon's egg. Among the debris was one that stood out from the rest. It was obviously the blade his partner's mother had made for him. It looked just like the old saber he carried, but with the tang exposed. The blade, about a yard long including the tang, looked like ceramic instead of steel. He picked it up and realized that it was lighter than metal but felt strangely more substantial than any other weapon he ever before held. He tucked it into his belt and took it with him.

He was a bit surprised to find himself still breathing easily after sprinting to the pasture. He hopped the low wall and quickly located the flock of sheep. He chose the largest and strode forward, intent on cutting it out of the flock and herding it to the clearing. He was just beginning to think that it would be a good idea to take several animals back when the dragon's hunger washed over him so suddenly that he almost doubled over from the physical sensation of it. He quickly used his mental skill to damp down the contact, but the urgency was unmistakable. He decided to bring just one animal and return for a couple more once she was sated.

He soon discovered that herding sheep was a learned skill, not an inborn talent. The next thing he learned was that herding one sheep away from the flock was nearly an impossibility. The individual he had chosen weighed nearly as much as he did, and he had no rope or other such material with him to make a collar to lead the animal. The sheep was extremely reluctant to leave the others of the flock. Every time he made a little progress in moving the beast away from the others it would take the first opportunity to rejoin them. The tug-of-war with the creature would have been comical if he had not had the little dragon in his mind alternately demanding and imploring him to hurry.

He chose a somewhat smaller one and decided that he would have to butcher it as best he could right there in the pasture and carry as much meat back as possible. When he grabbed the animal he remembered that the only blade he had brought was the one made for him by the mother dragon. Being somewhat reluctant to use that for something as mundane as slaughtering a herd animal, he decided to try and carry the sheep back alive. Grabbing the ewe's legs, its back legs in his right hand and its front legs in his left, he hoisted it over his shoulders with its legs dangling on either side. The ewe struggled very briefly then became quite quiet and placid. He moved back to the low, stone wall and stepped over. Then he started running back to the clearing where his young partner was waiting rather impatiently for his return. While the return trip was a bit slower with the extra weight of the ewe draped over his shoulders, Delno was still pleasantly surprised at how easily he moved, considering the handicap.

When he entered the camp, the young dragon rushed forward to meet him. While she was certainly a bit awkward compared to what he had seen of her mother, she was still able to move rather quickly, and was nearly dancing when he stopped and set the ewe on the ground. It was all he could do to keep her from pouncing on the sheep and trying to eat it alive.

He swiftly went to his gear and grabbed his belt knife and used it to cut the animal's throat. He made the cut so quickly that the ewe showed no reaction and just stood there dumbly as its life drained from its severed jugular vein. The young dragon reacted instantly to the blood, positioning herself to catch the warm liquid as it drained from the sheep's neck. He almost tried to restrain her, but then thought better of doing so, reasoning that the blood was probably as nourishing as the meat itself, and the act of drinking the blood seemed to take some of the edge off of her hunger.

As the sheep succumbed to the blood loss and finally lay down and died, he set about butchering it. As he gutted it, she immediately went for the entrails. While she had been in the throes of her hunger pangs, he had not tried to open the contact enough to communicate more than general assurances that she would be fed soon. Now he decided that he would try and converse with her.

"*I thought you would be more interested in the meat than the gut,*" he said.

"*I will eat the meat,*" she replied, "*but there are substances contained in the gut that can't be found in the meat alone.*"

"*You seem to be quite aware of your needs and how to fill them,*" he observed. "*Are all dragons born with such knowledge?*"

"*Dragons are born with certain. . .*" she searched for the right words, "*memories,*" she finally said. "*Such memories are imprinted on us before our egg is laid.*"

"*How much do you know?*" he asked. "*Do you have the full knowledge of an adult?*"

"*I have much to learn and much to grow before I will be an adult,*" she said. "*However, if you don't either cut up that carcass or get out of my way and let me feed, I will not be able to grow.*"

Delno realized that he had stopped working on the carcass while they talked. He returned to the task. He was just starting to skin the animal when she asked plaintively, "*What are you doing?*"

"*I am skinning the animal for you,*" he responded.

"*I will eat the skin with the rest,*" she implored, "*please just cut it into manageable sections and let me eat.*"

Chuckling as he worked, he did as she asked. He first removed one front leg, separating the shoulder joint and slicing it from the rest of the body. The dragon took it without ceremony, or manners, and devoured it quickly, bones and all. He removed the head and was laying it aside when she sighed out audibly and said mentally, "*There's no need to be dainty and great need to be quick.*" So he gave the head to her, and she made short work of it. After that, he simply cut pieces loose and gave them to her indiscriminately.

As her hunger began to abate, after she had eaten approximately eight stone of meat, he decided that he would have to either move their camp closer to the pasture or figure out some way to bring several animals at time to avoid a repeat of this morning's frantic run for provisions. When he mentioned this to the dragon, she merely thought that he should do as he felt best. Then, before he could speak with her further, she fell asleep. As he looked at her, he realized that she had eaten so much that he could see the outline of part of the meal through the skin over her belly.

He took the small portion of one back leg that she hadn't eaten, and, banking the coals from the fire, he placed that meat, wrapped in leaves, in the heat to bake for himself to eat later. Then, deciding she would be safe enough if he kept the link fully open, he left her sleeping while he went to move several animals to the camp to facilitate feeding her.

The trip, though uneventful, took much longer than his mad dash to procure her first meal. The sun was past noon when he returned to camp with three sheep and one rather disgruntled pig. He figured after a couple of days she would welcome the change in her diet, and he was sure that he would be ready for something besides mutton by then.

He sat down beside her and rested his hand on her shoulder. She moved into the touch. He decided that, though she was still very young, she was big enough to rest his head on her. As he did so, she sighed contentedly and soon they were both asleep.

In his dream, they were standing on a mountain top watching other dragons fly, and she was telling him her lineage. As she told him of her mother, she turned to him and said, "My mother passed on her name to me. I am Geneva, and I am bonded to you, Delno."

The dragon awoke with a start, dumping him fully on his back. Coming wholly awake in that instant, he knew that she perceived some danger. He jumped to his feet, hand on his belt knife. "*What's wrong?*" he queried, trusting that her senses were much keener than his own.

"*There are two creatures approaching from that way,*" she replied, nodding her head to indicate the direction.

While his hearing wasn't as acute as hers, the sound of the two beasts tramping through the brush was unmistakable. Realizing just how small his belt knife was, he reached for a log to use as a club. It was too late; the first of the two creatures burst from the bush and caught him full in the chest, taking him to the ground.

# CHAPTER 13

A S HE LAY on the ground, expecting to die horribly, the monstrous beast began to lick his face sloppily and breathe its foul breath on him. At that same moment, Nassari's voice said, "Oh, there you are Del, I was afraid even Chester wouldn't be able to find you: figured you'd climbed to someplace inaccessible."

The young dragon was just about to leap to his defense when he stopped her with a thought. Not fully understanding why, but knowing he was more annoyed than frightened, she held her place, but remained ready to strike.

"Nassari," he blurted angrily, "what the hell are you doing here?" Then giving a mighty shove at the huge dog, he growled, "Get off of me, Chester!"

Nassari started to respond to the question. "Well, I had rather thought. . . ." his words caught in his throat as he noticed the dragon. He raised his hand, pointing at her and trying to speak coherently, but what came out was just the syllable "wha, wha, wha . . . ?" before he was completely dumbstruck.

As Delno sat up, he looked at his friend. Nassari seemed to have lost his ability to move as well as his ability to speak, so Delno answered the question he assumed that Nassari had been trying to ask. "That, my friend, is a dragon." He was about to go on, but then thought better of it and let his friend stare mutely while he assimilated that little tidbit of information.

Chester tried to lick Delno's hand, so he grabbed the dog's tongue and held on. After almost a minute, with the dog trying unsuccessfully to extricate its tongue from his grasp, he let go. It was a rather disgusting way to make the dog stop licking him, but it worked without actually hurting the animal. Chester, realizing he wouldn't be allowed to indulge himself in licking Delno's hand, turned his attention on the strange new beast in the clearing. As he approached the dragon with his tail wagging and his tongue lolling, she hissed and struck out at him. Even though she was very young, she had a considerable mouth full of teeth, and Delno had seen her snap the leg bone of a sheep like a dried twig.

As he shouted "NO!" to both animals, the dog, reacting more quickly than its size would have seemed to allow, jumped back just out of range. Mentally he added, in a much softer tone, to the dragon, *"Please do not harm this creature. While he can be annoying at times, he is only a faithful pet and means you no harm."*

*"You have a pet?"* she responded, her mental tone sounding jealous.

*"No, he is my friend's pet, but I have known him since he was a puppy."* Then he hastily added, *"They won't be staying too long."*

While she resonated uncertainty, she settled down and stopped eyeing the dog as though he was her next meal.

While this was all happening, Nassari once again found his voice, "What in the world is that, and where did you get it?"

"It's a very long story, Nassari, one that I had hoped that I wouldn't have to tell you." He sighed resignedly, and after a moment's thought, said, "Sit down, my friend, and I will tell you everything."

While his ability to move was returning, Nassari had seen the dragon almost decapitate a dog that weighed nearly thirteen stone, and he was quite reluctant to get any nearer to her, so he simply dropped to the ground where he was standing.

"As I said, she is a dragon," Delno began, but was interrupted by waves of hunger that caught him off guard. Realizing that the hunger came from the object of the conversation, he reached out to her mentally, *"You can't be hungry again. I was told that you would eat a third of your body weight each day: you've already eaten nearly twice that amount!"*

*"Normally I wouldn't be so hungry. However, I used up all of my nourishment before my egg was laid, then I waited several days to break free of the shell. I have gone long without food and need sustenance; one more good feeding and I believe that my appetite will diminish some."*

Telling Nassari he would have to wait for his explanation, Delno fetched one of the sheep and cut its throat as he had done earlier. As before, the dragon caught as much of the blood as she could, and then waited, this time more patiently, for him to begin butchering the animal.

Once he had opened the animal's gut, and, much to Nassari's disgust, given the entrails to her, he started recounting his strange tale to his friend. The dragon ate much more daintily this time, for which he was grateful. The telling, punctuated by pauses as he butchered the sheep and fed the pieces to her, took more than hour. She ate less this time, and there was nearly half a sheep left when she told him the haunch he had just given her would be enough.

"*What am I to do with the rest of the carcass?*" he asked.

"*Leave it; I will eat it later.*"

"*It will turn quickly in this heat,*" he observed.

She chuckled mentally, "*While dragons are not scavengers of carrion, we have strong enough stomachs to eat meat that is slightly tainted.*"

Never being one to be ignored for any length of time, Nassari cleared his throat and said, "So you intend to keep this creature, and to head south?"

"Of course I do," he stated. "After all, what choice do I have?"

"You could let it go free and get on with your life right here," Nassari retorted. "After all, what do you owe the creature? You saved its life and the life of its mother. Haven't you already done enough?"

"*It,*" her anger at the insult would have been apparent without the mental link. Her sides were puffed out; instead of just the iridescent flashes of red as before, her overall color had take on a reddish tint, and her posture was frighteningly reminiscent of just before she struck out at Chester.

"*Calm yourself, dear one,*" he soothed. Out loud he said, in what he hoped was a stern enough tone that even Nassari couldn't miss his meaning, "**She** is not some dumb beast that I somehow captured. **She** is a fully aware being with intelligence and feelings. **She** can also understand every word you say, and **she** is quite insulted."

"It," he began; then, noticing the dragon's bared teeth, quickly corrected himself, "She . . . can understand every word?"

Delno nodded, "Her name is Geneva."

Having just seen the dragon devour half a sheep, and have no problem with even the thickest bones, Nassari shifted a bit uncomfortably and said, "My apologies, Geneva. No dragon lore is taught in the northern kingdoms, so I must plead ignorance and beg your forgiveness."

The dragon looked Nassari over intently, causing him to shift slightly to put Delno between her and himself in case the apology wasn't accepted. Delno found that he was perversely pleased with his friend's discomfort; like when they children and he would chase Nassari with a particularly nasty looking specimen of some bug or small reptile.

Geneva settled back down, and the reddish cast of her hide drained away. Nassari breathed a sigh of relief. "*Apology accepted,*" she said. Delno relayed the thought.

"So, Del," Nassari went on, "there's no way to talk you out of this?" Then he quickly added to Geneva, "I mean no offense to you, of course, it's just that I don't like the idea of my best friend going away and never seeing him again."

Fortunately, Geneva took no offense.

"I've told you, Nassari, I have no choice in this. She and I are bonded. The only way for that bond to be broken is if one of us dies. If that happens, the other will die also. Besides, I am looking forward to going south. I would probably have moved on anyway. This just gives me a definite purpose for going."

"Do you really believe all of it?" Nassari asked. "A bond that only death can sever, the prolonged life, all of it?"

"Yes," he responded, "I rather think I do."

"But, Del, magic? We've been taught all our lives that magic is evil and should be avoided, and here you go rushing headlong into it."

Delno took so long to consider his answer that his friend had begun to wonder if he would respond at all. Finally he said, "I can use a hammer to build a structure. If I use that same hammer to kill someone for no reason, does that make the hammer evil?"

Nassari considered his friend's words and then said, "A hammer is an inanimate object. It has no will of its own."

"Neither does the magic." He let that hang in the air for a few seconds before pressing on, "Nassari, all of our lives we've been taught that magic is evil, that it somehow corrupts a person and makes that person evil. In actuality, it is the person who uses magic for evil purposes who is corrupt. Like the hammer, the magic is merely the tool he uses."

Nassari looked as though he was not entirely convinced, but he didn't pursue the argument. "Having your life prolonged at the expense of the dragon seems a bit one-sided to me. How does that balance out?" he challenged.

"Well, I'm not exactly sure that you or I would ever consider it balanced, but, according what I've been told, female dragons abhor being alone, but nature has forced them to shun their own kind for the good of the species. So, since they would rather live a shorter life than solitary one, they choose to bond with humans."

At this point Geneva began speaking to him, and he relayed her words to Nassari. *"You see, magic itself can manipulate energy, but it can not create life. The extra life that the rider gets must come from somewhere, and since there is such open flow of magical energy between the dragon and her rider, it is logical for that life to come from her. It is something that all bonded female dragons understand and accept as the price we willingly pay for the companionship and love we receive from the relationship."*

Nassari thought about this for a few seconds and then asked, "If magic can draw this energy from you to him, couldn't you, or he, draw this energy from other sources, like the herd beasts or some such?"

While Delno thought this sounded a bit too much like being a parasite for his liking, even he was surprised by Geneva's almost violent reaction. She drew herself up as if she was ready to strike and roared at Nassari. Mentally she said, and he translated, *"Only the vilest and most evil practitioners of magic would do such a thing. To take from another in such a way is worse than being a parasite. At least a parasite is born to be what it is: a person who sinks to that level does so by choice. He puts himself so far above the rest of the world that he feels that he has a right to drain away what nature has given them for his own use. He has no concern for other life and becomes an entity that is an enemy to all and should be hunted down and destroyed."*

Delno soothed her mentally while Nassari, more frightened than Delno had ever seen him, apologized.

"I meant no harm in the question," he said, "it was merely an academic exercise. You see, until about two hours ago, I hadn't given much thought to magic at all."

Geneva calmed down and said, *"It is all right; I'm sure your friend meant no harm, but I am young and my emotions can swing strongly. It is abhorrent to me, as it should be to all thinking-feeling beings. Fortunately, it is an extremely difficult thing to do, and most magic users who acquire the mastery of magic required for such a practice are not inclined to do so."*

Never being one to leave well enough alone, Nassari went on, "I don't wish to offend, but what about the animals you eat? You are killing them anyway; why is draining their life such a bad thing?"

Geneva began to bristle at his question, but calmed down as Delno pointed out that Nassari was simply asking questions out of ignorance. She answered, "Nature has produced predators and prey. When an animal is born as a prey animal, it is natural that at some point in its life it may be killed and eaten. Even predators may be eaten by larger predators, and eventually all animals are eaten by scavengers if they die of old age. That is the natural way of things. When an animal dies, whether it is killed by another or succumbs to old age, its life energy returns to nature and the animal will be reborn. If you take that life energy, then it can not return to nature, and it can not be reborn until you die. It is a perverse practice that places the life energy of those drained in limbo. Some even believe that doing such condemns the poor creature to complete oblivion, unable to ever be reborn."

After listening carefully to Delno's translation of Geneva's thoughts, Nassari found he was both willing to accept the dragon's explanation, and rather fascinated with her overall philosophy on death and rebirth.

He was also quite curious about how the dragon, herself new born to the world, could have such extensive knowledge.

Delno didn't wait for Geneva; he supplied his own answer to his friend's curiosity. "The old female told me that all dragons are born with some racial knowledge. I believe that she also imparted a great deal more than is normal to Geneva just before she left."

At his explanation, Geneva nodded in an almost human manner, so he continued. "You see, females have some special bond with the last female offspring they bear. That dragon child is to carry on the female's name and her family honor. That's why that dragon carries the name of the mother."

Again the dragon nodded in affirmation.

Nassari was about to ask another question when Delno interrupted him. "Nassari, my friend, I know that you are always one for seeking new knowledge, and I see that you could easily spend the next week asking questions, but we must move on. What has brought you out into the wilds to find me? I thought you had a political campaign to run."

"Very well," Nassari replied, "one last question and I will answer you."

Delno nodded and Nassari asked, "Why can Geneva not speak? You told me her mother spoke directly to you."

Delno was himself a little puzzled and looked to Geneva who said, "*I don't speak because I am very young. In six or eight weeks, when I have gained some physical maturity, I should be able to hold up a reasonable conversation.*"

After relaying the answer, Delno said to Nassari, "Now it is your turn to answer my questions."

"Well, there is no great shake up, I assure you. I haven't given up politics and decided to join you on the road. I simply saw that my candidate would win hands down and decided that I could take a bit of time off." Then he added with a slight bow, "So, here I am."

"You have to tell me how that worked out. You made it sound as though we would be working like farmers at harvest for the next two weeks if I had run for the office."

"So I thought we would," he responded. "However, when I took my candidate to the council to present him, he got into a shouting match with one of the other prospective candidates. Before the council could call for order, he had struck the other man in the face hard enough to nearly knock him unconscious. The whole thing ended in a furious brawl. It took a dozen town guards to restore order."

Delno was shocked. "So they disqualified your candidate? But, you said he was sure to win. I don't understand."

Nassari laughed out loud. "Who said anything about disqualified? The crowd loved it. He put up such a good fight that he's a sure winner for the open seat." Then, still chuckling, he added, "Perhaps you were right about not being a good politician."

"But, fighting in the council chambers?" Delno was more flabbergasted than ever.

"Del, have you never gone to a council meeting?" When Delno shook his head 'no' he continued, "Shouting matches are frequent and actual fist fights are common among the council members, although the town guards assigned to the council do try to keep real bloodshed to a minimum. Hell, Del, half the people who attend council meetings only go there to cheer on their favorite member in the brawls that break out." Then he added with a laugh, "The fact that the soldiers would vote for one of their own wasn't the only reason I wanted you, the retired soldier and hero, to take a seat on the council; I figured that you could hold your own in a fist fight against a bunch of merchants and politicians."

Delno just shook his head, convinced more than ever that he had made the right decision.

"Anyway," Nassari went on, "after that, I did a quick poll and realized that the only way my man can lose now is if he falls and breaks his neck. So, I thought I would look you up and spend some time together before you leave. Of course, I had to do some detective work and enlist Chester to find you."

Geneva, realizing that the conversation had shifted away from her and her kind, and, being full of fresh meat, curled up and went to sleep as the two friends continued talking into the night.

# CHAPTER 14

ELNO WOKE EARLY the next morning. Geneva was already awake and finishing the carcass of the sheep from the previous evening. "*I thought they wouldn't be staying long,*" she said, a definite note of accusation in her voice.

"What was I supposed to do? I couldn't very well tell Nassari to walk home in the dark. Besides, there's something I want to do in town, and I thought I might ask Nassari to stay and watch out for you until I return."

"*I don't need looking after like some human infant,*" she said indignantly.

"*You are certainly formidable enough to discourage most predators. I doubt that even a bear would face off against you. But there is always the possibility that a hunter might happen by, and with your hearing to give advanced warning and Nassari's gift of the tongue to put him off the scent, you would remain undiscovered, which is the point of staying so far from town in the first place.*"

"*I don't like it when you are gone away so far,*" she said peevishly.

"*And I don't like being away from you, Dear Heart, but I need to get a few more provisions for myself, and I would like to get a few things in preparation for moving on our way. I promise I won't be any longer than necessary.*"

As Geneva was about to respond, Nassari got up and made his way to the bushes. The dragon snorted, and Delno took that as the closest he would get to an actual affirmative response from her on the subject.

As Nassari stumbled back into camp, Delno told his friend of his plan to visit the city, and Nassari reluctantly agreed to stay with Geneva. Then, quickly killing another sheep and cutting off several nice pieces for his friend to cook for himself and the dog, he placed the rest of the meat within easy reach of the dragon. With everything he could do done, he started his trip to town.

He set a brisk pace for himself and was again surprised at how easily he seemed to maintain a stride that should have quickly tired him. He decided that increased stamina must be one of the side effects of the bonding that the old female had hinted at. At the rate he was traveling, he was able to reach the city before the sun was even half way to noon.

Upon entering the gates, he made as direct a course as possible through the twisting streets to a metalsmith he knew. Approaching the shop, he could hear the sound of steel ringing on steel. As he entered, he could feel the heat of the forge, and wondered how people could stand to do such work during the summer months.

It took several moments for his eyes to adjust to the relative darkness of the place. Besides being a large space to provide light for, the smiths liked to keep ambient lighting dim inside so that they could accurately judge the temperature of the piece they were working by the color and brightness of the hot metal. The shop was filled with different projects in various states of completion. Several journeymen and over a dozen apprentices were working at the different jobs assigned to them. The youngest, and least experienced, were pumping bellows at the forges or fetching and carrying whatever materials were needed, while the more experienced were actually wielding tongs, hammers, or other tools. Standing in front of a large slate was a man who reminded Delno of the big bears that plagued the herders in the wilder parts of the country. The man wore braces on both of his legs and walked with an awkward rolling gate that did nothing to dispel the ursine image. Seeing Delno, the huge man, Elom, smiled and waved to him.

Delno approached the man a bit cautiously. They had been friends for years. Elom had joined the military because of their friendship. Delno had not only been present during the attack that had resulted in Elom's injuries, but he had been in charge, and he still felt quite guilty about it.

Seeing Delno's caution and concern, Elom said, "Still blaming yourself for that ambush, Corporal? Sorry, I forget it's Lieutenant now." Elom, still smiling, used the title of rank as a show of respect, which only heightened Delno's feeling of guilt.

"Actually, it's neither. I've given up the army life all together. As for the ambush, if I'd been a better leader, it might not have happened."

Elom grimaced and said, "Corporal, if you'd been less of a leader and less attentive, the ambush would have been a hell of a lot more successful, and we'd not be around to be having this conversation." The big man shook his head and said, nearly shouting, "Damn it, man, if you'd just look at it objectively, you'd realize that you did the best anyone could have under the circumstances."

Delno would have been ready for Elom to hate him, but the man's gratitude only made his own sense of shame worse. "If I'd sent more scouts ahead, we might not have walked into that narrow ravine in the first place."

"Nonsense," growled Elom, "you led us where you were ordered to lead us, and...."

Delno cut him off, "And you paid a dear price for my obedience to orders, and the fact that I pushed you right under those falling rocks."

"Oh damn it all, give it a rest, will you? You pushed me out of the way. I tripped and the big rock that would have crushed my skull and killed me crushed my legs instead. You saved my life, and I can still get around my father's shop and do my work just fine."

Delno opened his mouth to make further objection but Elom spoke first. "You saved my life. Then, when you couldn't shift that boulder off my legs and pull me to safety, you stood over me despite the arrows whizzing around your head and fought off seven enemy soldiers who would have liked to finish me while I was laying there helpless." Then he added in a loud, dangerous voice that invited no argument, "You are the reason I'm standing here alive today, and I'll have no man, not even you, Corporal, saying any different or even hinting that you did anything wrong that day."

Delno looked around and realized that all work had stopped and that everyone in the shop had heard the exchange. All he could do was smile and reach out to clasp hands with his friend. Elom returned the smile, and clasping Delno's arm, pulled him close and picked him up off the floor, wrapping his huge arms around him in a bear hug. He was sure he could feel his ribs bending under Elom's forearms and wondered briefly, before he was released, if he might be safer if Elom had held some animosity for him.

Once Delno's feet were again on solid ground, and his ribs were no longer in that iron-solid grip, Elom sent an apprentice for beer and led Delno to a table. The big man refused to speak of anything until the two of them had raised full glasses and toasted their old unit and those friends who had not returned from the war.

Elom looked him in the eye and said, "Now then, what brings you to my father's shop?"

"I thought this was your shop. I'd heard that your father retired." he responded.

"Aye, he retired, but I will always think of this shop as his. It was he who built this with his own hands, and it was he who taught me the trade and made me the finest journeyman metalsmith in the realm, and while it was you who saved my life during the war, it was he who raised me to be man enough to put aside my self pity and get on with my life when I returned. So this is, and always will be, my father's shop."

Delno had always admired Elom, but that speech elevated the man greatly in his eyes. They simply sat and stared easily at each other for a moment, and then Delno raised his glass for one last toast, "To your father," he said.

The big man smiled and raised his glass and they finished the beer.

"Now then," Delno spoke up, "I have a blade that needs some finishing touches, and I know no better man to do the job."

"A blade?" Elom said. "If you want a blade, I'll make you one that will be unequaled anywhere."

"This blade is unequaled," he responded, then hastily, to avoid any insult to Elom, he added, "Though I'm sure your metals are the finest, this blade is of a different material."

Whether he took any insult Delno couldn't tell, but he was certainly intrigued, and said, "Different material, you say, but fine enough to warrant further work? That's interesting. Let me see what you've got there."

He handed it, bundled in some rags, to the smith. Elom unwrapped the blade and was immediately fascinated by it. He examined it carefully from every angle. Finally, he said, "If this is what I think it is, you've got yourself a treasure here. Where did you come by it?"

"It was a gift." he replied. Then he added, "From a very special lady whom I believe was of regal lineage."

Elom raised his eyebrows and smirked.

"We weren't involved that way. I saved her life and the life of her child. In return, she gave me the blade."

He decided that the truth would be a bit much for the man to handle and said nothing further, even though Elom obviously wanted to hear the whole story.

"Well, if this is what I believe it to be, she must have been a very well placed lady, indeed."

"What do you mean?" Delno asked.

"Well, I have seen the like only once, years ago, before we ever met. In fact, I was just a young lad myself. My father did everything himself in those days, and I was his only apprentice. I was working the bellows and this man comes in looking for the smith. He was a small man, but walked like he was sure of himself, completely at ease without being cocky. I called my father, and the man introduced himself and said he had need of a good craftsman. Then he brings out this sword. It didn't look like any metal I'd seen, but that wasn't too surprising since I was so young. I figured that my dad would know what it was. That was the thing though; my father had never seen the like. The man said it was a Dragon Blade."

Elom stopped to refill their glasses from the pitcher and then went on. "It's some kind of ceramic that comes from down south, I reckon, but how they make it, I don't know. It's harder than any steel. In fact, my father ruined two of the finest quality steel drill bits trying to make a hole so he could rivet a new guard to the tang."

"So, are you saying that you can't work with it at all?" Delno asked.

"Oh, I'll be able to set you up all right. I'm not just braggin' when I say I'm the best. But you need to remember this; that blade will out live anything I can add to it. A few hundred years from now, your great-great-however–many-times-removed grandson will have to find another clever smith to redo the guard I'm going to make for you." Then Elom lowered his voice and added, "The legend of those blades says that they aren't made of ceramic at all."

Delno raised his eyebrows and leaned closer to listen. After looking around to ensure that none of the other craftsmen were eavesdropping, Elom continued, "They say that the dragon blades are made from the shell of the egg of a dragon using dragon's fire and magic." After letting that hang in the air between them for a moment, he went on. "From what I remember about my father working on that fellow's Dragon Blade, I almost believe it."

"You have a remarkable memory of those events," Delno said.

"I should," he responded, "it was after the man came back and retrieved the sword that things starting going so well for my father. The man was quite impressed by the work, and said my father should be thrice blessed for his fine skill. After that, we suddenly found ourselves with so much work that we had to start taking on new apprentices. It seemed that every caravan master who needed work done saved as much of it as possible for our shop. As our business grew, our fame grew, and then our business grew some more . . . I heard rumor that the man himself was somehow linked to dragons or some such. Don't know if it's true, but it sure feels good to think he was some kind of nobility."

He sat for a moment thinking, then added, "You might want to remember that when dealing with this lady of yours."

"I'll keep all of that in mind." Delno said quietly. Then he added, "How long do you think it will take you to make the guard?"

"In a hurry, are you?"

"Well, I have to go away soon, and would like to have the blade with me when I leave."

Elom thought about this for a moment before saying, "Well, if you'll be traveling, you'll be better off with a better blade, so I'll get this one done quick as I can. Will two weeks be too late?"

"No," he replied, "I'll be around that long, though I won't be in town. I have some new duties that require nearly all of my time right now."

The big man chuckled, "It wouldn't have anything to do with a certain lady whose life you saved, would it?"

Delno chuckled back, "It would, my friend, but not the way you are thinking." Then, after a moment's thought, he added, "Elom, do you think you could have a suitable scabbard made for the blade? Not anything too ornate, but something that fits its grandeur and will be serviceable under hard wear."

"Aye, I know just the craftsman to do the job. After all," he smiled, "I don't wrap the blades I make in anything but the best."

After concluding their business, they sat and talked for some time. It was lunchtime when Delno finally got up to leave. Elom insisted that they have lunch together, so it was nearly an hour after noon when he finally said good-bye.

In parting, the big man said, "It's been too long since we last spoke. Don't be so long in coming around next time. You're always welcome here."

"I'll remember that, my friend," he said as he left the smith's shop and headed out into the city.

His next stop was the herbal market where he bought a good supply of herbs, both for cooking and for medicinal purposes. Then he moved on and replaced the canvas satchel that Geneva had so easily shredded in her frenzy to get to the meat inside. After that, he replenished his supply of bacon and jerky, and then added some flour, salt, and other such staples to his portable larder.

He then found a shop where he could purchase some maps. While the maps of Corice were quite good, the only ones he could find of the southern lands were incomplete. When he inquired of the shopkeeper if he had any better, he was told that the caravan traders had purchased the best weeks ago. He did find one that showed the kingdom of Palamore, and though it, too, was less complete than he liked, he bought it as well as a good map of Corice. "At least," he thought, looking at the scale of the map, "Palamore isn't a large kingdom."

His last purchase was made at the stockyards. He was quite capable of walking, but having his own mount and a stout pony for a pack animal would be helpful when he finally began his trip south.

As he rode back to his camp, he thought a great deal about the story Elom had told him. He wondered if perhaps Geneva's mother had come this way because it was familiar territory. He didn't know how he knew it, but he was absolutely sure the man with the Dragon Blade had been Corolan. For some reason, this comforted him. He had been going to that spot where he had first met the dragon for many years, since he was very young. Perhaps it was the shared knowledge of that place that had somehow fated him to be there for Geneva's mother in her time of need. Then he thought to himself, "Perhaps you are looking for connections where there are none." Still, the thought remained and occupied his mind all the way back to camp.

# CHAPTER 15

RETURNING TO CAMP he found that all was relatively well. At least, Nassari and Chester were still intact, and Geneva wasn't too peevish at being left so long. She had eaten the meat he left for her and slept most of the day.

There were still several hours of daylight left, so he built a large fire and then butchered the pig. He cut several sections of meat. First, a large roast for the evening's meal, which he intended to share with Nassari and Chester, then several smaller cuts that he placed so that they would smoke and dry as they cooked. The smaller cuts, once properly salted, would keep for quite some time if left wrapped. The largest portion of the animal he set aside for Geneva to eat the next time she got hungry.

He didn't have any potatoes, but there were cattails growing in profusion near the stream, and the roots would make a good substitute. Nassari helped him gather them. They also gathered greens, and Delno spotted some ripe fruits that would make a fine desert when pan-fried with a touch of sugar and some of the cinnamon bark he had bought in town.

Once the meat was spiced, herbed, and set to cook, they sat back and talked while waiting for the meat to be done enough to start cooking the vegetables. They had just settled down to their conversation when Geneva bolted up onto her haunches, lifted her wings as if for flight, raised her head to the sky and began to produce an ululating wail in several different tones at once. The eerie sound seemed to be felt as much as heard.

When she first started to move, Delno had initially reached for his knife, but now he went slack and looked to the sky as his dragon was doing. Nassari was alarmed and began to ask what was happening, but Delno held up his hand to silence him.

The strange wailing continued for several moments. Then, as suddenly as she had started, she stopped. She furled her wings and lowered her head to her chest. Though Delno needed no explanation, she seemed to need the mental contact so she told him, *"She who was my mother has passed to shadow."*

Delno quietly relayed the information to his friend, and then went to comfort her. He leaned his head against hers and said, *"She will be remembered."* Then they stood that way for a time. Even Nassari, generally glib at almost any occasion, silently waited out of respect for them.

It took a while, but the mood finally passed, and they all settled back down and tried to return to what they were doing.

"If I might ask," Nassari queried, "how did she know her mother had died?"

Delno was uncertain, especially since he had felt something then, too. He was about to ask Geneva if she felt like answering questions when she spoke, *"All dragons can feel the death of another dragon. The closer you are, both spatially and genetically, the more you feel the death."*

By this point Nassari was no longer disputing anything either psychic or magical about dragons; he'd seen more things out of the ordinary in the last two days than he had seen in the entire course of his life to that point. Showing remarkable concern for the feelings of another, especially for him, he asked the dragon, "Do you mind talking about this?"

Geneva was quite willing to talk, so he pressed on. "I don't understand how you knew, but I do accept that you did know. I didn't go to the war, never been much for that sort of thing. I did help with the war effort with the rest of the people who stayed back. One thing I saw time and again was that sometimes women just knew when their son or husband had been killed or seriously injured. I suppose that it's a trait that we sometimes have in common."

He paused, and seeing that Geneva was actually interested, he continued. "Tell me though, if you don't mind, how is it that a female dragon knows when she is bearing her last female offspring?"

The dragon was thoughtful for several moments before answering. *"Unlike human females, female dragons can feel every part of their bodies. They can even feel what sex the offspring in an egg is from the time of concep-*

tion. They know whether or not they will be capable of rising to mate again. So they know when a clutch will be their last. In the case of she who was my mother, she knew that even though she may have had the strength to rise again, that she would die after her eggs were laid because her rider had been slain."

"Well, that explains a lot, but what happens if a female dies unexpectedly? Does her line die with her?"

"If she has no daughters, yes." Then after composing her thoughts she added, "All dragons know their lineage, but only the last daughter actually carries it and her mother's name. So, if she has daughters, they will know she has passed to shadow, and they will know that she left no one to carry the lineage. The youngest daughter will then take the mothers name and continue the lineage, though some of it may be lost because the connection wasn't as strong between them. To ensure that no lineage is lost, or at least as little as possible, the youngest daughter will take a quest to find her sisters and collect their knowledge, because some may have knowledge that others don't."

By this point in the evening the meat was nearly done, so Delno cooked the vegetables and set the fruit to cook. When the vegetables were done, they sat down to the feast. Though it wasn't served in a fancy hall, it was, as he had promised his friend, fit for royalty. The main course was absolutely delicious and the dessert was just complex enough to complement the food without overpowering it.

Chester, who was actually a very well trained dog, didn't beg, but waited patiently, although he drooled excessively, until the humans had finished, then he happily ate whatever was left.

Nassari looked as though he was about to attempt to ply Geneva with more questions, so Delno interrupted him before he could start. "You know, my friend, you'll have to return to the city tomorrow."

Nassari stared thoughtfully at the fire for a moment, then said, "I know, Del, I can't stay. The more people there are here the more likely we might attract attention from others. I just hate to leave you alone out here."

"In case you hadn't noticed, I'm not quite alone."

"Yes, but you do have to leave her alone occasionally," he started, but Delno interrupted him.

"Nassari, you should give up politics and become a scholar. You've become absolutely enamored with studying this young dragon."

"You're right, of course," he said. "I am finding it harder by the moment to tear myself away from such a fascinating subject. Do you realize that soon she will master speech and I won't even need you to translate? Why, you could go about your business, and I could collect volumes of information without even bothering you."

Delno laughed, but Nassari cut him off, "Please Del, you can't just shut me out of this."

Delno looked at his friend seriously and said, "Nassari, I have no idea how long I will be gone. I don't know how far I have to travel. I've already been told that the road I will travel on will most likely be dangerous. I can't allow you to accompany me, old friend." Then, seeing the crestfallen look on the man's face, he added, "I'll tell you what though; once I get south and get the least bit settled I'll send word to you of where I am. Then, if you still want to come, you can hook up with a caravan and travel by safer roads."

Still disappointed, Nassari conceded the point and let the subject drop. They spent the remainder of the evening talking about their shared experiences and then retired for the night. The next morning, after being sworn to secrecy, Nassari left.

# CHAPTER 16

ONCE THEY WERE alone, Geneva decided to try her wings. Delno watched, alternately delighted and amused as she went about figuring how to get off the ground. She got a bit frustrated with his snickering every time she stumbled trying to take off.

"*I'd like to see you do better*," she said, and snarled.

"*Your indulgence, Dear Heart*," he chuckled, "*I know you are doing your best. All parents of young children find the child's first steps amusing.*"

"*I am not a human child, and you are not my parent*," she said testily.

Delno decided it would be best not to argue further. Instead, he found some simple tasks to occupy his time, and cover his chuckling, while she continued to try and get airborne.

After several more tries, she finally found herself aloft. Flapping madly, she managed to gain some altitude and began to awkwardly circle the camp. "*Delno*," she called, "*I've done it. I'm flying.*"

"That's marvelous," he replied, beaming with great pride. "*You look absolutely majestic up there.*"

"*Well, after all, I am made for this*," she said, showing great pride in herself.

She lifted her head to roar with delight. Unfortunately, the action shifted her body enough that her aerodynamics changed and she lost altitude quickly. With her belly brushing the bushes, it was all she could do to convert the downward plunge to a controlled crash landing. As her front claws dug into the soft ground of the clearing, her front feet tried to grip to slow her forward progress and her hind end, unchecked in its speed, kept going, and she ended up flipping over and landing flat on her back.

Delno ran to her at once, terrified that she had hurt herself. "Are you all right?" he implored both aloud and mentally.

"*Yes,*" she said, "*I'm fine.*"

"*Here, let me help you.*" Rather than roll her over one of her wings they decided that rolling her over vertically would be better. As she raised her head, he moved up between her shoulders and pushed. He was surprised that she didn't refuse his assistance. "You've got to move your tail to the side so that we can get you upright," he grunted as he continued pushing. She was heavier than he thought. She must have gained two stone in as many days.

Once they had her back on her feet, he again inquired whether or not she had sustained injury. "*Only to my pride,*" she answered somewhat indignantly.

"Well, Dear Heart," he said, chuckling a bit, "*perhaps you had better put your pride away until you have mastered landings.*"

She glared at him for several seconds and then said, "*I am going to try again. I will be hungry when I finish practicing. Perhaps you should get some food ready.*" She was being pointedly nonchalant.

He quickly embraced her before setting about his task. Such a simple gesture, but it embodied his feelings perfectly. She knew that no matter how much he might tease her, he loved her and was proud of her. She set about her practice with renewed spirit.

When the morning's practice was finished, Geneva ate with great appetite. After gorging herself, she curled up and napped. Delno felt that, since she was asleep, he might try his luck at fishing in the stream.

Later that day, with several nice fish cleaned and roasting, he practiced his awareness of the magical energies around him. Reaching out, he was able to feel all of the creatures within half a mile of camp. He could sense and see the energy of the stream and the fire. He could even sense the bushes and trees.

Once he had eaten, he began to work on a reed flute. Later, when he realized that Geneva was going to sleep through the night, he decided to turn in early himself, and he went to bed just as the light failed and full night came on.

The next morning he woke to the sound of Geneva moving about. She was awake early and eager to get a start on flying practice. She ate, for her, a small meal, explaining that she didn't want to be weighed down or tired.

Again, there wasn't much for Delno to do. He watched her and gave enthusiastic encouragement whenever he could, but he was just an observer. Though she had a ways to go before she would master the mighty leaps that her mother had executed, her take offs had improved a good deal in just the one day. Once aloft, she was a beautiful sight indeed. She was really getting the knack of flapping just enough to gain altitude and then gliding. Soon she was circling the camp like a soaring bird.

After watching her all morning, Delno was proud of her accomplishments, though he was also secretly pleased that she would practice for several more months before he would be expected to ride with her. While her take offs were still a bit choppy, if she didn't improve her landings before she had to do them with his added weight, they would both be grateful for his ability to use magic to heal the injuries.

While she hadn't ended up on her back again, she did regularly overshoot her intended landing site and plow into the bushes. One time she even hit a tree hard enough to upset several small arboreal rodents that were nesting in the branches. Delno wasn't sure, because she was blocking some of the contact, but he suspected that she had quite a few bruises from her practice session.

Again she ate heartily and then went to sleep. Delno was beginning to think that the old dragon had either been mistaken or deliberately mislead him about how much Geneva would eat. He was just hoping that the food would last until she started hunting.

Thinking of this, he decided that he should bring several more animals from the pasture while she was sleeping. This time, he brought the remainder of the pigs—there were only five—and four sheep. It took the rest of the afternoon to move them. He knew so many animals would be a handful to care for in the confined space, but the way Geneva was eating, he figured the numbers would diminish rapidly.

The routine established itself pretty quickly. Awake early, eat lightly, practice flying, eat heavily, and sleep. Delno decided that since he was nothing more than a third wing as far as the flying lessons went, he should do something to maintain his own physical fitness. He built a practice pell. Nothing elaborate, just two logs tied together in the shape of a cross that he could practice sword cuts on. Then using a stout stick of about the same length as his saber, he spent his mornings practicing. In the afternoons, after Geneva had fallen asleep, he would do calisthenics and then go for a run to keep in shape, and to tire himself out.

In the late afternoons, he whittled while he waited for his food to cook. At first he whittled his stick sword into a more exact imitation of the real thing to facilitate his practice. That only took a couple of afternoons, though, so he started whittling other pieces of wood into shapes. Some of the pieces he merely whittled into more perfect abstracts of the original, but some began to take on images of the things around him. He was developing quite a knack for carving small figurines. Many of the images were birds, and bears, and there was even one rather good rendering of Chester the dog. One, however, he worked on a little here and little there, and it was taking on the shape of a beautifully carved dragon, just readying herself for flight.

Later in the evenings before retiring, he would play his little flute. Sometimes Geneva would wake;' she appeared to sleep less heavily now even after a good meal, and just lay and listen to him making music. Sometimes, when the mood struck her, she would hum along quietly in the strange multi-toned way of hers. Delno enjoyed making music by himself, but he especially enjoyed it when she joined in.

Nearly two weeks had passed, and Geneva was flying extremely well. She was still having a bit of trouble with take offs and landings. She was getting a bit discouraged by that until Delno pointed out that she was growing so fast she was now nearly twice as large as when she had first started flying, and that her change in size was apparent from day to day.

"I believe," he told her, "*that what is happening is this. You are growing so fast that your senses are having trouble keeping up with where your extremities are in space. Once your growth slows, you will be as graceful as any other dragon.*" Then he added, letting his pride in her come through fully, "*In fact, I'll wager that you'll be more graceful than most.*"

Geneva rose up on her haunches proudly. "*Do you really think that is what's happening, Dear One? You aren't just trying to make me feel better, are you?*"

"My dearest Geneva, I wouldn't lie to you even if I could. Think about this: every morning I can see how much you've grown overnight. Every morning you start off a little clumsy. Every morning the clumsiness seems to wear off a little quicker, as if your senses take a few tries to catch up to your new dimensions."

"*That does make sense,*" she replied.

After saying this, she sank back on her haunches and launched herself perfectly. After flying so high that she was a tiny speck in the sky, she soared for almost another hour, learning to look for and ride thermals.

She ended her practice session by spectacularly swooping down on, and neatly killing, the last sheep in the clearing. Then she ate the whole thing before settling down to rest.

Later that evening, when she awoke, Delno asked her, *"Do you think you could fly to the pasture and get your own sheep tomorrow?"*

*"I believe so. Why? Getting tired of fetching the food?"*

*"No, not really, but I do have to go back to town tomorrow. I have to retrieve my Dragon Blade. Also, I would like to get news of the road, if possible, since it seems that you and I will be traveling soon."*

This time she wasn't apprehensive about his going to town. *"I can feed myself, Dear One. Just don't be gone too long."* Then she teased, *"If I get lonesome, I might eat your pony out of frustration."*

Delno chuckled. She had wanted to eat the pony two days after she had devoured the last pig. She was less than fond of mutton, and it had taken some convincing to keep her from pouncing on the animal. In fact, he had finally had to threaten that if she did so, she would have to carry his gear herself.

*"I'll hurry,"* he promised, laughing.

Then he put his flute to his lips and began to play a soft melody that the two of them had developed. He was delighted when she joined in, and they played together for a while before settling in for a good night's sleep.

# CHAPTER 17

ALL ACTIVITY CAME to a halt as Delno entered the smith's shop. One of the journeymen came over to him quickly, led him away from the door, and bid him sit down in an alcove from where he could no longer see the street. The young smith quickly explained that the mastersmith was quite busy and would be with him shortly, then left him alone. He was surprised by the reception and wondered what could be wrong that he would be shuttled out of sight and ignored like this. His answer wasn't long in coming.

There wasn't much activity going on in the shop. From what he could see from his poor vantage point, it looked as though everyone was watching what was transpiring between their master and someone else. He could hear Elom arguing with the person now as they walked in the back door of the building.

"That blade is of the south and shouldn't be in your possession," said a nasally voice with an accent that Delno couldn't place.

"I told you," Elom responded, "that blade is a commission from a customer. If you think that customer has done something wrong, then you need to go to the city guard. If they come and tell me there's a problem, I'll relinquish the blade to them. Then they can take it to the courts, and the courts can decide if you have a just claim. Otherwise, you can take your inquiries and your money and shove them both up your arse."

The man's voice took on a dangerous edge, "You would do well not to make insults, smith." He had made the title sound like a slur.

"And you would do well to take your hands off of me, little man," Elom replied in a voice that left no room for negotiation.

The man started stringing together syllables into strange words. Realizing that the foreigner was about to use magic to harm Elom, and that despite his great physical size, he would be unprotected, Delno stepped out of the alcove and said, "I wouldn't do that if I were you." As he said that, he also reached out mentally and scanned the thoughts of the man.

Delno didn't allow the contact to last longer than a second. As he pulled his own senses back, he felt the man reaching out mentally to scan him and slammed the "door" shut so hard the other fellow flinched and reached up to his head as if he had been struck. In the brief contact, Delno had discovered that the young man, in his early twenties, wasn't extremely well trained in magic.

As the young mage, who was dressed in a manner Delno had seen among caravan traders from the south, stood glaring at him, another southerner, similarly dressed, stepped forward from an alcove like the one Delno had been led to earlier. This man was older, mid-thirties, and much more heavily armed. He wore at his side a large bastard sword. On his back, over his right shoulder, could be seen the hilt of what appeared to be a short sword. There were several daggers on his belt, as well as knife hilts sticking up from each boot. In Delno's experience, only two types of individual carried that many weapons openly. Either he was very good with edged weapons, or he simply wanted to appear dangerous. While Delno didn't get the feeling of easy confidence that being very good would warrant, he knew it was best not to take chances in such situation.

"Now then, gentlemen," he said, laying his hand almost nonchalantly on his saber, "What's all this about?"

Elom was only momentarily surprised by his appearance. He said, "I'm sorry, Corporal. It's all my fault. One of my journeymen was looking at that blade of yours while one the caravan merchants was here. . . ."

The little southerner cleared his throat and said, "If that blade is yours, where did you get it?"

"You are in a poor position to be asking questions or making accusations." Delno responded. "Suppose we start over. I am Delno Okonan. Who are you?"

"You will answer *my* question, you pompous. . . ." the young magician started to say. His older friend, realizing that all of the men and older boys in the shop had taken up weapons, said in a loud clear voice, "Enough!"

The younger man looked like he was about to make an angry reply when the elder went on. "There is no reason for uncivil behavior here. I am Farrel," he executed a polite bow, "and this is my traveling companion, Cheeno." At a look from Farrel, the young man stiffly nodded his head; not exactly polite, but Delno was willing to let it go to avoid a fight.

"Now then," Farrel went on. "We are from a small kingdom in the south. Perhaps you have heard of Palamore?" Delno's surprise was apparent, and Cheeno jumped on it at once.

"You see, he does know! It was he who stole the blade." He raised his hand to make some type of motion and started again to string syllables into "magic words." Unfortunately for him, he had forgotten his close proximity to the smith. He suddenly found himself unable to speak; in fact, he found it impossible to move air through his throat at all with the smith's massive hand clamped so tightly around his neck.

Cheeno's eyes shifted to Farrel in a silent plea for help, but the older man found himself suddenly staring at nearly a dozen improvised weapons in the hands of the journeymen and older apprentices.

The whole tableau had become ridiculous. Delno, not wishing to be, even indirectly, responsible for the deaths of two men from the very place he needed to go said, "Please, we obviously have a misunderstanding here. Perhaps if we all calm down we can get this settled."

No one moved; however, Cheeno was beginning to turn a purplish shade.

"Elom," Delno said, stepping forward and placing his hand on the big man's arm, "Please, let him go."

Elom looked at him as if he'd taken leave of his senses. "Do you realize what he was about to do?"

"Yes," he replied. "I do, and I'll handle it." Then turning to everyone else he said, "The rest of you, put away your weapons; there'll be no bloodshed here today."

As Elom reluctantly released his grip on Cheeno, the would-be mage slid to his knees still gasping for breath. It was apparent to Delno that Elom had squeezed much harder than was necessary and that the poor man's windpipe had been crushed. He dropped to his knees in front of the stricken man and, hoping that his new skills were up to the task, he quickly examined the injuries. Then, having a good idea how much energy to draw, he used some energy from the forge and gathered it to himself and used the word "HEAL" to release it. Cheeno stopped choking and drew a deep gasping breath. After several more breaths, his color began to return to normal.

Elom looked at Delno as if he had suddenly sprouted an extra head, but he didn't say anything.

Standing up, Delno turned to Farrel and said, "Well then, let's get this straightened out, shall we?"

At a hand motion from Elom, the rest of the men in the shop returned to work, though they stayed alert, ready for any trouble. The four men then moved to one of the alcoves where they could talk without being overheard.

Farrel again bowed before being seated, then said, "Two years ago, in our country, a sword was stolen. I believe that we all know now that we are speaking of the Dragon Blade." He didn't make it an outright accusation, but the implication was that he believed Delno's blade to be that missing sword.

"This blade had belonged to a dragon rider who had been of the royal house of Palamore. That rider died over three centuries ago, and the blade has been passed down in the royal family since. Since it was stolen, all caravan guards have been charged with keeping watch for the blade to surface." He paused and waited to see if Delno would admit to having the blade. When nothing was said, he continued, "As you know, that blade cannot be changed by human means. So even if the guard and pommel are altered, the blade will remain the same."

"I see," said Delno. "That makes everything clear. There is no problem here. The blade our smith has honorably been protecting for me has never been in Palamore."

Cheeno found his voice, "Never been in Palamore? Do you expect us to believe that you simply found it while walking one day?"

Delno couldn't quite stifle a snort of laughter, "That's much closer to the truth than you realize."

Cheeno looked at Farrel, "How long are we going to listen to this rubbish? If they won't give us the blade willingly, then we should send word to Palamore. We'll see if their king is willing to go to war over a trinket."

Delno smiled at him and said, "So far, Cheeno, I've been very tolerant of your insults, but if they continue, I can use the same energy I used to heal you and put you right back down on that floor unable to breathe."

Cheeno's eyes widened, he opened his mouth to reply hotly, but controlled his anger. Instead, he said, "Dragon Blades are completely unique; made by dragons. A female dragon breathes fire on. . . ."

"On the shell of a baby dragon while using magic to outline and strengthen the blade. When the young dragon hatches, the blade breaks away from the rest of the shell perfectly intact." Delno finished for him.

"If you know that, then you also know that it has to be done on an intact egg. The mother dragon will only do that if two conditions exist." Cheeno said smugly. "If the rider bonds with the young dragon while she is still in her shell, which is very rare indeed. The second condition is that the rider has proven himself worthy of such a gift." He paused for a moment, and then said, "There aren't more than a dozen such blades in existence. Each one is worth a king's ransom."

"Proven himself by doing something like saving the mother dragon's life?" Delno let the question hang in the air.

Elom's jaw dropped. He stared so hard that Delno was almost afraid that his eyes would burst from the effort.

Delno looked at the bigger southerner and said, "Describe the blade you are looking for, Farrel."

Farrel, now somewhat unsure of himself said, "It is a long sword. Over a yard in length, and double edged."

"Well, this will be settled in a moment then," Delno replied. "If you can look at the blade that is here and positively identify it as the one you seek, you may take it with our blessing. Then, turning to Elom, he said, "Show them the blade, my friend."

Elom turned to a journeyman who had been nearby pretending to use a large hammer to cold work the edge of a rather nasty looking boar spear and sent the man to get the blade. The journeyman was gone only a minute. When he returned, he handed a large bundle to Elom.

When Elom unwrapped the bundle, two blades were inside. One was the Dragon Blade, the other, a large *main gauche*. Both were in fine scabbards of hardwood overlaid with tooled leather. The tooling on the leather of each scabbard, while not excessively ornate, was a depiction of a stylized dragon.

Taking up the saber, Elom drew the blade from the scabbard. It was truly beautiful. The blade was unchanged, a slightly curved, single-edged saber, but the guard was exquisitely done. It had been cast in bronze. It was two dragons, their bodies meeting under the handle to protect the fingers, their necks curving up and around so that their heads touched to form the front of the guard on top, their tails intertwined to connect the guard to the base of the handle. Their wings, partially unfurled, further protected the hand. The Dragons were then reinforced with a nickel-steel alloy to protect the fine casting from being marred when turning a strike. The handle itself was leather wrapped and tied with the same nickel-steel alloy.

The blade of the *main gauche* was, of course, made of steel, and fully one foot long. The hilt, though similar in style to that of the sword, was one dragon. The tang of the knife went through the dragon's body and the head and neck of the dragon formed the top of an S while the tail formed the bottom of it. The wings were slightly unfurled to complete the guard; again, the same nickel-steel alloy protected the bronze. The pommel, though, was a simple bronze cap heavy enough to use as a bludgeon if needed. The handle of the knife was the same type of wrapped leather and metal as the saber.

"I knew that such a sword was called a Dragon Blade," Elom said. "That's why I chose to use dragons when I formed the guards. The tanner who made the sheaths saw the drawings I had rendered for the castings, and worked the leather accordingly. Since no drill bit will penetrate that material, I had to cast the sword in the mold with the wax and then pour the bronze in around it to make sure the guard was secure. I worked in bronze for strength and laid that nickel-steel into the wax before I set it in investment. After the wax was baked out, the bronze poured into the mold and filled in the empty space. The nickel-steel will reinforce the bronze at the edges to prevent wear, and the two metals won't separate if you have to use them. These blades may look too fancy for use, but they're fully functional."

The two southerners were awestruck. They simply stared as Delno took possession of his blades.

Delno could find no words suitable for the craftsmanship exhibited here. "Magnificent," was all he could say, and that came out as a whisper.

Farrel was the first to move or speak. He rose from his seat, and dropping to one knee, he said, "We have wronged you. We have falsely accused you of thievery and lying. We are shamed. I will not even ask your forgiveness. What we have done is unforgivable."

"Nonsense, man," Delno responded. "How many Dragon Blades are there?"

He took the man by the forearms and helped him stand before continuing. "As far as you knew, all were accounted for except the blade you seek. It was a mistake; show me a man who has never made a mistake. Come, let us put it behind us and be friends."

"That is a much kinder response than I expected or deserve," he said. Then he glared at Cheeno.

"Yes, well, I, too, am sorry. If we had described the blade we sought, this could have been cleared up quickly without all of that unpleasantness." Cheeno said, rubbing his throat.

Delno realized that Farrel was staring at the Dragon Blade, so he handed it to him hilt first.

Farrel was so shocked by the gesture that for a moment all he could do was stare slack jawed. Finally, at Delno's insistence, he took the handle and examined the blade reverently.

"I have only seen two other Dragon Blades in all of my travels," he said, "and never before have I been allowed to touch one. You honor me, sir."

After first allowing Cheeno to hold and examine the blade, Delno then took a couple of half-hearted practice swings to feel the balance, which was perfect. Then he turned to the southerners and said, "Gentlemen, if you would excuse me for a few moments, I will finish my business here. Perhaps then we can talk further."

Farrel nodded his head and said, "We would very much like to talk to you as well. We will await you outside." Turning to Elom, he added, "Mastersmith, your skill is unsurpassed in any kingdom. I will sing your praises to all who will listen." Saying this he turned, and, beckoning Cheeno to follow, left the shop.

Delno was about to speak when Elom spoke first, "Is this all true?" he asked. "Are you mixed up with magic and dragons and the lot?"

Delno had never wanted to have this get out, but he had decided early on not to lie if directly confronted with it. After all, if you always tell the truth you don't have to remember what lie you told to whom. So he nodded and said, "Yes, my friend, it is, all of it."

"But how?"

Realizing that he would have to tell the big man, especially if he expected him to keep quiet about it, he quickly told Elom the story. Even the short version took nearly twenty minutes.

For his part, Elom kept his silence until Delno had finished, then he asked, "So, you're going away for good then?"

"Yes," Delno said. Then, when Elom didn't say anything, he asked, "You're not going to try and talk me out of this?"

Elom laughed, "No, I am not. The last time I tried to talk you out of something it was the army. The next thing I knew, I was on a parade field with some training sergeant calling me names and making me run in circles. If you're going south, you'll have to do it without me." He crossed his massive arms over his chest and stood there daring anyone to try and contradict him.

Delno laughed out loud and, grasping the big man's arms, said, "You're a good man and a good friend, Elom. I'm going to miss you." Then, remembering what he had come for, he asked, "So then, what do I owe you for the work you've done?" After seeing the work, he wasn't even sure he could afford it.

Elom just shrugged, "You don't owe me anything." Delno started to protest, but was cut off, "Think of it as a goin' away present. Besides, when those two flappin' southerners start spreadin' this story, I have a feeling I'll be so busy I'll have to take on more apprentices."

"You've done so much, and that *main gauche* was completely unexpected; surely there is something I can do to repay you."

"There's no payment I'd take for it. Work of that sort isn't done for money. As for making the extra blade, I recalled that you prefer to use a large-bladed dagger in the off hand rather than a shield, so I simply took the liberty. Never been one for that style myself, always preferred a shield, but since it's the style you use, I'll sleep better knowin' that you've at least got a good piece of steel between you and trouble."

They stared at each other for a moment before Elom said, "There's a blessing, some call it a curse, that goes, 'May you live in interesting times and come to the attention of powerful people'. Well, blessing or curse, that seems to be your fate, Corporal. I hope you have good fortune, and if you're ever back up this way, stop in and we'll tip a few glasses to the old unit."

Delno started to speak, but Elom waved him on and then turned and walked off into the shop.

# CHAPTER 18

A S DELNO STEPPED from the shop into the dazzling sunlight, he was momentarily blinded and almost ran right into the two men he sought. He had half expected them to have gotten tired of waiting, but they were just outside the door as they had said they would be.

"It is good of you to wait for me, gentlemen, I apologize for keeping you so long," he said.

"Not at all," Farrel responded. "We have much to ask you, and I believe that you have many questions as well."

Cheeno, looking around nervously, added, "Perhaps it would be best to have our conversation some place less public."

Delno said, "You're right, of course. Tell me, where are you staying? I could finish the rest of my business in town and meet you later."

"We stay with the Moreland caravan. We are camped on the eastern edge of your city, near the trade road."

After ensuring that he had a thorough description of their camp and would have no trouble finding them, he bid them farewell and made his way to the market. He added to his supply of herbs and spices, and bought some sweet bread to munch as he wandered among the shops and stalls. He bought a decent-sized cast iron pan with a lid. The pan could be used to either roast or fry foods. Then he kept moving among the vendors. One stall caught his eye, so he stepped under its awning and began examining the goods exhibited there.

The stall was full of small figurines. Some were done in porcelain, some in rougher clay, some were carved of wood, but the pieces that really caught his eye were carved out of ivory. They were small; any of them could easily fit in the palm of the hand, but finely detailed. Most were of different sea creatures of which he'd only heard tales. Some were of sea creatures he had never even dreamed of. One in particular was of a lovely figure of a female with the torso of a woman and the lower body of a dolphin.

He had just decided that he needed to conserve his dwindling money when he saw a small set of three knives, just the right sizes for the carvings he liked to work on. "How much for those?" he asked the portly little merchant.

"Oh, there's some fine quality steel, sir," the man said in an oily voice that set Delno's teeth somewhat on edge. "There's none finer to be found. Come all the way from the south they do. I couldn't part with them for less than half a gold crown."

"Half a crown!" he said, stepping back as if the case had suddenly caught fire. "Ten whole silvers? They must be more fond of steel in the south than we are here in the north. That's half a week's wages for most men."

"But sir," the man purred, "Those blades have to be shipped all the way on the caravans. Surely you can understand the expenses involved."

"Expenses or not, I'm sure one of Elom's advanced apprentices could make a similar set, and it wouldn't cost me half a crown. I'll give you three silvers for them."

"Three silvers!" the man exclaimed. "If you are going to rob me, sir, you should at least show me the courtesy of drawing your weapon. I couldn't possibly part with them for less than eight silvers."

Warming to the game, Delno responded, "Now who's being robbed? I'll give you four silvers."

"Seven, and I'll go no lower."

"Call it five and we've a deal."

"I can appreciate that you know the value of money, so give me six, and we can seal the bargain." Saying this the little man pushed the pouch containing the blades half way across the table but kept it covered with his palm rather than withdrawing his hand.

"Done," said Delno.

As he opened his belt pouch to get the money, one of his carved figures fell out. The man snatched it up before he could retrieve it.

"Now this isn't bad work," the vendor said. "Did you carve this?"

When Delno nodded, he said, "You have a knack for carving. This is good."

"It's just something to do when I am not otherwise occupied."

"Well," he said, turning the little figure of a hawk about to take flight this way and that, "If this is the quality of the work you normally do, bring them to me, and I'll give you a silver for each one."

Delno hadn't been sure why he'd carried the pieces to town, but was now glad he had. He pulled another bird, a bear, and the small image of Chester out of his pouch and showed them to the man, who then agreed to take them all. He was a little reluctant to sell the dog because he had thought about giving it to Nassari, but the merchant was willing to trade the knife set for the four pieces, so he let pragmatism win over sentimentality.

He was just getting ready to leave the stall after stowing his carving knives away when two southern merchants walked up to the kiosk and began examining the figurines as they talked. He didn't mean to eavesdrop, but they weren't attempting to keep their conversation quiet, so he listened.

"I tell you, I know what I saw," said the taller man.

"You couldn't have seen such a thing. It must have been a large bird," said the other.

"I know the difference between a bird and a dragon. I was raised in a kingdom that is unfortunate enough to have three of those damned beasts in residence," stated the first with an air of authority.

"Better watch how you speak of such things, my friend," the second admonished, "there are many from the south here who would not take kindly to such talk."

"Phah, they believe the old children's tales of benevolent riders who protect the weak. They haven't lived under thieving riders who fatten their beasts at the expense of poor herders while helping themselves to whatever they want, be it merchandise or women."

"Still," his smaller friend went on, "you'd do well to remember that dragons and riders are still revered in many kingdoms. You could find yourself in a death match if the wrong person over hears you."

The tall man made a rude sound, "Those fools from Palamore? That whole kingdom is populated with half-wits, and that king of theirs isn't even *that* bright."

Making a shushing sound, the smaller man cringed and looked quickly around to see if anyone close by had taken offense.

The taller man went on unperturbed. "The only thing they care about is that damned sword that was stolen. Stolen right out from under the noses of their *elite guards*, at that." He said the words elite guards as though he were talking about something he needed to scrape off the bottom of his shoe. "They'd be better off forgetting the damn thing and getting on with the business of replacing that numbskull king of theirs."

The smaller man, eager to change the subject before anyone who might take offense could hear, asked, "So, what makes you think you saw a dragon?"

"I've been bored lately, so I thought I would do some hunting. I was told the undeveloped lands to the north would offer the best prospects, so I took my bow and headed off in that direction. I followed the road for a few miles, then began to look for game trails. I was also watching the sky in case I should spy any likely game birds. I had just stopped to rest when I saw the dragon. I was extremely surprised, and first thought my eyes must be playing tricks. However, it circled a couple of times, giving me ample opportunity to confirm what I had seen. Then it flew very high and soared for almost an hour before returning to the forest. I almost went looking for its landing place, but I've heard that wild dragons can be very dangerous, and if it was with a rider, I wanted to have even less to do with it."

The two turned and walked away from the awning, and by the time Delno could see that they had resumed their conversation, they were too far away in the crowd to hear what they were saying. He wanted to go after them, but could think of no way to follow them without attracting attention to himself. Since attracting attention was what he wanted to avoid, and, since he and Geneva had already attracted more attention than was good for them, he decided to try and learn more from other, friendlier, sources. He already knew enough: the man had seen Geneva flying, but knew nothing more than a general area where she could be found. It was time to move his camp.

As he turned to leave, the merchant laughed and leaned toward him conspiratorially, "Dragons is it? More likely he chewed on the wrong mushroom while hunting. I'll wager that by this evening it will be a dozen dragons." Then he added with a chuckle, "Probably with golden swans in attendance and a couple of fairy princesses thrown in for good measure."

Delno laughed suitably at the merchant's joke and bid him good day as he started off at a brisk pace. He had one more thing to buy, and then he'd get out of town as quickly as he could. He'd spent more than enough time in Larimar for one afternoon. Also, he was going through more money than he really should without knowing how much he would need when he headed south soon. He took some comfort in the knowledge that this carving skill he had developed could earn him a few honest coins if needed.

He was anxious to get to the caravan from Palamore, so, after stopping at a bowyer and buying a new re-curved bow and quiver of arrows, he left the city. As he got through the gates, he decided to try and contact Geneva. He wasn't sure he could do so from this far away, but he could still feel her presence in his mind, so it was worth a try.

As he strapped his purchases onto his horse, he reached out to her, *"Geneva, can you hear me, Dear Heart?"*

*"Yes, quite well, are you near?"* came her reply.

*"No, I am just leaving the city gates."*

*"Then you will return soon?"* She sounded happy at the prospect.

*"Not as soon as I'd like,"* he told her. *"Something has come up, and I must stop at one of the camped caravans and make some inquiries."*

*"I don't like the sound of that,"* she said flatly. *"If there is trouble, I can come to you."*

*"No, that's part of the trouble, Dear Heart, you've been seen, by one who is familiar with your kind."*

*"Familiar?"* she replied.

*"Yes, familiar enough to know a dragon when he sees one, and he's not favorably disposed to dragons or riders from what I could gather."*

*"Not favorably disposed? And you're going to meet him? Why not just walk into a bear's den? It might be quicker for both of us. I should come to you."*

*"NO!"* He looked around quickly, realizing that he had shouted that out loud as well as mentally. There were a few people near the hitching posts, but they assumed the horse had done something wrong and paid no further attention, so he quickly went on. *"Please, stay put. I am not going to meet that man. I am going to meet some men from Palamore. Since they **are** favorably disposed to dragons and riders, and since we must go there anyway, I am hoping to arrange to travel with them."*

*"I would still feel better if we were together,"* she said.

"So would I, but that isn't wise right now. Please, Dear Heart, stay and watch the camp and I will be back soon, hopefully with good news. When I return, I will tell you everything."

"Very well, but I don't like it."

"I don't like it either, but that's the way it is. Please, be patient, watch our possessions, and take special care not to be seen," he implored. "I'll let you know the minute I start back to camp."

"Very well, but be careful, Dear One." Her voice betrayed her concern.

# CHAPTER 19

AS DELNO APPROACHED the camped caravan, he noticed that their horses were kept in a makeshift corral, so he moved toward them. Seeing an older lad of about sixteen tending the horses, he raised his hand in greeting, and, smiling, he approached. The boy seemed a bit wary. Delno spoke as he got near him, "I'm here to speak with Farrel or Cheeno. May I tie my horse here?"

The lad looked a bit uncomfortable, but shrugged his shoulders and said, "I'll have to ask the chief handler; I'm just a hired hand."

The boy then went off around a nearby wagon and was gone for several moments. He returned on the heels of a man who was probably twenty years older than Delno. The man walked right up to him, extended his hand and said, "I'm Willy, Chief Animal Handler for this outfit."

Delno reached out to return the handshake and the older man grasped his forearm just above the wrist. It felt a little strange, but Delno returned the gesture and the man smiled and shook his arm gently. "I'm Delno Okonan," he said. Apparently there would be some new customs he would have to get used to in the south.

Willy walked to Delno's horse and looked him over while he spoke. "Nigel tells me you're visiting and would like to tie your horse with ours."

Delno waited a moment to see if the man would continue speaking, but Willy just opened the horse's mouth and looked inside.

"Well, yes," he said. "I'm just here to talk with Farrel and Cheeno and would like to make sure that my horse has fresh water." When that got no reaction, he added quickly, "They're expecting me, and I can pay for hitching the horse."

Willy stiffened and said with some formality, "I guess customs are different around here concerning such things, so I'll take no offense, but we from the south don't expect payment from guests."

Delno quickly apologized, "I meant no offense, certainly, I just didn't want to put anyone to any trouble on my account."

The southerner looked at him for a moment, then his smile returned and he said, "No offense taken. Different kingdoms, different customs. You'd think after traveling with caravans for over twenty years I'd get used to it." He then began lifting the horse's feet and checking them. "No offense, Delno, but I have to make sure that your horse isn't carrying something that will cause problems for mine."

"No offense taken. I do my best to take good care of him, but I'm not a professional handler. I appreciate you looking him over."

Willy, finishing with his inspection of the horse, appeared pleased with the compliment. He turned to Nigel and said, "Take the gentleman's gear off of his horse and put the horse in the small corral where there's fresh hay and water. Stow his gear in my wagon." Then to Delno he said, "When you're ready to leave, just find Nigel, or whichever boy is on duty, and they'll get you saddled up and ready to travel." He turned to leave, then stopped, and, remembering his manners, he again clasped Delno's forearm in the southern style and said, "Good to meet you," then turned and left without another word.

Delno retrieved the bundle with the Dragon Blade, but left the rest for Nigel to stow in the wagon. He stood staring around at the camp. The wagons were huge: Delno had seen apartments in the city that were smaller. "That must be why they need so many animals; it would take at least eight large draft oxen to haul one of those behemoths just on dry road," he thought. The whole camp was laid out like a small town. He looked around to ask Nigel where he might find the men he was looking for and discovered that he was completely alone. Apparently, Nigel was an extremely efficient lad.

Delno decided that wandering toward the center of camp would probably be best. After all, even if he didn't find Farrel or Cheeno, he was sure to find someone who could point him in the right direction. Turning thought to action, he strode off in what he hoped was the right way. He walked past several wagons. Most of them appeared to be a combination of living quarters and cargo vehicle. The living quarters on most of the vehicles had canvas sides that were raised like awnings to shade the interiors while allowing air to circulate freely.

He was starting to enjoy this look at a culture so different than the one in which he grew up. Thus, with his mind occupied in such peaceful surroundings, the attack was totally unexpected. There was a fierce growl as a large dog lunged at him out of one of the wagons. Even though his bond with Geneva had heightened his reflexes slightly, his reaction, while quick enough to save his hide, didn't save his tunic. The ferocious dog clamped down on the material and shook it, ripping the clothing right off of his body. As he stepped back, he lost his footing and fell. He rolled, both to protect his throat and to get leverage to leap up to deal with the dog. The dog, however, was quicker than he thought; it jumped on his back and started to go for his unprotected neck.

There were shouts from several people at once. One older man hobbled over, and, swearing at the dog, grabbed it by the collar and pulled it back before it sunk its teeth into Delno's flesh. A middle-aged man with an air of authority swore at the older man, "Damn it all, Jared, I've told you to keep that mutt tied when there's apt to be visitors about."

"Well, what are 'visitors' doing wandering around? They shouldn't be allowed in camp," the old man spit out defiantly.

"Right," the first man said, "Not allowing visitors into camp would be a great way to encourage trade, now wouldn't it?" Then he added, "You damned old fool. Just tie that dog before I stick a boar spear through it. I've had all the trouble out of that animal I'm going to tolerate." Then he added in a quiet voice that left no doubt who was in charge, "If that dog of yours causes any more problems for this caravan, you'll either put it down, or go your own way. Understand?"

The old man didn't say anything, but the look on his face was more fear than defiance. The other man took that as an affirmative and turned to Delno.

"Here, now, let's get you back on your feet," he said, and, reaching down, he grabbed Delno's arm and hauled him up.

As Delno stood, everyone went silent and stared slack-jawed at him. More precisely, they stared at his right shoulder. He looked to see, wondering if perhaps the dog had injured him and he hadn't felt it. As he looked just above his right breast, he realized he had completely forgotten about the dragon mark. He had been bathing in the wee hours of the morning or late at night and hadn't looked at it in the light in almost two weeks. It was now about two hands wide and about the same height, and looked like a tattoo of a bronze dragon standing on her hind legs, wings extended, ready for flight, only a little blurry around the edges.

"Well," he thought, "The cat, or should I say dragon, is out of the bag now."

He was just about to apologize for disrupting the camp when Farrel stepped through the crowd and said, "I suppose introductions are in order." He waited for a moment. Then, since no one moved or shifted their gaze, he went on, "This is Delno Okonan," he said to those assembled. Then turning to Delno he introduced the middle aged man, "This is the Caravan Master, Roland Moreland."

Delno, embarrassed and keenly aware of his lack of a shirt, extended his hand. The Caravan Master took his forearm in the southern style and shook. It was still a moment before he could find his voice, when he finally did he said, "My apologies, Rider. This incident should never have happened. I'll see that damn dog destroyed for this."

Delno was taken aback by the respect, near reverence, and by the oath to destroy the dog. He said, "Apology accepted, though it isn't really necessary." Then, glancing at the stricken face of the old man he added, "Please don't destroy the dog; I'm sure it only thought it was protecting its property from a stranger."

Roland met his gaze for a moment, then gave a slight nod. Looking over his shoulder, he said to the dog's owner, "You're damn lucky this Rider is a forgiving man, Jared. Otherwise, that blasted mutt of yours would be dragon dung by tomorrow." Then, turning back to Delno, he said, "Well, we should get in out of the sun, and get that covered up before any of these Northerners see it." Turning to those milling about, he said, "Off to your own business with the lot of you, and mind you, keep this to yourselves." Then he looked back at Delno and said thoughtfully, "You look to be about my size." Turning to a boy of about ten, he said, "Tim, fetch one of my best shirts and bring it to the meeting tent."

Delno tried to say that he would make do with his own torn garment, but Roland waved his objection aside saying, "That shirt is done in right and proper." Then, again looking over his shoulder at the old man, he said, "Don't worry; Jared can pay me for the shirt in penance for not controlling his animal."

Jared, happy to have gotten off with such a light penalty, nodded his head and hauled the dog back to his wagon and tied a large rope to its collar.

The Caravan Master and Farrel led Delno to a sizeable pavilion almost in the middle of the camp. The side awnings could be lowered for inclement weather but now were raised to increase the shade and allow air movement inside. There were nearly a dozen tables under the canvas, and Roland gestured to the chairs at one of them.

The boy, Tim, came running up breathless with a shirt draped over his arm. He started to hand the garment to Roland. "My shirt's intact, boy, it's him that's walking around barebacked," he said, inclining his head toward Delno. "Give the shirt to the Rider."

The boy approached him cautiously and held the shirt out for him to take. He accepted the garment and said, "Thank you, Tim."

The boy was awestruck that the Rider had not only thanked him, but had actually used his name, and just stood there staring like a dimwit. Roland, smiling, admonished the boy gently, "Don't stand there staring, lad, go and fetch us some of that chilled wine." The boy seamed reluctant to move, so Roland shoved him gently and said, "Go on now, be a good lad and do as you're told."

As Tim ran off for the refreshments, Delno looked at the shirt. It was made from a light material. Though not silk, it was certainly as light and almost as luxuriant. Instead of being a pullover tunic like his own garment, it was slit all the way down the front and buttoned up. He had seen nobility wear such garments, but the amount of work and material that went into them put them out of the price range of the average Corisian. He thanked Roland profusely for such a gift.

Roland said, "It's the least I could do for an honored guest, especially since your own shirt was destroyed during an attack that should never have happened. I'm just glad you're such a forgiving man and don't take offense at my fault in this."

"Well," Delno replied, "I don't see how it is your fault anyway."

"I'm Caravan Master, everything that happens here, good or bad, is my responsibility."

Having been a military leader, Delno could certainly understand that sentiment.

At that moment, Tim and another boy arrived with two trays laden with food, wine, and extra glasses in case someone else joined them. Both boys were thoroughly pleased with themselves when Delno smiled at them in thanks for their effort.

He put the shirt on and fastened the buttons before taking a seat with the other two men while Farrel poured wine into glasses. Delno raised his glass and said, "To hospitality and new friendships."

The other two men raised their glasses as well. After the toast, Roland Moreland asked, "So, what brings a Rider to my tent this day?"

"Well, gentlemen," Delno said, "I'm sure you are aware of the feelings of the locals toward anything to do with magic." When they raised their eyebrows and nodded, he continued. "My situation here has become, at best, precarious. My partner and I must travel south, and soon. I know that your caravan must also begin the journey before long. I would like to travel with you to Palamore."

Both men looked thoughtful, but neither was quick to respond. They all sipped their wine for a few moments before Farrel finally spoke up, "So, if you wouldn't mind telling us, what is your dragon's name?"

Delno thought about it for a moment, then, seeing no harm in answering the question he replied, "Her name is Geneva."

Roland sat up straighter for a moment and opened his mouth to protest, then his whole posture changed, and he sank back into his chair and hung his head. "So," he said, "Corolan and his dragon are dead?"

Delno nodded and was about to ask how they knew Corolan, but Farrel spoke first. "You see, Delno, Corolan was well known in Palamore. As is the habit of many Riders, he didn't live in any one place but traveled from kingdom to kingdom, somehow seeming to know when he was needed. However, Palamore was his ancestral home. Our current queen is descended from the same family as Corolan, as is our good Caravan Master."

Roland interrupted, "Tell me, Rider, how did Corolan die? Were you there?"

"No" he answered the second question first, "I wasn't there when he was killed. He was killed by something that his dragon called Roracks somewhere in the south. He was shot with a poisoned arrow."

Farrel leaned forward, "I don't understand. If Corolan was killed in the south, why didn't his dragon die there with him? The Rorack's territories are far to the southwest; how did she end up here in the north?"

Roland waved him to silence and sighed, "Perhaps it would be best if you start at the beginning, Rider. Then we can make sense of all of this."

At this point, Cheeno joined them, poured himself a glass of wine, and sat down quietly to listen.

Again Delno found himself telling the tale of how he met the mother dragon and became bonded to his Geneva. Since Roland was Corolan's relative, Delno decided he had a right to know everything, so he left out no details. The telling of the tale to this point took over an hour. At a couple of points, Cheeno started to interrupt him with questions, but was silenced by either Roland or Farrel, for which Delno was grateful.

When he finished, Roland was the first to speak. "You have acted honorably toward my family, and for that I thank you. Your actions show that Geneva made the right choice when she chose you to bond with her last daughter. Though I didn't know Corolan as well as I would have liked, I'm sure that he would be pleased with the choice as well."

"Thank you, Roland," Delno said, "From the start I've been afraid of making a mess of this whole affair."

"Well," Roland responded, "You've been handed a rough lot of tiles to play, but so far you seem to have done all right considering you were left to raise a hatchling by yourself with only minimal training."

"Indeed," Farrel observed, "I'd say you've done better than could be expected."

Delno said, "Well, I haven't done as well as you think. Geneva has been seen."

All three men were suddenly concerned. "Tell us about it," Roland prompted.

Delno told them about overhearing the conversation between the two Southerners at the market. When he was finished, Cheeno spoke, "They must have been from Horne. I've traveled to that kingdom. Their lands border on the Rorack's territory, so their king gives the three riders there a great deal of freedom to do as they please because their presence keeps the Roracks in their place. The farmers take offense at having to feed the dragons, but there isn't enough large game to sustain three great predators in such a small area, and without the dragons the whole kingdom would suffer repeated attacks from the beast-men. I wonder how the farmers would like having their herds stolen, their farms razed, and their wives and daughters kidnapped and taken as slaves to those monsters, those who aren't killed outright, that is."

Delno was quite interested in Cheeno's comments. He had started to wonder if the riders in question were of the sort that Geneva's mother had warned him about. Now he saw it from a different perspective. "Of course," he thought, "The truth probably lies somewhere in the middle."

Roland interrupted his musings, "Well then, Rider, what's to be done about your request to accompany us?"

Farrel looked surprised. "What's to be done? He's to accompany us to Palamore, of course," he said as if any other course of action would be madness.

"Not so fast." Roland retorted. "You may be one of the king's chosen, but I'm still Master of this caravan."

Both Farrel and Cheeno began stammering arguments but Roland said, "Enough," in a commanding tone and both men where silent. He went on, "Having a dragon along will attract attention. It will make the caravan look very rich. A very rich caravan is a temptation to bandits. If the dragon were old enough to help protect the wagons and stock, I wouldn't hesitate. However, this dragon is very young: barely able to hunt. We'll not only have to protect the caravan, but the dragon as well, and, even if we hire extra guards, I'd still be very surprised if we get through unscathed."

Turning to Delno, he said, "I'm sorry, Rider; you've done well by my family, and it shames me to refuse you. If it were just me, I'd travel with you and help you as best I could, but I have to think of all the other people who look to me. I'm responsible for their safety and their profit. I can't risk all of that."

Delno looked the man in the eye and said, "You are acting honorably toward your charges. I can't fault you for doing what's best for those to whom you have sworn oaths of service. Having been a commander in the army, I understand such decisions."

Roland was genuinely pleased to hear that Delno understood and took no offense. Farrel was not happy, and said, "Caravan Master, as you know, I am charged with looking for the Dragon Blade that was stolen. While the blade we found here is most assuredly not the one I seek, I do believe that fate has sent this Rider to us for a reason. If you send him away, I would see it as my duty to leave the caravan and accompany him."

Roland looked at Farrel for a long moment before responding. "If that is how you feel, then you must do your duty as you see it."

"Gentlemen," Delno spoke up, "I will not be the cause of any hardship or hard feelings here. When I think more about this, I realize that it is probably best for Geneva and I to make our way south by ourselves. The fewer of us in that procession, I believe, the better. We will travel light and avoid others, and so avoid attracting more attention than we have already done." To Roland he said, "You have acted honorably, both to me and to those in your charge, and I can find no fault with your decision." Turning to Farrel, he said, "I greatly appreciate your offer to go with me, but I cannot allow it. I will be fine. I may be a novice dragon rider, but I am not helpless, and the caravan will be better off with you along as protection." Turning back to Roland, he added, "The only maps I could get of the south are quite incomplete. If I could buy a decent map from you, or you could have someone who has skill at such things fill in the one I have, it would be most appreciated."

Roland smiled broadly and replied, "I'm sure we can accommodate you."

Then, while the four of them drank the rest of the wine from the pitcher, Roland had Delno's gear brought in and set one of the women to filling in his incomplete map. It took her over two hours, but when she had finished, he was quite impressed. She had filled in every detail and added footnotes explaining all the roads, fords, and mountain passes. He felt bad about not paying for such fine work, but Roland wouldn't hear of it, so he settled for praising her skill highly and accepted the map as a gift.

It was late afternoon when he left the caravanners, but he felt that now he was finally ready to start his journey.

He talked with Geneva as he rode back to camp. Relating the day's events in detail took quite some time, and he was nearly there when he finally finished the tale. "*I am sorry, Dear Heart, I had expected to retrieve my sword, purchase a few things, and return before noon.*"

"*I'll hate you later, Dear One,*" she teased.

He got the impression that she was immensely pleased about something, and when he asked what it was she responded, "*I was flying again today. I flew further north away from camp to avoid being seen. When I got hungry, I found and caught on of those elusive deer that live in these woods. I am really getting the knack of flying and hunting for myself.*"

"*That's wonderful news,*" he said. "*Tell me, Geneva, do you think you are ready to start our journey south? Would you be unhappy if we left right away?*"

"*Well,*" she said, "*I wouldn't want to leave this instant. I just ate a whole deer and would like a nap first. As far as being unhappy about leaving, the only thing here that we wouldn't take is the last three of those scrawny sheep, and I would be glad to put some more distance between myself and them.*"

Delno laughed out loud; she really didn't like mutton. As he entered the clearing, he said, "*Have your nap, Dear Heart, I will get the camp*

# CHAPTER 20

AS GENEVA STIRRED from her slumber, he began tying his packs onto the pony. There was certainly more than he had originally started with, but it was still a light burden for the animal. After securing the packs, he saddled his horse.

He had started to pack away the Dragon Blade, but then decided that since their days of hiding were rapidly coming to an end, he would rather have the sword at his side in case he needed it. He hung it from his left hip and then put the *main gauche* on the same side. He preferred a cross draw on the longer blade, but wanted the smaller one at his left fingertips.

The other thing he kept out was his bow. It was made of horn and hardwood. It was short, but wickedly powerful. Even though the shopkeeper had reduced the price because so few men could draw it comfortably, it had still been hideously expensive. The draw weight had to be nine stone. Delno had tried the draw in the shop and found that his dragon-enhanced strength was up to the task. It and the quiver of arrows were now hanging from a quick-release strap on the back of his saddle within easy reach.

Finally, after one last check, he decided they were as ready as they would ever get, so they set off, heading toward the city. He coaxed his horse into a fast walk; the pony, with its shorter legs, had to almost trot to keep up. He wasn't worried about the smaller animal though: these tough mountain ponies were bred for hard work under adverse conditions. This would be good exercise for the little beast, but shouldn't over-tax its abilities.

The city gates would be guarded at this hour, but shouldn't be locked, since no state of emergency existed, so he decided rather than go several miles around, he would travel right through the middle of town. Geneva could fly ahead and meet him on the other side with no one the wiser. He had also written a letter to Nassari explaining where he was going and how Nassari might be able to travel with the caravan if he wanted. He even included a letter of introduction that should get the caravanners to look favorably on his friend joining them. He would leave the letter with the gate guards and they would, for a few coppers, make sure it was delivered.

They were silent on the first leg of the trip. Geneva wasn't used to flying at night, and needed to concentrate to get her bearings. He was happy for the solitude, as it gave him time to ponder some of the small questions that had been puzzling him. As he approached the city gates, he told Geneva to fly ahead and find a safe place to land while he continued through. She flew on, and he exchanged pleasantries with the guards, one of whom knew him from the army, and that man agreed to deliver the letter. The rest of the trip through Larimar was completely uneventful. He soon caught up with Geneva, and they were truly on the road this time.

"*I've been thinking, Dear Heart,*" he said.

"*I hear that some consider that a dangerous occupation.*" She was beginning to develop a real talent for sarcasm.

"*Some would caution that traveling with a dragon is not a smart thing to do also,*" he responded.

She chuckled mentally, but let him go on with his thoughts. "*I've noticed certain things in the last couple of weeks,*" he continued. "*First, I've gotten stronger, faster, more agile, and I tire less easily than before.*"

"*Those are all benefits of being linked to a dragon,*" she noted.

"*Yes, I figured as much. However, I've also noticed other things.*"

"*Such as. . . ?*" she prompted when he paused.

"*Such as,*" he replied, "*my carvings. I've always done okay whittling pieces of wood into recognizable shapes, but to achieve a high enough degree of skill to sell my carvings in so short a time?*"

She was thoughtful but kept her silence while he went on. "*Then, there's you.*"

"*What about me?*" she asked.

"*Your mother told me that you would eat less and that you wouldn't be able to hunt for yourself until you were a month old. From what your mother said about dragon growth, I have the impression that you are larger than other dragons of your age, also.*"

She considered her answer carefully before speaking. "*I'm not sure, but I believe that the magic flows much more strongly between us than normal. That allows the energy of the world to flow more powerfully through us, making us stronger. I believe that that also explains how your carving skills got so good so quickly. The magic enhances your spatial perception as well as your other senses and physical characteristics. While the enhancements aren't enough to make you super-human, I'd say they put you in a fairly elite class.*"

She paused for a moment, then continued, "*As for my impressive growth, it's happening for the same reason. Again, I am just guessing, but I am probably at the equivalent growth of about five to six weeks for one of my kind.*"

"*If I get my longevity from you, does that mean that the increased strength I have attained comes from you also?*" He was concerned that their relationship might actually harm her.

"*Calm yourself, Dear One,*" she soothed. "*Remember what I said, magic cannot create life, so your extended life has to come from somewhere? Strength, stamina, and other physical characteristics are different. The energy flow between us enhances them as a byproduct of the link. You are taking nothing from me. In fact, I believe that I am gaining some benefits in those aspects just like you are. Think of it like running water through a stream; the bigger the stream bed, the more water can flow.*"

"*Delno,*" she suddenly sounded alarmed, and he instantly became alert for danger, "*There are three men about three hundred yards ahead of you.*"

He stood in the stirrups and strained his vision. "*I only see one,*" he replied.

"*The other two are trying to hide on either side of the road. I can see them because I can see heat as well as light. To me, they glow like beacons.*"

"*Perhaps I can go around and avoid them all together?*"

"*No, I don't think so. I believe that the one standing in the road has seen you.*"

Delno considered his options. He could return to town, but he would lose much of the night doing so. He could simply wait here and let them make the first move, but that would also take time he would rather not lose. He said aloud as well as mentally, "*Oh well, nothing for it but to push on and get this over with.*"

Making a quick check on his bow and quiver, he started forward. To Geneva he said, "*Stay out of this Geneva. I am armed and have had a great deal of training with weapons; I'll do better knowing you are safely airborne than if you try to help me.*"

"*There are three of them,*" she responded, sounding a bit hurt.

"*Yes, but they believe they have surprise on their side. It'll put them off when they realize I am prepared for all of them. Besides, if I need you, you will be much more impressive swooping down from out of nowhere than if you walked up by my side.*"

His last statement soothed her hurt pride, so she reluctantly agreed to be reserve air support.

Delno briefly considered breaking the horse into a run, but then thought better of it. While a charging horse is an impressive sight, it was full dark, and they might have laid a rope across the road. The last thing he wanted to do was lose his horse to a broken leg and be left on foot to deal with three highwaymen. He continued forward at the same pace he had been maintaining since leaving camp.

As he came within ten yards of the man standing in the middle of the road, he stopped. The man waved as if this were just a natural meeting of two travelers. When he didn't move any further forward, the man said, "You can advance, rider, the road ain't blocked."

"Oh, I think I like it so well right here that I may set up camp," he quipped.

The would-be robber, as tall as Delno though not as filled out, looked perplexed. "There's nothin' to be scared of; I don't bite."

"Ah, but I do," Delno replied. Then he added, "Why don't your friends come out where I can get a better look at them? Are they shy?"

The man didn't look as though he was pleased by the question. He said, "I've got no friends here. I'm all alone."

"Really?" Delno replied, "Then you had better get away from there because there are two men, one lying in the brush on either side of the road, and I don't believe that their intentions are exactly honorable."

The man looked as though he would either swear violently or perhaps cry. Delno went on talking casually, "I know your friends are there. I know that you are lying in wait for unsuspecting travelers. Now you know that I am not unsuspecting, so I would advise that you and your friends move along and find easier prey."

The man didn't seem to know when to quit. He said, "I tell you, I'm alone."

Delno pulled his bow from behind him and nocked an arrow, then said, "Then you won't mind if I shoot a few arrows into the clump of brush off to your right, and couple more in the brush on your left, will you?"

The man stared at him for a moment and then said, "Iffin you want to waste your arrows, I guess you can."

Geneva said, *"The man on the right is moving slowly toward you, the one on the left is moving further out into the field."*

In a loud voice, Delno said to the man in the road, "I am tired of this game. If either of your companions moves another inch, I will put this arrow right through your chest." After saying this, he drew the bow and aimed carefully.

There was no movement. They all stayed perfectly still until the slender man's will broke. "All right," he said, "You boys git up and come out of those bushes before I end up a pin cushion." When neither of them showed himself, Delno stood in the stirrups and fine-tuned his aim. The man swore and then screamed almost hysterically, "I said you two git up here, now."

The other two, neither of whom had seen his twentieth birthday, stood and walked over to stand next to the first man. Delno was a bit disgusted with the lot of them. He moved closer, but stayed out of reach, and he kept the bow ready. He could now see that his suspicions had been correct; there was a rope stretched across the road. If he had tried to charge past, the two hidden boys would have pulled the rope tight and tripped his horse.

"In this kingdom, it is my right to leave your decapitated corpses beside the road, and I could collect a bounty for your heads," he said. "Smart highwaymen are a bane to trading; stupid highwaymen like you are just idiots and should be killed before they have a chance to breed." Then, noticing the resemblance between the man and the boys, he added, "I can see I'm too late to stop you from breeding."

After letting them sweat for a few minutes, when all three were shaking with fear, he continued, "I should take you back to the city and turn you over to the guards."

At this suggestion, both of the boys actually started crying. The older man, who he assumed he was the father, fell to his knees and starting begging, "Please, sir, don't turn us over to the guards. We didn't want to harm no one, we just needed to get some money, and there's no work we could find. We wouldn't have hurt you, honest."

"Wouldn't have hurt me? Suppose you had tripped my horse and I had broken my neck in the fall?"

The man looked completely abashed at this suggestion. Apparently, the thought that they could accidentally cause injury or death hadn't occurred to them.

"Fortunately for the lot of you, my business is too pressing to return to town at this point. I'm going to send you on your way, though I should tie you up and leave you here with a note to whoever finds you." As he kicked the horse and clucked at it, he added to the three men, "Go to the docks in town. If you are willing to do hard work, they are always looking for men to load and unload cargo. What ever you do, get out of the robbery business. You're really lousy at it."

The three men couldn't believe their good fortune. The older man said, "Thank you, sir. We will git out of this here business, I promise. We'll go to the docks come first light, I promise."

Delno continued on his way, hoping the man wasn't lying through his teeth. Either way, he didn't have any more time to spare for those three. As he kept the horse walking at the same brisk pace as before, the three *reformed* robbers kept jabbering thanks and promises until he was out of earshot. For all he knew, they kept jabbering even then, but he no longer had to listen to them.

The excitement, though a bit unwarranted, had drained him more than he would have expected. To rise to such a state of readiness only to find out he was dealing with halfwits had left him feeling the hours and miles he had traveled since he had awoken at dawn the previous day. He asked Geneva to look for a suitable place to camp not too far from the road. When she found one, he followed her to it.

Once at the clearing, he did little more than remove the saddle from the horse and the pack from the pony and hobble the two animals to keep them from wandering off. He was too exhausted, both physically and mentally, to actually make camp. It was a warm night, and there wasn't a cloud in the sky, so he simply rested his head on Geneva's front leg, and they went to sleep.

# CHAPTER 21

DELNO WOKE THE next morning expecting to find himself covered with mosquito bites. He was pleasantly surprised to find that wasn't the case. When he thought about it, he realized that since he had begun associating with dragons, he hadn't been bothered by any such pests. He pondered this for a few moments while he quietly went about his morning rituals. He would have to ask Geneva when she woke up if she knew anything about this.

One of the things he had told Geneva to look for in a campsite was a close supply of fresh water. This was not a problem here in the north near the mountains. Even in the summer, the runoff from the higher peaks kept most of the streams bubbling along nicely. So, after building a small fire, he retrieved his kettle from his pack and went to the nearby stream to get water.

As he was about to fill the kettle, he noticed several pan-sized fish swimming lazily and feeding off of a plant that was growing so near the bank it was partially in the water. As he got nearer, he realized why the fish had come so close. They weren't eating the plant; they were eating the beetles that were crawling down the plant stems to drink. He didn't know what prompted him to do it, but he decided to try and grab one of the fish before he scared them off filling the kettle.

He knelt down slowly and held his hand over them. As he'd expected, his appearance caused the fish to move off into deeper water. He sat patiently with his hand still in position to grab and waited until their hunger and his lack of movement lulled them into returning to feed. He didn't have long to wait. Within minutes, several of the fish moved back under his waiting hand. Though he had never before been fast enough to do this, his hand shot forward like the neck of a wading bird and he grabbed one of the creatures and threw it up on the bank. He sat on his haunches for a moment just looking back and forth from his hand to the flopping fish. "This dragon magic definitely has advantages," he said out loud to no one. He briefly considered trying for a few more fish, just for sport, but decided that it would be wrong to do that to the fish when he already had enough for his breakfast. Instead, he filled his kettle, and, slipping two fingers into the creature's gill opening, he returned to his fire.

First, he put some of the grounds he had brought into a cheesecloth sack, which he then submersed into the kettle. Then, placing the kettle on the edge of the fire, he went to his pack and got his frying pan and some bacon. Just a small piece of bacon would go well with the fish, and the fat would lubricate the pan. As the bacon was heating, he set about cleaning his catch with his small belt knife. After removing the head and tail, he gutted it and found treasure. Inside, the fish was laden with delicious roe. He carefully cut that away from the rest of the gut and put it aside while he removed the fins and filleted the meat. All of the scraps; gut, fins, bones, and skin, he saved in case Geneva wanted them. Then he fried the fillets, adding the roe only as the meat was just reaching perfection; he wanted the roe to be cooked but not over done. Not wanting to unpack any more of his camp gear, he improvised a plate by turning the cast iron lid upside down and using the concave underside. As he poured his drink, he lamented that he had no way to lighten the brew. He much preferred cream and sugar. However, since there were no milk cows about, and sugar was nearly worth its weight in gold here in the north, and he didn't even have any honey, he resigned himself to drinking it black.

Geneva woke while he was eating. "Good morning," he said to her.

"Good morning to you, too," she returned. Then she sniffed and asked, "What are you eating?"

"Fish. I saved you the gut and some other parts if you like. It's not much more than a morsel, I'm afraid."

"That will be fine. Thank you for thinking of me."

"I always think of you, Dear Heart."

She beamed her pleasure while he gave her the pieces of fish he had saved for her. Then she said, "While that was very good, Dear One, I'm *afraid that it only made me even hungrier than I already was. I shall have to hunt this morning. I flew a great deal more last night than I'm used to, and I feel completely empty."*

He chuckled and said, "I had assumed as much. Go and hunt. We are still close enough to town that we would probably meet people on the road if we traveled today anyway. I think that until we are farther into the wilds, we should continue traveling at night. So gorge yourself if you can. Then we can set out again after you have slept off some of the meal."

*"That makes perfect sense. I shall try not to be long hunting, but I am very hungry."*

Without another word, she rose up on her back legs, and, gathering herself, lifted her wings for the down stroke and launched. Delno watched all of this and marveled at how graceful she had become in such a short time. He had also watched more carefully this time, noting the way the muscles moved under her hide. He was curious and wanted to figure out how her body worked. He had paid a great deal of attention to other animals, including humans, in this respect. He realized that all the other animals he had seen and studied that were not bugs were four-limbed. Even birds' wings were nothing more than front legs adapted for flight. Geneva, on the other hand, was a six-limbed creature. She had hind legs, front legs, and those marvelous wings. As far as he could tell, other than insects, dragons were the only six-limbed animals on the planet; therefore, it didn't make sense that they existed in nature, but here they were.

When she had gone, he cleaned his utensils and stowed them away. Then he spent some time stretching out his sore muscles. He hadn't thought that riding for several hours would leave him so stiff when he had been working out so much in the previous two weeks. *"Different work, different muscles,"* he thought to himself and continued stretching. After stretching, he decided to practice his saber work. This time he used the Dragon Blade instead of the wooden practice blade. Last night had been a farce, but it reminded him that there were real dangers on the road, and, as his old training sergeant used to say, "A false blade gives false confidence."

He was amazed and pleased with how well the blade performed, and he was surprised at how well he performed with it, especially since, until now, he had barely handled it. He spent nearly two hours practicing before he finally decided that he had done enough this day to familiarize himself with his new saber. He went to the stream and, finding a place wide enough and deep enough, he took off all of his clothes and washed himself thoroughly, then he washed the clothes, and, upon returning to camp, hung them on bushes to dry in the sun.

He was just beginning to worry about Geneva being gone so long, even though he could sense her, and she didn't feel distressed, when she landed awkwardly in the small clearing. He was about to ask if something was wrong when he saw that she was clasping the carcass of a small wild pig in each of her front feet. Then he noticed that she was also somewhat distended from the meat she had already eaten. He watched with something approaching awe as she began eating one of the pigs she was clutching. As she finished that one and immediately moved onto the second, she noticed him staring.

"I told you I was famished," she said sheepishly.

Delno laughed and said, "Eat, Dear Heart, we have a lot more traveling to do tonight."

When she had eaten about half of the second pig she said, "I am full. If you would like, you may cut some of this meat for yourself. What you don't eat, I will eat later after I have slept."

"Thank you," he said, "I suppose a small piece of the haunch would make a nice supper before we have to travel again." He drew his belt knife and began cutting a small roast from the hindquarter of the carcass. When he finished that task, he set the roast down and built a new fire on the ashes of the old. Then, as Geneva drifted off to sleep, he retrieved his herbs and spices, mixed some, and rubbed them into the meat thoroughly. Then he put the meat in his covered pot and set it aside to wait until the fire died down to embers and was suitable for cooking the roast.

He looked over at his sleeping partner and was almost shocked at how large she had become. He knew she grew overnight, but she was now so large that he doubted that any predator on the planet, except another dragon, would have the gall to even consider attacking her. Her talons had gone from the formidable little daggers he had noticed when she had first hatched to something more akin to his *main gauche*. Her fangs, now visible even when she closed her mouth, were as long as his outstretched hand when measured from his wrist to his fingertips. Her sheer bulk was already bigger than his horse, and that didn't include her wingspan. If he had to sum up her appearance in one word, that word would be "formidable."

Then, retrieving his new carving knives from his gear, he began looking for a suitable piece of seasoned wood. He found a piece that nearly screamed at him. As he looked at it, he could clearly see the animal inside just waiting for him to remove the excess and free it. He took the piece and settled down where he could watch Geneva sleep while he worked. He then lost track of time while he carved on the piece. When he stopped for a break, he realized that the fire had died to embers, so he put the covered pan in the center, and, using a flat piece of wood, he piled the embers up almost to the lid so that the meat would heat evenly from all sides. He lamented that he hadn't looked harder for a lid that was dished on top so that he could pile some embers on it also. He made a mental note to look for one at the next town they came to on their journey.

He started to settle back down to his carving, but decided to try and nap since he had awoken early and would be riding long into the night. So he settled down, half reclining against Geneva's side and closed his eyes. The dragon wriggled slightly in her sleep, snuggling against him.

Soon he and she were again standing together on that same mountaintop where Geneva had told him her lineage and her name in their dreams. He didn't know how this worked, but he was sure that, while they remained asleep, they were actually sharing this dream and were conscious of each other on a different level. At first, neither of them spoke this time. They simply stood and watched the other dragons soar in the strange reddish light. He noticed, too, that there were other dragons sitting or laying on other ledges, and when he looked off in the distance, he could see other mountains. It was a bit like sunset through swirling clouds, but the light didn't grow brighter or diminish, as if the sun never set in this dream world.

Finally he turned away from the light and faced Geneva. "What is this place?" he asked.

She smiled at him and said, "This is a collective Dream State of the dragons. As a Rider, you are able to come here with me because our bond is so strong. The other dragons you see soaring or perched are also asleep, and together we all create this place."

"How are we able to talk here? When we are awake, we talk with our minds."

She snorted a little laugh and said, "We are talking with our minds. This whole place is in our minds. Here, our 'mind bodies' simply conform to our expectations, so we appear to speak out loud."

Delno tried to count the other dragons, but found that they tended to move about too much. Even the mountains seemed to move. He gave up counting, but was sure there were more than a dozen. As he looked at another mountain, he noticed that there was even another Rider here. He waved. The other Rider saw him and nodded in acknowledgement, but that was as much interaction as the man seemed to want.

He considered this for a time and then asked, "What about the other dragons here? Can we speak to them?"

"I communicate with them, but they choose not to communicate with you, for now." Then she turned directly to him and said, "You see, Dear One, many of the other dragons who come here are what men call 'wild' dragons. They come here to indulge their desire for companionship. It is not as fulfilling as having companionship in the waking world, but it does ease the loneliness."

"Wild dragons," he said. "Are there males here as well?" He began looking about somewhat excitedly.

"Males don't feel the loneliness as females do," she responded, "They rarely come here. Those who do are usually quite young and haven't established a territory of their own yet. They don't stay long."

As if on cue, a small brown dragon appeared and Geneva said, "There is a male."

Delno looked more intently. The male was only about half the size of the females, not much larger than Geneva, and looked surprised to be in this place. He noticed Delno watching him, and, snarling, dived at him in attack. Geneva roared a warning, but was more amused than frightened. The male dragon, however, pulled out of his dive, and, looking a bit frightened, faded completely from view.

"Male dragons succumb to the territoriality even here," she said. "That is one reason they don't stay long; here that behavior isn't tolerated."

"He seemed frightened of you," Delno observed.

"Well, you can't really be hurt here, but males aren't as intelligent as females, and he was young, so he might not have realized that." Then she said, "Males have good reason to be frightened of an angry female. We are bigger, stronger, and more likely to deal a death blow than another male would be." At his look of surprise, she added, "Though it shames us, female dragons are harsh. In our defense though, we have developed this way to ensure the survival of the species."

"But the way your mother talked about mating flights I had assumed the male could be a danger to the female. She hinted that if the male outright rejected a female, it could result in injury."

"She told you the truth, but you didn't have enough information and misinterpreted it. A male dragon is not a direct threat to a female. However, during a mating flight there are several females vying for the attention of the male. They participate in aerial contests of agility, grace, and stamina. The male will choose the one that excites him most during the contests. Just competing in the contests is enough to quell the mating drive. If one female does something that makes the male reject her outright, she creates the danger that the male will then refuse to mate with any of them and leave the area. If that is the case, the frustration of rising to such a heightened emotional and physical state only to be denied even the opportunity to compete can drive the other females, especially the 'wild' ones, to turn on the offender and attack her."

He again turned to watch the dragons soaring, but she said, "We must go now."

"It feels as though we just arrived," he responded.

"Yes, but we have slept long, and if we do not return to the waking world soon, your dinner will be burned, and you will have to eat cold jerky. If that happens, you will be grumpy, and I don't wish to travel with a grumpy companion. Besides, I want to eat the rest of that pig and have a bath before we go."

As Delno stared at her, she, and the rest of the Dream State, faded to black. Then he came fully awake right where he had fallen asleep. He quickly moved to the fire, and, using the rag that had until recently been his tunic to protect his hand, he pulled the pan out of the heat. As she finished the pig, in a couple of bites, he removed the cover from the pan. The dragon had been right; if he'd waited much longer, the meat would have been ruined.

As she walked to the stream to bathe, he remembered his question from this morning. *"Geneva,"* he said, *"perhaps you can answer a question for me."*

*"If the answer is within my knowledge,"* she responded.

*"Very well, since the day I met your mother I've been living in the wilds, often sleeping under the stars. We've been camping in areas that have a great deal of water where mosquitoes and other such pests flourish; however, I can't remember being bothered by them during that whole time. Why is that?"*

She thought about it for a moment then said, *"Sorry, Love, I have no idea. I am not bothered by such things, and there is nothing in the knowledge that my mother passed on to me that hints at an answer to your question."*

*"Hmm,"* he said thoughtfully, *"I wonder."*

"Wonder what?"

"Well, I have noticed a slightly musky odor about you, and, when I think about it, your mother had that smell about her also."

"Are you saying that dragons stink?" She sounded a little offended.

"Not at all, my dear," he replied hastily. "In fact, I find the scent quite pleasant. More like a very fine perfume, light as butterfly wings, but it lingers pleasantly."

"How very poetic, thank you," she said a little sarcastically.

"I'm serious," he declared, feigning indignation. When Geneva only chuckled, he went on with his thought. "Perhaps this scent, that I find so pleasant, is a natural defense that dragons have as protection against such annoyances."

"Perhaps," she replied. "We have no way of knowing, and since we can't prove your theory one way or the other right now, if you are finished eating, could you come down here and scrub the area between my wings? I'm having trouble reaching it, and it itches terribly."

Delno joined her at the stream. She had, even though it had only been a few moments, wallowed the bottom out enough to make it deeper. He told her to wait a moment while he removed his pants. The last thing he wanted to do on a warm humid summer night was spend several hours in the saddle wearing wet trousers. Then he waded in and immediately attacked the offending dirt that was causing her such distress. He noticed that the skin under the dirt appeared to be flaking off. As he scrubbed, a couple of scales, each larger than his own palm, even came loose.

"Geneva," he said with some concern, "are you sure everything is all right? Your skin is flaking off here, and you just lost two of your scales."

To his surprise, she laughed out loud for the first time in her life. "Yes, my overly protective partner, I am fine. As you have noted, I am growing bigger every day. Well, I am actually outgrowing my hide. My skin can't keep up so it sloughs off in patches to be replaced with new growth. Usually I just roll on the ground, or rub against trees and rocks. It's nice to have someone to rub the parts that are hard to reach." Then she added, "Thank you!"

"Of course, Dear Heart, any time."

This new revelation only brought more questions about the nature of dragons to his mind. He decided that the questions could wait, though, as he moved out of the water and retrieved his pants. He didn't want to be preoccupied while he packed. Last night's lesson was still fresh in his mind, and he wanted his packs tight and everything in just the right place in case something else happened. If he were accosted again, he doubted he would be so lucky as to be set upon by more idiots. The bandits who tended to work farther out from town were not so stupid and traveled in larger numbers.

He finished packing, and they moved out once again as the sun disappeared completely from the sky. He set the same pace as before, figuring that at such a rate they would probably be able to make seven or eight leagues before they would need to find a campsite. It ended up being much closer to seven leagues when exhaustion forced him to have Geneva find a place for them to rest.

# CHAPTER 22

"**Y**OU ARE GRUMPY *this evening*," Geneva said. "*Remember what I said about traveling with a grumpy companion?*"

It was almost morning, and they were just making camp after only traveling, by his estimation, a little more than three leagues.

"*Of course I'm grumpy,*" he said. "*We've been traveling for six nights; each night we traveled for a longer period of time, and each night we've traveled less distance. At this rate, we won't make Palamore by late winter!*"

"*Well, it's not my fault,*" she retorted. "*I am bigger than both of those beasts put together,*" she said, inclining her head toward the horse and pony, "*and I can travel many times the distance they can in a night!*"

He sighed and said, "*I am sorry, Dear Heart, it's not your fault, and I shouldn't take my frustrations out on you. You're right, of course; the horse and pony are actually slowing us down at this point. Unfortunately, you still aren't strong enough to carry your weight and mine, too; otherwise, we could probably have made the whole trip in less than a fortnight.*" Then, in frustration, he said out loud, "Hell, if it weren't for that eight-stone pack on the pony's back, I could probably walk faster on my own feet!"

She knew he hadn't been speaking to her, but she responded to his last statement with a question. "Are we sssure that you can'th ride with me?" She had just started to speak out loud in the last couple of days and still tended to lisp around her fangs, which, at this point, were a bit too large for her mouth.

The lisp made him smile, "No, Dear Heart, on this I must remain firm." As she started to object, he raised his hand to quiet her. "We've had this discussion already. You may be maturing extremely fast for one of your kind, but your mother told me that it would be six months before you would be ready to carry a rider. I will not rush that. Suppose we overtax your growing muscles and bones, and do permanent harm?"

"I carry a great deal of weight when I fly with the animalsth I kill back to camp before eating thhem," she replied.

"*I know you do, but I am heavier than most of the animals you carry back, and we would be traveling much further each night,*" he said. Then he added, "*A one-year-old horse appears almost fully grown, but if you start riding it before it is about three years old, you can damage the bones that are still growing, causing it to have problems for the rest of its life, perhaps even permanently ruining the animal for riding.*"

"I am not a horse," she pointed out.

"*I know you are not a horse, Geneva, but I also realize that I know so little about dragons and their growth that I can't say whether or not you carrying me in flight would do you harm, and I would rather err to the side of caution.*"

She knew, from three consecutive nights of repeating this conversation, that Delno would hold firm on this point, so she shifted the topic. "*Then what are we to do if we wish to increase the distance we can go in the time we have to do it?*"

"*The farther we get from the cities, the more danger of being waylaid by bandits, so we need to travel at night to avoid being seen. However, the farther we get from the cities, the worse the road gets, and the slower the horses have to go to avoid injuring themselves stepping in a pothole. The slower the horses travel, the longer we are traveling in the wilderness putting our selves at risk of attack,*" he mused. "*I can see no other way; we will have to start traveling during the day.*"

He was exhausted, but he was too frustrated to sleep, so he unpacked a few camp supplies, still opting for not erecting the tent, since there wasn't a cloud in the sky, and then gathered wood for a fire. Once he secured the horses, he settled down and read his map by firelight. "*If I am judging the landmarks and distances right, we are about one day's travel from this small village,*" he indicated the spot on the map with his index finger.

Geneva's vision could range from miles to just a couple of feet from her eyes, though when she viewed a small object that close she tended to look with one eye or the other, so she was able to see the point on the map.

"This village is right at the southern border of Corice. I will stop there and get more supplies and see if there is any news of the road ahead. It is the full dark of the moon now, so it will be another week, at least, before the horses will be able to see the road well enough in the dark to make good headway, so today we will begin traveling before full dark to try and make up time we will lose once night has fully fallen if we don't reach the village before dark. After we have rested and I have resupplied at the village, we will start traveling during the day."

"I still think we would be better off leaving the horses. . . ." she started, but he cut her off.

"I won't hear of it. We've been over this every night for the last three nights. Me riding you is out of the question until I can be sure that doing so won't damage your growing wing bones, muscles, and spine."

They stared at each other for a long moment until Geneva shrugged her shoulders in a surprisingly human-like gesture and gave up on the argument. She lay down and lowered her head to rest. Delno pillowed his head on her front leg and closed his eyes. Soon they were both sound asleep.

Later that morning, she hunted and returned with one small deer haunch that she allowed him to take enough meat to make a nice roast from, and then she slept again. He cooked his meat and ate quietly. Shortly after noon, he began breaking camp in preparation of her waking. When she woke, he made sure she was ready for the day's journey, and then gave her instructions.

"I need you to fly ahead and scout the terrain. Fly high enough to avoid being seen, but stay low enough to still be able to see enough detail to warn of any danger. Then find a suitable campsite near the town. Once you have done that, you should hunt and eat well. We may be at that camp for more than one day, so make sure it is fully concealed and you are well fed. If I can travel fast enough, I may be able to get to the village early and conclude my business there before nightfall, and thus we will be able to move on tomorrow. Otherwise, I will join you at camp, and we will leave the day after."

"Very well," she said. "I will do the scouting; you just get some haste out of those little beasts." Without another word, she launched herself into the air and was soon just a tiny speck in the sky.

He pushed the horses into a trot and maintained that pace for over an hour. Finally, he relented and allowed them to slow to a fast walk. After another hour, they came to a ford, which meant they were only about four leagues from the village, and he waited long enough for them to drink their fill before pushing on. He'd made good time, and he had several hours before the summer sun would set, but he decided to join Geneva at camp rather than continue to town. Some of these out-post villages closed up fairly early, and he didn't want to have to explain himself to gate guards any more than was absolutely necessary. Also, he knew Geneva might still be peeved at him, both for not relenting about riding her, and for the way he had ordered her about this afternoon. He wanted to join up with her and make sure she wasn't still upset.

"Good evening," she said as he entered camp.

"Good evening to you, too," he responded. "Is everything all right?"

"If by all right you mean am I over being angry, then yes. I know that your arguments against us flying together are based on sound logic and are for my own protection, and your instructions this morning made good sense. Although I didn't get over being angry with you until after I had eaten, so I'm afraid that I didn't save you any meat."

Delno laughed a little and said, "That is not a problem, Dear Heart, I passed a fruit tree a short way back and found enough ripe fruit lying on the ground to make a good supper. Being human, I need more than just meat anyway."

That night things were much happier in camp then they had been in the preceding few days. Delno even finished the carving he had started after their first evening on the road: it was a wild boar with wicked-looking tusks. He was quite pleased with how it turned out. He had erected the tent this time, but he used it to stow his gear, preferring to sleep under the stars with his head pillowed on Geneva's leg.

He again went with her to into the Dream State, but this time they barely spoke to each other. He was more than content to sit with her and watch the other dragons soar, and conversation seemed unnecessary.

# CHAPTER 23

THE NEXT MORNING he woke later than he had planned, but it was still plenty early enough to go to the village. He told Geneva that he had decided to forgo breakfast in camp, as there would surely be a bakery or some other shop where he could buy something to eat. After assuring her that he would be as quick as possible, he started off on foot, preferring to leave the horse where she could watch over it rather than trust it to some stranger in a strange town. The last thing he did as he left the camp was caution her against being seen, which she took good naturedly as him being over-protective, and then he was on the road by himself.

He had chosen his garments carefully. Both pairs of trousers he owned were of the same sort, the standard britches worn by most working people in Corice. He had three shirts, the fine one given to him by Roland, one tunic that was fairly new, and one that, though still serviceable, was patched and stained. He had worn his best pants, and had opted for the better of the two tunics. He had rejected the patched and stained tunic because he didn't want to look like a beggar, and had passed on the finer shirt because he didn't want to look like a wealthy traveler, either.

Though it only took him about half an hour to reach the village gates, because of his late start the morning sun was quite high in the sky. The gates stood open, but there were two guards on duty. The guards eyed him somewhat suspiciously as he approached. "Where are you going on such a fine day, and on foot?" one of the guards asked him.

The gate-guard's tone hadn't been exactly friendly. Delno didn't see any reason to cower from the man, so he straightened his shoulders and said, "I am going into the village to replenish my supplies." Almost as an afterthought he added, "I am on foot because I trust my horse to my friends in camp more than I trust it to strangers."

The guard didn't appear to like being addressed in that manner and said, "You'd do well to keep a civil tongue when speaking to guardsmen. What's your name and where are you from?"

"I am from Larimar, and my name is Delno Okonan, formerly Lieutenant Okonan of the Corisian Army, now retired, and you would do well to take your own advice concerning your tongue."

The other guard stepped forward and said, "Apologies, sir, he didn't mean any harm, he was just doing his job. I thought you looked familiar, sir; I was at Stone Bridge." He paused and whispered to his friend who turned red from embarrassment.

Delno was surprised that he hadn't recognized the second man. He smiled and said, "I'm sorry I didn't recognize you sooner. Parnell, isn't it?"

The man was genuinely pleased that Delno had remembered his name. "Yes, sir, I was in the squad that was sent to relieve you and ended up fighting at your side. You stopped one of the enemy from running me through with a spear when I was already down with a sword cut to my leg." He turned to the other guard and said, "If the lieutenant hadn't been the man he is, I wouldn't be here to tell the tale. I owe him my life!"

Delno said, "Nonsense, man, if I remember correctly, you took a sword stroke that was meant for me. I just did my best to return the favor. It was you who saved my life, and, I believe I put you in for a commendation for that."

Parnell's companion was, by this time standing with his mouth open, staring at both men wide-eyed.

Parnell said, "That you did sir, and I got a promotion out of it and am eligible for a small pension when I finish my time here."

Parnell and Delno both just looked at each other in silence for a long moment. Then Delno said, "I'm glad you're still alive, and I'm even more pleased that you are doing well. I wish every one who was with us on that bridge could have been decorated. There were so many acts of bravery among all of you men that some of them got forgotten. Every man who was there is a hero many times over."

Again they looked at each other. Delno's eyes were shiny and Parnell had a tear trickling down his cheek. Finally, they both came to attention in unison and saluted each other.

The first guardsman then said, "I beg your pardon sir, but we're on the edge of the wilderness here. Vagabonds and robbers aren't unusual in these parts, and we have to ask those questions of everyone, and you in work clothes and wearing a rough beard. I should have done better by you."

Delno reached up and rubbed his cheek and realized that he had been so preoccupied, first with his lack of progress, then with getting to the village, he had not even remembered to shave. He was wearing six days worth of whiskers. "No harm done. I suppose it's necessary out here, and I suppose I do look a bit like a vagabond." They all laughed a little.

Then Delno thought for a moment and said, "I skipped breakfast in camp to get an early start, and because I've eaten camp food since leaving Larimar. Is there a shop close by where I might buy a pastry, or at least some bread with butter?"

Both men must have eaten their share of camp food as well, because they smiled at his complaint and told him where he could get both. He bid them good day and walked through the gate.

Parnell called out to him before he got too far away, "Sir, if you're still in town after I get off duty at two o'clock, I'd be honored if you'd let me buy a round and drink a toast to the men on the bridge."

Delno replied, "Only if you let me buy the second round."

Parnell answered, "Done! I'll go to the Hog's Head Inn when I'm off duty and look for you."

Delno knew that it was an extravagant waste of time, but he also knew how much it would mean to the man, and he knew how much it would mean to him. He waved his assent and then continued on his way.

The village was larger than he thought it would be. Of course, being situated at the junction of two trade roads would make it a prosperous community when the caravans were traveling. He quickly located the bakery the guards had told him about and bought a couple of sweet rolls. He then left the shop, munching the sticky breads while he walked.

He wandered around town checking the shops and stalls that were selling all manner of trade-goods. He found the pan lid he'd wanted, and then replenished his supply of herbs and dry goods. He bought some hard bread. It wasn't as good as the softer breads, but it would keep for several days on the trail and be a welcome addition to his diet of mostly meat.

By the time he had finished shopping, it was near enough to two o'clock that, after getting directions, he began to make his way to the Hog's Head. When he entered the tavern, he saw that Parnell hadn't arrived yet, so he stood at the bar and ordered a glass of beer. There were quite a few men in the place; most looked like traders of one sort or another. He just stood at the bar and listened to what he could hear of the conversations going on around him.

One man was telling his companion that the mountain passes had remained blocked by snow longer than normal this year because of the extremely cold winter. His companion agreed and said that if it happened again next spring, it would play bloody hell with trading. Another group was discussing the prices of trade goods in the city of Larimar. Still another group was discussing brothels in the various towns and cities they planned to visit. While he was somewhat amused to hear them, no one was discussing road conditions and possible dangers on his chosen route.

He was thinking about mingling and asking a few questions when Parnell entered the tavern. Seeing Delno, the soldier smiled and waved, then joined him at the bar. "Sorry I'm late," he said, looking at Delno's half empty glass of beer. Then he turned and ordered two drinks for them. When the drinks arrived, they each took up a glass, and since custom gave the buyer the right to make the toast, Parnell said loudly, "To the men of the First Corps, living and dead, who held the Stone Bridge of Highland Pass."

Not noticing that several men suddenly went silent at a nearby table, Delno said, "Heroes, one and all," and touched his glass to Parnell's. Then both men drained their drinks.

Delno called the barkeep to order another round, but before he could say anything, one of the group who had watched him and Parnell spoke up. "Heroes, one and all," he mocked. "Lucky, bloody, cowards if you ask me." By his manner of dress, Delno surmised that he was from Bourne, though he was obviously too young to have been in the army during the war; he was no more than seventeen. He was also rather drunk.

Both Parnell and Delno turned toward the speaker. "Cowards?" Delno asked. "You'd call brave soldiers who held their position against ten times their number, 'cowards'?" Then he continued, "Lad, you should look around and notice where you are, then you should go somewhere and sleep off the drink before you make someone angry."

One of the other men at the table, older and not so drunk, tried to get the boy to sit down and be quiet, pulling on his sleeve. The boy wasn't interested in being quiet and jerked his arm free so violently that, in his drunken state, he fell backwards and ended up sitting down hard enough to bite his tongue and draw blood.

The whole thing might have blown over except that three more men from Bourne walked in at that moment, and one of them was apparently the boy's older brother, and rather hot headed. He looked at his brother who was unable to speak, and so just pointed at Delno. The elder brother took the gesture and the boy's bloody mouth to mean that Delno had hit the lad and started forward. Things might have still been smoothed over because the man who had tried to quiet the boy quickly explained what had actually happened, and the older brother started to relax. Unfortunately, the younger boy regained his voice but not his senses and told his brother about the toast.

The older brother, himself still not much more than a boy, stalked up to Delno and said, "So, you think that those bastards on that bridge were heroes, huh?"

Parnell spoke up, "We were on that bridge, boy. The lieutenant here was given a medal of valor for his bravery."

"My father died on that bridge," the young man responded.

Delno said, "A lot of good men died on that bridge, son. Both groups fought valiantly, and fiercely; being on different sides doesn't change that."

The young man responded, "Don't speak of my father and his companions in the same breath as those Corisians who died like the dogs they were." His hand was on his belt knife.

Delno's words came through clenched teeth, "You've reached your limit youngster; you have no idea how far this can go. You're not in Bourne now; you're in Corice, and you'd do well to remember that."

The Bournese who had first tried to avert trouble grabbed the young man by the arm and said, "It's time we leave, Karl."

Karl would have none of it. He shoved the man away and pulled his knife and said to Delno, "You're wearing enough blades, hero, pull one of them, and we'll settle this."

Everyone in the room except Parnell and Karl's younger brother backed away. In Bourne, if a man is old enough to make a serious challenge, he's old enough to fight the duel, so even his countrymen refused to intercede.

Delno shrugged. He stepped into the middle of the room where the tables had been hastily pulled aside to make space for the duel. The barkeep made a feeble attempt to get them to move this argument outside, but gave up when one of the men from Bourne waved for him to be quiet.

Karl was agitated by Delno's reluctance to pull his own blade. He began taunting his opponent. "What's the matter, *hero*, afraid to pull your blade and fight? Or are you just showing the same bravery that you showed on the bridge?"

As always happened to him when a situation turned deadly, Delno wasn't excited. He could remain calm through the thick of the toughest battle, and then he would shake like a leaf in the wind afterward. He was in that calm place now. He responded to Karl's taunts, "Oh, eager to die, boy? The men from Bourne seemed eager to die that day, too."

"You, shut up," Karl said through teeth clenched so tight it was a wonder that they didn't break.

Realizing he had struck the right nerve, Delno continued taunting him, but still didn't draw a weapon, "They had us outnumbered more than ten to one, and they kept throwing themselves at us."

Again Karl said, "Shut up."

Delno taunted him further, "They kept throwing themselves at us, and we kept cutting them down like wheat at harvest."

Karl's response was a nothing more than an animalistic growl.

"The bridge beneath our feet was slick with their blood and still they kept coming, and they kept dying."

Karl could contain himself no longer. He roared like a wounded bull and lunged at Delno with his knife, trying to gut him like a fish. This was exactly what Delno had been waiting for. He stepped slightly to the side and pivoted, allowing the knife to go by; it passed so close to his belly that it nearly found its mark, but that, too, was planned. As the knife missed by a fraction of an inch, Delno turned and allowed his hand to travel down the youth's arm until it naturally came to rest at the juncture between hand and wrist. Then, gripping the knife hand above the blade, he pivoted and pulled. The boy lost all forward momentum and was forced to turn and stop; he was, however, off balance and bent forward. Delno then took the younger man's knife hand in both of his own hands and pulled hard. Karl nearly flew back the way he had come, and as he did so, Delno held onto his wrist and allowed the boy's momentum to cause him to flip over his own arm. The boy landed heavily on his back on the floor. Delno quickly stepped over him, still holding his hand and wrist, and used that leverage to roll the lad onto his stomach. Then he placed his leg under the youth's arm, and, taking the knife from him, put the tip of the blade to the back of the young man's neck.

He looked at the other men from Bourne and said, "Will first blood end this, or do I have to kill this boy?"

The man who had tried to avoid trouble said, "First blood will settle it. We'll handle it after that." All of the other men in the party nodded in agreement.

Delno briefly thought about nicking the lad's neck, but then changed his mind. He quickly reached back with the blade and drove it an inch into the boy's right buttock. He then released his hold and stepped back.

Before Karl could dishonor himself by attacking his opponent again, his companions grabbed him and restrained him. Delno turned to the man who had answered him, and, handing him the knife, said, "Give this back to him after he's calmed down."

Two of the Bournese escorted Karl and his younger brother out of the tavern while the others helped move the tables and chairs. Once the furniture was arranged the way it had been before the fight, the men approached Delno and Parnell. The one who had tried to avoid trouble in the first place said, "I'm Jon, and those two hot heads are my brother's sons. I came in here to retrieve the younger one, Sam, before he got himself into trouble. I guess I didn't do such a good job."

"Older boys can be like that sometimes," Delno responded. "They want to prove that they're men and end up proving that they have a ways to go. No real harm done."

"Still," Jon said, "you'd have been well within your rights if you had killed Karl, but you didn't. For that I'm grateful. I wouldn't have been able to face his mother if he'd died in some stupid brawl."

Delno met the man's gaze for a moment, then said, "I've seen more than enough killing to last me a lifetime. He lost his father and wants to somehow make sense of it. He's looking for someone to blame, someone to hold responsible. Hopefully he'll learn something from this."

Jon thought about Delno's words for a moment and simply said, "Hopefully," before nodding his head and walking away.

Parnell shook his head and said, "I guess that we tend to forget that those were men we were fighting. Men with families and jobs and such, just like us."

Delno only nodded, and then waved the barkeep over and ordered two more glasses of beer. This time, he and Parnell toasted the men of both sides, living and dead, who had served honorably.

Nearly five hours had passed since the sun reached its zenith when he walked back into camp. He had little to show for his trip other than his replenished supplies. His time spent at the tavern had produced no news of note about the road ahead, and the other events while there had left him introspective almost to the point of depression.

Geneva had picked up on his mood long before he even left the tavern, but had not interrupted his brooding, hoping the walk from town would put him in better spirits. Now that he was back at camp, she said, *"Care to talk about what's bothering you?"*

"There's not much to talk about," he replied, *"I let some young man, a boy really, goad me into a fight over something I should have put behind me two years ago."*

She sensed that he wasn't finished but didn't prompt him, knowing that he would talk about it in his own time.

After a few minutes he said, *"I seem to be destined to define my life with my blade. Everything I have done that is considered to be of worth I've done with a sword in my hand. The 'Hero of Stone Bridge'—Hah! I was scared nearly to the point of wetting myself that day."*

"So you were afraid that day?" she asked.

"I was terrified," he responded, "I had to fight the urge to turn tail and run all during the battle."

"So, are you saying that you are a coward?" she asked.

"Well, I certainly didn't feel like much of a hero," he responded sarcastically.

*"I may still be very young, Dear One, but I do know that the absence of fear is insanity, not bravery. Facing your fear and doing what must be done in spite of it is the mark of a brave man."*

He was quiet for a long time. She waited patiently without pressing him to go on. Finally he said, *"I don't want my life defined only by the strength of my sword arm."*

Geneva stared at him for a moment, then said, *"I love you, Dear One, and I will help you define your life in any way you see fit."*

Delno simply placed his arms around her neck and hugged her tightly.

# Chapter 24

THE NEXT MORNING Geneva left to hunt while he was cleaning and stowing his gear in preparation for travel. She returned within an hour to find him shaving. She had fed somewhat lightly, and she observed that an early start would be better, and said she could hunt again before nightfall, reasoning that since their travel routine was changing, her feeding routine would have to change also. Delno couldn't fault her logic.

This time, it was she who suggested that she scout ahead, so they were able to start their travels this day without tension.

As with Larimar, he decided that it would be quicker to just travel right through the middle of town. He stopped only for a few moments to talk with Parnell before making his way along the main street to the gate on the other side of the village. The village straddled the road leading north to Larimar. The actual crossroads was about two hundred yards beyond the southern gate. Delno passed through and then continued straight when he came to the crossroads, taking the most direct route south.

If they stayed on the main roads, they would have to travel over two hundred leagues before reaching the borders of Palamore. About ten leagues ahead, the road turned east for several leagues, following the natural contours of the land. If he cut cross-country when the road turned that way, he could possibly save time, but he would be subject to whatever the wilds threw at him. Of course, cross-country would present the best hunting for Geneva. Once again, he found that he must make a choice that might cause more problems than it solved. He decided that he would call a halt about noon to rest the animals, and he and Geneva could discuss it. After all, they were partners and she had shown a remarkable amount of good sense this morning.

After traveling all morning without a break, he reached out mentally for Geneva and found the contact as strong as if she were right beside him. *"Dear Heart, I would like to halt and rest the animals, and my buttocks, for an hour or so. Is there a place were we can meet together that is somewhat hidden from the road?"*

*"There is a place about four hundred yards from where you are now that should work,"* she responded.

She guided him to a clearing about fifty yards from the road. She joined him within a few moments. Again, he was awed by how large she had grown, and by her grace and beauty. He watched carefully as she landed to see how the muscles moved under her hide. He was actually starting to get a feel for what muscles were responsible for which movements of her wings.

*"I have an itch between my hips that I'm having trouble reaching,"* she said.

Delno laughed softly and dug into his pack. *"I got something while I was in the village that might help,"* he said. He brought a small bundle to her. He unwrapped the bundle to reveal a stiff-bristled brush and a small covered jar. He then began using the brush to remove the flaky skin that was causing the itch. Then he opened the jar and applied a small amount of the oil that was inside to the patch of new skin. Geneva sighed in contentment and beamed pure joy and love to him, thanking him for his thoughtfulness.

Once her immediate concerns had been attended to, he told her about his ponderings and asked her opinion on whether or not they should leave the road and try to cut cross-country.

"At thish point," she said out loud, "I believe tshat we tshould shtick with the road."

"Really? I would have thought that you would have been for cross-country."

Again her common sense came through, "Normally I would, but the land around here is still crissh-crossht with thstreams. You will looth time fording them. Later, when the land ith more open, and there are more thities, we can leave the road."

"Again, Dear Heart, your logic is flawless."

"I wishth my thpeach was likewithe," she complained good-naturedly.

"I'm sure it will improve once the growth of your jaws has caught up with those fearsome teeth of yours," he said, laughing with her.

The next week went quite smoothly. Delno had met several travelers including one fairly large caravan, but Geneva had seen them well before they had the opportunity to see her, so she remained undiscovered. He had been able to get some news of the road and found that there was little to fear from bandits for a while, though it was always wise to be vigilant. He'd even been able to trade a few things with the caravan, bartering several carvings he had finished.

They had settled into an easy routine that was not unlike the one they had at their original camp. Geneva would eat a small meal of whatever she had left from the day before, and then they would travel. He and the horses were able to go about six to seven leagues before they would make camp for the evening. She would then hunt while he cooked his own dinner. While his dinner cooked, he usually worked on carving, then later he would play his pipes, usually accompanied by Geneva. While Delno was sure that fate had not made him a Dragon Rider to be an idle traveler peddling his carvings, he was equally sure he could get used to this life.

Another week passed without incident. The road turned sharply east and wound its way along for several leagues. He and the horses were approaching the last bend where the road turned back to the south when Geneva's warning brought him to a halt.

"What is it?" he asked.

"There are seven men who appear to be accosting an older man just around the bend in the road," she responded.

"That doesn't exactly sound fair," he said. "Perhaps we should have a look."

In the last week Geneva's growth had continued, and she was now large enough to be very dangerous, and her scales were thick enough to stop an arrow. He said, "While I am sure you can take care of yourself, Dear One, and me, too, for that matter, I would still prefer that you stay hidden unless I really need help."

"I don't like you walking into danger alone, but I understand. Besides, as you have pointed out before, I'd be much more impressive swooping down out of the sky than walking beside you like just another pony."

He chuckled and thanked her for her understanding. He kept the same pace as always as he rounded the bend. It wasn't difficult to make out what was going on. There were seven men, ranging in age from two older boys to one middle-aged man, all dressed about the same. The other four were roughly Delno's age. The eldest one had an older man pressed up against a small wagon while the others were going through the wagon's contents, throwing things carelessly on the ground, heedless of what they might be breaking. The older man was pleading with them to be careful of his property.

The men were so intent on what they were doing they didn't notice Delno's approach. They were quite surprised when he spoke. "I'd ask what's going on here, but I hate stupid questions, so let's just move on to, 'Let that man go and leave now if you wish to live.'"

Saying this, he swung his right leg over the horse in front of himself and jumped down. It was a style of dismount taught in the Corisian army when you were riding a horse that wasn't trained for combat. As he landed on his feet, he drew his Dragon Blade with his right hand and his *main gauche* with his left. He was an impressive sight; six foot three inches, well muscled, holding the two blades like he not only meant business but knew how to conduct it.

The men were unsure what to do next and didn't immediately move. They looked to the older bandit for guidance. Instead of telling the men to attack, the older man drew a wicked leaf-bladed dagger and placed it to the other traveler's throat. "One move out of you, my fine fellow, and this man dies. You boys get his weapons, and then we'll see what goodies he's packing on that pony."

Delno looked at the nearest man, "I wouldn't be too quick to obey those orders if I were you." The man, who had started to take a step in his direction, stopped. "You see," Delno went on, "I may be a Good Samaritan trying to protect a fellow traveler, but I don't know that man. I'm not likely to relinquish my weapons just because your leader puts a knife to his throat. The first man that tries me dies."

The older robber opened his mouth to speak and suddenly screamed in pain and keeled over. Everyone looked. The leader of the bandits was now on his knees holding his groin, which was bleeding, and the man he had been threatening was holding a small but wicked-looking curved blade in his right hand.

Delno looked at his new ally and raised his eyebrows. The older man shrugged his shoulders and smiled sheepishly.

Then Delno turned back to the other bandits and said, "Well, now, that puts a new light on things, wouldn't you say?"

They all drew their weapons and one said, "You'll both pay for that."

Delno realized that the older man wouldn't be able to hold his own against the younger bandits now that he no longer had surprise on his side. He called out mentally, *"Geneva, I can look out for myself, protect our new friend."*

As two of the younger highwaymen moved toward the old man the rest of them advanced on Delno. Suddenly, the two screamed in fear and dropped to the ground as Geneva, roaring, swooped down just over their heads and grabbed the elder traveler. She then flapped her wings and carried him away from the fight. Even though he was ready for it, Delno was still surprised. The rest of the men were dumbstruck.

*"You certainly know how to make an entrance, Dear Heart,"* he said.

*"I do my best,"* she replied, *"but if this man doesn't stop squirming to get a look at me, I'm going to drop him."* The old man, who had initially been startled by her appearance, was now completely enthralled by her. She landed and set him down as gently as possible about fifty yards from everyone else and moved as quickly as she was able back to the fray.

One of the men recovered, and, drawing a short sword, lunged at Delno. Delno used his *main gauche* to block the blade and brought his saber up under his opponents chin and thrust it into the right side of the man's neck, then he swung his arm to his right, nearly decapitating his assailant. He instantly moved on to the next attacker, again blocking and then thrusting his saber into that man's chest.

The other four hadn't quite recovered from Geneva's appearance, so they were standing still as she approached, bristling and ready to fight. She still had a lot of growing to do, but for the uninitiated, she was more dragon than they had ever wanted to see. Three of them broke and ran, and the fourth fainted. She was about to run them down when Delno called her back.

*"Let them go, Dear Heart, I don't think they will trouble us again today."*

*"As you wish, Dear One, but I would prefer to know where they are when we resume our travels."*

*"I'm sure,"* he responded, *"that wherever they are they won't want to find you again."* Then he laughed out loud. *"You were wonderful. You nearly frightened me, and I was expecting it."*

She chuckled and said, *"Yes, I am rather pleased with that performance."*

Delno was surprised to see the old man walking toward them. He didn't appear to be afraid at all. In fact, he appeared to be completely enchanted with Geneva. Before anyone could speak, though, the unconscious man groaned and sat up. Delno had his blade to the man's throat before he could move another inch. "Move and you die," he said.

The old man walked directly to the dragon, wide-eyed, and oblivious to either of the bandits who were still alive. He walked completely around her twice, appraising her. Finally, he actually walked right up and placed his hand on her scaly side. Then he said, "Magnificent, absolutely beautiful, I've never seen anything so wonderful."

Delno, his blade still at the bandit's neck, cleared his throat and said, "Perhaps we should. . . ."

Geneva hushed him and said out loud, "Don't interrupt him, he's doing jusst fine." Her lissp had almost completely disappeared in the last week.

Delno wouldn't have thought it possible, but the man's eyes actually opened even wider. He said, "You can sspeak as well, you're sentient? Why, you're more marvelous than I'd even dared hope."

Delno was getting a little annoyed, "We need to finish up here and resume our trek," he said.

Geneva snorted, "There's no harm in hearing what the nice man has to say."

At that moment, the older bandit groaned loudly and rolled over. The front of his trousers was soaked with blood. Delno turned to the younger man and said, "Get your friend on his feet and get him over there," he pointed to a sspot a few feet from the wagon.

The younger man, wary of the dragon, did as he was told. As he helped the older man to his feet, something fell out of the man's trouser leg; Delno looked and saw what it was. The old man had emasculated the bandit with that curved blade of his.

Their former victim turned to the bandits and said, "So, not so tough now, huh? Now that it's not just a defenseless old man you're facing."

Delno looked at the body parts lying on the ground and said to Geneva, *"Judging by that evidence, I wouldn't exactly call him defenseless."*

*"Don't you pick on him,"* she said.

*"Wonderful,"* he exclaimed, *"a little flattery and you have a new best friend,"* he teased.

She made a rude noise he hadn't thought she was capable of but otherwise ignored the comment.

No one moved or sspoke for several moments. Finally Delno said, "Well, what's to be done with these two?"

The old man looked at him and said, "I would gladly have killed them during the fight, but to do so now feels too much like murder for my taste, though I am loath to leave them free to prey on others."

Delno understood the sentiment. In fact, he was in complete agreement. If there were soldiers about, he would have no problem turning them over, but killing them in cold blood, though they would be within the law to do so, just wasn't in his nature.

Finally, he looked at the two men and said, "I have no reason to let you live, but I feel that killing you while you are helpless would be sinking to your level. We are too far from any city to turn you over to the authorities, and I cannot afford the delay in taking you along. Besides, I feel that your companions would eventually overcome their fear of my scaly friend and come looking for you."

Before he could continue, Geneva spoke up. "I can eat them."

The two men looked terrified at the suggestion.

Delno said, "You aren't serious?"

"Of course not."

Out loud, he said, "The last bandits you ate gave you indigestion."

"Yes, well, there is that, but I am very hungry this time," she said.

To the men, he said, "I've wasted enough time on you; be on your way. Mind you, though, if you ever cross my path again, I won't be so kindly disposed toward you."

The two men got up quickly, and, with the elder leaning heavily on the younger, they walked away as fast as they could.

Delno, Geneva, and the old traveler stood and watched them until they were out of earshot, then the man turned to Geneva and said, "Would you really have eaten them?"

She did her best to approximate a smile and said, "No, but they don't know that."

Their new friend laughed out loud and said, "You are an amazing creature. I've read about your kind, but I haven't had much opportunity to study dragons personally. The last dragon I had the opportunity to observe was when I was still a boy." Then, remembering that they hadn't been introduced, he said, "I'm Nathaniel; my friends call me Nat."

She looked at him for a moment and then said, "I am Geneva, and this man, my Rider, is Delno."

Delno extended his hand and Nat started to grasp his hand in the northern style and then tried to switch to the southern arm grasp. As the poor man got more flustered, Delno closed both of his hands over Nat's and said, "Pleased to meet you."

Nat grinned, and said, "I'm sorry, I'm not very good at social interaction. I'm a doctor and usually deal with people who are more interested in getting help than exchanging pleasantries."

As he turned to survey the remains of his belongings, he said, "I would dearly love to talk with you at length," he turned to Geneva, "especially you, my dear, but I must salvage what I can from this mess."

Delno was about to offer to help when the poor man nearly wailed out, "Oh, my poor pony."

They all stepped around to the front of the small wagon, and there, still tied into the harness, was a pony with several arrows sticking out of its side. The animal was obviously dead.

Nat shook his head and said, "I tried to run when I saw them, but they just killed the poor beast and stopped me anyway."

Geneva said, *"Delno, we have to help him."*

*"Calm, Love, I have no intention of just leaving him here."*

Then he said to Nat, "The pony that carries my pack is also broken to harness, at least according to the man I bought him from. He should fit that rig just fine, and, since it seems from the direction your wagon is facing that we are going the same way, we can at least get you to the next town."

Nat said, "I don't know how I am ever going to repay you. You've saved my life, you've introduced me to this wonderfully beautiful creature," at this he pointed to Geneva who sat up straighter, "and now you are providing me with transport for myself and my possessions. I am a simple doctor; please don't take this wrong when I say that I hope I never have opportunity to repay your kindness."

Delno smiled and bent to the task of removing the dead pony from the harness. Then he unstrapped his pack from his own pony, stowed it in the wagon, and hitched the animal to the wagon. While he was doing that, Nat salvaged as much from the mess as he could, explaining that the jars and such that the bandits were throwing around so casually were full of medicinal herbs. Once the pony was hitched, and all that could be salvaged was stowed, Delno suggested that they put some distance between themselves and the site of the bandit attack.

Geneva looked at Nat's dead pony and said, "It seems such a waste to leave it laying there."

Delno was afraid that Nat would take offense and was surprised at the older man's response. "I had an attachment to that animal while it was alive, but I do not believe that you eating it is offensive." Then, at Delno's look of surprise, he added, "After all, if we just leave the poor beast here, scavengers will only eat it anyway; I'd rather she get the nourishment."

Delno, shrugging, then pulled the arrows out of the stricken beast's side so that they wouldn't get in Geneva's way. He looked at the arrows and found them to be of inferior quality for his use and tossed them aside. His own bow was much too powerful to use them; his arrows were longer and had steel nocks to prevent the string from simply splitting the shaft when he fired them.

Neither he nor Nat wanted to search the bodies of the bandits. It was probably a waste if they were carrying anything useful, and by law they were entitled to anything they found, but it just seemed too much like lowering themselves to their attackers' level. So they simply mounted up without another word.

With Delno on horseback and Nat driving the wagon, they left Geneva to dispose of the carcass. Delno pushed the animals harder than he would have liked, but he wanted to put some distance between the dead bandits' live companions and themselves. The pony, although unaccustomed to pulling so much, appeared to take it good-naturedly, trotting along. When they stopped more than an hour later, the harness was wet with sweat, but the beast looked like it could continue if asked to do so.

# CHAPTER 25

AFTER THEY HAD moved the wagon off the road at a small clearing and made camp, Delno reached out for Geneva mentally. *"Where are you, Dear Heart? I would have thought that you'd have made short work of that carcass and joined us by now. It's been over two hours."*

*"I will be along shortly,"* she replied, *"I am just taking care of a few details that you missed."* Then, sensing his puzzlement, she added, *"I will explain shortly when I arrive."*

"Were you communicating with your dragon?" Nat asked delightedly.

"Yes," he answered, "how did you know?"

"You appeared as though you were concentrating on something, but you had a distant, somewhat unfocused look in your eye." He seemed pleased with his deductions.

Delno chuckled and was about to say more, but Geneva's arrival interrupted him. She landed gracefully. "Now then," he said out loud, "care to tell us what details you were attending to that kept you away for so long? I thought we had pretty much cleaned up after ourselves."

"I decided to do something with the bodies of the men," she said. Seeing their astonished looks, she added, "Don't worry, I didn't eat them. I did carry them off so that their companions will assume that I ate them, though. I thought that doing so might make them think twice about following us."

"That's amazing," Nat exclaimed, "I knew I was right!"

Both Geneva and Delno looked at him. Then Delno asked, "Right about what?"

"Oh, I'm sorry," he said, "I tend to think out loud sometimes. It's a habit I've gotten into from spending so much time alone. There is some debate among my colleagues about the intelligence of dragons. Of course, up until now, it's been a purely academic debate based solely on information we have gathered from the books written on the subject." He then went silent as he became lost in thought while watching Geneva settle herself into a comfortable position.

"Um, some debate. . . ." Delno prompted.

"Oh yes," he said coming back to the moment. "There's debate about whether dragons are actually sentient beings capable of independent thought or if they merely *borrow* the intelligence of their rider."

Geneva snorted at this, showing her disgusted opinion of the second theory.

"Oh, I don't hold to the 'borrowed intelligence' theory myself, mind you," he said quickly. "I have always argued that dragons are sentient. Your actions, my dear, prove that you are intelligent and quite capable of independent thought."

Delno was curious and asked, "How is it that these others can know of the existence of dragons and not believe them to be intelligent?"

"Well," Nat responded, "those people I've argued this point with are scholars who have only read about dragons in books. I'm afraid the books deal much more with care, feeding, and dragon anatomy than they do with dragon intelligence. Those books that do deal with the behavioral aspect of the species are written as second hand accounts of the deeds of dragons and their riders and are looked upon as legends more than any kind of factual accounts."

"Care, feeding, and anatomy?" Delno asked thoughtfully.

Before Nat could respond to Delno, Geneva spoke up, "Surely these men don't assume that these books are definitive?"

"Oh, I'm afraid that most do, my dear," Nat said sadly. "You see, these men don't travel much, and therefore, don't get the chance to make their own observations. Even I, who have traveled quite extensively, have never been close enough to a dragon before today to actually speak with the creature. Up until now, the closest I've come is having spoken briefly to one or two Riders," then he added, almost to himself, "They don't seem to have much need of my medical services."

"Tell me, Nat," Delno inquired, "how extensive are the books that you have seen concerning dragons, about their growth and anatomy I mean?"

"Oh, they were quite extensive," he responded. "The care of dragons, at least in southern libraries, is a fairly common theme in most books concerning dragons. As for anatomy, that's a little less common, though there have been at least three dissections, and those are well documented in at least two volumes I've studied."

Geneva bristled and said, "Dissections?"

Nat was a bit shaken by the ferocity she put into the question and said, "I'm sorry, Geneva, I don't mean to make light of the death of any dragon, but the poor dragons who were dissected had died of either natural causes or wounds. Other bonded dragons and their riders decided that not doing an autopsy would be a waste of an opportunity to learn, since the anatomical knowledge gleaned had such potential to help living members of the species. It was all done with the utmost respect, I can assure you."

Geneva considered the point then settled back down. "Yes," she said, "I can see the advantages to such an action."

Delno said, "You know, Nat, perhaps there is a way that you can repay us for helping you." He then told the older man their entire story from the beginning, only leaving out the details that had no bearing on the present situation.

When he had finished, he said, "So, you see, I have almost no training when it comes to dragons, yet I find myself as a rider. Your knowledge would be invaluable if you would agree to teach us what you know."

Nat thought about it for so long that Delno was worried that the man would refuse. Then the physician smiled broadly, and said, "I know that I owe you my life and should agree to your request outright, but I will only teach you on one condition."

Delno was taken aback by the man's response. "What is your condition?" he asked.

"That you take me with you on your travels," Nat said firmly.

It was Delno's turn to be thoughtful. Finally, he asked, "Why would you want to accompany us? Surely you have other concerns more important than following us around the country-side?"

Nat smiled, "Actually, my friend, I don't." He drew a deep breath and sighed before continuing. "A while ago I took an apprentice. The man was nearly a journeyman physician then, and he's been with me for more than two years. He is quite capable of taking over for my practice, and his elevation is merely a matter of formality at this point."

"So you'd prefer to travel rather than settle into a quiet retirement?"

Nat laughed out loud, "Quiet retirement? If I simply retired, I would just spend my time traveling and studying anyway. One can only learn so much sequestered in a library. By traveling with you and Geneva, I can study dragons first hand and perhaps write a definitive book on the subject."

Delno smiled at Nat's reasoning, but said, "While I can appreciate your position on this, and I think that you would be an intriguing traveling companion, I don't think I can take on the responsibility."

Nat sat up straighter and said, "No one is asking you to be responsible for me. I will pull my own weight, I assure you."

Geneva said, "There is no reason he can't come along. It might be a good idea to have a physician with us, anyway." Mentally, she added, "*You never know when you might find yourself in a bar fight and end up unconscious.*"

Delno glared at her, and Nat said, "There, you're out voted, two to one."

Delno looked from one to the other and back again. Eventually, he said, "Fine, since you are both so adamant about this, I will relent, but you will have to purchase your own supplies and carry your own weight."

Nat beamed like a child who had just been given a particularly wonderful new toy. He turned to Delno and said, "My house and practice are in Orlean. Since that is the closest city, and you have already offered to take me there, it won't be out of the way, so we can rest, re-supply, and I can make arrangements for my apprentice to take over for me."

"How long do you need in Orlean?"

"Not long, I should be able to put everything in order within a fortnight"

"A fortnight," Delno groaned. "We're already behind schedule. I want to get to Palamore as quickly as possible."

Geneva spoke up, "Since we are going to Palamore to find someone to train us, and we have now found someone to do just that, we no longer have need of such haste."

Delno rolled his eyes and said, "If I didn't know better, I would swear that you two had somehow met in secret and conspired together." At Geneva's stare, he threw up his hands in resignation, "Fine," he sighed,

"We stop in Orlean while Nat makes his arrangements. As for me, right now, I am hungry and would like to find something for dinner."

"No problem," Nat said, "I have some salt pork and plenty of herbs and spices. There are also some edible greens growing at the edge of this clearing that will make a nice salad. You get a fire going, and I'll start preparing the food."

Once the fire was ready, the food didn't take long at all. Within an hour they had a nice meal ready. They ate in silence and then cleaned up the utensils. After dinner, Delno and Nat talked about dragons for quite some time, mostly growth, feeding, and development. Delno told Nat his thoughts about dragons being six-limbed creatures and wondered that they existed in nature at all.

Nat was thoughtful for a long time before finally responding. "According to what I've read, dragons aren't naturally occurring creatures."

Geneva, who had appeared lost in her own thoughts, turned her head toward him and paid closer attention. Delno asked, "If they aren't natural creatures, how did they come to be here?"

"That, like most dragon lore, is a subject of much debate," he said. Then he sighed and continued, "According to all of the books that make mention of the origin of the dragons, they were created by using magic to blend other unrelated creatures until the species of dragon was achieved. Some claim it was a magical experiment gone awry, others claim that it is a magical experiment that was entirely successful."

"How is that possible?" Geneva asked.

"Well," he began, then added hastily, "and please don't take offense, either of you, but long ago there were practitioners of magic who make even the most adept present day masters of magic look like fumbling apprentices. There are hints that there were wars waged between mages that rearranged the very world itself. Mountains were raised up as barriers only to be thrown down a day later. The courses of rivers changed in an instant to wipe entire cities from the map. Even the seas were made to boil to sink fleets of war ships. Some of the mages who wielded such power actually thought of themselves as gods, but they were still only men, subject to all of the desires and other pettiness of any other member of the species."

He paused to sip some water before continuing. "Then one group of mages finally realized that such power couldn't be left in the hands of men, so they began to develop spells that would forever limit the amount of magic one man could wield. There was, of course, an opposing group who worked against them. The war between the two groups was the most devastating of all. All life on the planet was nearly destroyed. By the time the first group had emerged victorious, there were only a few small isolated pockets of life left. The mages who had sought to save the world by limiting the potential power of magic users now found themselves called upon to combine their own powers to try and restore the planet. The did their best to restore the land, then they brought forth the species they had managed to save in those few places they had been able to protect and repopulated the world.

"In the end, though, these once noble mages began to put themselves above the other creatures of the world. Again they vied for power. This time, however, their power was limited. Each one could only do so much by himself, and when they worked together they found themselves fighting with their own allies for control. That is why one mage, or it could have been several mages working independently from each other, that point isn't exactly clear, set out to create a species that would have access to magic but could be controlled. He used different species and magically combined them. The first attempts failed miserably. The books don't really describe them, but the more fortunate of them died shortly after birth. Later attempts produced things like trolls, but they were merely resistant to magic and hard to control. By combining men and elves with trolls they got the Roracks; more intelligent than trolls, but still unable to directly use magic and completely untrustworthy. At this point, the records that survive are very sketchy about which species were combined, but eventually they came up with dragons before the experimenters were hunted down and stopped. Their creations were thought destroyed with them, and indeed disappeared from history for over a thousand years."

He paused for a long time lost in his own thoughts, then suddenly seemed to realize that he had not finished, and, smiling embarrassedly, he continued, "Then, of course, those created species reappeared. The Roracks were the first. They swarmed down out of the mountains and attacked everyone they could find. It was during these wars that men found the dragons. The dragons hated the Roracks, and fought them whenever they could. At some point during that war, certain men found that they were able to bond with female dragons, and they formed partnerships. Eventually, they also found that once they were bonded, they were capable of wielding more magic than either could do alone, though even bonded they aren't as powerful as the mages of old. Together though, they were able, working with the men and elves, to push the Roracks back, though they have never been able to fully defeat them." Then he added, as an afterthought, "Of course, the trolls were found at some point, but since they lack real intelligence, they aren't a threat except to lone travelers or small groups who venture into their territory."

"I didn't know elves ever took such an active role in human history. I thought they tended to keep to their own lands and ignore the rest of the world," Delno observed.

"So they do, now. It wasn't always so, though. If it weren't for the elves and their ability to control their environment, the mages could never have preserved so much during the mage wars. What was saved was saved on Elvish territory. Of course, their powers were limited by the same machinations that limited human use of magic, and now they have withdrawn to their own realm and ignore us for the most part, though they still send out hunting parties to cull the Roracks."

They were all thoughtful for a long time. Delno finally said, "Nat, I don't want to contradict you, but your tale speaks of a time that must be thousands of years in the past."

"Tens of thousands" Nat corrected.

"Tens of thousands," Delno said, "how can you be sure it's not just fables? I have visited libraries; the oldest books I've seen are several hundred years old, and those are falling apart. I can't imagine that you've seen actual accounts that were written at the time."

"Ah," Nat responded with a smile, "You haven't been to some of the libraries that I have. The elves have ways of preserving written knowledge that we have either lost or never had."

Delno was a bit incredulous, "You've been allowed in an Elvish library? I thought elves were a bit standoffish toward humans."

At this point, Nat said, "Since we will be traveling together, and you have been honest with me, I suppose it's time for me to return the consideration." Then he pulled up the gray hair that came down nearly to his collar. Underneath his locks, his ears were slightly pointed. "Not many elves travel much beyond their own borders. Of those who do, even fewer choose to dally with human women. Apparently, my father was a bit lecherous for one of his kind."

Both Delno and Geneva stared at the man. Nat then told them, "My mother was lovely young farm girl when she met my father. He was tall, handsome, and I suppose somewhat mysterious to a simple girl like her. He stayed around for a few weeks, and then left, not knowing she was pregnant. She died shortly after giving birth to me. I was initially raised by my mother's parents, but they never liked the idea having a half-elf bastard in the family. I was kept hidden from the community. What I can remember of the time wasn't all that pleasant. Then, when I was four, my father returned and found me. He couldn't bring himself to leave his son to the care of unloving grandparents, and they were happy to be rid of me. I spent the rest of my childhood traveling with him. He was a good man, even affectionate. He taught me about both the worlds he traveled through, elvish and human. As his son, I was allowed access to the libraries I have mentioned. When I became old enough to make my own choices in life, I decided to become a healer. I studied with both the elves and the humans and became the best healer I could. In my time as a physician I've not only ministered to the sick and injured, but also taught nine apprentices. I believe I've done enough for my fellow men and elves, and now I want to accompany you and indulge my own curiosity."

Delno couldn't help but ask, "Nat, just how old are you?"

Laughing mischievously, Nat answered, "I am one hundred and thirty-seven years old."

Delno shook his head in wonder, "I wouldn't have thought that you were more than fifty.

# CHAPTER 26

THE NEXT DAY they stayed at the camp because there was a thunderstorm which left Geneva grounded. Delno and Nat were forced to spend the day inside Delno's small tent with barely enough room to sit comfortably. They swapped stories about their lives, and generally got to know each other. After the noon hour passed, and the storm showed no sign of abating, they ate a cold meal, and then napped for a bit.

By evening, the rain had slacked off but not stopped. They munched on jerky while they talked about dragon anatomy. "From what I've read," Nat was saying, "the muscles that extend and flex the wings simply overlay the normal, four-legged muscle structure. There are extra lateral muscles that attach at the pelvis, and then attach to the wing at the pinion joint. That's why the hips are so large; the pelvis is bigger to accommodate the extra muscle and sinew. The same goes for the breastbone and collarbones. The muscles that attach to the front legs are still there and still separate from the muscles that run over them and pull the wing in the downward part of the stroke. The flight stroke works very much like a bat. The lateral muscles relax and the extra deltoids pull the wing forward and up, then the extra pectoral muscles pull the wing down while the lateral muscles assist in the down stroke and pull the wings back. The whole motion from beginning to end is rather like using a butterfly stroke to swim, although not quite so exaggerated."

Since she was outside the tent, and it was hard to actually talk to both men, Geneva said to Delno, "*I would like to know more about growth and maturity.*"

Delno translated her thoughts, and Nat told her that he would answer what questions he could.

*"Ask if he can settle our dispute about flying together,"* she said.

Delno quickly explained about their argument and especially his concerns about her bone growth.

Nat thought about it for a moment before answering. "Well, from what I've read, bone growth doesn't seem to be an issue." Delno could feel Geneva's smug feelings of triumph, but Nat continued, "The problem, as I understand it, is," at this Geneva began to deflate somewhat, "that putting too much weight on the dragon too early can overtax the muscles, and, especially, the sinews. Once this happens, it can take months or even years to get them back to normal. The biggest drawback is that you wouldn't even know there was a problem until those muscles were put under some extra stress, such as the more acrobatic flight required when fighting, and then the muscles and sinews could fail, causing a fatal plunge."

Delno had to work very hard not to say, "I told you so." He consoled himself with saying, *"I'm very glad we were cautious, Dear Heart."*

*"So am I,"* she responded. *"Point for you, Love."*

They continued talking for a while, then Delno decided that it had been too long since he had practiced reaching out with his senses magically. Geneva and Nat were talked out for the time being anyway, so they respected his desire for quiet. He reached out and found that he could easily feel everything around him. The storm itself, though nearly spent, was immensely powerful. The lightning flashes that were still happening sporadically in the distance were nearly "blinding," and he had to dampen his senses to observe them.

Then he concentrated on seeing the living creatures in the area. He could see farther now than before: his range had increased to nearly a mile. There was nothing on two legs within range of his "sight," which was a relief. He did find that there were quite a few rabbits in the thickets around camp, though. After he pulled back to himself and reported his findings to both of his companions, he left the tent to go and make a couple of snares to try and get a rabbit or two for the pot.

When he returned to the tent, he was a bit surprised to find Nat playing softly on a stringed instrument the like of which he had never seen. It had a neck and body, but it was more akin to a mandolin than a guitar, though it was larger and had eight strings. It was extremely well made, and had a tone that was extraordinary. The physician was quite adept with it, also. Delno was quite content to just listen to him for a while.

After about half an hour of listening, he reached into his pack and brought out his pipes, which he held up as a request to join in the music making. Nat smiled and nodded and Delno began to play along. It was hard at first to keep up with the haunting tune and somewhat strange modulations that the half-elf's nimble fingers were making, but he caught the hang of it, and soon they were playing quite well together. Nat almost stopped playing when Geneva added her multi-toned voice to the melody, then he smiled broadly, and they all played together for a couple of more hours.

When they stopped, Delno asked Nat where he had gotten such a wonderful instrument. "I made it," the physician responded.

Delno said, "You are full of surprises, my friend. You are an accomplished physician, musician, and now instrument maker."

Nat laughed softly and replied, "When you study music with the elves, making your own instrument is part of the training." At Delno's look of surprise, he added, "My father insisted that I learn more than one skill, so I studied music and archery as well as medicine."

"He encouraged you to broaden your horizons. He sounds like a good man. I'd like to meet him."

The smile on Nat's face this time was rather sad, "I wish you could have met him, but he was killed by Roracks down in Horne."

The look on Delno's face was stricken, "Nat, I'm sorry. . . ."

"It's all right; you couldn't know that he was dead."

"I feel like crap for bringing it up all the same."

Nat's smile turned a little brighter, "Don't feel bad, you honored him with your sentiment." He had finished putting his instrument into its case, and he climbed into his blankets and said simply, "Good night, my friend."

Delno said good night and blew out the candle. Then he reached out to Geneva and said, "*Good night, Dear Heart*"

"*Good night, Dear One, sleep well.*"

Delno felt Geneva beside him and looked around. As soon as he saw the reddish light and the swirling clouds, he realized he had again joined her in the Dream State. "It's good to be here tonight," he said to her.

"Yes, it is. I felt your uneasiness before you fell asleep. What is troubling you, Love?"

Delno told her about his conversation with Nat, and how he inadvertently reminded the man of his dead father.

She considered it for a moment then said, "I do not think he faults you for that."

"I know," he responded, "In some ways that only makes it worse."

"I wouldn't worry too much about it, Dear One. Nat may look old and frail, but I have a feeling that he cultivates that image to avoid trouble. I think under it all he is a very tough and capable man."

"I have a feeling that you are right," he said.

He then put the incident out of his mind. That was easy to do here in the Dream State. The whole place radiated tranquility.

Geneva spoke up, "There is another male dragon. This one is much older; that is unusual."

Delno looked where she indicated, and there was a male, larger than the first he had seen. This one was deep blue, almost black. This time he tried to be careful about being seen. He didn't want to anger the dragon, not only because he did not want to disturb the peace of this place, but also because this dragon was much bigger and more dangerous looking than the youngster had been. Intellectually, he knew that the dragon was no threat to him, but he still didn't like the idea of facing those teeth and claws if the old boy got angry. After all, there had to be some way to affect others here, because Geneva had said that the females wouldn't tolerate bad behavior, so they had to have some way to stop it.

He thought about that for a while as he watched the male. Then he realized that the male had seen him watching and didn't appear to care. He told Geneva about his musings and asked her how the females kept order here.

"As I have told you, this place is a construct of the females' minds collectively. If several females decide that a male, or even another female, is causing trouble here, they simply use their minds to force them to leave. It isn't a physical expulsion. No one can get hurt; the offender is simply blocked from staying and returns to his or her sleep."

She seemed a bit preoccupied, so he asked, "Geneva, are you communicating with the other females now?"

"Yes."

"Do you mind if I ask what you are saying to each other?"

"Not at all," she answered, then paused so long he thought she was waiting for him to actually ask the question. Just before he did so she said, "I am speaking with them about something I would have liked to have talked about long before now. I have been gathering information about our training."

"Are they telling you anything useful?" he asked.

"Yes, tonight they are willing to discuss this. Before now they wouldn't talk to me about it."

"Wouldn't talk about it? Why not?"

"Because they didn't know me. At first, only the wild dragons would talk with me, and they can't answer my questions about training with a rider because they simply don't know. Before the bonded females wouldn't even speak to me; they had to get to know and recognize me first. Now they know me, and they are willing to help."

He started to ask another question but she cut him off, "Dear One, I would love to indulge your questions, but you are distracting me from my conversation with a particularly knowledgeable older bonded dragon."

He contented himself with simply sitting by her side watching the other dragons soaring for a while. Suddenly, the old male began spewing forth fire and soared in a tight spiral: it was an impressive display.

Geneva chuckled at him and said, "He's displaying his readiness to mate. He's also broadcasting the place where he can be found in the waking world. It doesn't happen often, but sometimes males do come here and do that, at least the older and wiser ones do."

As they watched, the male and several females faded from view. Geneva said, "I think that's my lot; the female who was instructing me is in mating heat and left to find the male."

"Well," he said, "you have to admit the old boy was impressive."

"Yes," she replied, "he was. Even I was stirred, and it will be quite some time before I am ready to rise to mate." Then she continued, "We will leave now, you return to sleep, Love, it will be dark for several more hours."

Everything faded to black and Delno drifted back into normal sleep until the sound of chirping birds woke him.

# CHAPTER 27

THE NEXT DAY the road was an ankle-deep quagmire, so they decided that traveling would be more strain on the animals than it was worth. There were two plump rabbits in the snares, so they decided to stew them. The problem came when they discovered that all of the deadwood in the area was thoroughly soaked.

They were about to give up on the fire when Nat's face lit up and he said, "Couldn't you use magic to dry the wood?"

Delno thought about it for a moment and said, "I don't know, I've never given it much thought. I suppose it's possible, but up until now my training has been limited to telepathy and simple healing."

Nat responded, "Yes, but according to what you told me about your training, your first attempt at healing resulted in burning the patient's foot. Couldn't you use that same energy to heat the wood enough to dry it?"

Delno thought about it and said, "I suppose if I tried hard enough, I could probably heat the wood enough to turn it to ash. I'll give it a try." Then he added, "To dry the wood, not turn it to ash."

Both Geneva and Nat chuckled at his small joke.

While looking at the wet wood that was piled near the tent, he reached out and looked for a source of energy large enough to generate the heat he needed. There was no fire to draw from, and, while there was water nearby, it flowed very slowly and didn't release much energy. He was about to give up when he remembered about the ground. He reached down with his senses. There it was, an enormous amount of energy, some coming from the roots of the plants that were drawing the rainwater up into the stems, but also a great deal of energy from the earth itself, many times more than he estimated he would need.

He opened himself up as a conduit and began channeling the energy from the earth. At first it was difficult, as if the energy was resisting the flow. He bent his will toward the task, but kept himself open so that the energy would flow through and not gather within him. It began to move slowly but picked up momentum quickly. After a minute, the wood began to shimmer before his vision; he realized that this was a simple heat mirage such as you see on a hot day. Then steam began to rise, just a little at first but increasing steadily. Nat and Geneva both encouraged him, so he continued. The steam ceased to rise and the wood began to smoke and char, then, suddenly, what a few minutes before had been a pile of wet timber burst into flame. He quickly shut down the contact, afraid that he really would turn their firewood into ashes.

Geneva was smiling and Nat was actually clapping like a child who has just seen an illusionist perform a neat trick. Delno bowed to his audience and said, "That concludes our show, please, there's no need for applause, but feel free to throw a few coins if you like."

Nat laughed and said, "I guess we'd better get those rabbits cleaned and in the pot before the fire burns down. It might also be a good idea to pile up some more wood near the heat so we will have a dry stack for later."

While Nat bent to the task of cleaning the rabbits, Delno gathered more wood and stacked it near enough to the fire that it would dry. Nat was delighted when Geneva asked for the entrails of the animals he was cleaning. He enjoyed giving them to her and watching her eat. He kept the skins though, explaining that he had not only the expertise, but also the chemicals available, to cure them properly. He then went on what he called a "weed-walk" while Geneva excused herself to go hunting since she had not done so the day before, and she was famished.

As Delno chopped herbs for the stew, he thought about magic. He decided to try and keep himself more open to the energy around him while going about his daily tasks. After all, it would be a very valuable asset to be able to keep his awareness high, if he could do so without leaving himself open to attack or intrusion. Thinking of how he had read Cheeno, and then been able to block the young mage before he could turn the tables, he reasoned that what he was trying now was possible and mostly a matter of practice. He also figured that since magic would be more common in the south, he should start practicing now before they actually reached any southern cities.

Nat returned to camp with a bundle in his hands. He explained that a "weed-walk" was simply walking about in the nearby fields and looking for any plants that would be useful, whether they were for cooking or medicine. The bundle contained quite a few herbs; rosemary, a bit of sage, some wild onions, and the greatest treasure of all, a bulb of wild garlic. Garlic was very hard to cultivate in the north and was hideously expensive, so Delno hadn't had any in quite some time. He was surprised that Nat had found the stuff.

"Oh, you find it here and there in these parts occasionally," Nat said. "The caravans take it north with other trade goods. If they find any fungus on any of it during the trip, they will throw out the whole sack to avoid the fungus contaminating the rest of the load. Often half of what they discard is still good, and, if the weather conditions have been favorable, some of it will take root. The last two years, the winters have been hard on the other side of the mountains but the mountains themselves have shielded these lands from the harsh weather. Still, garlic doesn't flourish here. We were very lucky I found this: a few days from now it would most likely have been dead from the drowning it got yesterday."

After putting the stew on the fire, Delno and Nat talked quietly for a while. Delno was curious about the elves and their lands. He explained that, until recently, he'd always thought of elves as mythical, not real, and asked Nat to tell him more.

"There's not much to tell, really," Nat was saying, "The elves keep to themselves, tending not to trust outsiders. They practice magic, but the magic they practice is mostly concerned with the land and the plants. They have a way at woodcraft that seems magical to those who aren't familiar with it. They can blend in with their forests so well they can nearly disappear while you're watching them: they just seem to fade from view."

"And that's not magic?" Delno asked.

"Not really," he replied. "They make clothing out of the natural materials available to them, and they make it in patterns that blend with their surroundings. They move in a way that fools the eye. As they move farther away, the camouflage is so good that your eye loses the ability to distinguish them from the background. I learned some of the techniques when I studied archery, though, to be honest, I was much better at music." He laughed softly.

"What are they like, as a people I mean?"

"Well, that depends," Nat responded. "When I first met them, I had been traveling with my father for several years. I was about nine when he decided he needed to return home to 'recharge' himself, as he put it, so we traveled to his homeland."

He was thoughtful for a moment; Delno had decided that the man organized his thoughts in bits and filed them away the way that some businessmen filed records. Then Nat started speaking again, "The elves usually like children just fine, but since I was a bit older and half human, they were a little standoffish at first, almost as if they were reluctant to get attached to me. Perhaps it has something to do with the fact that they live about seven hundred years. Maybe they don't want to become emotionally involved with someone they know they will outlive."

"I can almost understand the sentiment," Delno said. "I've been thinking about that a bit lately myself."

"Well," Nat responded, "there are no guarantees in life, my friend. The possibility that one person in a relationship may die is no reason not to get to know someone."

Delno smiled and said, "You're right, of course, though no one likes to think of the possibility of losing a friend or loved one. But I'm interrupting you, please continue."

Nat smiled. "Eventually they warmed up to me, and I began to learn some of their ways. We stayed there for nearly six years before my father felt it was time to travel again."

As Nat finished his thought, Geneva flew in for a landing.

Delno had kept his senses open, and he felt Geneva getting close. He was quite pleased because he had managed to keep the contact only going one way, so she didn't know he was scanning her.

Geneva settled herself down and told them that she had eaten a very large deer and a wild pig, and that she was now quite tired. She settled down to sleep without another word.

Delno and Nat kept quiet so as not to disturb her. Delno found a piece of wood in the pile that was dry that had an owl waiting to be freed from the surrounding material, so he retrieved his carving knives and bent to the task. Nat went about setting the rabbit skins into some chemical mixture to cure in silence.

Later that day, after he and Nat had eaten, and Geneva was fully awake, she began telling them what she had learned from the old female the night before. Nat was so interested in the Dream State that he plied her with so many questions it was nearly an hour before she actually got back to her original subject.

"According to the old female I was speaking to last night, there are certain signs to look for that will indicate when I am mature enough to carry a rider. As my wing muscles mature, the bulges they produce in my hide will become more pronounced. To some extent that is already happening, because I not only hunt each day, but fly to keep up with you as well."

Delno sat upright and asked, "Is it possible that we have already overtaxed you?"

"I asked her about that and she didn't think so. She believes that, since young wild dragons push themselves much harder than bonded dragons, I have simply been living up to my potential, and that such extra exercise will only be good for me in the long run."

"That is interesting; there is a book owned by the elves that hints that riders tend to coddle their dragons and thus delay their development. Unfortunately it didn't go into great detail, but it did mention that young dragons living in the wild are subject to much greater physical stress and appear to mature faster," Nat interjected.

"Yes," she agreed excitedly, "that old female, she's seen more than two millennia on this world, seemed to think that young bonded dragons are, for the most part, allowed to laze around and do nothing but indulge their appetites these days. She said that the training regimens could do with some revamping."

"Perhaps it is a good thing that we have been our own teachers so far, otherwise we might have allowed you to lounge around and be lazy," Delno teased.

"Yes," she said dryly, "and you might have taken up something as sedate as carving for a hobby and let your muscles go slack as well."

Nat chuckled and said, "I wish some of those stodgy old scholars could see the two of you talking and teasing each other; there'd be no further doubt about the intelligence of dragons then."

After they had all finished laughing, she continued. "The first thing to look for is a change in the color of the iris of the eye. The blue that you see now will change to my mature color, probably sometime after my third month. Then, when my wings are roughly three times the length of my body, not counting my neck and tail, I will be mature enough to begin carrying you. She did caution that I should not carry you for more than two hours a day for the first few weeks, and that we shouldn't try aerobatic maneuvers for at least a month."

Nat was curious, "What color will your eyes become when they change?"

"They will simply not be the fixed blue that you are used to. They will most likely be bronze with hints of both red and green, since those were the colors of my parents. But they will also change color with my mood," she said.

"That sounds convenient," Delno responded, then he added, "I wish all females came with such an easy mood indicator."

"Yes," she said, "just make sure you watch closely; if they ever turn black, hide."

# CHAPTER 28

THE NEXT DAY there were two more rabbits in the snares. They gutted them and gave the entrails to Geneva, then wrapped the carcasses in light cloth to keep the flies away and hung them on the wagon to age until they reached their destination that evening. Neither of the men had yet grown tired of rabbit stew, and they still had quite a bit of garlic left, anyway. The roads were passable, so, with Geneva assuring them she would eat lightly and join them soon, they packed and renewed their travels. They were less than a day's ride from Orlean, and both men looked forward to sleeping in beds under a real roof.

Once on the road, Nat began to ply Delno with more questions about dragons and magic. Delno found this quite amusing, since the reason they were traveling together was so that he could learn from the physician, not the other way around. He didn't begrudge the questions, though. The half-elf had an almost childlike curiosity that was somewhat refreshing, and Delno had to admit that he did enjoy the man's company. He might be bonded with a dragon, but he was still human and still craved the company of his own species to some extent.

"So, tell me Delno, do you think you could use magic to shield yourself from attack?"

He thought for a moment before answering, "I'm not exactly sure how to go about it, but I believe that since I can project the energy in a form that can heal a wound or start a fire, I should be able to create some form of barrier that I could impose between an attack and the intended target."

"Sounds like a handy trick if you can work out the logistics," Nat responded. "Perhaps you could try when we stop this afternoon."

"I believe I will," he said. "Perhaps if I project the energy like an invisible wall. . . ."

Geneva broke into his musings, *"Dear One, there is a large group of mounted men approaching ahead of you. They are heavily armed and appear to be dressed in uniforms. I will stay out of sight unless I am needed."*

Delno relayed this to Nat, who said, "I won't know for sure until I see their colors if they are from Ondar, but they are most likely a patrol sent out from the garrison in Orlean. They patrol these roads as often as possible, though not often enough, otherwise we wouldn't have met those bandits the other day. This group is actually further out than I expected to see them."

Delno could now barely see the soldiers if he stood in the stirrups and strained his vision. They were still nearly a mile distant. They decided the best course of action was for Geneva to do as she said and remain hidden while they continued on their way. After all, if the soldiers were simply a mounted patrol, they had nothing to fear and something to report. If the men were more than a simple patrol, they would have more on their minds than stopping and harassing innocent travelers.

As the soldiers got close enough that Nat could actually distinguish their livery, they did, in fact, appear to be Ondarian. They were a squad of thirty men, led by two sergeants who were under the direction of a lieutenant. The lieutenant appeared to be younger than Delno by a couple of years. As they drew near enough to exchange greetings, the lieutenant raised his hand and one of the sergeants called out, "Troopers, halt!" in a loud, commanding voice.

The young officer, the older sergeant, and several of the mounted troopers moved forward in a practiced maneuver that put them close enough to be effective if they had to draw weapons, while the remaining men sat on their horses with readied spears and bows.

Nat harrumphed in an almost disgusted way, then said, "Really, Robbie, tell your men to put those weapons down and relax; you know I'm no threat."

The officer looked a bit ashamed, but the sergeant spoke up, "Sir, we may know the healer, but the man with him is a stranger."

The younger man turned to the sergeant and said, "I'm sure that one man doesn't pose a great threat to thirty of His Majesty's best troopers, and he is traveling with someone who has proven himself a friend to everyone in this squad several times over. Perhaps, Sergeant, we can dispense with formalities, just this once."

The sergeant snorted his disapproval, but turned to the troopers and said, "Stand down, men."

Nat laughed quietly, then looked at the sergeant and said, "That's better, Norman."

Then he asked the man in a scolding tone, "How's that leg holding up?"

The man half shook, half nodded his head sheepishly and said, "It's healing just fine. Thanks for asking."

Nat wouldn't be put off so easily, "I know I told you to stay off of it for two weeks, and here you are ten days later riding with a patrol. Any further problems?"

He looked decidedly uncomfortable and said, "Nah, no pain since the first couple of days." Nat gave him a stern look and raised his eyebrows, so the man continued, "I just couldn't stand sittin' around on my bum any longer, so I rode out with this patrol. I figured sittin' on a horse would still keep me off the leg, and I'd be doing *something*."

Delno noticed that the men within earshot of the conversation were being careful not to let the sergeant see them smiling at his discomfort. There was a bit of an awkward silence while the poor man squirmed under Nat's stare. Delno spoke up to deflect attention from him. "I am Delno Okonan, from the Kingdom of Corice, specifically from the city of Larimar. I am traveling through your lands on my way to Palamore."

Norman nodded to him in gratitude for deflecting everyone's attention. The Lieutenant rode up beside Delno and extended his hand, "I am Robert Williamson, lieutenant with the Ondarian military garrisoned at Orlean. My friends call me Robbie." Delno, not sure whether to shake in the southern style or the northern, extended his arm far enough for the younger man to take it either way. They shook in the southern style.

Robbie turned to his sergeant, and told him to give the men a break while he talked with the travelers, then turned back to Delno, "Palamore, you say? I can understand the caravans traveling in this beastly heat, but what brings a man of Larimar so far under this broiling sun?" His manner was open and his smile genuine, and Delno found he liked the man immediately: he reminded Delno a bit of Nassari.

"Oh, I have business with someone who is there, and, since that man can't be persuaded to come to me, I must go to him."

"Well, since our good friend and physician Nathaniel finds you fit company to travel with, I suppose we won't delay you for any reason," he said, smiling broadly. "Still," he added, "There's something about that name that rings a bell." Then he looked over his shoulder and called out, "Sergeant Smith, come here please."

The younger of the two sergeants rode up quickly and saluted the officer, then he nodded to Delno and Nat. He was about Delno's age.

"Tell me, Sergeant," Robbie inquired, "you've traveled in Corice, does the name Delno Okonan mean anything to you?"

"Oh, that it does, Sir," the man responded, wide-eyed. "Lieutenant Delno Okonan is famous, sir. He was decorated several times during the Corisian/Bournese war, and won the Medal of Valor for his bravery at 'The Battle of Stone Bridge.'"

Delno groaned, "Guilty," he said, "though it is just Delno Okonan now. I've retired from military life."

"Retired?" Robbie asked, "Why in the world would you retire with such a record?"

"I had reached the highest rank possible, in fact, higher than is usually possible, for one of common birth, so I gave it up for other ventures." While Delno liked the man's open curiosity and easy manner, he hoped the officer would take the hint and let the subject drop.

As Sergeant Smith moved back to the ranks, Robbie said disgustedly, "Oh, that noble birth crap is lunacy. You should stop in at the garrison; here in Ondar, we promote based on merit. If you'd consider joining up, we could get you a commission based on your record, and I'd bet you'd be captain in no time."

Delno felt a surge of gratitude when Nat spoke up and interrupted the conversation. "Robbie, I'm sure that my companion would love to sit here and discuss the merits of a military career all day, but we must get to Orlean, and I'm equally certain that you must get back to your patrol." Then, as a parting shot to the older sergeant, he said, "And you mind that leg Norman, or I'll put you on bed-rest and see to it that your officers enforce it."

Norman nodded and waved.

Robbie wasn't quite ready to let the subject drop and said, "I'll let you go on one condition. You promise that you will have dinner with me at the garrison tomorrow evening, and that, in the mean time, you will give some serious thought to my suggestion."

To avoid any further delay, Delno reluctantly agreed. Then, after telling the officer and his senior sergeant about the bandits they had encountered, they shook hands again, and then each group set off in their previous directions. Delno noticed as they passed the men that many of them were looking at him with something akin to awe. Sergeant Smith must have been gossiping.

Though they met a few other travelers since they were so close to town, the remainder of the trip passed without incident. It was late afternoon when they reached the city gates, and Nat exchanged pleasantries with the guards. Then they went directly to Nat's home, which also contained his offices. His apprentice was busy seeing patients, so Nat showed Delno to a guest room and then set about putting away the herbs and chemicals he had brought along. Delno offered to help, but the physician refused, insisting good-naturedly that he knew where everything went, and Delno would be more of a hindrance than a help with the task.

Since Nat had turned the rabbits over to his housekeeper to cook, the horses were being attended at the stable near the healer's home, and Geneva was just settling down to eat in a secluded spot near town, Delno decided to have a look around.

"Don't go too far," the housekeeper, a plump woman with a pleasant face and broad easy smile, said to him, "the stew will be ready before dark."

Delno thanked her and stepped out of the door, then quickly crossed the small yard to the street. Orlean wasn't as big as Larimar, but it certainly wasn't small either. The main road, though not cobbled, had gravel and ash spread on it, and was, for the most part, kept in good repair, though the recent rains had created a few muddy spots. The main street, like most large towns, appeared to be mostly lined with shops of one kind or another.

As he walked along, he thought more about using magic to shield. He had been practicing keeping in contact with potential energy sources. He had also tried doing some things using his own personal energy and found that he could accomplish quite a bit that way if the need arose, but it would leave him drained and tired.

He continued playing with the idea of shielding, imagining a shield like a large invisible, unbreakable window between himself and some attack. He was lost in his musings when two horses carrying young riders, apparently racing, heedless of the danger they presented to others, came around a corner and ran right past him through a large puddle. Without really thinking about it, he put up shield. It was more a reflex than a conscious action. The large clots of mud that the horses had kicked up flew right at him and suddenly stopped, as if they had hit a window, about six inches from his face and chest.

People were yelling at the careless youths on the horses; he, however, had forgotten all about them. He stood transfixed by the sight of the mud sliding slowly down the invisible wall he had erected. He reached up and put his hand on the wall where one of the mud clots was sticking. It didn't feel quite like anything he'd ever experienced: while it was solid, it felt as though it were slightly pliable, as if it was almost alive under his hand. He glanced around and realized that several people were pointing at him and the mud that appeared to hang in the air. He quickly let the energy go and the mud fell to the street with a wet sound. Deciding that he had drawn enough attention to himself for his first day in town, he quickly retraced his steps back to Nat's home.

He found Nat sitting in a comfortable chair in the front room of the house. He started to speak up and tell him what had occurred outside, but as he stepped into the room he realized his friend wasn't alone. As he came through the doorway far enough to see the whole room, he found a tall slender man of about thirty-five sitting in another chair. He immediately bit off his comment and apologized for interrupting.

"Nonsense, my friend," Nat said, "This is Pearce, my apprentice." Then he added, "Soon to officially be the physician in residence here. I was just telling him our tale, and that he will be taking over everything when I take to the road."

Delno extended his hand to Pearce, and the man grabbed his arm just above the wrist. Delno returned the grip.

"Now then," Nat said, "I had just finished explaining about Geneva and your need to travel. I'm afraid that it's put Pearce in a bit of a quandary. He wants to be elevated to full healer, and he is proud that I am willing to write the letters of credential, but he is a bit upset that I will be leaving with you so soon."

"I could have earned a letter of credential several years ago," Pearce explained, "but I chose to study under Nat for good reason: he's the best healer in the kingdom, and the best herbalist this side of the Elven territories, not to mention that he and I have become very good friends."

"I am convinced that Nat is an easy man to become good friends with," Delno responded. "We've only traveled together for a few days, and there is an ease about our growing friendship that would have taken months to achieve with anyone else. He's an extraordinary man."

"I've noticed the same thing," Pearce said.

Nat blushed at the praise. "Really gentlemen, I'm only an old scholar who wishes to indulge his own curiosities for a while."

They all shared a laugh; then Delno asked Pearce, "So you know about Geneva? What are your thoughts on that?"

"I think it's a wonderful opportunity, and I envy you both. You, because here in the south nearly every boy dreams that he will be chosen to bond with a dragon, and this one," he indicated Nat, "because he will have an opportunity to study such a rare and wonderful creature first hand." Then he turned to Nat and exclaimed, "You are not to sneak off in the night and disappear and keep her all to yourself, you old scoundrel! I will not agree to any of this if I don't at least get to meet her before you go."

Nat held up his hands in feigned innocence.

Delno promised that he would take Pearce to meet Geneva the first chance they could get to do so. Then he told them about his experience with the magic in the streets of Orlean. They were both impressed and insisted on a demonstration. Soon they were happily throwing anything in the room that was small and unbreakable, which happened to be a chess set that was on a table nearby, at the invisible barrier that he had erected in front of himself.

The housekeeper was disgusted at the pile of small items on the floor when she came to announce that dinner was ready. "You men are just boys with bigger bodies. Worse; at least I can bully boys into not throwing their toys around the room and leaving them for me to pick up," she said.

They apologized and picked up their own mess before going to dinner.

# CHAPTER 29

THE NEXT MORNING Delno woke early, as he was used to doing, but was loath to leave the comfort of a real bed after sleeping rough for so many weeks. He lay in bed just listening to the sounds of the city coming awake for nearly half an hour before Geneva finally said, somewhat petulantly, *"Are you going to come and see me today, or will I have to be alone until you tire of that comfortable bed?"*

"I will come see you, Dear Heart, as soon as I've had my breakfast." Then he added, *"Nat's apprentice would like to meet you as well. If he isn't too busy with patients, would you mind if I bring him along?"*

*"Only if he does not mind if I hunt and eat first. We are too close to the city and game is scarce. I didn't have nearly enough to eat yesterday,"* she complained.

*"I am sorry. I will look into the possibility of purchasing some herd beasts here to supplement your diet."* Then he quickly added, *"Don't worry, Love, I won't buy sheep."*

She was satisfied with his responses to her concerns and her mood softened. She maintained contact while she soared happily away from Orlean in search of suitable game.

After breakfast, since Geneva had just killed several wild boars and would be some time eating them, he wandered to the garrison to make inquiries about meeting with Robbie later. He had forgone wearing his Dragon Blade in town for now, leaving it secured in the cords supporting his mattress, but he did carry his *main gauche*.

The garrison was housed inside a stockade near the main gate of the city. While the city walls were stone and mortar, the stockade walls were made of wood. The first thing he found when he entered was a number of men practicing with blunted swords, spears and other weapons. On one side of the large central yard was an archery range and some men were practicing there, also. One man waved for him to come over. It was the sergeant, Norman.

He approached and asked, with a large smile on his face, "Aren't you supposed to be staying off your leg?"

Norman made a rude sound, then a worried look came over his face, and he said, "You won't tell the healer, will you?"

Delno held up both hands and said, "Don't worry, man, I won't sic Nat on you." Then he chuckled and continued, "I've grown quite fond of the man, but he's a regular wild boar when he puts his mind to something."

"Don't I know it," Norman sighed. "A spear broke during practice, and the broken haft got me in the leg. That man expects me, the senior sergeant here, to sit on my bum and let these lads get lazy for a whole fortnight."

Delno nodded seriously to Norman, but almost laughed at the two men who were smiling and rolling their eyes at his comments behind him.

Just then, Sergeant Smith approached with some urgency. "The Captain wants to see you, Sarge," he told Norman. Then, noticing who it was that Norman was speaking with, he hastily saluted and said, "Oh, Good morning, Lieutenant."

Delno returned the salute out of reflex, then said, "It isn't lieutenant any more, but good morning to you, too, Sergeant."

The Senior Sergeant excused himself and left Delno with Sergeant Smith.

They talked for a few minutes about garrison life, then a bit about the city in general, then the man asked Delno, "So, sir, are you going to take our lieutenant up on his offer and join the Ondarian army?"

Everyone stopped what they were doing and listened. Delno was so sure that nearly every man in the garrison had bet one way or the other on the answer to that question he could almost hear the coins changing hands.

"I've actually thought a bit about that," he said, "and, as much as I'd like to belong to such a fine group of men as this, I have other business that prevents me from doing so. I'm afraid I'm going to have to disappoint your lieutenant."

Several of the men appeared quite pleased with the answer, while many looked equally disappointed. Then a voice spoke up from behind, "Oh, I don't think I will be disappointed until you are so far out of the city that I can't find you and continue trying to persuade you to join us."

As Delno turned to face the speaker, he found, of course, that the cheerful voice belonged to Robbie. "Lieutenant, good to see you this morning," he said as he extended his hand.

"Well," the man replied, "providing that you haven't come to tell me that your business is pushing you on before we can have our dinner, the pleasure is all mine."

"No, nothing like that. I'm just wandering around and getting to know the city. Also, I wasn't sure what time I was supposed to be here this evening."

"Oh, yes, I never did give you a specific time," Robbie responded. "Terribly sorry about that, six o'clock would be good, if it's no inconvenience."

"Six would work well for me," Delno said.

He was about to leave when Delno, on impulse, asked, "Robbie, could I ask a favor?"

"Certainly, if it within my power to grant it."

"Could I train with your men while I'm staying in Orlean? That bit of unpleasantness on the road the other day reminded me that I should keep my skills honed."

"Well," the lieutenant responded, "I suppose that I should tell you that you would have plenty of opportunity to train if you joined us, but instead, I'll just hope that getting to know the men on the training field will persuade you to become one of us. Now, while I'd like to chat more, duty calls, if you'll excuse me." They saluted, and he walked off to attend to his tasks.

Delno was offered his choice of any of the practice swords on the nearby racks, from which he chose a saber. He was offered a small shield, but declined in favor of a blunted short sword that wasn't that much larger than his own *main gauche*.

At first, even though he had told them that he wanted to train seriously, the men tried to take it easy on him. However, as he dispatched his first three opponents in short order, and without breaking a sweat, the men began to make more realistic attacks. While his dragon-enhanced strength and reflexes did give him a bit of an edge, he soon found out that Robbie's boast from the day before about these men being the best wasn't just brag. Soon he was not only sweating, but also hard pressed to defend himself against the young men. When they stopped two hours later, he was completely worn out, and he had a few bruises from the blunted blades that he would be feeling later.

He further impressed the men when he simply joined them at the communal water trough and dipped his head right in like everyone else. He suspected that Robbie, though likable enough, was one of those officers who considered himself too good to wash the sweat off his body in the same water that the men used. He was so comfortable that he almost removed his shirt to wash his chest and underarms before he remembered the mark he bore. Instead, he quickly thanked the men for practicing with him and left the compound, promising to be back the next morning.

He reached out for Geneva. *"Are you ready for company, Dear Heart?"*

*"I have eaten and I am awake. I would like to spend some time together,"* she responded.

*"I told Pearce that I would bring him if he is able to come. I will stop and see; either way, I will join you shortly."*

He quickly made his way to Nat's home and found Nat and Pearce both there and unoccupied: they agreed to accompany him. Geneva was hiding less than a mile from the main gate in a very thick section of woods. The men decided to walk, which was Delno's preference anyway, since the walk would loosen muscles stiffened by the hard workout he had just completed.

Pearce's reaction to his first look at Geneva was very much similar to the reaction she had gotten from Nat. The words marvelous and magnificent were used repeatedly. Geneva was positively aglow with pride as the two men continued to praise her beauty and stature. Delno was rather amused and chuckled to himself at her reaction to the flattery. Although he did have to agree with one of Nat's observations: she had certainly grown again overnight. While she still had some ways to go to reach her full adult size, she was visibly larger than she had been when they had last seen her yesterday before meeting the patrol from the garrison.

*"From what your mother told me of dragon growth,"* he said, *"I would estimate your age at more than four months, rather than under two. I am pleased that you are growing so fast, but I'm afraid that such a growth rate may be harmful to you."*

"I spoke with that old female I told you about again last night," she responded. "She believes that I am growing so fast because we are so strongly bonded. The magic is flowing so powerfully between us that it is greatly accelerating my growth. She feels that I should be able to bear your weight soon."

Nat spoke up, "I don't believe, from what I've read, that she is growing at the normal rate of a newly hatched dragon. I can only hypothesize that the magic that flows so well between the two of you is causing her growth to be accelerated."

Both Geneva and Delno laughed out loud. At the puzzled looks from the men, they quickly explained about their private conversation.

"Remove your shirt, please," Pearce said to him, sounding rather clinical.

"What?" Delno responded.

"Oh, I'm sorry, I tend to forget that we aren't in some laboratory studying inanimate objects," he replied. "I would like to see your Dragon Mark. So, if you would please remove your shirt. . . ."

Delno shrugged and, crossing his hands, grabbed the hem of his tunic and pulled it up over his head. The Mark was even more perfect than the last time it had been shown to others. The lines were crisp and clean and it looked like a fine tattoo in the perfect likeness of Geneva about to take flight. It was a little larger than before.

"Absolutely amazing," both Pearce and Nat said together as they examined the mark.

Delno stood so long under their combined scrutiny that he began to feel uncomfortable, so he asked, "What is amazing? It's a Dragon Mark. You had to know what it would look like."

"That's just it," Pearce said, "We thought we did know what it would look like until you removed your shirt."

Noticing Delno's puzzled expression, Nat spoke up, "Forgive us, my friend, we tend to forget that you haven't read the same books we have. According to all the literature on the subject, that mark, this early in the bonding, shouldn't look like much more than a wine-colored birth mark, perhaps in the vague shape of a dragon."

"According to one book," Pearce added, "if the bond is strong, it could even be starting to take on some of the dragon's color."

"Your mark, Delno," Nat added, "you can not only recognize that it is a dragon, you can specifically recognize that it is Geneva, as if it were portrait drawn by a fine artist."

"For the mark to be so pronounced," Pearce interjected, "speaks of an extremely strong flow of magical energy between the two of you."

"That is the only thing that could account for Geneva's extremely rapid growth," Nat concluded.

They measured her dimensions from nose to tail and wingtip to wingtip. They estimated her weight. They even measured her teeth and claws. Pearce helped Nat write up their findings as they did so.

Although, by the estimation of the two scientists, her growth was that of a dragon of about four months, her wing-to-body ratio was still not right for mounted flight, and Delno would not even entertain the idea of rushing that. He was adamant, as always, on the subject: they would not risk flying until they were sure she was developmentally ready.

They spent the rest of the afternoon with Geneva, and it was more than four hours past noon when they left. Delno hurried home. He was amazed that he actually felt like it was home to him, and he quickly bathed and donned his better pants and his best shirt. Then he walked to the garrison. He arrived shortly before six o'clock.

Robbie met him in the practice/parade yard and led him to the officers' quarters. The table was set for three and the lieutenant quickly explained that the captain of the garrison would be joining them. Delno fervently hoped the men wouldn't try to gang up and brow beat him into joining the army.

It was a quarter of an hour before the captain of the garrison arrived. He quickly apologized for his tardiness, explaining that something had come up that required his immediate attention, then he shrugged and said, "The problem with running an outpost such as this one is that it's big enough to need a full staff but not funded enough to merit such, which means that I have to personally attend to problems that would normally be handled by junior personnel."

Delno nodded. The man appeared sincere and he could sympathize with him.

The food and wine arrived and was served by two young enlisted boys. Delno was surprised by their age. The older of the two couldn't be more than fourteen. When he mentioned this, the Captain laughed easily and said. "Oh, don't worry, we don't conscript young boys into our army. It's been an extremely dry year, and the farms around here aren't doing so well. The boys are the youngest sons from two of the farms. We need someone to do some of the minor chores here at the garrison; in return for their labor, they get food and clothing and are paid a stipend. The work is not nearly as hard as the work they would have to do on their families' farms, they eat better, and we also teach them to read, write and do basic mathematics."

After toasting each other, they settled down to a rather good, if simple, meal of roasted wild boar and vegetables. There was even a nice gravy to go with the potatoes.

The Captain said, "So, the men speak highly of your performance in the practice yard this morning. You're good with a blade, and they are all interested in that two-bladed fighting style of yours. Does your participation mean that we will be seeing more of you here at the garrison?"

Delno started to answer, but the lieutenant spoke up first. "Actually, sir, I was hoping to recruit Lieutenant Okonan into the Ondarian army. From his record in Corice, I think he'd make a first-rate officer here."

The Captain turned to Delno and raised his eyebrows in inquiry.

Delno shook his head sadly and said, "If I didn't have such pressing business in Palamore, I would certainly be tempted. There is a camaraderie here at the garrison that I must admit that I have missed since I retired from military service, but I'm afraid that I have to be about my original errand as soon as possible."

The senior officer asked, "So tell me Delno, why did you retire from military service? It certainly wasn't old age, and you didn't look the least bit infirm this morning."

He was about to answer when again Robbie spoke up, "It's that old noble birth nonsense that the North clings to so strongly. The man had reached the top of his career as a lieutenant because he wasn't born a nobleman, despite the fact that he'd proven that he was better than any four of the noble-birthed put together. He chose to retire rather than be stuck for twenty years as a junior officer. I don't blame him myself."

"Thank you, Robbie," the Captain said, then turned to Delno and asked, "Is that the whole of it, then?" As Robbie opened his mouth to respond, the Captain held up his hand and the younger officer remained silent.

"Yes, that's pretty much it," Delno said. "It wasn't money or rank so much though, really, but the lack of companionship." Robbie didn't seem to understand, and the Captain appeared to be waiting patiently for him to continue, so he went on, "I could find female companionship if I wanted, it wasn't that; it was more just being alone in a garrison full of men. Sometimes a man needs to be able to sit around and have a few drinks with friends, maybe throw the tiles. In my situation, I wasn't accepted by the other officers because I wasn't a Peer, and I wasn't accepted as one of the men because I was an officer. With all those people around, I was still alone. So I gave it up when my term ended and went home."

The Captain nodded and said, "And then you got home and found that you were still alone because none of the people there knew anything about what you'd been through during the war. To them, you weren't the same person they had known before you enlisted."

Delno nodded and smiled, "You've been through this yourself."

"Yes, I've been through it and seen other men do the same," he said. "I am the son of a blacksmith. Never did take to it though, especially working over that hot forge in the summer. Joined the army when I was sixteen. Earned my stripes first, rose to the rank of sergeant. Then I earned my collar as a field promotion and it stuck. Went from Second Lieutenant to First Lieutenant during a border war over ten years ago. I tried to go home after the war, too; lasted about a year before I came back and earned Captain chasing bandits all over the back country."

"So you see, Delno," the younger lieutenant spoke up, "a man of your prowess and reputation could do well as an officer in the Ondarian army. I'm sure that a quick letter to...."

"Oh, let the man alone, Robbie," the Captain said, "you can see by the look on his face he isn't interested in joining the army." To Delno, he said, "You see, Robbie here *is* of noble birth. He got it into his head to try and marry a girl whose father didn't find Robbie's family up to the standards he had set for his daughter. The girl's father used his connections to have the poor boy reassigned here hoping the daughter would get over the whole thing and find someone her father found more to his liking."

Robbie was noticeably uncomfortable with his captain telling Delno the story, but held his tongue. The Captain continued, "Robbie knows that if he can find someone to take his place in our little backwater garrison, he could then have his father use some influence to get him reassigned to a less provincial posting. He has high hopes that you will join, knowing that your record will guarantee you a commission, and that they will then station you here, making it possible for him to leave."

Robbie didn't look up from the table as he said, "It's not like I'm trying to get the man to do something dishonest. He is without a position, and the army could use a man of his experience and prowess." His final words on the subject were almost mumbled, "I think it would be good for all concerned."

The Captain laughed easily and Delno couldn't help but laugh with him. Then the Captain clapped his lieutenant on the shoulder and said, "Cheer up, man, it's not the end of the world; I've written stellar reports on your performance since I've been your commander, and your tour here is up in eleven more months regardless. Then I'll do what I can to see you stationed in the capital city of Ramira."

With the real reason for Robbie pushing Delno so hard to join the army out in the open, the rest of the evening was extremely pleasant. Even Robbie's mood improved considerably after a couple of more glasses of wine. When the Captain observed that the two boys serving them were nearly falling asleep on their feet due to the late hour, they rose from the table.

"Well, good night, Captain, it was a real pleasure meeting you and Robbie. If I could join, I would, but I do thank you for inviting me."

The Captain responded, "Well, since you are training here, you will have to stop calling me 'Captain' and start calling me by my name: it's Winston. Perhaps I will be able to join you on the training field soon. I would like to try myself against that two-bladed style of yours; it's somewhat common in the southwestern lands of Horne, but we don't see it much around here. Perhaps we'll get the chance to spar. Good night to you both." He turned and strode away.

Robbie thanked him for coming and showed him to the gate. "I'll try and get out to the yard tomorrow; perhaps you could teach me that style you use. Good night."

Delno walked quickly and quietly to Nat's and let himself in. He went straight to his bed, but didn't sleep for some time, thinking about how life could have been different if he'd come to the south after his term of enlistment ended instead of going home. Then he realized that if he had, he would not have met Geneva's mother, and he couldn't even begin to think about not being bonded to Geneva.

"Fate."

"What, Dear Heart?"

"Fate, love, it's what brought you to me. If you had come south at that time instead of going home, you wouldn't have met these same people and the prospect of joining them wouldn't have happened." Then she said the word again. "Fate."

"You are right, of course," he responded, "and I would rather be bonded to you than anything else I can think of. Perhaps Fate isn't such a bad thing."

# CHAPTER 30

DELNO WOKE EARLY the next morning, and, this time, he was eager to be up and moving. Nat's housekeeper was just coming in as he was leaving. "Oh, Missus Gentry, I'm glad I found you now. I have some clothes that need to be cleaned; I've laid them out. If you could have them cleaned and have any mending they need done I would greatly appreciate it. I won't have time to have breakfast this morning, so I will find something in town."

Missus Gentry was in early to receive the grocery order. She assured him that she would personally take care of his laundry, and he left the house headed directly for the garrison, wanting to get there early. This day he also carried his bow and the six practice arrows he had purchased with it. The practice arrows were exactly like the other arrows, except the tip was just a rounded piece of metal that was the same weight as the deadly double-bladed arrows that could be used for hunting or war. He intended to see what his new bow could really do, and, if possible, get any needed instruction from the archery master of the garrison.

While the night watch was ending their shift, the garrison proper was just getting into full swing. The men he met insisted that he join them for breakfast. He didn't want to use garrison supplies, but was assured by Sergeant Smith that it would put the garrison under no hardship. They were well supplied and often shared their provender with travelers, so he ate with the men.

First light found him in the practice yard with a blunted blade in each hand facing his first opponent: it was Sergeant Smith. This Sergeant

Smith was quite different than the good-natured, gossiping sergeant he had met. Despite his boyish good looks, this man was all business.

The two opponents circled each other, wary of the blades that were ready to strike. The sergeant, normally smiling, showed no emotion on his face of any kind. He was nearly impossible to read. Delno also became aware that there was quite an audience gathering. As he started to identify the men he knew in the audience, the sergeant took advantage of his momentary distraction and lunged with his sword. Delno turned the blade with his short sword easily enough but that had been a feint, the real danger from the attack was the sergeant's shield. The man had expected him to block the blade and strike, so he caught the saber, allowing it to glance off his small shield and then tried to use the edge of the shield to strike at Delno's face. The counter attack with the shield was unexpected and nearly succeeded. Delno had seen this ploy before and was able to recover in time to prevent the blow from landing, barely.

They circled again; this time Delno didn't let the audience distract him. He watched the sergeant closely. Again the man's face told him nothing. Delno shifted his concentration to the man's chest. Again the sergeant attacked without warning, and again Delno deflected both attacks. The sergeant used the small shield nearly as efficiently as a weapon as he did the hand-and-a-half sword in his right hand.

Delno settled back and watched the man's feet. At first, there was still no hint of the man's intentions, then he noticed a slight movement just before an attack. It wasn't much, and it was difficult to read—a lesser swordsman would most likely miss it, but it was there, and once Delno had figured it out, the sergeant may as well have been telling him with words exactly what he was about to do. His opponent lunged again, but Delno was ready. He shifted at the last possible second when the sergeant was completely committed and let the larger blade slide by and used both of his own blades to go after the shield. This time he managed to dislodge the shield, breaking the strap that held it to the man's arm.

Unfortunately, in the process of taking the man's shield, he lost his own saber. The sergeant switched to a two handed grip on his sword and lunged again. It was all Delno could do to get out of the way of that eight-pound blade. The opponents circled and the sergeant lunged time after time. It took several attacks before Delno was again able to read the sergeants coming move by paying attention to the man's feet: once he had it though, he simply waited for the right attack.

Sergeant Smith's feet moved first, then he brought the blade back and up to make a powerful downward slice. This was precisely what Delno had been waiting for. He dropped his short sword and raised both hands and stepped inside the swing of the blade. Their arms met, and the sergeant's arms slid harmlessly down Delno's while Delno swung his hands down and around to bring the blade between them. Then he grabbed the man's wrists and, before Smith could react, Delno stepped forward and brought his opponent's arms in front of him. Then, with his opponent off balance, Delno stepped even farther in and brought the man's arms up and over their heads. Then he pivoted while still holding the sergeant's hands and brought them back, sword still in them, beside the man's own head. He simply pulled the man's arms back, making Smith fall backwards while taking the sword from him. Then, with the sergeant lying on his back, before he could react, he placed the sergeant's own blade to his throat.

The sergeant looked up and smiled, and Delno smiled back. Then, moving the sword away from the man's throat, he reached down and grasped his hand, helping Smith to his feet. It felt like the entire garrison was an audience, and they were all now clapping at the performance the two men had just put on. The Sergeant said, "That was a neat trick; you'll have to teach me that one." His words were almost drowned out in the applause and cheers from the men around them.

As the noise subsided, Winston stepped forward and said, "Well, I see you've disarmed our Weapons Master; good work." He shook Delno's arm. "If I didn't have to go and meet with some city officials, I would ask you to spar with me; unfortunately, duty calls. I hope to see you soon."

Delno stayed and practiced for another hour before moving on to the archery range. Several of the men were quite interested in his bow, and he let them try the draw. None found it comfortable, and they all walked away shaking their heads and talking about it to each other. The targets they had were barely suitable to stop the practice arrows he was using.

Norman, it seemed, was the Archery Master. While he was impressed with the quality of the bow, he scoffed a little at the strength of the thing, saying, "You can have a bow that will shoot through a giant oak tree, and it'll do you no damn good at all if you don't hit what you aim at."

He then worked with Delno for over an hour on his stance and how he actually drew the bow. By the end of the first lesson, the Senior Sergeant actually pronounced him fit to train.

He left the garrison tired but quite happy.

He then found a clothier in town and bought three tunics made out of the same fabric as his good shirt. The material was much lighter than the material of his heavy northern-made tunics, but was still strong and serviceable.

He also bought two more pairs of pants made of a denser weave of the same material as the tunics. They were of an interesting design. Instead of using a drawstring that ran around the waist like his other trousers, they were tighter through the hips, which kept them in place once the fly was buttoned. The clothing was expensive, but both pairs of trousers he owned were thick, because they were made with northern weather in mind. Also, the one pair was beginning to get a little threadbare. While he hadn't traveled that far south yet, it was hotter than he was used to and he was still planning to travel even farther. The new clothes would serve him well.

As he left the clothier he reached out to Geneva. She was pleased with herself, and he soon found that she had located a good hunting range. The recent rains had enticed many large wild animals down from the nearby foothills to the rivers. Geneva was quite happy to report that she had fed well and didn't think that hunting would be a problem for at least another week or so. He decided to join her, and they spent the afternoon together. He was even able to find two nice pieces of wood for his carvings.

They managed to settle into a very easy routine over the next few days. He would train hard with the soldiers at the garrison in the mornings, and then join Geneva in the afternoons, sometimes with Nat, or Pearce, or both. The evenings were usually spent with Nat and Pearce discussing dragons and magic.

His magic was improving as well. He had found that he could improve on his shield by completely surrounding himself with the energy. He could make a shield strong enough that normal fire had absolutely no effect on it. He wondered if dragon fire were hot enough to still cause harm through it, but since he needed a fire-breathing dragon for that, and it would still be some time until Geneva could oblige, much to Nat's disappointment, that experiment would have to wait.

He was on the practice pitch one morning when several townsfolk ran into the garrison shouting for the soldiers to come. It took several moments to calm them enough to learn that there was a dragon and rider just outside the city gate. Delno had been sparring with Winston and Robbie and simply fell into step with them as they headed for the source of the commotion. "If it really is a dragon and rider, you're in for quite a treat; this isn't a sight you see in the North, my friend," Robbie whispered to him.

When they reached the gate, it was nearly impossible to get through because of the crowd. Norman smiled to his commanding officer and said, "Allow me, Sir." The Captain put his hands to his ears and nodded his head. Norman open his mouth and shouted out in the same 'Senior Sergeant' voice that he used when training large groups of men, "MAKE A HOLE!" Then only slightly softer, "Make way for the Guard." People hastily moved aside.

Winston said, "Thank you, Sergeant," and walked through the 'hole' past the startled citizens. Just outside the gate, the officers and Delno were joined by the Territorial Governor who resided in Orlean, as well as several members of the city council. They walked a few more paces forward and Winston stopped short. The Governor, who had been trying to talk with one of the Council Members, nearly walked right into him and was about to complain when all conversation was simply forgotten. There, directly in front of them, was a gorgeous royal blue dragon. The muscles under her hide moved slightly as she repositioned herself, and he could see flashes of iridescence, mostly reds and greens. The only other mark she bore was a reddish orange splash, rather like a starburst, on her head between her eyes.

The Governor took a step forward, a very small step, and opened his mouth to speak, but the rider spoke first. "Where is the Dragon Rider?"

Delno estimated that the Rider would be about average height once he dismounted, but that was the only thing average about him that was visible. His hair was so black it shone blue in the sunlight. His eyes were a piercing, deep shade of brown. He had high cheekbones, and a narrow, well-sculpted nose, and his skin was the color of dark chocolate. He was wearing a fur-lined jacket and Delno thought he must have been boiling in this heat. As if reading Delno's thoughts, the man began to unbutton the coat. He was seated in a saddle of simple leather and wearing a plain, unadorned sword, the hilt of which was quite visible over his shoulder.

"Come, come," he said, "Where is the Rider? I don't have much time to waste."

"R-r-rider?" the Governor managed to sputter.

"There's no need to hide the Rider from me. I know the dragon is here; her Rider can't be far off." He scanned the crowd. Delno knew at once that he was scanning their minds as well as their faces. He was especially looking at the older boys present. Delno shielded himself and reached out to shield both Pearce and Nat who were in the crowd. To his delight, he found that both men were already protecting themselves.

Finally, after several moments the rider pointed to Pearce and said, "You." Then he repeated the same to Nat, "You." Then, looking at Delno, he said, "And especially you, step forward."

"*Careful, Love, this dragon is much older than I am,*" Geneva said to him, then added, "*I am coming.*"

"No, stay where you are, I'll handle this."

She ignored him this time. With a strange dragon present, and not knowing that dragon's intentions, she would not listen to his words of caution.

Winston made a quick gesture to his Senior Sergeant, and the man motioned the nearest soldiers into action. They moved quickly between the blue dragon and Delno. Winston spoke up, "I am Winston Eriksson, Captain of this garrison. What is it you want here, Rider?"

The Dragon Rider shook his head, "This is ridiculous," he said, "Tell your men to put down those weapons; if I intended to harm you, you'd all be ashes by now. I merely want to talk to the Rider of that dragon."

As if on cue, Geneva roared and landed less then twenty feet from the blue dragon. "You will state your intentions," she said, "if you try to harm my Partner there will be much blood spilled this day."

The older dragon snarled back, "You are no match for me, youngster, calm yourself."

"I may be a youngster, but I am not only large enough to destroy your rider, I am too close for you to stop me before I can do it." Geneva responded. "So, if there is to be trouble here this morning, we will all die together."

While Delno wasn't happy with the way things were progressing, he had to admit, to himself anyway, that he was quite impressed with Geneva.

The other Rider held up his hand and said, "Peace, both of you. No one here wants trouble. As I've said, we're here to talk." To Delno he said, "Control her, man, before this gets out of hand."

Delno said, "Looks to me like *she* has the situation under control." At the other Rider's look of consternation, he said, "If you are really here to talk, why don't you dismount, and we can have a conversation like civilized men?"

The man's demeanor diminished considerably and he said, "You're right, of course." Saying that, he unbuckled two straps that were attached to his belt on one end the saddle on the other and climbed down. Once on the ground, he removed his heavy jacket and said, "Whew, it's good to get out of that thing. You need the warmth when flying, but here on the ground you can boil in your own juices wearing it."

He stepped a few paces forward and held his hand extended toward Delno. Delno, much to the Senior Sergeant's disapproval, stepped forward and grasped the man's arm. "I'm Delno Okonan, and this, he said, pointing with his left hand at his dragon, "is Geneva."

Delno was surprised at the man's reaction. The other Rider's face fell and he just stood staring for a long moment. Then he hung his head and said, "Then it's true; Corolan is dead." It wasn't a question. Then he looked back up at Delno and said, "I'm sorry. I knew through my dragon that it was so, but I didn't want to believe it without proof. Since Geneva wouldn't carry her mother's name if Corolan and his dragon were still alive, I can deny it no longer." Then, still clasping arms with Delno, almost as if he needed the support, he drew a deep breath and sighed before continuing, "I am Brock Ard, and she," he indicated the blue dragon, "is my Partner, Leera. Leera is a daughter of Geneva's mother, and I was a student and good friend of Corolan." Then he looked around as if remembering the crowd, "We have much to talk about, but perhaps it would be better if we did so with a smaller audience."

At that point, Winston stepped forward. The Senior Sergeant was nearly beside himself that the man had stepped out of the protective ring of soldiers. The Captain said, "Yes, Delno, we have much to discuss. Perhaps we can move this conversation to the relative privacy of my office at the garrison?"

Delno smiled sheepishly at the officer and then raised one eyebrow at the Rider in inquiry. The other man nodded his approval, and they each turned to their dragon.

"*Geneva, you were very brave standing up to that older dragon like that. You were also very rash. That situation could have gone very badly if she had decided to attack,*" he said.

"*That is why I threatened her rider instead of her,*" she responded. "*I landed so close that even if she had flamed me I would still be able to kill her rider and therefore her. It presented a standoff so that they would have to settle the situation by talking rather than fighting.*"

Knowing that the argument would get him nowhere at this point, and wanting to talk with the other Rider, he said, "Very well, but we aren't at odds now, so relax and don't insult her."

"Her? What about her insulting me? I'll give her 'youngster.'"

"Please, Dear Heart, we may have an opportunity to get some real training here. Besides, she is your older sister."

Geneva snorted and said, "Very well, for the sake of training I will try to be nice."

Delno found that the other Rider, and everyone else, was waiting for him, so, he patted Geneva affectionately on the snout, and they all moved off in the direction of the garrison. When they reached the compound, the soldiers, at the Captain's orders, turned and barred the way, stopping everyone until Delno spoke up and told them to allow Nat and Pearce through. At a nod from Winston, the soldiers let the physicians accompany them. The Governor was quite put out by this, since no one seemed to feel that his presence was necessary, and he was left standing outside the garrison with the rest of the crowd.

# CHAPTER 31

THEY ALL WAITED until the two young boys who served as orderlies filled everyone's glass with wine. Then the Captain raised his glass and said, "Welcome, Rider, to this outpost."

Everyone sipped their drinks. Brock turned to Delno and said, "I would very much like to hear how you came to be a Rider, and how you came to be here."

"Yes," Winston agreed, "That must be an interesting tale. One that I'm sure you would have gotten around to telling your friends here at the garrison eventually."

Delno felt like a child caught with his hand in the cookie jar. He looked around at the faces in the room, and found that the officers and sergeants of the garrison were looking back with expressions like they felt betrayed. He was glad that he had insisted that Nat and Pearce be allowed in; otherwise he wouldn't have any moral support what so ever.

He drew a deep breath and then began retelling his story from the beginning. Since, this time, he had to stop at certain points and answer questions during the telling, it took more than two hours and several glasses of wine to finish. When he had finished, the Rider plied him with even more questions, and, after making sure he knew every detail of Corolan's death that Delno knew, he seemed particularly interested in the Dragon Blade.

"So, tell me," Brock asked, "Why did you decide not to carry your Dragon Blade? Is it safe where you are keeping it?"

"To the first," Delno replied, "I didn't think it was a good idea to reveal myself as a Rider, which the blade would have done; especially since I'm only technically a Rider because, up until this point, Geneva has been too young to ride." Then he turned to both officers, and both sergeants, and offered as an apology, "I was afraid that making the presence of an immature dragon common knowledge could put us, and therefore our new friends, in danger. I felt it was best to keep it a secret at least until Geneva and I started flying together. I didn't want to cause you and your men any trouble; you've all been so good to me."

Winston smiled and the other men nodded in satisfaction at the explanation. The other Rider said, "From the look of Geneva today, I'd say she was ready to carry a rider. If she is as young as you say, then your bond must indeed be strong. We'll have to get you into the air soon."

Delno was delighted to hear this and started to respond, but Brock was quicker, "Now about that Dragon Blade. . . . ?" he prompted.

"Oh, yes," Delno replied, "it is hidden at Nathaniel's house."

The other Rider was a bit perturbed, "It isn't under lock and key?" he asked incredulously.

To everyone's surprise, it was Nat who replied, "Nonsense, man, the quickest way to advertise that you have something worth stealing is to go to great pains to lock it up. My home doesn't even have locks on the doors; therefore, no thief in his right mind would even suspect that there is anything inside worth taking."

'Very well," Brock conceded reluctantly, "I accept that the blade is safe. Now that it is widely known that you are a Rider, though, there is no further need for you to hide. You should start wearing the sword."

Delno shrugged, seeing no reason to argue with the older Rider, though he did wonder that the man was so obsessed with the Dragon Blade. While it was an incredible blade, it had no special powers that Delno had yet discovered.

Brock then said to everyone, "The day wears on and Delno and I still have much to do. So, if you will excuse us, we will be about it."

Delno was about to object, but Winston spoke up, "Yes, this has all been very interesting, but we are still a working garrison. Another patrol needs to be organized and sent out, and I must see to it. The bandits around here won't give us a holiday simply because we've met some new friends and wish to spend the day drinking wine."

Everyone suddenly seemed to remember that they had lives to get back to, and, now that the excitement of meeting the new Rider was ebbing, they should be about their normal activities. Nat said to the Riders from the doorway, "When you two are finished and ready for food, please join us for dinner this evening; I'll tell Missus Gentry to prepare for extra company." Then he left without another word; Pearce left with him.

Delno left the office and went to Nat's home, at Brock's request, and retrieved his Dragon Blade before joining the other Rider outside the city gates.

"You may want to start strapping that to your back instead of carrying it on your hip," Brock said by way of greeting. Then he added, "I find that it makes it easier to draw while mounted." Then, reaching out he said, "Let me see the blade."

Delno was a bit taken aback by the man's gruff manner but handed him the Dragon Blade.

"A saber, hmm," he said, "Well, to each his own. A saber's a good general blade. Heavy enough to turn the stroke of a larger sword and still light enough to be fast. I prefer a long sword myself. Still, the work on the guard is exquisite, and you say he made you a dagger to go with it?"

Delno handed him the *main gauche*.

After examining it, Brock shook his head and said, "There's more than just craftsmanship in that work; the man puts so much of himself in his art that it's a type of magic. I can feel it; the blades nearly sing with it."

Delno looked at the blade on Brock's back. It was indeed a long sword, and, while finely made, it was of steel, not a Dragon Blade. Brock laughed at his scrutiny and said, "No, I don't carry a Dragon Blade myself. I was bonded in the normal way; stood in a circle with several other lads, all of us shaking in our shoes, and waited for her to choose." He reached up and patted Leera's snout affectionately. "She didn't have much of a choice, I'm afraid; most of the other lads were useless. They were only included in the circle because their fathers were influential in the city, so it was either me or that pimply-faced baker's son."

"I might have chosen him, too; he had a good mind and good heart, if only he hadn't been so ugly." Leera teased.

Brock and Delno both laughed, then Delno asked, "So tell me, why all the fuss over the Dragon Blades? I mean, I know they are virtually indestructible, but they have no other magical powers that I've found. Why all the bother?"

"You really are uneducated about all of this, aren't you?" Brock responded. Then before Delno could speak out in offense, he added, "I'm sorry, I forget that I'm not training some boy who's just bonded with a hatchling. You and Geneva have done quite well for yourselves, all things considered, but you still have a lot to learn, and you'd do well to just pay attention when someone with nearly five hundred years of experience is willing to teach you."

Delno quelled his irritation and listened.

"The Dragon Blades are not magical in the sense that most people think of the word; they don't ignite flammable materials on contact or some such nonsense," he said. "The female who makes one uses magic to do it, otherwise the fire she uses during the process would just cook the baby dragon inside its shell when she breathes on it; however, the magic doesn't stop there. During the process, the magic protects the un-hatched dragon. After the hatching a small measure of that protection is passed on to the bearer of the blade."

He looked Delno in the eye and said; "You said the Dragon Blade that had been stolen from Palamore was a long sword, right?" At Delno's nod, he continued, "Ever wonder why you got a saber and not another long sword?"

"I supposed that it was because I was carrying a saber. I assumed that she made the blade in the likeness of the one she saw that I already had."

Brock snorted, "Assume makes an 'Ass' of 'U' and 'me,'" he said. "Assume nothing when dealing with dragons or magic, and when deal-ing with both together be especially careful to verify your assumptions." He paused to let that register before he went on, "The female who makes the Dragon Blade lets the magic connect to the Rider she is making the Blade for and the magic shapes the blade to his specifications. You are most comfortable with a saber, so that is the blade you got, but it was the choice of the magic, not the dragon."

After a pause, Brock resumed the lesson; "That Dragon Blade is so special because, like the dragon herself, it is bonded to you. In my hands, the blade would certainly be more effective than it would be in the hands of just anyone else: mostly because I've had nearly half a millennium to practice, but also because I am a Dragon Rider. The magic suffused into the blade would recognize that and react accordingly. In your hands, the hands of the Rider it was made for, it will nearly come alive. In your hands, it will have the power to break steel, or even penetrate the scales of a dragon. Your dragon-enhanced abilities may not make you superhu-man, but that blade should give you an edge over a normal one whenever you use it."

Delno looked at the blade, turning it over and over in the sunlight. It didn't shine like polished steel, but it gleamed with a luster that seemed almost alive. When he concentrated on it, he realized that it felt very similar to the way the magic shield wall had felt. He smiled.

"Don't get cocky," Brock said sharply. "That blade may give you a small advantage in a fight, but so does real time spent on a practice pitch. The two things that can always offset a magical advantage are skill and luck. You can prepare for the one by spending your own time practicing. The other, well, it's best to keep your wits about you, especially when luck seems to be favoring your opponent.

"One last thing about Dragon Blades, and then we're through with that lesson for now. The second thing that makes a Dragon Blade so special, and perhaps the most important, is that it is a symbol of great power and authority. That's why they are so carefully guarded, and why the blade in Palamore was stolen."

Delno started to open his mouth to say something, but Brock held up his hand to forestall any further discussion. "We've spoken enough about swords today. It's almost noon and I want to get you into the air, and now is as good a time as any."

"Is Geneva ready? I don't want her harmed."

"Man, have you really looked at that dragon lately?" Brock responded. "While I do have to admit that Leera is slightly smaller than the average female dragon, she is still plenty large, and Geneva is nearly a match for her in size."

Delno did look then and was amazed. Geneva was standing near Leera, and he was astonished to see that she was so close in size to her older sister that the difference was moot. He said to Brock, "I guess I haven't really looked at her lately. I see what you mean."

The older Rider had been rummaging through his pack and was holding two blankets and a coil of rope. "You don't have a proper saddle, so we'll have to make do with these. Give me a hand." Saying that, he began folding the blankets into large triangles. Then he tied the triangles together and told Delno to ask Geneva to lower herself as much as possible. Delno had worried that she would balk at the other man's gruff manner and at having the makeshift saddle tied on, but she eagerly complied. She was so anxious to fly with him riding that she was having trouble sitting still. Eventually the rig was secured and he was ready to mount.

Brock looked him over and said, "Those clothes are a bit light, but we won't be flying high today, so they should be all right, but you need to understand that it gets cold as you gain altitude. Even on a hot summer day, you'll need a winter coat when you start getting a mile or more up into the sky."

Delno was nearly dumbstruck. He hadn't thought about how high dragons could fly. He had simply 'assumed', there was that word again, that they wouldn't fly so high that he would need any special riding gear.

At Brock's direction, he used Geneva's front leg as a step and climbed up into position just as he had with the dragon's mother only a few short weeks ago. Brock had left the ends of the rope long on either side and now used those ends to tie around Delno's thighs to prevent him from accidentally falling off in flight. He said, "You'll want to use straps, even in normal flight, at least until you get used to flying. I've been doing this a long time and still strap myself on, though I prefer to use a safety rig that attaches to my belt rather than tying around my legs for normal flying. I find it more comfortable on a long flight, but others don't; it's a matter of personal preference."

Then Brock mounted Leera and said, "One last thing before we get airborne: the winds in the air are different than the winds here on the ground. Sometimes they can hit at an odd angle and cause the dragon to tumble, which can make you drop like a stone. If that should happen, don't panic, and don't try to help her figure it out; just lie down as flat as you can over her neck and keep quiet. Let her natural instincts take over and you'll be fine."

Geneva sank down on her haunches and said, "*Brace yourself, Dear One,*" then shifting to full voice, she yelled, "Here we go!"

She gave a mighty push with her back legs as her wings beat downward. Delno's head snapped back on his shoulders with the force of the takeoff. Then he noticed that the walls of the city seemed to be falling away from them as they rose higher. He looked around and saw that the trees were getting smaller also, and still they climbed into the sky. Geneva wasn't speaking to him, but he was aware of her elation, both at flying and at finally having him riding with her.

He called out above the wind roaring in his ears, "This is wonderful! It's everything I'd hoped it would be!"

Delighted at his encouragement, she surged even higher, then her demeanor changed slightly and she said, "*Leera and Brock say that I have* flown high enough and that we need to make some maneuvers and then return to the ground."

Delno could sense her desire to disobey the directives and said, "We need to listen to them, Dear Heart—they have a great deal more experience then we do. There'll be many more hours of flying for us in the future; we don't need to do it all at once."

"But I want to do it all at once," she said mischievously. "This is what I was made for; but you are right, there will be plenty of time."

Brock and Leera then put them through some basic maneuvers before finally telling them to land. Geneva glided down and landed quite gently almost in the exact spot from where they had taken off. Delno unstrapped himself and then removed the improvised harness from Geneva, paying close attention to how it was rigged.

"Good first flight," Brock said as he approached. "Now help me get the saddle off of Leera, then you can carry my pack to our quarters."

Delno stared at the man. Finally, he said, "Your quarters? I didn't know you had quarters here in the city."

Either Brock was much denser than Delno suspected, or he was being deliberately thick. "Oh, I'll be staying with you, and Leera will find herself a nice clearing."

"Don't you think that you should first check with Nat? It is his house after all."

"If there isn't room, I'll take your bed." The man was so full of himself.

"My bed?" Delno asked. "You're rather sure of yourself, aren't you?"

"Look, Delno, I have decided to stay and spend some of my time teaching you and Geneva. It's customary that you ensure that your teacher has a bed and food. I'm not asking you for the world, and if your funds are too low to provide for me, I will pay my own way. All I ask for in return is simple respect." There was no humor in the older Rider's voice, but there was no belligerence in his eyes either.

"Forgive me, Brock," Delno responded, "We have been on our own so long that I tend to forget that we are still little more than babes in the wilderness. If Nat has no other bed at his house, you shall have mine." After saying this he bowed to show his respect.

Brock said, "Good, you understand the role of student and teacher. We've made a good start, I think." He then returned the bow.

Delno gathered up the other Rider's gear, including the saddle, which was about twice the weight of a saddle for a normal horse, and the two men walked toward the gates. He looked over his shoulder and saw

Geneva bow her head submissively to Leera. Apparently, the two drag-ons had just concluded the same conversation that he and Brock had.

"This is especially hard for them, you know," Brock observed, "As the keeper of her family's lineage, Geneva is technically above Leera in sta-tus, but they must put that aside, even though their instincts tell them differently, so that Leera can take the role of teacher. It will be a strain on them both, and it's up to us to help them through it."

"Head for the garrison," Brock said abruptly.

Delno was surprised, "Why?"

"Because you need a real saddle, and I've noticed over the years that small garrisons like this one, especially when commanded by someone who has some brains, like your friend Captain Eriksson, tend to cut their expenses by choosing their soldiers carefully. If you wanted a fancy saddle for some kind of parade or other such nonsense, I'd tell you to go to the nearest leather worker in town. Since what we want is something that is serviceable and made with some thought toward the comfort of the rider during long use, the garrison will probably have the best man for the job. In the long run, it's more cost effective for them to find a sol-dier who has the skill than it is to contract for the work with the locals. If they have no one who can do the work, we can go elsewhere."

Winston was delighted when they returned and personally took them to the garrison's leather worker at once. With Brock's help, the saddle maker was able to draw up a set of plans for a general-purpose saddle that should adjust to Geneva's present dimensions and still leave room for her to grow.

When Delno said that he would use belt straps like the ones on the other saddle Brock objected, "You can't know what you will prefer until you've tried both, and even I use leg straps when doing aerobatics. There-fore, the design we've come up with has provisions for both." Then in his sternest teacher's voice, he continued, "Remember what I said about assuming anything? Just because I do things a certain way doesn't nec-essarily mean that it's the best way for you. You need to examine every-thing before making such a decision."

Once the saddle was commissioned and the price settled, the man would take nothing for his labor, and only charged for materials. The leather worker said that he would give the job top priority, but even so, it would probably take a week to finish the work. Brock assured him that there was no reason to rush, and since a failure of equipment at a mile or so off the ground could prove fatal, quality over haste was preferable.

The man was wide-eyed at the thought of being so high off the ground and assured them he would take that into consideration.

Then Winston said; "Well, I guess you'll be too busy to continue sparing with us in the mornings, Delno. . . ."

Before he could say more, Brock spoke up; "He will not be too busy. Being a Dragon Rider is more than parking your arse in a saddle and letting the dragon do the work; physical training is an important part of the regimen. If you'll have us, Captain, we'll both be on the pitch bright and early."

"Excellent," Winston replied, "I'll also be honored if you'll both join me for breakfast before training." As the two men nodded their acceptance, he said, "Good, I'll see you at six in the mess hall." He then saluted and walked back to his office.

They continued on their way. Fortunately, the saddle maker wanted to keep Leera's saddle as a guide while he worked on Geneva's, so Delno wouldn't have to carry it to Nat's home.

As they walked, Delno asked; "So, why are you doing this for me?" At the look that suddenly came over the other man's face, he hastily added; "Not that I'm complaining, mind you. I'm very grateful that you are taking time to teach me, but you were obviously on some errand when you arrived here. Why would you abandon that to teach a stranger?"

"Well," Brock said thoughtfully, "You're not exactly a stranger. Leera and Geneva are sisters, and that almost makes you family, but that isn't the reason. I was on an errand. I was looking for a boy of about fourteen who bonded to a hatchling about a year ago. Someone whose methods I don't exactly approve of was training the lad. The boy finally got tired of being battered and brow beaten and took off. I was hoping to find him and see if he is all right. If I had found him, I would have offered to let him accompany me for a time, try to undo some of the training he's already had."

Brock pointed to a well and they angled toward it. After he had gotten a drink, he continued, "Leera told me she sensed a young dragon nearby; she was sure the youngster was bonded but was shut out almost instantly when she made contact. At first we thought we had found our missing lad, but since I knew who I was looking for I realized right away that we hadn't and decided to find out who was here."

"That's why you were looking so intently at the boys in the crowd," Delno observed as they continued walking.

"Aye," he said, "It was a bit of a shock when I found you instead. Once you had told me your story, I realized that fate must have played a hand in bringing me here. I decided to train you, if for no other reason than because I owe Corolan and Geneva's mother so much. Besides training me, they saved my life once."

"Saved your life? Care to elaborate on that?"

"Got myself in a bit of a nasty situation one time. Remember what I said about not keeping your wits about you when luck is favoring your opponent? Such things can happen when you live for centuries and try to do right in the world. Fortunately for me, Corolan was near enough to come to my rescue." Then he added, so softly that Delno wasn't sure he had even meant to speak out loud, "Wish I could have been there for him."

"Also," he shifted back to the original subject, "I'm training you because, as a Dragon Rider, it's my responsibility. Once you've been trained and have some experience, you'll be able to do the same if the need arises. There's no code that requires it, but it is the right thing to do."

The rest of the walk passed in silence. When they arrived, Nat was happy to see them and assured them he had room enough for another guest. Missus Gentry showed Delno where to put his teacher's things, and then Delno showed Brock to the bathing room to wash for dinner.

# CHAPTER 32

DINNER CONSISTED OF good food punctuated by interesting conversation. Both Nat and Pearce were brimming over with questions about dragons. To Brock's pleasure, and near astonishment, they were very much interested in the mundane aspects of the species, such as care, feeding, growth, endurance, and how high they could actually fly. He said he was so used to people wanting him to tell epic tales of heroic, draconic deeds that he found their plain curiosity about the species quite refreshing. After nearly two hours of discussion at the dinner table, they all retired to the sitting room.

"Now, Delno," Brock said, "you will tell me what you know of magic."

They spent the next hour and half with Delno telling the older Rider what he had been taught and what he had learned on his own. The telling was, of course, punctuated by questions on specific points. Then Brock decided that a demonstration was in order. Delno first presented a shield wall, which the older man tried unsuccessfully to punch through with a dagger. After that Delno placed a shield around his hand and arm, and held his hand over a burning candle for several minutes with no ill effect.

"We've tried it with even hotter fires," Delno said, "though we haven't had the opportunity to try with dragon fire. It should work even against that much heat though, if the energy can be maintained."

"Yes," Brock said thoughtfully, "I've seen such a shield used to stop dragon fire, but maintaining the energy is the key."

218 •• DRAGON FATE

Everyone looked at him expectantly, waiting to see if he would elaborate on his thought. Finally, he said, "All right, I've seen a mage fighting against a rider. The mage used such a shield and it worked, until he was distracted and the shield collapsed mid-breath. The man was ashes before he got a chance to correct his mistake."

"That sounds horrific," Pearce said.

"That may be," Brock responded, "but that mage had already killed dozens of innocent people and was trying to take control of a barony that would have placed him in a strategic position to make a move on the kingdom itself. It wasn't like the Dragon and Rider simply took it in their heads to see if they could cook the nearest magic user for fun."

He turned to Delno and said; "That's a lesson to remember from both sides. On the side of the dragon, you work with your partner and try and distract the mage while she does what dragons do. On the other side, don't let yourself get distracted, and know that you have to maintain the shield until the flame stops."

"How long can a dragon sustain a flame?" Nat asked.

"Well, that depends on the dragon," he responded. "Dragons can maintain a flame for seven to twelve seconds, average is about ten seconds." Then he added, inclining his head to Delno, "For those who haven't had the benefit of being able to read the books about the three dissections, a dragon produces flame by secreting chemicals. The chemicals are made in two glands. If the dragon were standing like a man the glands would be above the kidneys and behind the lungs. In that raised portion between the shoulders, just behind where the rider sits, is a muscular bladder that the glands squirt their chemicals into. The chemicals mix and create a gas that is then forced through two tubes to muscular valves at openings in the back of the dragon's mouth. The gas ignites on contact with air, so that when the dragon sprays the chemical what we see come out is fire. Dragons can breathe fire ten to twelve times a day depending on the size of the dragon and her access to good food, water, and mineral licks, or mineral-laden water."

"So, what chemicals does the dragon produce?" Delno asked.

"To be honest," Brock replied, "I neither know nor do I particularly care. I suppose that would be a question for our two scholars here."

They both turned to Nat and Pearce. Both men shrugged their shoulders and looked at each other.

Finally, Nat spoke up. "There are any number of chemicals that, when mixed together, can make different gasses, some flammable, some merely poisonous, some completely inert. But I have no idea which, if any, gas burns on contact with air."

"It is also possible," Pearce interjected, "that there is some magical component of which we are completely unaware."

"That's always possible when dealing with dragons," Brock conceded.

Nat sighed, "I wish I could get a sample of those chemicals and do some experiments."

Delno and Brock laughed. Then Brock mentioned that it was quite late, and that he and his student had to get up early. Everyone agreed that going to bed was a good idea.

The next morning Brock looked through Delno's things and told him to bring his older pair of work pants and one of his heavier tunics as well as the lighter clothes he was wearing. Then they left the house and quickly hurried to meet the officers at the garrison.

They ate a light breakfast in the mess hall with the officers. Brock was able to give them quite a bit of information from his observation of the surrounding country at altitude, for which they were grateful. While the information didn't pinpoint any possible bandit hideouts, when added to their already extensive knowledge of the countryside, it did give them some ideas about where to concentrate their next few patrols.

After breakfast, they joined the officers and men in the practice yard. Brock was pleasantly impressed that the officers trained just as hard as their men. They each sparred with the officers, and then Brock sparred with Sergeant Smith, who gave him quite a battle even though the sergeant lost. Delno was then surprised to find out that it had all just been a warm-up. He still had to spar against his teacher.

As the two dragon Riders squared off, all work in the compound ceased. Men started whispering to each other, and Delno was certain that there was a fair amount of betting going on.

He stood with his saber held on guard and his short sword ready to block. Brock opted for a long sword and a small targe. They circled slowly, then suddenly Brock made a lighting fast series of thrusts and lunges that Delno was hard pressed to defend against. His defense was successful though, and they settled back into warily circling each other. Then, as before, the older Rider made another series of attacks, and, again, he defended. Then Delno made series of advancing attacks that caught the smaller man somewhat unawares; however, the attacks didn't find their mark.

They settled into kind of a pattern, circle, attack,—circle, attack. The morning wore on and neither man showed any sign of fatigue other than the sweat that was soaking their shirts. Suddenly Delno noticed an opening, an almost imperceptible lowering of the shield arm, and he quickly took advantage of it. Just before he connected, he noticed a slight smile appear on Brock's face, and he knew he had been baited. As Brock blocked the attack with his shield, he swung his sword up hard; it was all Delno could do to block the counter attack with his short sword. Even though he blocked the blow, the blades clashed so hard that his hand was nearly knocked numb from the impact and he almost lost his grip on the short sword. He quickly disengaged his saber from the targe and reversed his grip on it and, spinning around, stabbed back toward his opponent's ribs. He was sure that the move had worked, as there was a satisfying thud when the blade impacted, and a grunt from behind him, but at the same time, his opponent's blade caught him just under the right shoulder blade.

The Weapons Master called out, "HALT!" and both men stopped and lowered their weapons.

The match was determined a tie, since no one could decide which blow had hit first, but both blows could easily have been fatal if they hadn't been using blunted blades. The duel had lasted over an hour. All the men were applauding the performance. No one was unhappy: since the contest was declared a tie, all bets were off, and none of the spectators had lost any money.

"That's enough sword work for today," Brock said. "We won't do archery this morning, either; I want to get you back into the air before noon."

They saluted each other and bowed. Then they both walked to the trough and removed their shirts. Delno's Dragon Mark stood out clearly for all to see. Looking at Brock's dark skin, Delno could just see the tops of the blue wings of the Dragon Mark above the waist of the man's trousers on his right side.

They then went to the stable, where the leather works was housed, to fetch Leera's saddle. The saddle was where they had left it, but it had been thoroughly cleaned and looked to have a fresh coat of black polish on it. Brock was quite pleased, and asked the leather worker, Brandon, who had taken such good care of his gear.

"Well, I supervised it, but the two lads who work as orderlies, Jim and Tom, they worked a good while into the night on it," he said. "They'll be bragging about polishing a real dragon saddle for years to come, I expect."

At that moment, the two boys entered the shop somewhat hesitantly, not knowing if the Dragon Rider would be pleased with their work on his equipment.

"Come here, boys," Brock said in his usual gruff manner.

The two boys entered staring at the ground, afraid to meet the man's eyes.

"Look at me, both of you." When the boys looked up, he continued. "You did some fine work on that saddle. I'm pleased to see there was some leather underneath all that dirt. Thank you." He then handed each boy a small silver coin.

The two boys were so relieved and pleased that all they could do was bow and thank the Rider repeatedly.

Finally, Brock said, "Enough, we don't need any fishing corks here right now, so you two stop bobbing up and down, and go get yourselves some time off, and then spend your money on something fun and completely worthless."

The three men laughed as the two boys ran off to do as the Dragon Rider had told them.

Delno then gathered up Leera's saddle and their other gear, and they left the garrison and headed for the city gate. Delno was working a kink out of his shoulder from the hit he had taken. He was pleased to note that Brock was also taking some pains to make sure nothing bumped his ribs where his own blade had found its mark.

"That was some decent sword work you did back there," Brock said. "Enough practice and you might actually be good, eventually," he teased.

"Yes, enough practice and I might actually score that hit without you being able to make a counter strike."

The older man smiled and rubbed his sore ribs. "You did tag me pretty good. That was a nice move, reversing your blade like that. Is that something you learned when you were in the army?"

"Partly," Delno responded, "It's not a normally practiced move, but the Weapons Master in my company said I had a bit of a knack for the blade and taught me some extra things. That move has saved my life a couple of times."

"Well," Brock retorted, "it wouldn't have saved you today. I hit you pretty good myself. You'll want to remember that in the future. You won't normally find yourself going up against another Rider, but there are swordsmen out there who are a match even for our enhanced abilities."

"Then what should I have done?" he asked a bit peeved.

"Well, there are a lot of things you should have done, including using magic. What you shouldn't have done was let me bait you into attacking on my terms."

"I didn't think to use magic," Delno responded.

He was shocked by Brock's response. The older man grabbed him by the left shoulder and spun him around so forcefully that he dropped the gear he was carrying. Their faces were no more than an inch apart as the older man nearly shouted, "That's right, you didn't think, and if that had been a real blade you would be dead and Geneva would be tearing this town apart to find me and get revenge before she herself suicided."

They stared at each other for a moment, then he continued, "You need to know this; there are men who have the skill to fight effectively against you. Some of those men would kill you just to be able to say they had beaten a Dragon Rider."

Then he softened a bit, and let go of Delno's shoulder, and took a step back before going on, "As a Dragon Rider, it's your duty to protect innocent people from those who would prey on them. A lot of those same men who would kill you for bragging rights would also use innocent people, such as your friends, the healers, or those two boys at the garrison, any way they please. You can't protect anybody if you're dead. If staying alive means using magic to do so, then use magic. You are a Dragon Rider; you can't risk yourself in frivolous duels, or waste time fighting someone who kills for pleasure. Killing is done because it's necessary and honor has damn little to do with it. People are depending on you now."

Delno hung his head and said, "You're right, of course. I've never felt honor in killing, but I am capable of doing it when necessary. I suppose I was simply enjoying our duel because I knew that it wasn't a real death match. I have taken your training frivolously, and I apologize. I will treat future lessons as real."

They stared at one another for a moment, then Brock nodded and said, "Good, get the gear, I still want to get into the air before noon."

They called the dragons, and Brock declined Delno's offer to put the saddle on Leera, saying, "Even if she'd let you, I'd rather do it myself. Remember, the main thing keeping you safe when you're a mile off the ground is that saddle; never trust it to someone else."

Once Leera was ready, Brock supervised Delno in rigging the blankets on Geneva. Then, at the older Rider's instruction, Delno donned his loose, older trousers over his newer pants. Then he put on his tunic over his shirt and tucked it into the trousers before he tied the drawstring. Then Brock tossed him a scarf and had him wrap it around his neck and tuck it into his tunic. While he was layering his clothing, Brock had been tucking in his own clothes and putting on his heavy jacket and gloves.

"You want to do everything possible to keep the air from circulating under your clothes when flying," the older Rider said. "If you can trap a layer of air you'll stay much warmer. If we get back in time, you should stop by a clothier and see about getting a jacket and some gloves, but make sure the gloves are long enough to tuck your sleeves into."

Delno was starting to sweat a little by the time he was strapped on to Geneva and Brock pronounced them ready to leave. He was beginning to think that the precautions against the cold would kill him by heat prostration when Geneva gathered herself to push off the ground. He did remember to brace himself so that his head didn't snap painfully as she launched into the air.

They rose quickly, and this time Geneva was allowed to fly much higher than the day before. By the time they reached a half a mile, he was beginning to feel more comfortable in the layered clothing. By the time they reached a mile and half, and Leera relayed that they were high enough, he was beginning to think that he might have to send north for some real winter gear if he was going to do much flying.

Leera and Brock then put the pair through a series of maneuvers that might have caused Delno to lose his lunch if he'd eaten before they started the lesson. The one he hated the most was what Brock called a barrel roll. After Geneva made several unsuccessful attempts, and then managed the maneuver twice, he knew why they called it that; he felt as though someone had stuck him in a barrel and rolled it down a hill. They did several more stunts, and then Brock had them fly forward as fast as possible. Once Geneva had reached her maximum speed, he instructed them to climb as steeply as they could. This, of course, caused a stall, at which point Geneva simply let instinct take over, and she fell over backwards and rolled until she was upright again.

"Leera says that maneuver is designed to quickly get you facing the reverse direction while evading pursuit or missiles," she said.

"Really? I thought it was designed so that Leera could find out what I'd had for breakfast," he responded.

After the last stunt, Leera relayed that they should land on a hill not too far distant. Geneva angled her flight in that direction. Delno was glad to get to a lower altitude; his hands and ears were nearly numb from the cold. In fact, he was so cold that his teeth were chattering. Once on the ground, Brock told Leera and Geneva to fly off and practice some more, while he and Delno continued their lessons on the ground.

Once the Dragons had gone off, Brock said, "We're going to work on magic. I wish I were better at it myself, so that you would get some real instruction, but, for now, I'm all you've got. To start with, we're going to work on healing." Then he smiled and said, "You really did tag me good; I think you broke my rib."

Delno smiled and said, "Let me see."

This time, when he examined the injury magically, he could clearly see an area that was reddish around the wound. As he looked deeper, he realized he could actually see the broken rib. It was broken in two places, just above and just below the point of impact, and the bone at that point was spider-webbed with smaller fractures. Delno was amazed; the man must be in agony but didn't show it. He described what he saw to Brock. Then he judged how much energy it would take to heal the fracture and called it up from the ground. He focused and spoke the word "Heal" and the rib reassembled itself like a child's jigsaw puzzle. While his patient hadn't let the pain show, he did expel an audible sigh of relief as the broken bone was mended.

"Well, since you know to look into the body and not just at the blood or bruise, I'm not going to go into healing any more," Brock said. "You're already better at it than I am. Let's move on to that shielding you do."

They practiced shielding for a while. Brock was more interested in him being able to get the shield up fast than he was in how strong it actually was. "Know this," he said, "your dragon's scales are tough. They can stop a normal blade, partly because they are about as strong as steel, but partly because normal people like men and elves just don't have the strength to push a piece of steel through them. Arrows, unless they come out of a really powerful bow, won't penetrate either, and I've only met a handful of men in my lifetime who were capable of drawing such a bow. The problem comes with the angle of attack and the general health and fatigue of the dragon."

Delno listened intently, knowing that the information that the older man was giving him could save his and Geneva's lives.

Leera landed nearby. Delno looked for Geneva with some concern and reached out to her. He could feel her but she was engaged in hunting. "Relax," Brock said, "she's only hunting; she exerted a lot of energy today. She's still young and needs to eat a lot. She'll be along shortly."

Then he continued the lesson. "A dragon in good health and not fatigued has tightly overlapping scales that are nearly impervious to most mundane attacks. Dragons are immune to disease, but they can be injured. They are especially vulnerable on the bottom of the feet where the scales are small and subject to a lot of use. An injured or hungry dragon fatigues easily. When a dragon is fatigued, the scales can get slack. When that happens, they are still overlapped, but an arrow or other missile can slide between them if it comes from the proper angle. If you are in a situation where your dragon is fatigued, and there are many archers on the ground, you will want to angle your shield under her to protect her until you can withdraw. You may have to get that shield up quickly: that is why I'm more interested in speed than strength. It should be second nature for you to do it. Remember, a weak shield is still a whole lot better than no shield at all; the membranes that hold the scales in place are tough, and if an arrow has to pass through a weak shield first, it may not have the power left to get through that membrane even if it slides between the scales. Also, always remember, *you* have no scales at all. You can always add more energy to a weak shield; just get the thing in placed as fast as possible."

Then Brock called Leera over and told Delno to put a strong shield around a scrub tree that was standing alone on top of the hill. When the shield was in place, Leera gathered herself some, and then, extending her neck, she breathed forth a cone of fire that was a most impressive sight. The cone was nearly fifteen yards long and went from the size of her head at one end to about thirty feet in diameter. As she started to flame Delno began counting to himself, "*One-one thousand, Two-one thousand, Three-one thousand. . . .*" The flame lasted eleven seconds. The fire didn't touch the tree; it parted about four feet in front of it and then curled around behind, but the tree remained unharmed, protected by Delno's shield. When Leera's flame was spent, they both thanked her for helping.

"That," Brock said, "was a very good shield. I have placed a steel breast plate out as a target for Leera and one blast of her flame turned it to a bubbling puddle."

"I knew from talking to Nat that a dragon's fire was hot," Delno responded, "but I had no idea how hot."

"When Geneva is old enough to produce flame, you will have to be careful when practicing so that you don't accidentally hurt yourselves or start a fire. It's best to practice somewhere that has very sparse vegetation and make darn sure that she breathes with the wind and not into it."

They approached the charred patch around the tree. Delno noticed that there were now bits, and small sheets, of glass on the ground from where the sandy soil had melted under the dragon's breath. He whistled and said with a touch of awe in his voice, "That is a very impressive weapon."

"Yes," Brock responded, "but it has its drawbacks. On the ground, the contours of the terrain can throw the fire back in your face if you aren't careful. In the air, she can only breathe down and back."

Delno thought about it for a moment and replied, "I can understand that; once the flame leaves her mouth, it is subject to the air currents, and, like smoke, it will slow quickly. If she breathes ahead of herself while in flight, she will then fly right into the fire. If she turns her head to breathe over her shoulder, she endangers her own rider and her own wings."

"You catch on fast. Just remember those things and take it slowly when Geneva starts flaming, and you should be fine." Then the older man added, "Also, always remember that she will not be able to flame more than a dozen times in a day, possibly less, so make sure you are certain of your target, and don't waste the chemicals. It is a limited weapon, but is very effective when used on a low pass over large groups."

Delno found that idea distasteful, and it must have showed on his face, because Brock put a hand on his shoulder and said, "I know, it's not a pretty thing to think about, but then, neither is watching your forces die on the enemies' pikes because you haven't stomach to do what must be done."

"The problem I've always encountered is that the troops on both sides are usually just men; they have a lot more in common with each other than they do with the leaders who send them to fight and die," Delno responded.

"Then you're ahead of some I can think of. It takes most Riders a while to learn that lesson, but I tend to keep forgetting that you're a combat veteran and former officer; most new Riders are little more than children." Then he paused and collected his thoughts, "So, tell me, if you don't want to fight, why do you train so hard with the blade and magic?"

Delno spoke carefully, as if mentally picking his way through a field full of traps, "I practice to keep my skills honed so that I can protect those people and causes I care about."

"So, there are causes you would consider worth fighting for?"

"Of course," Delno replied, "I'd be a fool to think otherwise, but fighting isn't always the only answer."

"No, it is not; that is why I have told you to examine all angles before making assumptions. That goes for everything in your life, not just magic."

"I have fought in a war that nearly ruined the economy of two kingdoms. I was decorated for my valor several times over and promoted beyond my station in life for my abilities. In the end, nothing had changed in the two kingdoms except that a lot of good men had died on both sides." They looked at each other for a long moment before he added; "I won't define my life with the edge of my blade."

"That is why Dragon Riders rarely get involved in wars, because they are usually fought over territorial disputes or some such. Typically, Riders only get involved when there is a clear cut act of unprovoked aggression." The older man sighed and said, "Look, Delno, as a Dragon Rider you wield great power. With that power comes great responsibility. There will be many who will come to you to help settle their squabbles, whether they be kings, governors, or just men who feel they have been wronged. Some will expect you to 'ride forth and slay their enemies'; some will expect you to have the wisdom to decide other types of disputes. Not everyone can be right, and not everyone can be wrong. It often seems, that in any dispute, the truth of the matter usually lies somewhere in the middle. Don't make decisions until you have all of the facts, and if you have to choose sides, pick your side very carefully."

At that point, Geneva arrived and settled down to rest while her meal digested some. Delno picked up a few of the now cool pieces of glass, saying that Nat and Pearce would be interested in the flame demonstration, and that neither of them would ever forgive him if he didn't bring them back a souvenir.

Then the men gathered some fruits that were growing nearby and ate them for lunch. The fruit was orange with a tough rind, and had a taste that was more savory than sweet.

After lunch, they discussed magic again. Delno learned that he could gather energy from clouds, especially storm clouds, and from the wind itself. He practiced that for a while, then, while Brock and Leera went flying together, he tried using a variation of the shield to push objects. He was having some success when Brock landed and said it was time to return to the city, so, once Delno was mounted and strapped in, they flew straight back with no extra practice, and Brock kept their flight mercifully low to avoid the cold.

Once in town, Delno immediately went to the clothier to look for a jacket and gloves.

"Jacket and gloves?" the shopkeeper asked, "Why in the world would you want a jacket and gloves in this weather?" The man obviously thought that Delno was not quite right in the head.

"Obviously, you've never been a mile and half off the ground while moving at nearly four times the speed of a galloping horse, or you wouldn't ask such a question," Delno retorted. At the man's incredulous look, he said, "Look, man, either you have what I want and will sell me the items, or I will go elsewhere." He then flashed several gold coins and made a show of putting them away in preparation of leaving the shop.

"Ah, let's not be hasty, I may have something in the back. Let me just go and look." The man might be leery of dealing with a lunatic, but the difference between outright insanity and acceptable eccentricity is usually the number of coins in a man's purse. "Now don't go away, I'll be right back."

The merchant returned in short order with several coats, and two pairs of gloves. Delno bought a lined coat with a fur collar, fur lined gloves, and even a knit hat that would cover his ears. He left the shop poorer, but happy, and the shopkeeper would undoubtedly enjoy telling everyone just how crazy the Dragon Rider was.

That night at dinner, after telling Nat and Pearce about the performance of the dragon's breath, and his shield, he was pleased with how delighted they were when he presented them with the souvenir glass he had collected. Nat and Pearce wanted to talk far into the night, but both Riders claimed fatigue and retired early.

# CHAPTER 33

DELNO WOKE EARLY; there were still a couple of hours until dawn, but he couldn't get back to sleep. He decided to have a bath before starting the day, since he had the time. He went to the bathing room and pumped the tub about a quarter full with cold water, then he used the second pump, which pulled water from a supply tank that was warmed by the kitchen stove, to pump it full of enough hot water to be comfortable before he got in to soak.

*"Ah, you are awake, Dear One, I was hoping to have a chance to talk with you before you started training today."*

*"What are you doing awake, Dear Heart? I thought you'd sleep long after the meal you had yesterday."* While he was happy to have her company, he didn't want her distressed in any way.

*"I don't sleep like I used to after eating now, Love. I woke up and was pleased to find you awake and alone, so I thought perhaps we could talk."*

*"Then we shall talk to your heart's content."* Then he quickly added, *"While I have enjoyed sleeping in a real bed, I think I sleep better lying on the ground with my head pillowed on your foreleg; I have missed being near you."*

*"I have missed you, too. So, how do you like flying with me? I have had a wonderful time, though I am sorry if the maneuvers upset your stomach."*

He laughed, *"Oh, that, I was only teasing, Love; I will get used to it, I'm sure. In the mean time, my stomach will survive, providing I remember not to eat just before a flight."*

She laughed mentally and said, *"We are fortunate that our new teachers found us. I am learning much from Leera, and you seem to be benefiting from your training with Brock."*

"Yes, Brock told me they had been looking for a young lad who had run away from training when they found us."

*"Oh, yes,"* she replied, *"Brock's son, Connor. Bit of an upset about all of that."*

"Brock's son!?" he had nearly shouted that out loud. "Brock didn't tell me the boy was his son!"

*"Then I hope I haven't done wrong by telling you. Leera didn't seem to think it was any kind of secret. I thought you knew."*

"No," he said thoughtfully. "He mentioned that he was looking for the boy, and that he hadn't approved of the methods the lad's teacher had been using to train him, but he never mentioned the lad's name or that he was his father."

*"Perhaps then,"* she responded, *"you shouldn't ask him about it then. If he wanted you to know, he would most likely have told you."*

"Perhaps," he agreed, "for now, anyway."

They continued talking until the water in the tub got cold, and Delno was distracted by drying himself and getting ready for the day. He told her that they would see each other later as he met Brock and they headed to the garrison for breakfast and physical training.

Once on the pitch, they practiced with the men and officers for a time, and Sergeant Smith then asked Delno to teach him the move he had used when they first sparred. All practice stopped as Delno demonstrated the move several times. Brock was fascinated and insisted that he be taught as well. Soon the men were paired up, and Delno walked around correcting peoples' technique as they took turns throwing and disarming each other.

After about two hours, he and Brock again squared off. This time, however, Brock announced that they would only work on their technique and reflexes today. This would not be a sparring match. Even though this wasn't a pitched battle like the day before, they still had quite an audience since they were each demonstrating techniques that were foreign to the troops of the garrison as well as each other. They found themselves easily trading off roles as both teacher and student.

When the older Rider called a halt to sword practice, he decided that this morning they would take time to do a bit of archery.

When Brock saw Delno's bow, he asked, "Where did you get this?" He seemed quite impressed.

"I bought it in Larimar just before I left."

"Well then, my young student, you are simply full of surprises." Brock replied. "This bow was made by a member of the Archery Guild in Horne. They only sell a very limited number of these bows each year. This must have cost you a fortune."

"The man I bought it from in Larimar said he got it as part of a shipment he bought trading with a caravan some time back. No one he had shown it to could comfortably draw it, so he had discounted it. Even with the discount it was still very expensive; I almost didn't spend the money."

Brock looked the bow over carefully again and then tested the draw. He asked for an arrow and took a practice shot that flew straight and true right to the bull's eye. He handed the bow back to Delno and said, "Keep that safe; it's worth a good deal more than that merchant charged you for it, and it will serve you well in the years to come."

They practiced archery for over an hour. It was just past noon when they reached the city gates. They were surprised to find a small crowd gathered there. The crowd had gathered because the dragons had anticipated them coming earlier and were lounging just outside the gate. Apparently, curiosity had overcome the people's fear of the dragons, though the onlookers were keeping a respectful distance.

As they approached, the crowd started babbling to themselves. Then someone asked, "Are you going to fly on them today?" The question came from a boy of about twelve.

"Yes," Brock responded. "We are going to fly today. You can stay and watch, but there won't be much to see."

A young girl of about nine, probably the boy's younger sister judging by the resemblance, asked Delno, "What's it like to fly on a dragon?"

Delno chuckled and said, "Well, I guess it's like flying on a bird, only bigger."

He turned to walk away toward Geneva, but the little girl grabbed his sleeve and said with a giggle, "No one can fly on a bird."

Delno smiled and replied, "You're right, of course, no one can fly on a bird."

The girl, still holding his sleeve and giggling, started to say something else, but a young woman, too young to be her mother but still bearing a resemblance, said, "Enough Julia, let the Rider go, you're bothering him."

"I am not!" the girl insisted, "He's a nice man, and I like him."

Delno looked into the young woman's eyes and said, "She's no bother." Then he smiled at the little girl and said softly, "But I really do have to get to work now."

The young woman took Julia's hand, and the girl reluctantly let go of Delno's sleeve. Then Julia said, "Can't we stay and watch them fly, Jennie? Please!?"

Delno smiled at Jennie and said, "It will only take us a few minutes to rig up, and then we'll be off. We won't be back until late this afternoon, so she'll be easier to manage once we're gone."

The young woman returned his smile, and still looking at Delno, said to the girl, "All right Jules, we'll stay until they're in the air, then we have to go."

Julia looked at Delno and said, "Oh, thank you!"

Delno smiled at her and winked, then turned to Geneva and began rigging the improvised saddle.

One of the older boys in the crowd said in a belligerent voice, "How come you don't got a saddle like the other fella? You poor or smumthin'?"

Delno found the question and the tone of voice annoying and started to respond that if the boy thought he could make a saddle faster then Brandon at the garrison, he was welcome to try. Instead, he simply shook his head and said, "Yes, boy, I'm poor or something," enunciating his words very carefully.

Another of the older boys slapped the offensive youngster in the back of the head, and while Delno didn't think violence was a good idea, he couldn't help but want to thank the other lad.

Julia's brother asked Delno, "Why are you wearing a coat and gloves? Aren't you hot?"

Delno turned to him and said, "Here on the ground, yes, but up there," he pointed to the sky, "it's pretty darn cold." Then, seeing Julia watching wide-eyed, he made a bit of a show of putting his knit cap on his head and pulling it over his ears.

They were soon in the air, and the crowd got smaller as they got higher. Once they had put several miles between them and the city, Brock and Leera again put them through the same series of maneuvers as the day before.

After they had successfully completed them, Geneva said, "Brace yourself, Love, Leera says we are to do the dive she taught me yesterday. Just lay low and hang on!"

Geneva pulled her wings in much closer to her body and pointed her head downward. As she picked up speed, the angle of her dive increased. Delno watched with growing concern as they moved faster and faster towards the ground below them. Then, when he was certain that they would crash and be killed, she extended her wings a little and turned herself upward, pulling out of the dive about a hundred and fifty feet off the ground. She was absolutely elated with the maneuver and roared her pleasure.

*"Wasn't that fun!?"* she asked.

"Oh yes, Dear Heart, that was a lot of fun," he said. "Could you just do me one small favor, though?"

*"Of course, Dear One, anything you need."*

"Well, the next time we fly over that particular piece of ground, do you think you could fly lower and slower? I'm sure I left my stomach back there somewhere, and I'd like to look for it."

She laughed out loud and said, *"Don't worry, Love, you'll get used to this eventually."*

They spent over an hour flying until Brock signaled them, and Leera relayed the message to land. This time they landed on another hill that was covered with rocks. As Geneva went to hunt, he and Brock began another magic lesson.

Brock had him review shielding for nearly an hour before he was ready to move on.

"This time," Brock said, "you will work on magical attacks. Hopefully, you will never need to use one, but it's a good idea to know how, just in case. Now then, since you will be using enough energy to kill another human being, you will aim at rocks."

At Brock's instruction, Delno gathered energy and then released it with the intention of stopping a beating heart. The first attempt was extremely weak: they couldn't even see the energy hit, and there was no mark on the rock.

"What are you holding back for?" Brock demanded. "Is this more of your not wanting to kill unnecessarily?"

"No," Delno responded, annoyed, "It is a little hard to gauge how much energy it takes to stop the heart of a *rock*."

"That may be, but why are you trying to gauge it so closely? Your intention here is to kill your opponent; don't be afraid to put some energy into the effort."

This time, Delno let his annoyance fuel his magic, and drew much more energy. Then he concentrated on the spot on the rock for only a second and, pointing his finger for focus, he released the energy with the word, "KILL."

There was a flash of light, and the energy struck the rock like a lightning bolt. The specific point on the rock exploded, blasting a hole in it about the size of a man's fist, and little shards went flying. The boulder itself, about four feet in diameter, split into three large pieces.

Delno looked at Brock, and asked innocently, "Was that enough energy?"

"Yes," Brock answered, "if you wanted to kill an entire herd of oxen. Now, do it again, and this time tone it down somewhere in between the first two attempts."

They practiced for another hour before Brock was satisfied. Then they had a light lunch and sat for a while.

"So," Brock said, "You looked a bit uncomfortable with the crowd this afternoon."

"I don't like hero worship when it's merited, and I certainly don't like it when it's for something that is totally outside of my control. Those people think we're special because we're Dragon Riders. To me that's like thinking we're special because we eat and breathe."

"Well, I can see your point on the one hand, but I can see their point on the other."

Delno raised his eyebrow.

"You have to remember, Delno, that to those people we *are* special. There are only about a hundred bonded female dragons alive in the world at any one time. We were chosen by those dragons because we are special. We have the magic within us to make the connection."

"Are you saying that there aren't others who have enough connection to the magic? That we are the only ones?" He looked at the older man incredulously.

"No, of course not." Brock answered, annoyed. "There was also a large bit of luck involved. If we hadn't been where we were at the time that our dragons hatched, they would have chosen someone else. But fate put *us* there and not someone else. Fate has singled us out to be special."

"So, what does that mean then?' Delno asked. "Does that mean we have to like scenes like that one in front of the gates today?"

"What it means, young Rider," Brock explained, "is that what happened in front of the gates today is part of our lives. As I've told you, being a Dragon Rider is a big responsibility."

"It's our responsibility to accept that type of nonsense?"

Brock snorted and said, "Of course it is. Didn't you see those people? Most of them were commoners; their lives are set, the chance that they can improve their situation is slim. They need heroes to worship; it gives them some hope in their lives. If they can, even for a moment, get us to notice them and acknowledge their right to be people, then they are elevated in their own eyes. It isn't much when you take a moment to talk to people like that, but to them, it's everything. It helps them to feel some self-worth and dignity, and those are two things that everyone deserves to feel."

Delno was thoughtful for a moment, then said, "I really hadn't thought about it from their point of view. I guess you're right. I just grew up as one of them, and then had all of the rest thrust upon me. I never liked having people back in Larimar worship me for being a hero, but when I think back on it now, from their point of view, I see that buying me a pint of beer and drinking with me elevated them because the 'hero' had joined them. They needed to borrow a bit of my fame to raise themselves because they had no other options."

"That's right," Brock said, "only the vain, shallow people like it, but the rest learn to accept it when they learn to look at it from the other point of view."

They sat in silence for a few minutes and finally Delno, though he wasn't sure why, asked, "So, care to tell me a bit more about the boy you were looking for?"

Brock just looked at him so long that he thought the man wasn't going to answer. Then the older Rider said, "Well, I guess Geneva told you then, huh?"

"One of the few things I have managed to learn about dragons is that you have to be really specific about what is a secret and what isn't," Delno replied.

"Well, it wasn't so much a secret as me not wanting to burden others with my problems. The boy was born out of wedlock to a woman I had known. He was my son. Besides the fact that he looks enough like me to remove doubt, Leera said he has my scent, and the dragons aren't wrong about such things. His mother couldn't keep him, and I couldn't drag him all over the world with me, so we fostered him. I saw him whenever I could, and when he came of age, he was presented as a candidate at a hatching. I wanted to train him, but his foster parents thought that would be a bad idea, and the rider who took the job helped them persuade me. I guess the boy was a bit hurt that his own father wouldn't be his teacher, but he did all right in the beginning from the reports I got."

"You said that you didn't think much of the Rider who was training him. In fact, you hinted that the man might even be abusive."

"Well, I didn't really mean abusive, at least not in a malicious sense. That Rider is a bit harsh, as much on himself as on anyone else. He wouldn't beat the boy physically as a punishment, but his training methods are much harsher than mine." He thought for a moment and then said, "He's a good man, basically. He never takes what isn't due and serves whatever community he stays in well, only asking food and lodging for his troubles. He lives a pretty austere lifestyle." He paused again before continuing, "Oh hell, his heart's in the right place, but I sometimes think he keeps his brain in the wrong end of his body."

Delno chuckled and said, "I don't know the individual, but I'm familiar with the breed."

Brock nodded and continued, "I should have insisted on training the lad myself, as his father, it's my right; but I let those who had actually raised him make the decision. I guess in the end I did the same thing I did in the beginning; I left my responsibilities to others."

Delno shook his head and said, "I don't believe that; you are a responsible man. After all, look what you're doing here; you've taken on the responsibility of helping me."

"Didn't stop to consider all the angles before assuming again, I see," Brock responded.

"How so?" Delno asked.

"Well, by stopping my search and taking on the responsibility of teaching you, I might just be avoiding the responsibility of finding my son."

"If you feel the need to move on, Geneva and I can take care of ourselves. You've taught us much already."

"Aye, I've taught you much, and you've taught me a thing or two also. I think this time has been good for both of us. I also think that, right now, you still need me more, and it most likely isn't hurting Connor to have a bit more time to cool off before he's found."

"I have a feeling that when you're ready to find him it won't be a problem for us," Delno said. When Brock asked for an explanation of that comment, he only smiled and said, "I have my ways, when you're sure you're ready."

# CHAPTER 34

THE TWO RIDERS and their dragons settled into a routine over the next few days: breakfast and physical training at the garrison, followed by flight training and magic practice in the afternoons.

On the ninth day of their training, they were sitting in the dining hall with Winston, and Delno said, "You know, my friend, we should pay for the meals we've eaten here."

"Nonsense," Winston retorted, "it is the custom of this kingdom that Dragon Riders are afforded every courtesy that can be spared. Food, and lodging if needed, is included in that custom. We can afford the small amount of food the two of you eat here. Besides, now that it has become common knowledge that there are two Dragon Riders staying in Orlean, bandit attacks have dropped off sharply." Then he laughed and added, "I'd go so far as to say that there hasn't even been a pick-pocket operating around here in a week or so. We should probably get you a voucher for services rendered."

Delno laughed and said, "We'll call it even then."

After working out with the men for about two hours, Delno and Brock squared off with each other. This time, Brock gave no orders not to spar, and told Delno to defend himself. Then he started circling until he was ready, before he once again made a series of quick attacks. They quickly settled into the pattern that they had settled into on the first day. This time Delno wasn't going for the bait; he had something to show his teacher today. When Brock dropped his guard this time, Delno moved in to attack, but that was just bait of his own. As he got close, he used the energy he had stored up, and, using the modified shield, he pushed hard enough that Brock was knocked off his feet. The move was totally unexpected, and the older man was splayed out before him. He quickly stepped on his opponent's right wrist and placed his practice saber at the other Rider's throat.

Brock's look of startled surprise quickly turned to a smile, and he said, "You've been practicing some new things when I wasn't looking."

"As you've said, I'm full of surprises," Delno replied, as he reached down to help the other man to his feet.

When they had cleaned up, they went to the stables and found that Brandon had completed Geneva's saddle. It was beautiful: done in black leather, it was simple but elegant. It had a seat that was wide enough to be comfortable even during a long flight, and fenders long enough to protect his lower legs from chafing against her scales, and it was fitted with both thigh straps and the same belt and harness set up as Leera's saddle. If the thigh straps weren't in use on his legs, they could easily be rigged to tie gear into place. Everything on the saddle was double stitched with good heavy cord. The overall effect was a very serviceable saddle that should be quite comfortable and last for years without major repair. Delno thanked Brandon profusely for the work. The man actually blushed at the praise, saying that he was just glad he could be of assistance to the Riders.

They carried their saddles out of the garrison toward the city gates. The young woman, Jennie, was there to watch them take off. She had taken the habit of being there when the Riders came from their morning practice to join the dragons. She had even been waiting near the gates on several occasions when they returned in the late afternoons. This morning, as on many of the previous mornings, she had brought them biscuits and honey to take with them for their lunch. As usual, both Riders greeted her and thanked her for the food, and, as usual, she barely seemed to notice that Brock was even there. She wasn't rude to the older Rider; she simply had eyes only for Delno.

They saddled both dragons, and Delno and Geneva were both delighted with the fit and feel of the new saddle. Geneva was so pleased she was actually dancing from foot to foot in anticipation of flying with a proper rig on. Once airborne, they did a few maneuvers, which Delno found much more pleasant with the comfort and stability of a real saddle. Also, he was really getting used to flying. He was even starting to like the acrobatic maneuvers. They didn't fly long before Brock had Leera relay that they were to land on the rocky hill.

Delno dismounted and approached his teacher expecting to start another magic lesson, but Brock said there would be no lesson today. He was just about to explain when both dragons sat up fully alert.

As Brock communicated with Leera, Geneva said, "*There are two Dragons and their Riders at the city gate; they are looking for Brock. We must go.*"

Delno looked at Brock and the older man shrugged and said, "I guess we'll find out when we get back to town."

They quickly mounted and took wing. Geneva had grown so much in the last nine days that she was now noticeably larger than her older sister. She was actually pulling ahead when Delno said, "*Brock and Leera are our Teachers; we should let them lead the way, Dear Heart.*"

"*You are right, Love, I had forgotten that I had grown so much bigger than she.*"

Geneva adjusted her flight to let Leera get slightly ahead of her, and Delno saw Brock smile and salute them for the courtesy.

When they reached the city, it was the same near-bedlam that occurred the day that Brock had first appeared. Delno shook his head and said, "*You'd think, after having two Riders in town for so long, these people would learn to relax a bit.*"

Geneva laughed out loud as well as mentally and he said, "*What's so funny, Love?*"

"*Leera just relayed the same message from Brock almost word for word.*"

Delno looked at Brock, and they simultaneously shrugged their shoulders and smiled at each other.

The two Riders at the gate were, of course, completely new faces to Delno, but he saw that Brock recognized them. They landed near the newcomers, who were already on the ground, and dismounted.

The new pair were surprised to see Delno. Apparently, they had been expecting someone else; most likely, they had expected Brock's companion to be his son, the missing Rider.

Realizing that the other Riders were startled to find a completely unknown person with him, Brock said, "Riders, let me introduce my student; this is Delno, and his Bond-mate Geneva."

The looks on the Rider's faces told Delno that they, too, understood the significance of Geneva's name.

Brock said to Delno, "This is Simcha Samuelson, and Marguerite Killian."

Delno wasn't sure how it was done in the south, but he grasped the woman's arm first as was polite in the north. No one took offense, so he then grasped the man's arm and shook with him.

Marguerite said, "Most people call me Rita; the full name is just too much of a mouthful."

Simcha only nodded to him and then turned to Brock and said, "We have much to discuss," then he looked at the crowd and added, "*Privately.*"

This time even the soldiers from the garrison held back. One Dragon Rider was one thing; four was more than any of them seemed willing to handle. Winston smiled at Delno as if to say, "Our Dragon Riders can handle this one."

Delno spoke up, "We can talk at Nat's home; it's about as private as we're likely to get."

Rita, a small pretty woman, just about five feet tall, with olive skin, long black hair, and dark eyes, who looked to be no more than her early twenties, just shrugged her shoulders and said, "This isn't my town; I'll defer to your expertise, Handsome."

Delno was a bit startled by her forward manner, but he extended his arm to her anyway. He realized that her apparent age had nothing to do with her actual years. A Dragon Rider wouldn't even be middle aged until she was twelve to fifteen hundred. If this young lady had bonded at twelve or thirteen, she was probably quite a bit older than he.

Simcha ignored Delno and looked to Brock who said, "Don't ignore the man, Simcha; he's a Rider and knows the town better than we do."

"I thought you said he was your student," the man responded, as if student meant something like a cross between a child and a pack animal. Delno was rapidly coming to the conclusion that it might save time to just avoid the rush later and start disliking the man now.

"I misspoke; I meant that he *was* my student." Then he turned to Delno and said, "That's what I was about to tell you before we were called back. Today is graduation day as far as I'm concerned. There's still more you can learn, but I'm confident that you will learn those things just fine. I've taught you what I can, and I've seen Riders who were a whole lot less prepared turned loose on the world." Then he extended his hand to Delno and added, "Congratulations. A teacher usually gives his student a gift at this point, typically a blade. I can't give you a blade that will even come close to the one you're carrying, so all I've got for you on such short notice is my blessings."

As he returned Brock's grasp, he said, "Your blessings are plenty and mean more to me than any trinket would. Thank you."

Then he turned to the other two Riders and said, "If you'll follow me, we can go someplace more . . . *quiet.*"

Rita took Delno's arm and said, "You lead, Handsome, and I'll follow."

Simcha snarled, "For the love of . . . You're over a century old, woman; get your glands under control."

"Simcha, Darling," Rita responded with smile, "when I am nearly seven hundred years old, I hope that, like you, I am so good at minding my own business that I have plenty of time left to mind other people's business as well."

Delno smiled at the petite woman; Brock merely shook his head, while Simcha glared at all three of them.

Delno began walking toward the gates and saw Jennie standing there; to his surprise, she was smiling and talking with Robbie and hadn't noticed Rita. Jennie looked up, and there was a flash of irritation when she noticed that the female Rider was holding Delno's arm, but then Robbie said something to the young woman, and she laughed and turned back to him, ignoring the Riders completely.

Brock leaned closer and whispered, "Looks like your lady friend has found a new interest."

"Lady friend?" Rita said, "I hope I'm not going to get you into trouble, Handsome."

"She's not my 'lady friend,' she's a young woman who was taken with a Rider. She brought me some biscuits and honey. I discouraged any-thing else; it would have been taking advantage of the situation." Then he noticed that Jennie and Robbie were virtually ignoring everyone and everything around them. "Robbie is a good man, and closer to her age anyway."

Rita smiled and replied, "Hmm, good looks, and he's got ethics; the more I learn about you, Handsome, the more I like what I see."

Simcha growled, "Maybe some of the ethics will rub off on you, Rita."

Delno stopped walking, but before he could turn on Simcha, Rita firmly shoved him in the direction they had been heading and said, "Ignore him; arguing only encourages him to rise to ever greater heights of self-righteous arrogance."

Simcha glared at Brock and said, "If that boy were my student, I'd take him to task for acting that way towards his superiors."

Delno had had enough of this pompous ass. He turned on Simcha and said with a smile, "I give respect where it's due; perhaps you missed that lesson."

Simcha's face began to turn pink, edging toward red.

Not wanting to be left out when it was Simcha who was on the receiving end, Rita piped up, "Besides, Darling, if *you* were his teacher, he'd likely be running loose in the countryside hiding from any Dragon Rider within a thousand miles."

Simcha's face went from pink directly to purple and the only sounds he appeared capable of were incoherent sputterings.

Rita was quite pretty, and Delno was sure she was fairly intelligent, but she didn't know when to leave well enough alone. She looked at Brock and, without skipping a beat, said, "Speaking of which, have you had any word on Connor? Any idea where he might be now?"

Simcha's hand was on his sword hilt, and Delno thought that the man was actually going to draw steel, but Brock quickly stepped into the middle of the three of them and said, nearly shouting, "ENOUGH!" All three were startled and he continued, almost whispering so that the crowd could not hear his words, "You will all keep your insults to yourselves, and your tempers under control. Simcha, if you draw that blade, I'll personally disarm you in front of all of these people."

Simcha moved his hand away from his blade, but continued to glare at Delno like the whole incident was somehow his fault. Delno wanted to point out that the man had brought it upon himself, but doing so would accomplish nothing, and Brock was right; this was not the time or place. He shrugged and led the other three Riders toward the gate.

As they passed the crowd, Nat nodded and said, "Delno, the sliding doors of the sitting room are fairly thick and should provide you with a quiet place to talk. I'll tell Missus Gentry to get some refreshments and make room for our newest guests."

Both Delno and Brock thanked the healer as he preceded them to the house so that he could make arrangements with his housekeeper. Delno lightly touched the half-elf on the shoulder and whispered, "I apologize for bringing this to your home."

Nat just smiled and replied, "It's not a problem. I'm sure everything will sort itself out in short order."

Missus Gentry set a tray of refreshments on a small table and said, "If you need anything else, I'll be about the house seeing to quarters for you all, but just pull the bell rope, I'll hear." Then she drew the thick sliding doors shut as she left.

The four Dragon Riders sat without talking for several moments. Brock looked expectant, Delno was curious, Simcha looked angry, and Rita looked a bit bored. Finally, Brock broke the silence, "Well, I'm sure you two didn't team up and come here simply for a visit."

Simcha snorted and then said, "We came here to find you." They all waited for him to continue, but he had apparently said all he was willing to say.

Brock rolled his eyes, and Rita said, "Well, that certainly explains the whole situation."

Simcha glared at her and replied, "If I wanted to tell my business to anyone other then Brock, I wouldn't have asked Brock to speak with me privately. If I'd wanted to include some youngster in this, I would have said so."

By this point even Brock's patience was starting to wear thin. He was about to say something when Rita spoke out in an exasperated tone, "Well, this is also my business, and I have no problems with Delno being present. So, since you won't tell them what this is about, I will."

She then turned to Brock and reported, "Chureny, Derrick and Quincy down in Horne have sent out a call for help from any Rider who can come. The messengers mentioned that they couldn't locate you and asked if we would watch for you as we traveled. It seems the Roracks have been massing and are now attacking human settlements in unprecedented numbers. The three normally staying there have only barely been able to stem the tide. They are saying that if they don't get help soon, the whole country will fall to the beast-men."

Simcha sat up and said, "Damn it, woman, I said that our business was private. If word of this gets out, it could cause a panic through the rest of the kingdoms."

"And just how do you think word will get out?" Delno asked rising from his seat. He was getting thoroughly tired of Simcha's nonsense.

Brock held up his hand and said, "Delno, please, let me handle this." Then he rounded on Simcha and said, "You've finally done it, Simcha; you've even pushed me beyond my limits. I've pronounced this man a fit Rider, and you're still treating him like either a child or an outsider. You not only insult him, you insult me, and you are breaking rules of hospitality that have served this civilization for thousands of years. Either you get yourself under control, or you can go on your way now."

"I won't fall for your baiting, Brock," Simcha responded. "You can't have been training this boy for more than three weeks, less most likely; how can you pronounce him trained? His dragon isn't even mature yet, despite her size."

Brock stared at Simcha for a long moment before answering, "This is no boy who was presented to a hatchling at twelve or thirteen years of age. Delno is a full-grown man of twenty-seven years, and he's a seasoned warrior. Further, he has led more men into battles in his four years of military service than you have in your seven hundred years as a Rider. He is the Rider of Geneva, carrier of her family's lineage. Named Rider by Geneva's mother, and you know damn well who her Rider was. What's more, Geneva's mother saw enough worth in him to present him with a Dragon Blade; even you don't carry an honor such as that." He paused to let that sink in.

Rita, who was sitting so close to Delno that they were almost touching, now looked at the saber hanging on the younger Rider's belt and whistled.

Brock continued, "I can pronounce him Rider after a fortnight because he has accomplished so much by himself that there was very little to teach him. He has acquired more wisdom in his twenty-seven years then some Riders acquire in a thousand. Geneva may not be old enough to breathe fire yet, but she can now outperform Leera in the air, and I'll bet that even you and Janna would be hard pressed to beat them in an aerial contest. Finally, I have as much right to pronounce a Rider fit as anyone else. So stop making an ass of yourself."

Simcha had just settled back and looked like he might start being reasonable until Rita said, "And, judging by your recent record, Simcha, I don't see where you feel you have the right to argue."

Simcha again turned nearly purple and rose to his feet. Brock stepped in between the two and glared at Rita so hard that Delno was afraid the man might strangle her on the spot. Instead, Brock said, "Rita, you are simply baiting Simcha on purpose, and that is completely counter productive. I have no choice but to make the same ultimatum to you; either behave yourself, or leave."

Rita closed her mouth and sat silently, Delno looked at her and realized that she was very cute when she was pouting. Then he shook his head to clear his thoughts and set his mind to the reason the four of them were gathered.

Everyone was again silent, and Simcha had returned to his seat. Delno got up and poured drinks for them all. The beverage was a fermented fruit punch that was popular in Orlean. It was made from mixed fruits that grew in the orchards around the city. There were also sandwiches, which he distributed.

After they had eaten a bit, and everyone had drunk a glass of the mildly alcoholic beverage, Brock said, "Now then, let's talk about the troubles in Horne."

Simcha shifted forward in his seat and said, "Well, from what we've been told, the Roracks have been attacking settlements, not just isolated farms and outposts this time. According to the reports, they've hit targets as big as towns, and down there the towns are pretty heavily fortified. They're also better organized than ever before. Usually their raiders are haphazard and hit targets of opportunity. Now they're coming on like properly drilled military with a definite purpose in mind. They seem intent on pushing the borders of their own territory further into Horne rather than looting and then going home. The other strange thing is that, in the past, they spoiled everything, more burning than looting, and they always burned crops. This time they're not being so destructive. They only burn houses and crops if they have to retreat, like they want to keep them if they can and only burn them to deprive the men from having them if they're losing ground."

Delno interjected, "From what I've heard of them, they're not that intelligent. Perhaps someone else is behind this and has found a way of controlling the Roracks."

Simcha snorted, "That would be a neat trick, especially since no one has been able to accomplish it in several thousand years," he retorted. "If you have nothing to add boy, keep silent."

Delno got to his feet and said, "Damn it, man, I fought bloody battles in a war for two long, hard years up north. I've seen my share of death and destruction. One thing I've learned is not to discount anything just because it hasn't been done in the past. Think what you're saying. What's the alternative here? Are you saying the Roracks have suddenly evolved into a more intelligent species?"

Simcha started to reply angrily but Brock cut him off, "Delno's got a point. If there isn't someone organizing them, then the alternative is that they are organizing themselves. I know that neither has happened in the past, but one must be happening now."

"I would much prefer," Delno responded, "that it is someone who has managed to organize them. At least then we might be able to find that individual and target him, and the whole thing would collapse. If they have somehow become smarter, then we will have to fight them until they can either see reason or they are all dead. The first scenario is much preferable."

"Perhaps," admitted Simcha, "It's just hard to imagine that after all this time someone has managed to organize these creatures into a cohesive fighting force. Also, it's a bit hard to believe that someone would want to do so."

"We can debate how this is happening until we're blue in the face," Rita put in, "but that doesn't help us decide about what to do."

"What to do!?" Delno said moving to the edge of his seat. "Innocent people are dying; what we do is go down there and help them."

"A man of action," Rita cooed, "careful, Handsome, I'm having trouble controlling myself."

Simcha let out a disgusted sigh, but held his tongue.

Brock looked at Delno very seriously and said, "You're not going anywhere near Horne right now."

"Not going anywhere near. . . ." he yelled jumping to his feet, "First you tell me about my responsibilities as a Rider, and now you tell me I have to sit by and let people die when I can help."

"Calm yourself, Delno," Brock replied. "Think this through. Simcha is right about one thing; Geneva isn't mature yet. If you go along, you'd slow us down on the trip. She's big enough to out-fly many adult dragons over a short span, but she hasn't the reserves for prolonged flight yet. She would have to stop frequently to eat. Then, once we get there, she can't fight effectively; she has no flame. The best you could do in the air would be to shoot arrows until your quiver was empty. Your magic is strong, but even that is just a drop in the bucket without her flame. Dragons are no good on the ground against large numbers of determined foes like Roracks; she'd be overwhelmed, and you'd both be killed. Without her, you're just another swordsman, even if you are a damn good one. The best thing you can do is stay right here and keep working with Geneva until she matures."

Delno sat back down and hung his head; he knew that Brock was right, but it didn't sit well with him.

"Besides," Brock said to him, "I have a task for you." At Delno's puzzled look he said, "It's more of a favor. I'll explain later."

Rita's lip curled in that pretty little pout again and she said, "Too bad, Handsome, I was looking forward to traveling with you." Then she turned to Brock, "We need to stay here long enough to let the dragons rest up from the flight up to find you, and while we get supplies and make ready to leave. I'd estimate that we need to stay about two," she glanced at Delno, "maybe three, days."

Delno was lost in thought and didn't notice: Brock and Simcha both rolled their eyes but kept silent.

# CHAPTER 35

"SO, SIMCHA," NAT said, "what brings you to our humble city, if I may be so bold as to ask?"

They had remained secluded until dinner time and had only had time to wash their hands and faces before sitting down to the meal. Nat and Pearce were brimming over with questions that they had not had the chance to ask earlier.

Simcha was not pleased with being asked his business, but he couldn't exactly deny that Nat had some right to know, since he had opened his house to the four Riders. "We have urgent business away to the southwest and have asked Brock to join us," he responded.

"Southwest," Nat replied thoughtfully, "Are the Roracks causing trouble again?"

Simcha became even more uncomfortable. He was used to people being somewhat afraid of Dragon Riders. Most people simply wouldn't have the audacity to question a Rider about his comings and goings.

Brock came to his rescue, "You are a fascinating man, Healer. You know more about the world than some Riders do, and your knowledge of dragon lore is so extensive one has to wonder if you have read some of the texts that are kept by the elves on the subject. Of course, one would usually have to be an elf, or a Rider, to get access to those."

Nat smiled and said, "Yes, I've led an interesting life." Then he changed the subject away from elves. "So, Rita, this is the first time I've had a chance to question a woman Rider. Tell me, are the expectations placed on you any different than those placed on the men?"

"That would depend on whose expectations we are talking about," she replied. "The other Riders don't treat me much differently than they do the men, but many non-riders have underestimated me because of my gender."

"Now I wouldn't have given it much thought if you hadn't mentioned it, Nat," Delno observed. "You see, in the north, women have nearly the same status in society as men. They can own property, run their own businesses, and even become politicians. The only thing they are kept from doing is serving in the military, though many of them still train in the martial arts, both with weapons and unarmed combat."

"Now that sounds like a very progressive society," Rita remarked.

"Well, when the Exiled Kings and their people moved north, they didn't take much with them," Delno said, "and the early years were quite harsh. At first, it was quite a struggle just to survive: a struggle that many lost. Those women who lost their husbands still had to live and raise their children. Those women who didn't lose their husbands often found themselves working right along side the men in their lives. The women proved that, except for sheer physical strength, they were just as capable as men in almost all jobs."

"But you find them lacking as warriors?" Rita asked.

"Well," he replied, "not me, personally, but it was decided early on that, unless the cities themselves were in danger, the women should not be burdened with military life. After all, they already carried the greater responsibility of raising the next generation. You see, in Corice, child rearing is not only considered a full time job, but a noble occupation." Then he hastily added, "By the time in our history that decision was made, women outnumbered men on the ruling council by more than two to one, and the king had died, leaving his only child, the queen, on the throne. She ratified the council's vote, and it has remained that way since. Young girls are required to train with weapons, especially bows. And they can, and do, serve as city guards or army reserve. The reserve positions don't pay, but since training is required twice a month, serving thus still counts toward the right to vote just like being in the army does for men. The reserves don't go to war, but if a force managed to fight its way to a city's walls through our men, they would then find themselves facing a large number of very good archers and swordswomen."

Rita smiled at him and proposed a toast to the women of Corice. Delno seconded the toast wholeheartedly.

"So the right to vote is earned through service in Corice?" Nat asked.

"Well," Delno replied, "a commoner can earn the right to vote by serving for at least eight years in the army, or some other job of that type such as city guard. Being promoted to officer earns you the right so long as you are honorably discharged even if you only serve four years: many noble-born men do that, since nobility start their military career as officers by right of birth. Since the crown always needs money, a person of any class can buy the right to vote if he has the gold. Many business people choose that option since they don't want to be soldiers, and they still want a say in how taxes are levied."

Nat was thoughtful for a moment before saying, "That's an interesting system. I knew you had kings, and I had just assumed that they ran the country through advisors like so many other kingdoms do."

As the physician said the word "assumed," Delno and Brock looked at each other and smiled.

The conversation continued to remain on safe ground for all concerned. Even Simcha actually stopped scowling and participated a little. Then, since the two new guests had been traveling, they all retired for the evening.

Delno went to his room and spent nearly an hour finishing a carving he had started a couple of nights before. Once the carving, a fox, was done, he decided that a bath would be nice. He got up and gathered clean clothing and a large bath sheet and went to the common bathing room that was at the end of the hall near the guest quarters on the second floor of the house.

The first thing he noticed when he entered the bathing room was that it was already occupied by Rita. The second thing he noticed was that she was naked from the waist up, and only wrapped in a towel from the waist down. While casual nudity wasn't common in Corice, it was more due to the ambient temperatures of the northern clime than modesty, so Delno wasn't shocked; however, since he was already attracted to Rita, he definitely took notice of her.

She simply smiled and said, "Oh, hello, Handsome."

Delno realized he was staring at her breasts and moved his gaze to her eyes, which looked to be full of mischief. "I'm sorry," he said, "I didn't know you were in here. I'll come back and use the room later."

"Wait," she said. As she stood, her towel fell to floor, "Don't go. I was just thinking it would be nice to have someone to wash my back."

Delno couldn't help but notice how beautiful she looked. Not overly busty, slim but nicely rounded. Even her Dragon Mark seemed to be in just the right place and perfectly proportioned. It was, of course, a red dragon, but this one was in flight. The dragon's head was just about an inch below her left breast, and the tail trailed about midway down her thigh, curling slightly to the outside of her leg. The Right wing wrapped slightly around her left side about halfway between her abdomen and her back, and the left wing spread across her abdomen until the tip just touched the edge of her belly button.

"Well," she said, "are you going to help me get the water pumped into the tub, or are you just going to stand their gawking like an adolescent boy who's just seen a naked woman for the first time?"

Without taking his eyes off of her he cocked his head to one side as if considering the options and asked, "How much time do I get to answer that question?"

One side of her mouth curled into a sardonic smile and she said, "Just man the pump, Handsome; I'll see if I can find us some soap and a loofa."

Delno moved to the tub and began pumping hot water, though he did angle himself so that he could watch her move around the room looking for the supplies. It wouldn't have taken her nearly as long to find them if she had asked him where to look, but, if she didn't mind putting on a show, he didn't mind watching. He said nothing and let her continue searching.

She found the soap and sponges and returned to the tub and pumped the cold water. When the tub was about three quarters full, she climbed in and sank down until her head was completely under water. Once her long hair was wet, she started applying soap to it. He helped her scrub her head and get the tangles out of her hair. Then he used the sponge to wash her back. When he finished with her back, he stood and removed his shirt.

She stood up in the tub and examined his dragon mark and asked how it had ended up so high on his body, so he quickly told her about the how the egg had hit him on the chest while being laid. She then spent several moments tracing the Mark with the tips if her fingers. The sensations were delightful.

Finally she looked into his eyes. Even standing in the raised tub, she was still a bit shorter than he was. He had to lean over to kiss her. At first, she simply wrapped her arms around him and up toward his shoulders and pulled his mouth to hers. They lingered like that for several moments before she reached to help him unfasten his trousers. Then he stepped into the tub.

Rita helped him bathe and they played together in the tub; wrestling gently, kissing, just holding each other. They stayed in the bath until the water cooled enough to be uncomfortable, then they dried each other and went to his room together.

He lit a candle and they sat down on the edge of the bed and he held her for several moments, just enjoying the feeling of being with her. Just as they lay back on the bed, Geneva broke into his thoughts.

"*Are you sure that what you are doing is wise?*" She sounded upset.

"*Are you jealous, Dear Heart?*"

"*Yes, but I'll get over that soon enough. That isn't why I asked you if you had thought this through.*"

"*Then what are you concerned about?*" Now he was truly puzzled.

"*The harsh Rider.*" She purposely didn't use Simcha's name. "*It was obvious this afternoon that he doesn't approve of her being with you. Knowing your talent for finding trouble when interacting with other humans, I thought you might want to be a bit more cautious.*"

Delno felt annoyed—first, because he didn't think that this was any of Simcha's business; and second, because he didn't think he needed a young dragon giving him advice on social interaction. It would have been better if this were just a case of simple jealousy.

"*I know what I'm doing, Geneva, and it will not cause any trouble I cannot handle, nor will it interfere in our relationship,*" he said. "*Now if you will excuse me, I'll see you tomorrow. Good night.*"

"*All right, Love,*" she responded. "*Good night.*"

The next morning he woke to the sensation of Rita's hair tickling his face. She was sleeping curled up nearly on top of him. Though he hated to do it, he gently woke her, and they dressed and walked into the hall.

Simcha was coming out of his room as the two of them emerged from Delno's quarters. He glared at them and then said, "So, I suppose you got lost in the night and just happened to walk into the wrong room?"

Rita looked him in the eye and said, "Think what you like, Simcha, but whom I spend my nights with is none of your business. Now, whether or not you have more to say, I'm not interested in hearing it. If you'll excuse me, I am going to find breakfast; I'm famished." She then stalked off without another word.

Brock, who had just stepped into the hallway, heard the exchange, and he looked as though he wished he'd stayed in bed just a few minutes longer. He gave Delno a questioning look, and Delno just shrugged his shoulders and turned to walk away. He hadn't taken a full step when Simcha snatched his shoulder and spun him around. Then the older Rider grabbed him with both hands by the material of his shirt and began shouting at him, "You think this is some kind of game, Pup?"

Delno had had all he was going to take of the man. He reached over Simcha's left arm with his right hand and grabbed the man's right hand while taking a step back with his left foot. This put the older man off balance and leaning forward on his right leg. Before the man could react, Delno pulled his hand over in a twisting motion while taking a large step forward with his own left foot and brought his opponent's hand and shoulder down to waist level, then raised the man's hand back up almost to chest level while placing his own left hand on Simcha's right shoulder. The result was that Simcha was now facing the other direction, bent over and off balance, looking at the floor, while Delno was upright in a stable stance. Delno then spun around and lowered himself to his knees, which caused Simcha to go down onto his belly. He then placed his open hand on the man's upper arm while bending the wrist back towards Simcha's own face almost to the breaking point.

Once he had Simcha pinned he said, "Simcha, I have accepted insult from you many times, but that is the last time you will ever touch me in anger. The next time you lay a hand on me I will break it off and keep it as a souvenir."

Delno then released his hold on the older Rider and quickly rose and walked away without looking back. He and Brock exchanged a look as he passed, but Brock said nothing, and Delno thought he noticed just the hint of a smile on his teacher's face.

When he reached the bottom of the stairs, Rita was waiting for him. She said, "What happened up there?"

"We had a quick discussion," he replied. "It's settled now."

"A discussion?" She responded, "It sounded like the two of you were coming through the floor. Where I come from, Handsome, we call that a fight."

"Well, where I come from the difference between a discussion and a fight is the amount of blood on the floor when it's over," he said. "Semantics aside, I handled it, and I don't think there will be any further discussion about the issue."

Rita smile mischievously, "Yes, I've noticed that you're very good at handling things." Then she asked, "Where do you find breakfast around here? I'm starving."

"Well, Missus Gentry runs Nat's kitchen, but she isn't in this early. Brock and I usually have breakfast with the officers at the garrison, and then do martial practice with the troops."

"Well, then," she said, taking his arm, "like I said before, Handsome, you lead, I'll follow."

As they walked to the garrison, Delno asked, "Rita, what is Simcha's problem? Why is he so dead set to keep you and me separated?" Then he stopped and looked her in the eye and asked, "You and he aren't. . . . ?"

"NO!" She cut that thought off quickly. "He and I never have been and never will be involved in that way." She took a deep breath and continued, "He was my teacher; at least, he was my first teacher. After four months of lessons with him, it took Brock nearly a year and half to train me properly. Simcha has never forgotten that I was his student, and I've never forgiven him for being my teacher. He was an ass then and another century of life hasn't mellowed him one bit."

They reached the garrison, so Delno let it drop and showed her to the mess hall. Winston and Robbie were waiting for them at the table. Apparently the officers had figured that all four Dragon Riders would join them, because they had six places set at one of the larger tables. Delno had just finished introducing Rita to the two officers when Brock and Simcha joined them. Brock introduced Simcha, and they sat down to eat. Simcha was stiff but polite, though he never once looked at either Rita or Delno.

After a light meal and a bit of pleasant conversation, they left the mess hall and joined the men gathered in the practice yard. Since practice was somewhat informal, Delno and Brock walked directly to the weapons rack and made their choices. Rita joined them, and chose a light long sword and small shield, similar to what Brock had chosen. Brock glared at Simcha until he, too, chose a practice weapon.

Rita whispered very quietly to Delno, "Besides not wanting to practice with the 'common folk,' he isn't very good. Brock's been trying to teach him for years, centuries I think, but he just isn't a swordsman." Then she added grudgingly, "Hell of an archer though, and he and Janna are good together in the air."

Then, leaving their live steel on the other rack that was provided for the purpose, they stepped out onto the pitch, and Sergeant Smith paired them up with opponents. Delno was paired with a man he had sparred with before, and while the man was good with a blade, as were all the soldiers in Winston's command, he wasn't that much of a challenge. Delno was happy for the opportunity to watch the other Dragon Riders.

Rita was right; Simcha was barely holding his own against the trooper he had been paired with.

The trooper Rita was sparring against made the mistake of underestimating her because she was a woman. He saw her gender, her small size, and her apparent youth, and thought he saw an easy victory about to happen. Rita, however, started dancing around her opponent with grace and beauty. Her opponent, a corporal Delno had faced before, was a very good swordsman, but no matter how many strikes he made, or how fast he struck, Rita's targ always seemed to be in the way of a score. Then he made the colossal mistake of letting her get slightly behind him: she struck faster than a snake and landed a blow to the man's lower back that would have killed him if she hadn't been using a blunted blade. Even through a layer of heavy-weight leather the blow nearly knocked him over. Sergeant Smith called them to halt. By this point, Delno was the only Rider left who hadn't dispatched his opponent, so he quickly finished the match.

The man who had been beaten by Rita was being ribbed by his comrades. He told them to just wait until their turn came up, and see if they could do better. Four more opponents stepped onto the pitch and the performances were repeated. By the end of the third set of matches, Simcha had been defeated once, and all of the men were now taking Rita very seriously.

After sparring with the men for over an hour, they stopped sword practice for a while, and Delno, as had become routine by now, took over and taught hand-to-hand. Rita especially enjoyed the Northern style of fighting that he taught since it relied on personal energy and body mechanics much more than physical strength.

After practicing hand-to-hand for nearly two hours, the Riders squared off against each other. Brock did the pairing, keeping Simcha and Delno separated. Delno first paired up with Rita. He found that she was indeed good, and, as he expected, she had learned her style under Brock's tutelage. Knowing that did give him some advantage, since he had spent time learning to defend and strike against her instructor. Even so, her speed and agility still made it a tough match. She had learned to actually use her small size as an advantage, getting inside of an opponents weapon when a larger person wouldn't have been able to do so.

The final blow wasn't with his sword. They had closed together and she had used a series of lightning fast strikes and cuts to get inside the arc of his main blade. He managed to lock up her blade with his and then pull her so close that she couldn't use her shield arm. Then he simply used a stabbing strike with his *main gauche*. By the point of the last strike they were so close together that his lips were almost pressed to her forehead. She looked up to congratulate him as he looked down and smiled, and they were almost kissing. They were both panting, and, in actuality, they were only taking a second to breathe before untangling themselves, however, from the outside of the embrace, it did look more like the moves they were making had nothing to do with sparring.

Brock had been taking it easy on Simcha, not wanting to humiliate the man in front of the troopers. Simcha wasn't applying his full attention to the match; he had been watching Rita and Delno as much as possible. As Delno made his final strike and they ended up face to face like that, Simcha growled and made a savage but clumsy attack, and Brock reacted instinctively; blocking the stroke and swinging his own blade up into the man's arm pit. Simcha grunted in pain, and Sergeant Smith called a halt.

Brock then paired Rita with Simcha and himself with Delno. For Delno, it was pretty much the same as before; circle-attack, circle-attack. He couldn't spare any attention while sparring with Brock, so he couldn't see what was happening with the other two Riders. He could barely divert enough attention to listen to them. Delno soon realized that Brock had intentionally kept them close enough to hear Rita and Simcha if he paid attention in the hope that he would be distracted trying to listen to the other match. "*Well, hate to disappoint you old man, but that isn't going to work,*" he thought. They continued circling and trying to find an opening in each other's defenses.

There was a thudding sound and a grunt of pain from Simcha followed by him saying, "Little whore."

Brock turned his attention to the other Riders for a second, and that was all the distraction Delno needed. He might have thought it an unfair advantage if he weren't so sure that his mentor had planned to defeat him the same way. He lunged and scored a hit that would have pierced the man's chest and stopped his heart if they'd been using live steel. Brock looked at him for a second, surprised he had been hit so easily, then lowered his blade and bowed. Delno returned the bow and the two men then turned to watch the other match.

They both realized right away that things were not right. Both combatants were completely absorbed in the match, but they were also both extremely angry. Two Dragons appeared overhead, circling the garrison; they were Janna and Fahwn.

Simcha began taunting Rita. "What's the matter, can't find your mark? Perhaps you'd do better if we were in a bath tub, or a bedroom."

Janna roared in anger, and Fahwn responded with her own throaty scream, but the antagonists on the ground ignored them both. Brock had that slightly distant look in his eye that told Delno he was in contact with Leera. He called out mentally to Geneva to be prepared to help Leera if this got out of hand.

"Perhaps," Rita taunted, "you should stick to beating your students into submission and leave the real fighting to those who do it well."

Janna and Fahwn tightened their circles above the practice yard. Leera and Geneva began circling also, but they were trying to stay between the other two dragons.

Simcha didn't say anything, but he made another one of those vicious but clumsy attacks, bringing his sword down on Rita's shield so hard that the shield split and the sound of her arm breaking was audible to all present. Rita screamed in pain and rage, and Fahwn did the same in the air. Fahwn tried to make a surge at Janna, but Leera stopped her by putting her own body in the way.

Simcha didn't relent. He wasn't a good swordsman, but he was a powerful man and weighed more than twice what Rita weighed. He swung again, this time aiming the blow at her head. She managed to get her sword up in time to block the strike. Leera kept Fahwn at bay, while Geneva stayed almost on top of Janna.

Sergeant Smith called out "HALT!" but Simcha paid no attention, moving again to strike at what he believed to be a nearly helpless opponent. Delno, realizing that Simcha was now only interested in punishing Rita, moved to intercede, but wasn't quite close enough. Fahwn was frantically trying to get around Leera. Leera may have been small for an adult dragon, but she made up for it in agility and experience.

Rita cradled her broken arm as best she could because of the pain, letting her guard drop considerably. Simcha moved more quickly than Delno would have thought the man was capable of doing. He raised his sword over his head in both hands and charged like a mad bull before

Delno could get a shield into place. Everyone watching was certain that, even with a blunted practice blade, the young woman would be horribly wounded if not killed. Just as Simcha smiled in triumph, but before he could swing the blade, Rita planted her left foot and kicked out with all her strength; her right foot hit Simcha in the groin so hard the man was nearly lifted off his feet.

This time it was Janna who screamed in rage and attacked Fahwn. Geneva didn't have Leera's agility or experience so she made up for it with sheer brute force: she rammed Janna so hard that the older dragon was nearly knocked out of the air. Delno winced at the force of the impact, which was so violent that it could be heard from the practice yard. He desperately wanted to communicate with Geneva and make sure she was all right, but he had to be content with the knowledge that she was still flying well and didn't appear to be in distress. Since he felt no pain from her, and he needed to help Brock deal with the situation on the ground, he kept quiet.

Simcha was doubled over in agony and Rita said, "*That* was for calling me a whore." Then she grabbed his right wrist and twisted it over her head and then down and around, flipping the man onto his back. Once he was down, she straddled his arm and used her legs to get enough leverage to pull his shoulder out of joint. "*That* was for breaking my arm." Then, before Brock or anyone else could stop her, she kicked him hard in the mouth. "And *that* was just because I've wanted to do it for over a hundred years, you self-righteous bastard."

The dragons were still in the air, but now that the actual combat was over they were more concerned about their riders than angry. Fahwn actually tried to land and get to Rita. Delno had to have Geneva make her back away so that he could help the woman. Janna was worried, but was now circling much higher with Leera keeping her from becoming a problem. It took several seconds, but Geneva was able to get Fahwn under control.

Brock bent down to check on Simcha while Delno took Rita under his arm and moved her away from the practice pitch. She smiled weakly and leaned into him for support. She had been putting a brave face on it, but her color was ashen and the sweat running off her face was now cold. She was going into shock. Delno laid her down on the ground and began examining her arm with his magical sense. He found that both bones had been shattered by the force of the blow. There were quite a few fragments and the shards had ruptured several veins and an artery. The arm was swelling nastily and already bruising. Her hand felt cold and was turning blue. He assessed how much energy he needed to draw and then spoke, "Heal." The fragments of bone knitted themselves together while the ruptured blood vessels closed and once again carried the blood to her hand and fingers.

The soldiers who were near watched wide-eyed as the bruising went from purple, to black, to brownish-green, to yellow, and then to normal while the swelling went away completely. Rita's color improved and she reached up with her right hand and touched his face and said, "Thank you, Handsome." Then she pulled him down to her and kissed him soundly. The men standing by cheered them.

Janna roared, apparently upset that Rita had been cared for while Simcha had not.

"Delno," Brock called from where he still knelt by Simcha, "I need you over here."

Delno got up and walked to Brock's side. His mentor looked at him and said, "I think at least one of his testicles is ruptured. I might be able to heal him, but I'd prefer that someone who is better at it try first."

Delno snorted, "Take him to Nat; he can remove them before they get septic."

"Delno, please," Brock replied, "I understand that you don't like the man, but I need you to do this."

Janna was nearly frantic with concern for her rider; it was all Geneva and Leera could do to keep her from trying to land in the garrison's court yard. Delno sighed and said, "All right, but I'm doing it for the sake of our friendship and the sake of his dragon. Make sure he understands that: I don't want this man thinking he owes me anything."

Brock nodded once in affirmation, and Delno knelt down and began working. One of the man's testicles had indeed been crushed completely. He called up the energy and healed the groin injuries. Simcha unfolded his body and sat up, still in pain but out of immediate danger. Brock then asked Delno to heal the dislocated shoulder and the split lip, but Delno refused.

"Those two injuries are not life-threatening. If he would like a healer to look at him, I'm sure that either Nat or Pearce would be willing to do so. As far as I'm concerned, those injuries can stay with him for a while. Hopefully, he will learn something from this," then he simply got up and walked back to Rita.

# CHAPTER 36

THE DRAGONS SETTLED down quickly now that their riders were no longer in danger. Geneva circled one last time. *"That was a near thing, Dear One,"* she said. *"You handled yourself well."*

*"I should have moved more quickly and gotten a shield between the two of them and this wouldn't have gone so far,"* he responded. *"That was quite a stunt you pulled up there: are you all right, Dear Heart?"*

*"Never underestimate the strength of a dragon, Love; I'm fine, though Janna may be sore for a few days."*

Delno could think of nothing to say to the last observation so he simply said, *"I love you Geneva. I'll be out to see you soon."*

The bronze dragon angled her flight to carry her just beyond the city gates and disappeared from view below the walls.

Rita smiled as he approached her. Her color was normal and she appeared to be completely healed. He stepped up very close to her and examined a small scratch on her forehead right at the hairline. He called up just a bit of energy and traced the scratch with his finger: it healed instantly as he did so. Rita lowered her eyes and leaned against him.

After they had embraced for a long moment, she stepped back and said, "Thank you. I was a bit worried for a time, and Fahwn was nearly frantic. I can heal injuries, but not as well as you."

"I hope that I never have the need to prove my skills on you again. I was nearly as worried as Fahwn. You should be more careful; I've only just found you; I don't want to lose you now."

"I don't think we've known each other long enough to be professing our undying love at this point," she said seriously.

"Who said anything about undying love?" he replied with a mischievous look in his eyes, "I just really like the way you look almost wrapped in a towel."

She smiled at him and winked. Then her look turned serious and she said, "Look, Delno, about the situation I've put you in the middle of here—"

He put two fingers gently to her lips to silence her and said, "Not now; later, when we don't have an audience."

She looked around and realized that most of the men of the garrison were still watching them. "People make jokes about how much women gossip," he said. "That's because they've never spent time around the men at an army post."

Brock had made a sling for Simcha and was leading him out of the garrison, probably to Nat's home so the healers could treat him. Delno knew that Brock was leery about treating deep injuries such as the dislocated shoulder because he had trouble using the magic to see deep into the body, but Delno also noticed that Simcha's lip was still bleeding a little. Apparently Brock had decided that healing normally might help Simcha's attitude some.

He and Rita walked to the water trough to wash. Delno had figured that she wasn't shy about nudity, but even he was surprised when she crossed her hands in front of herself and grabbed the hem of her tunic and began pulling it up over her head at the trough. Then he saw why: she was wearing a tight-fitting halter under the shirt that afforded her a little modesty. Still, Delno, and most of the troopers, couldn't help but notice that she was a lovely woman.

Winston joined them at the wash trough. Delno was sure that the man was itching to ask what the whole incident had been about, but to his credit, he kept his questions to himself. Delno did ask Winston if he could point Rita in the right direction to get some supplies for her upcoming journey. Winston assured them both that what she couldn't buy or have made at the garrison, his quartermaster could find for her at a reasonable price.

Winston stepped closer to Delno and said, "I don't want to be rude, especially to a Dragon Rider, but I would prefer that Simcha not practice here again." He was obviously a bit embarrassed to have to make such a request.

Delno replied, "Don't worry, my friend; even if he weren't recovering from injuries, I don't think Simcha would show his face around here after being humiliated in front of the men. However, if it will make you feel better, I will mention it to Brock discreetly; he seems to have some control over the man."

Winston thanked him, and then took his leave of them to get back to work.

Pearce, at Brock's request, had made arrangements for the garrison's orderlies to take all of the Riders' gear the day before. The boys had been both delighted and terrified at the prospect of actually removing the saddles from the dragons. The Riders had assured them that the dragons would be compliant, and that they only balked at having someone other than their own rider put the gear on them. None of the dragons had any problems with allowing someone other than her rider remove the saddles, since their riders were quite busy, and letting the orderlies remove the gear would make them more comfortable. The boys were absolutely delighted when, Fahwn, Leera, and Geneva readily talked with them. Janna had remained somewhat aloof, but even she had thanked the boys when they relieved her of her riding gear.

The saddles were in the leather works, so that was where Delno headed next. Much had happened since the previous afternoon, and he needed to fly out on Geneva and get his mind straight. He found Brandon and the boys there and saw that all the gear had been cleaned and polished. He thanked the boys and handed them each a coin before grabbing his saddle. Then he walked quickly to the city gates to meet Geneva.

The first thing he noticed was that Geneva and Leera had positioned themselves between Fahwn and Janna. The brown dragon was apparently quite angry with the red. He walked to them, and Janna glared at him, which elicited a snarl from Geneva.

"*Calm yourself, Dear Heart,*" he said. "*Her rider has been injured, and she is upset.*" Then he spoke directly to Janna, "Simcha will be all right. I healed his worst injury, and the others will heal on their own. He'll suffer no permanent damage."

"*He'd have suffered no injury at all if you had not taken up with the Female Rider,*" she replied.

"That is between me and Rita," Delno responded, refusing to be intimidated by the dragon, "He has no right to be upset." Then he added,

"If he has some feeling for her, he has a less then admirable way of showing it."

"Well, she certainly has no feeling for him other than contempt," Fahwn spat out. "The way he treated her when she was his student has assured that."

Janna retorted, "He treated her no differently than he's treated any of his other students, and they seem to have gotten through."

Geneva sighed, "Tell that to Brock's son."

"Enough," he exclaimed in exasperation. Then he added, "Janna, if you were injured earlier, I could try and heal you, if you'll let me."

Janna snorted and turned her back on all of them. Delno shrugged and began arranging the straps of the saddle in preparation for putting it on Geneva.

Fahwn looked at Delno and said, "Thank you for healing Rita; she was hurt badly, and I was quite worried."

He smiled at the red dragon. "I'm just glad I was able to do it. My magical training has been somewhat lacking."

"Well, you didn't seem lacking in any way today," Fahwn responded in a friendly tone. Then almost under her breath she added, "Or last night."

Delno wouldn't have thought it possible but both Geneva and Fahwn actually giggled.

"That's it," he said, throwing the saddle over Geneva's neck, and pretending to be angry, "there are too many persons who know the intimate details of my life around here. We're going as soon as I can get these straps fastened."

This time even Leera joined in, and the three dragons laughed outright. Delno rounded on her and said in a mock stern voice, "Oh, yes, you're supposed to be the responsible one, and here you are encouraging them." Then he said quietly to her, "If Brock wants me, I'll be at the hill were I first saw you breathe flame."

Leera smiled and winked at him in acknowledgement.

Within a few minutes, he and Geneva were airborne. The wind on his face was cooling, while the sound of it in his ears was calming. He said, *"It is good to be flying together without another accompanying us. So much has happened so fast it almost seems as if we haven't been alone together in years. Promise me something, Dear Heart?"*

*"Anything that is within my power, Love."*

"Then promise that as soon as we have gotten clear of some of our obligations we will go away from everyone else for a few days and just be together. I want to talk, and carve, and hunt, and sleep on the ground with my head pillowed on your foreleg, and not have to worry about anything for a while," he said.

"That sounds absolutely wonderful, Dear One," she replied, "but I have a feeling that now that our presence is common knowledge, we aren't likely to get the chance as often as we'd like."

"I'm afraid you're right" he responded unhappily.

Geneva flew straight to the hill and landed gently. Then, after he had removed the saddle, she laid down. She had chosen the spot carefully; there was a large patch of lichen next to her left foreleg that was so thick it was almost as comfortable as the bed he slept in at Nat's.

"Lie down and rest, Love, you're exhausted," she said.

He didn't argue. He simply lay down and rested his head on her foreleg and quickly became totally unaware of the world around him.

Delno looked around and saw mountains and the reddish sky. He realized he was in the Dream State. Geneva, as always, was beside him. As he watched a green dragon soaring, he said, "It's been so long that I had almost forgotten this place."

"Yes," she responded, "It's been nearly three weeks since I've brought you here."

"Are there many bonded dragons here today?" he asked.

"Not at the moment. Right now we are surrounded by wild females."

"I've been thinking," he said. "Why don't wild females find a human and bond?"

"Well, they could, if they chose to. The problem is that most humans are terrified of wild dragons. There are stories of wild dragons killing and eating humans. Those stories are false, of course, but they are believed by some. I suppose that if a wild dragon met a human and they talked and got to know one another, they might eventually bond. It would take much longer, though."

"Why would it take so much longer?" he asked.

"Well, a hatchling is eager to bond because it is scary to suddenly find yourself broken out of your shell and thrust into the wide world. She bonds because of the magical connection that runs between her and her partner, but the desire to do so is driven partly by fear of the unknown. She seeks a stable presence because she is, relatively speaking, small and helpless. Once a wild dragon has started hunting on her own, she has begun to understand that she can survive without help. It isn't until she has been alone for several years that she begins to long for companionship."

She paused while she organized her thoughts. "A very young female, once she has learned to hunt on her own, simply wouldn't be interested in having anyone or anything around until she is fully grown. Even then it takes some time for the loneliness to become a hardship. It is extremely rare to see a wild dragon under the age of four here in the Dream State. Once a dragon has begun to truly experience the loneliness, she might possibly be willing to bond if she could meet and get to know a human. However, dragon territories are very isolated; the chances of a wild female dragon actually meeting a human are extremely small."

"Why don't they leave their territory and go looking for someone then?"

"A dragon's instincts drive her to stay within her own territory unless she is looking for a receptive male to mate. Her instincts tell her that if she leaves her territory, not only does she risk angering another dragon who's territory she might invade, but she leaves her land, and thus her food supply, unprotected. So, they stay in their own territories and come here for what companionship they can get."

Delno started to ask more questions but Geneva stopped him and said, "Brock and Leera approach."

The Dream State faded to black and he woke up, but he kept his eyes closed, reluctant to move. He just wanted to spend some more time laying there. He could hear Leera land and Brock dismount.

Brock spoke to him from a few feet away, "Time to wake up, Delno."

"No," he said, "I'm sleeping, and you're just a bad dream. If I ignore you, you'll disappear, and I can stay asleep."

Brock laughed and said, "But if you ignore me, I'll go away and not explain what happened this morning at the garrison."

That did it; Delno sat up and looked at his mentor. Brock handed him a leather canteen and he took a drink of water. He handed the canteen back to Brock, who took it and sat down next to him.

They sat in silence for a few minutes before Brock finally said, "To understand what happened this morning, first you have to understand the culture that Rita was raised in. She comes from a chain of islands off shore from the southernmost part of Horne."

Delno started to open his mouth to speak, but Brock held up his hand, "Before you get excited, her people are safe from the Roracks, at least for now. The mountains that run along the western edge of this land branch in two at the northern borders of Horne. Each branch only runs about halfway down the country, one on the eastern side and one on the western side. Farther south, the land is almost flat and simply butts up against the sea on the west and part of the south. The Roracks live in the mountains. Besides, those monsters can't swim, they sink like a stone, so the sea in impassable to them."

He took a drink of water and then continued. "She comes from a large island off the coast. Their main source of trade is exotic fruit and pearls. In the culture of that island, it is quite acceptable for men and women to be a bit promiscuous. In fact, the two biggest taboos in their culture are child abuse and jealousy, in that order. Three or four times a year they have festivals and all work stops and they gather and have carnivals. During the day, the families do many different things together. Once the sun goes down though, the children are left with their eldest family members and the younger adults, whether single or married, go to houses that are only used during the festivals. There are no lights in the houses and it is almost pitch black inside. The adults who are in the houses freely participate in sex with as many partners as they wish during the night. It is so dark, and there are so many people from all over the island there, that they usually have no idea who they are with. That is why siblings take great pains to make sure that they go to different houses to avoid direct inbreeding."

Delno was thoughtful for a moment and then said, "My first reaction is to say that that is indeed a strange custom: it seems that it would create parents who have little concern for their children, since fathers can't be sure if a child is theirs."

"Ah, one might think that," the older Rider responded, "but it actually fosters quite the opposite reaction. Since you have no idea who has fathered which child, the men just take it that all children are theirs, and the children are treated extremely well. After all, would you allow your neighbor to mistreat the children in his house if those children might be yours?"

"When you look at it that way, it makes sense," Delno replied.

"It has worked for them for thousands of years," Brock said. "In fact, children are cared for and loved by nearly every member of society. Of course, there are drawbacks as well as advantages. Women who can't have children are objects of pity to the other islanders. Those women think less of themselves and feel unworthy of being loved."

"So, what does this have to do with Rita, over one hundred years removed from that society?" Delno asked.

"Well, she was selected by lottery to be presented at a hatching as part of a trade agreement. Like most of the children, she expected to be rejected and returned to her home. She was fourteen at the time. Obviously, she was accepted by Fahwn. Simcha was the Rider in residence in the area at the time, and he took her to train. It was hard on her from the start. To be taken from a society that treats children so well and turned over to a taciturn instructor who was incapable of showing her even the smallest amount of affection was a nasty shock, but the story gets much worse."

Brock paused while he took another drink from the canteen. Then he shifted his position and said, "I don't know if I should be the one to tell you this part of the story, but I'm pretty sure Rita won't, and you have the right to know since you are in the middle of it now."

He paused again, and Delno waited patiently for him to continue; it was a few moments before he drew a deep breath and went on with the tale. "Despite the culture shock, she did her best. The pair of them were growing together, but, as can sometimes happen, Fahwn matured at a phenomenal rate while it took more than five months for Rita to begin showing any real effects of the magic. Hell, usually a dragon isn't mature enough to fly with her partner before she is six months old, but Fahwn's growth and Rita's petite size convinced Simcha that the pair was ready for full training more than two months ahead of schedule. She worked hard at every task that Simcha set for her. She even snuck in extra practice when she could. She wanted so hard to please the man, to just get even a smile out of him. One day he put the pair through a series of maneuvers that taxed her skill, and the skill of her dragon, to the limit, perhaps a little beyond that limit. During a loop, her leg straps came undone, and she fell from about a thousand feet up. Fahwn raced after her to catch her. It was a near thing, but Fahwn caught her less than two hundred feet off the ground. Unfortunately, Fahwn was in a panic, and put a claw into the girl's lower belly when she caught her. When Fahwn set her on the ground, she was bleeding badly and in a lot of pain."

"Obviously, she survived," Delno observed.

"Barely," Brock responded. "Simcha isn't any better at healing than I am, but the man can be so damned stubborn about admitting his shortcomings. He managed to heal the external part of the wound just fine, didn't even leave a scar, but he didn't have the skill to look inside and see all of the damage like you do. The damnable part of it is he didn't bother to make sure she was seen by a healer, either. He just trusted that his skill was good enough because he is an experienced Rider."

Brock picked up a small stone and threw it angrily. "Damn it all, this all could have been avoided if he'd just taken the girl to a healer right away. Instead, he sent her to her bed that evening, and then started her right back into training the next day. The morning after that she collapsed, burning up with fever."

Delno got to his feet and began pacing. "How can he still be training Riders if he is so incompetent?" he asked. He was furious, not just at Simcha.

"Well," the older Rider replied, "he isn't trusted to train females any more, but you haven't heard the rest of the story, it gets worse."

Delno kicked at the lichen angrily before sitting back down.

Brock continued, "Fortunately for Rita, there was an elf healer in the area. Most elves don't travel outside their own lands, but this one had a habit of wandering. I brought him in to see her despite Simcha's objections. He examined the girl and said she had an infection. You see, until the bond between dragon and rider is strong enough, the rider doesn't share the dragon's immunity to disease. The Elf said that the wound had slightly punctured the girl's womb. He was amazed that she had lived long enough to develop the infection and not just bled to death. I remember he was quite upset. He admitted that the healing that was done at the time of the injury had saved her life, but he also said that the person should have realized his own limitations and had the girl seen by a real physician afterward."

Delno was shocked, "And after an incident like that he still has the audacity to act the way he does? The arrogance of the man continues to amaze me."

"Yes," Brock sighed, "Any way, the Elf was well schooled in the herb lore of his race and was able to save her life. I took over her training, and she learned to become a fine Rider. However, she was rendered sterile by the infection: she can never have children. Because of her society's customs, she feels inadequate and she has never forgiven Simcha for his part in that."

"Well," Delno replied, "I'd say she has a right to blame Simcha, since it is his fault."

Brock drew a deep breath and then said, "Yes, it is Simcha's fault, but three thousand years is a long time to let yourself be eaten up by hatred.

I don't want her to forgive and forget for Simcha's sake; I want her to move on for her own. That is why the other riders put the two of them together whenever possible. We hope that she will let this go and get on with her life, for her own good."

# CHAPTER 37

WHEN DELNO AND Brock returned to Orlean, Fahwn was still near the city gates, but Janna was nowhere to be seen. Once they had divested the dragons of the saddles and stowed the gear at the garrison, Brock went to find the quartermaster while Delno returned to the house. Rita was not immediately to be found, but he wasn't worried because he had asked Geneva to keep track of Fahwn in case they tried to leave without saying goodbye.

He found Nat in the sitting room. Pearce was busy with patients. He sat down in a chair across from the half-elf.

"Bit of a nasty time this morning," Nat said by way of greeting. "I had a hard time getting Simcha to hold still while I put his shoulder back into joint. I was going to stitch up his lip, but he simply stalked out without a word."

Delno said nothing, so the healer asked, "Rita really did that damage to him?"

"Yes," Delno replied, "she did. She did lot more than that, but I healed the worst of it with magic."

"I'd heard as much from one of the soldiers," Nat responded. "Care to tell me what happened?"

"They were sparring and let their emotions get the better of them. I think he instigated it, but she was more than happy to participate. It's an old disagreement." Delno didn't like keeping things from Nat, but this was really Rita's private business, and he had no right to tell the man more.

Nat sensed that Delno was uncomfortable with the subject, so he said, "We heard back from the College of Healers. They've sent Pearce his letter of confirmation. I just have a few final details to handle here concerning the house and my other business interests. We should be set to travel within the week."

"Nat," Delno slid forward in his seat and looked the man directly in the eye, "are you sure you're making the right choice? Coming with me, I mean."

"You're not going to change your mind about taking me along, are you?"

"I won't go back on my word to you," he responded, and the physician relaxed visibly. "I've come to realize, however, that I can not guarantee your safety, and I've grown quite fond of you, my friend. I don't want to lead you into danger."

Nat chuckled, "Is that what's bothering you? Well, you can relax; I can take care of myself."

"I've noticed lately that trouble and violence tend to be a part of my life regardless of how carefully I try to avoid it." Delno said.

"As you found out," Nat replied, "I could be run down by a horse stepping out of my own front yard. Delno, my father's people believe that you are born and you will die, but it's what you do with the time you have that makes you unique among your fellows. I will accompany you, my friend."

At that point, Rita came in the door. She greeted Nat warmly, then turned to Delno and said, "Hello, Handsome, I was hoping you'd be home."

Both men rose from their chairs, and Rita walked to Delno and held her hands up with her palms facing him, and her fingers splayed. He reached up and placed his palms against hers. They intertwined their fingers and smiled at each other. Nat suddenly remembered some work that needed to be done in the pharmacy and quickly excused himself.

Once they were alone, Rita said, "I really would like to explain about today."

"Rita," he said, "if you feel the need to talk to me, then I will listen, but you don't owe me any explanations."

"Then know this," She responded, "Years ago, when I was younger, something happened to me: something bad. I blame Simcha, and I've never forgiven him. I keep trying to stay away from him, but the other

Riders keep finding ways of throwing us together. I believe that they do this so that I will learn to forgive him."

She paused, unable to speak and tears began to fill her eyes. He pulled her to him, and she leaned against his chest and cried for a moment. He didn't interrupt her; he just held her and gave her support.

Brock came in quietly and looked at them. He raised an eyebrow in inquiry, and Delno just shook his head slightly to let Brock know that he hadn't told her what he knew. The older Rider nodded and slipped past the sitting room and went upstairs.

Rita stopped crying and said, "I might be able to put all of this behind me if the others weren't so dead set that I have to spend time with Simcha to get over it. It's like picking at a wound: if they'd just let me leave it alone for a while, it might heal."

Then she shook her head and continued, "The worst part of all is that since I've become a woman, I think that Simcha has decided that he has some feelings for me. I think that's why he reacted to us the way he did." She paused and then said as if she were spitting venom, "He's obviously jealous."

She took several deep breaths to get her emotions under control. "Now I've brought all of this to your doorstep: for that I am deeply sorry. I will be leaving sooner than expected, today most likely. I had hoped to travel with Brock, but I can't put you in this position."

Delno grabbed her by the shoulders and, holding her so that she was looking him in the eyes, he said, "You listen to me. You did not bring this on me. I have as much to do with what is going on as you do. We are both adults with all of our mental faculties. It's not like either of us has taken advantage of the other. As for Simcha, you are not responsible for his behavior, he is. As for you leaving early because of all of this, if you do, I'll follow you. I won't have you going off alone with the possibility that Simcha will go after you looking for revenge."

She stared at him for a moment then said, "I can handle Simcha. . . ."

"Like you did earlier?" he retorted.

Her eyes flashed angrily, but before she could start an argument, he spoke again. "Look, Rita, I have no idea how I feel about you. You excite me in ways that no other woman has ever done, and I don't mean just physically. I won't say something stupid like 'I love you', because I don't think a human being is capable of falling in love in such a short time, but I am thoroughly infatuated with you, and I won't allow you to take such an unnecessary risk. Wait until Brock leaves and travel with him.

Not only will that keep you safer, but it will give us another day or two together."

"You know, Handsome," she replied, "You make a pretty strong argument. I'll stick around long enough to think about it."

He bent down and kissed her passionately. She was surprised but not unresponsive. They lingered in the kiss for a long while. When they finally separated, he asked, "So how long do you think it will take for you to think about this?"

She shrugged, "No more than a day or two, I suppose."

He laughed and said, "How about I wash your back while you're thinking?"

"Are you trying to sway my decision?"

He replied, "Of course I am," as he wrapped his arm around her shoulder and led her toward the stairs.

"You are incorrigible," she said, as she willingly allowed herself to be led.

"You encourage me," he drawled, and they both laughed.

Later, as they were climbing out of the tub, they suddenly heard the sound of someone shouting. They moved to the door and opened it slightly to hear what was going on. The open door left them still unable to make out specific words, but it was obvious that the voice belonged to Simcha, and that he was angry. Delno decided to forgo drying himself and slipped his trousers on; Rita threw on his clean tunic, which came down nearly to her knees. Delno purposefully blocked her progress at the door with his arm and preceded her into the hall and down the stairs.

In the front entryway they found Pearce, Nat and Simcha. Pearce was trying to hush the Rider, but he would have none of it. He grabbed the physician by the front of his smock and said, "I don't give a damn about your patients. When a Dragon Rider asks you a question, you answer." He was punctuating every word with a shake of his hands and poor Pearce's head was whipping back and forth. "Now where is that alley cat of a woman and that young pup she's taken up with?"

"I'm right here, Simcha," Delno said quietly, "and if you don't let go of my friend, I'm going to break both of your arms."

Simcha glared at Delno and Rita. "You insignificant young pup. . . ." he began.

"I may be a young pup, and I have never claimed to have any real significance in this world, but you are still abusing someone I care about, and I am more than capable of carrying through on my threat." Saying this, Delno took a step toward Simcha just as Brock reached the bottom of the steps behind him and Rita.

"Simcha!" Brock said, "Have you lost your mind? You are guest in this man's home!"

"Guest?" Simcha sneered. He let go of Pearce and took a step toward the other riders. "Guest?" he repeated. "To be given shelter is the right of a Rider, and the duty of the lesser people of the land."

Even Brock was too appalled by the man's statement to try and rationalize Simcha's behavior this time. "Lesser people?" he asked. "Since when do Riders put themselves above those they are sworn to serve and protect?"

"Serve and protect?" Simcha responded. "They are no better than the herd beasts we feed to our dragons. We are superior to them in every way, and they are lucky we take the time to bother with them at all."

Brock shook his head sadly and said, "Simcha, I do believe that you have taken leave of your senses. Just where do you think the Dragon Riders would be without the people who support them?"

"No," he replied as he stepped even closer to the other Riders, "I have not taken leave of my senses, and I do believe that people such as these," he spoke with contempt and indicated Nat and Pearce, "are necessary. I also believe that the Dragon Riders could best serve these people by ruling them, not flying to their rescue every time they find themselves in trouble, and then begging for food and shelter that should be freely given."

Brock looked at Simcha as if seeing the man for the first time. "None of us has had to beg for food and shelter here. These good men have opened their home to us, fed us, and even given you medical treatment, and no one has even entertained the thought of recompense. Even at the garrison they give freely of their food, their time and even goods that are paid for out of their budget. And when offered payment, they refuse as if insulted, saying that no Rider who is a guest with them should have to pay for such things. I simply don't understand why you would rave on like you are doing."

"Oh, yes," he snarled, edging even closer, "they give freely to their *pet Rider*," he inclined his head toward Delno, "but then have him tell you to keep me out of the garrison. They don't even have the courage to come to me themselves."

Delno was suddenly aware of the man's proximity to them in the cramped entryway and put himself more in front of Rita while putting his hand on her stomach and gently pushing her back toward the stairs. He was quite pleased that she didn't resist and backed up at his silent request. He looked at Nat and motioned with his eyes for him and Pearce to withdraw from the entryway as well. Nat nodded and began moving surreptitiously toward the sitting room, pushing Pearce ahead of him.

"Can't you see it, Brock? Or have you been blinded by years of servitude to the masses?" He took another small step towards them; this placed him just at arm's length away from Delno.

"There is nothing wrong with my sight, Simcha," Brock replied. "I see things quite clearly, including the blade you have hidden in your sleeve and the fact that you are almost within range to use it." Simcha's eyes widened when Brock mentioned the blade he was hiding. "Not another step, Simcha," Brock warned.

Delno was grateful that Brock had pointed out the blade; he hadn't noticed it until then. Now that he knew to look, he could make out the outline of it in the man's sleeve and just see the point under the cuff. He motioned behind his back for Rita to continue retreating. He couldn't chance taking his eyes off of Simcha to check; he hoped she had complied.

Not only did he want her safe, he might need the room to move.

Geneva and Janna had taken to the sky the moment they sensed the trouble. They had then circled wearily waiting to see what happened. Geneva was hoping that Delno and Brock would resolve the issue without bloodshed.

"If you are determined to settle this with steel, Simcha," Delno said, "then let us do this like men and move to a more appropriate location."

Janna called out, "This time, Whelp, Simcha will kill that upstart rider of yours."

"He couldn't handle Rita in the practice yard," Geneva taunted the other dragon, "what makes you think the clumsy oaf is capable of defeating a real warrior?"

Simcha lowered his hand and said, "I like this location just fine." As the dagger slid down his arm and into his hand, he swung it up and forward while stepping into the attack. At the same time, he swung his left hand over and down towards Delno's face.

Simcha's attack would have been effective against a man who wasn't a seasoned fighter. Delno caught the older man's right hand with his left and left hand with his right, blocking both strikes. Simcha might be clumsy and underhanded, but he was certainly strong; it took all of Delno's strength to keep the blade out of his belly. It was only due to Simcha's weakness from having his shoulder dislocated earlier that Delno had been able to hold back the initial lunge. The sound of the dragons screaming in rage outside was muffled by the roof and walls but was still unmistakable.

As Simcha made his move inside the house, both dragons realized instantly that their riders were locked in mortal combat. Each knew that if she could kill, or at least severely wound the other, the distraction would give her partner an advantage.

Janna lunged without warning and caught Geneva with her talons on the right shoulder. She tried to get her teeth into her as well, but Geneva, screaming in pain and rage, swung her own head around, butting the older dragon hard right in the ear opening, forcing Janna away.

Leera and Fahwn were frantically trying to get in between the combatants.

Delno wanted to let his attacker push him against the wall, which would then make room at the foot of the narrow stairs for Brock to get into the game. Simcha, however, was not as out of control as he appeared: he was simply holding Delno where he stood, not allowing the younger Rider to make room for Brock to pass. Simcha then began pushing down on him, trying to drive him to the floor by brute force. A dragon screamed in pain, and Delno realized that it was Geneva!

Simcha sneered at him and said, "Janna has scored a hit, boy; looks like we'll have two for the price of one today."

Geneva had tumbled getting clear of her attacker and had to take time to right herself. Janna had used that time well; she was above and slightly ahead of the younger dragon now. She lowered her head and aimed a blast of fire at Geneva, hitting her. Her right side and wing were engulfed in the cone of flame. She screamed in agony and instinctively folded both wings and dropped like a stone. The maneuver saved her life. She was burned, but she was able to then extend her wings and arrest the fall. Her side and wing membrane were blistered, and moving was agony, but she could still fly.

Delno nearly panicked. He pushed with all of his strength, but was only able to hold his position not gain any advantage. There was another scream of pain from outside; again, it was Geneva.

"When I finish you, pup, I'm going to enjoy teaching your little slut a lesson." Simcha taunted.

Behind him Rita said, "There'll be a lesson taught here today, Simcha, as soon as I can get around at you."

Simcha raised just his eyes to glance at her and said, "You had your chance to join me, but laughed at my offer. Well, you're not laughing now, are you, little alley cat?" Then to Delno he said, "What's the matter, Pup, no fancy northern moves for this?"

The other two dragons had momentarily distracted Janna. Despite the almost crippling agony, Geneva pumped her wings as hard as she could to gain altitude. Janna got away from Leera and Fahwn by flaming at them; they avoided getting burned, and she singed her own wingtip in the process, but she had room to fly now. She chased Geneva as fast as she could fly. Geneva was ahead of and above Janna, but the older dragon wasn't worried because she knew that her opponent was too young to breathe fire. Janna stroked her wings as hard as she could but couldn't get any closer.

Geneva knew she couldn't keep this up; the pain was so bad she was afraid she might actually lose consciousness if she didn't end this soon. She knew that Janna was flying as fast as she could and was less than fifty yards behind and only about forty feet below her. She suddenly swept her wings in a back stroke; the force of doing that at such a high speed nearly ripped her wing pinions out of their sockets, and the pain it elicited from the burns made her dizzy. The effect, however, was like applying brakes on a wagon. Then, before Janna could react, Geneva folded her wings and literally dropped onto her antagonist's back. As they collided, Geneva sunk all four sets of talons into the older dragon's flesh. Her rear claws ripped horrible gashes in Janna's flanks, while her front claws sunk down into the flight muscles all the way to the bone.

Geneva then pushed off of Janna and opened her wings to catch herself. It was all Janna could do to glide in for a rough landing because of the severe damaged to her flight muscles. She hit the ground hard and just lay there on her belly. Geneva landed far enough away that she was out of range of the older dragon's breath. The other two dragons landed between them and watched them warily.

There was another scream from a dragon outside, but it was unclear which dragon it was, and Delno could not spare any of his attention to reach out to Geneva.

"Just this one move," Delno responded to Simcha's taunt.

He had used the slight distraction that Rita had provided to stabilize his footing. It wasn't much, but it was just enough to allow him to raise his knee sharply into Simcha's groin. The man grunted in pain, but didn't abate the force he was using to push his arms against Delno's hands. Delno was about to kick the man again when there was the sound of breaking pottery, and Simcha fell to the floor as shards of clay rained down around him.

Delno was surprised to see Pearce standing behind the man holding the base of what was left of a baked clay bust that had resided on a table in the sitting room.

"I guess he forgot about the 'lesser people' who were still behind him," Pearce said with a smile.

The older rider was only stunned, but Brock moved quickly and disarmed him and bound Simcha's hands with the man's own belt before he could recover and start fighting again.

Delno nodded to Pearce, and then turned to Brock and said, "Geneva!" before running from the house with Rita hot on his heels.

While he was concerned for Geneva, he couldn't help but think that they must look quite the pair, still wet from the tub, both bare footed, him wearing only trousers, and her wearing only his tunic. When he got to the city gates, all such thoughts fled his mind as he found Geneva wounded by Janna's fire.

Her whole right side, including her wing, was red and blistered, but fortunately there was no flesh burned away. She also had a gash about two feet long on her left front shoulder. He reached out to soothe her mind and was almost overwhelmed by the pain. He quickly began examining the wounds. This was more damage then he had tried to heal before, and he wasn't sure he was up to it.

Geneva caught his worried thoughts and said weakly, "*I know you can do this, Love; if doing it all at once is too much, do it in steps. The shoulder looks bad, but is not life threatening. If you work on the burns on my wing first, that will ease a great deal of the pain. Then it will be easier to help you work on the rest.*"

Rita stepped beside him and took his hand. He looked at her; she was crying. She reached up to his face and wiped the moisture from it, and he realized that he was crying, too.

Rita smiled and said, "No one is as good as you, Handsome, You can do this." She squeezed his hand a little tighter.

Delno examined Geneva's wing; the membrane was blistered with second degree burns, but the underlying structures were intact. He decided how much energy he needed to use and began trying to gather it; it was harder this time because the burn was so extensive. He was having trouble connecting to the energy of the world because he was so distracted by his concern for Geneva. He was frustrated because his concern was preventing him from doing the thing that would alleviate that concern.

A crowd had gathered nearby, including many of the men from the garrison who vocalized their encouragement to him. They began whispering, "Heal, heal, heal," over and over. Soon the whole crowd had taken it up as a chant. Even the two boys, Tom and Jim, from the garrison were there, tears streaming down their faces, chanting.

Delno realized that as the crowd chanted they released a tremendous amount of energy; he smiled and reached out toward the energy source and was rewarded with a surge in the power available to him. He concentrated on Geneva's wing, visualizing it as it should be, whole and healthy; he focused on it and said, "HEAL."

Everyone watched as the fluid in the blisters was reabsorbed and the redness and swelling went away. Within seconds, the burns were completely gone from her wing. Rita, through her own connection to the magic, realized what energy source he was using and began chanting, encouraging the crowd, who again joined in. They didn't understand how they were helping, but they realized they were and redoubled their efforts. Pearce and Nat had come to the front of the throng and were leading the chanting now.

Delno then concentrated on the rest of the burns. Healing her wing had broken through the concern and self doubt that had been blocking him. Within moments, there were no blisters or red areas left anywhere. He then moved on to the gash on her shoulder. He looked deep inside, identifying every bit of damage to all of the structures. Again, he drew on the energy that the chanting people were calling up and focused it on the wound. The blood vessels knitted themselves back together, the muscles were repaired, the skin closed, and the membrane that held the scales in place sealed itself. She even grew new scales where some had been completely ripped away.

A cheer went up from the crowd, and Geneva stood on her hind legs, raised her head skyward and roared with them. Rita literally jumped into his arms and wrapped her legs around his waist to get high enough to kiss him. He was congratulated and patted on the back so many times by the people who were there that he was almost afraid they might harm him in their enthusiasm.

Once the fervor had settled down, Brock called for his attention. He walked over to his mentor. Brock was holding Simcha by the shoulder. He had thrown a loose fitting rain poncho over the man so that it wasn't immediately apparent that he was still bound.

Brock pointed to Janna. The dragon was laying on the ground in obvious distress. As Delno walked closer, he could see the horrible gashes that Geneva had inflicted. He couldn't help but be impressed with what Geneva had done. It was a terrible sight, but Geneva, only weeks out of her shell, unable to produce her own flame, and wounded, had managed to severely wound and disable a dragon who had seven hundred years of experience on her.

As he began to examine the wounds, Simcha snarled, "Get away from her; this is your fault!"

Delno turned on him; he raised his hand to strike the man, then thought better of it. "No, you're wrong again. This is the direct result of your asinine behavior. You were never out of control as you would have had us believe. You know damned well that the dragons are linked to us, and you had to know that they would react the way they did. You were just too arrogant to consider the possibility that Geneva could harm her. You had hoped to not only kill me, but have Janna kill my Partner at the same time to save you from Geneva's vengeance once I was dead. You have brought this on Janna as a consequence of what you have done."

Brock nodded in agreement, and Delno continued. "I have the right, by law, to kill you now if I wish. But unlike you, I consider attacking and killing a helpless opponent to be murder." He paused for a moment to let Simcha consider his words before continuing. "No one here could rightfully blame me for walking away and leaving you to heal Janna yourself, even though your flimsy skills would most likely leave her a cripple unable to fly. However, I want you gone, and the only way that will happen is if you have a dragon to fly away on."

Without another word, he turned to Janna. The look in the dragon's eye was pure hatred. Leera reached out and put her front claws to Simcha's throat and said, "Know this, Janna; if you turn on him after he heals you, your Rider will be dead before he hits the ground." The fire in Janna's eyes died out; she laid her head back down in defeat.

The crowd had no interest in helping him heal the older dragon since the tale of Simcha's vicious attack on Rita earlier had become common knowledge. Delno didn't need their help this time, anyway. Since it wasn't Geneva, there was no panic from concern. He was able to pull the energy he needed from the world and heal the dragon.

By the time he was done, the troopers had retrieved Simcha's gear from the garrison, and Winston had even ordered that he be supplied with three days worth of food, and two canteens. As Brock untied the older rider's hands, Nat checked his shoulder to insure it had taken no further hurt during the struggle.

"You are free to go, Simcha," Brock said coldly. "Leave now and don't cause further trouble."

Simcha didn't say a word as he mounted Janna. Delno noticed that both Leera and Fahwn were standing as if they had a full load of flame ready just in case. Janna gathered herself up and pushed off the ground. They gained altitude quickly and were soon lost to sight. The three dragons declared the pair gone, and Fahwn and Leera, much to the delight of the people watching, turned and safely ridded themselves of the gas they had built up. Then the three Dragon Riders and two physicians walked back to Nat's house.

# CHAPTER 38

MISSUS GENTRY MET them at the door. "I'm going to tell you now, Mister Nathaniel, if incidents like that are going to become the norm around here, I'll be needing a raise in my pay." She surveyed the group, looking last and longest at Rita who was still wearing nothing but Delno's tunic.

Rita raised her eyebrows and said sweetly, "Is there something wrong with the way I'm dressed?"

Missus Gentry chuckled and said, "No, dear, if I still had the figure for it, I might dress that way, too. I was just looking at your hair thinking how pretty it would be with a nice comb. Come with me, I've just the thing."

Pearce and Nat looked at their housekeeper like they'd never met this woman before. Brock and Delno smiled as Rita, protesting weakly, was led away by the hand.

Missus Gentry called back over her shoulder, "There are refreshments in the sitting room, and a clean shirt laid out for the Rider. When the young lass and I are done, I'll bring some sandwiches in for dinner; that's all I'll have time to fix with all the excitement that's gone on." Then she and Rita went through the door to the kitchen.

Once drinks were poured, Nat said, "Normally, gentlemen, I wouldn't pry into other people's business so much, but since there was nearly bloodshed in my home, I believe that entitles me to a bit of an explanation.

"Well," Brock replied, "I actually am nearly as much in the dark as you are. Obviously, Simcha has come to believe that Dragon Riders should start governing the lands, but whether he is part of some scheme, or just delusional, I have no idea. Unfortunately, the one who might have gleaned some information from him in the last few days has been spirited away by your housekeeper." His last sentence elicited laughter from the other three men.

Since they would have to wait for Rita to flesh out the subject of Simcha's behavior, Pearce decided to indulge his own curiosity. "So, Delno, I noticed that you seemed to have a bit of trouble when you first started working on Geneva, what happened?"

Delno told them how he had been having trouble due to his anxiety until the crowd started raising energy chanting, and how he was able to use that energy for the healing.

Nat collected his thoughts for a moment and then said, "There are many cultures that use chanting to bond groups, to raise warriors to a fighting fervor, even to pray." He paused, thinking, then went on, "When you think about it, what is prayer but a kind of spell? Those who believe in such things pray to their gods for something, wording their prayers carefully to get what they want or need, and some religious groups use chanting specifically for prayer. So it does make sense that a large group of people chanting while focusing on a desired result will raise the energy to help achieve that goal."

At that moment, Rita and Missus Gentry came in carrying plates of sandwiches and assorted fruits. All conversation came to an abrupt halt, and all four men stared openly at Rita. Having spent some time with Rita, seeing her dressed for riding, or arms practice, or even dressed only in a towel, had not prepared them for the sight of her now. She was wearing a pair of tight dark pants and sandals. Over the pants she wore a bright red tunic that came almost as far down her legs as Delno's shirt had, but that was where the similarity ended. Where the man's shirt had been very loose fitting, this one hugged her upper body quite nicely, showing off her figure without being immodest. It was also open on the sides up to her waist so that when she moved the material would shift and reveal her tight pants and, consequently, her shapely hips. The tunic was edged with gold colored thread and the same thread was used for an embroidered dragon that was done so realistically it looked more like it was perched on the front of her right shoulder than embroidered there. The tail of the dragon wrapped, somewhat suggestively, around her right breast. Her hair was pulled back on the right side and held in place with a mother of pearl comb that was adorned with a cloisonné flower. All four men could only sit and stare.

When no one spoke up, Rita put her hands on her hips, stared back at them and asked, "What's wrong?" She was starting to get upset.

Missus Gentry laughed and said, "You may be more than twice my age in years, Child, but if you can't tell why these men have been struck dumb, then you are spending too much time around dragons and not enough time around the male members of your own species."

Delno was the first to break free of the spell. He rose and stepped to her and took her hands in his and said, "We were simply struck speechless by your beauty."

He led her to the chair next to his seat and poured her a drink. She and Missus Gentry exchanged looks and the housekeeper actually held her fist in front of her bosom with her thumb pointing upward before hustling out of the room. Rita sat demurely sipping the drink Delno had poured for her while Nat handed her a small plate, Brock offered her a sandwich, and Pearce held the platter of fruit for her to choose from. Once she had made her selections, they simply sat and ate in silence for a while.

Brock was the first to speak. "So, Rita, what exactly was Simcha talking about when he said that he had given you a chance to join him? What did you two talk about while you were traveling together?"

Rita collected her thoughts before speaking, "Well, mostly he talked about putting the past behind us and forgetting old differences, as if I would ever forgive him for what he did to me."

Pearce gave Nat a puzzled look, but the older physician had no more information about Rita's last comment than he did and could only shrug.

Rita continued, "He kept talking about how the world needed to change, that people needed to understand their proper place. He said that even the Dragon Riders didn't understand their proper position and that the world needed to be set right. Then, on our last stop, he told me that we were heading into a firestorm that would change everything, and that all Riders would have to make a choice." Then she looked directly at Brock and said, "He said that with my help we might be able to make you see the path ahead more clearly and that you might then join us."

Nat began, "I don't want to speak out of turn. . . ."

Delno quickly interrupted, "Nonsense, my friend, you are as much a part of this as anyone else in this room." At the puzzled looks from the other riders, he added, "I have never been much of a liar; I've always thought that if you always tell the truth you don't have to bother remembering who you told what lie to in the first place. That is why I decided early on, even when I felt secrecy was needed, that if I was directly confronted about Geneva I wouldn't lie. The only people in my life back in Larimar who don't know the real reason I left are my parents, and I only misled them because I know they are much happier not knowing the full truth, because I've never been able to successfully lie to them in my life."

He paused looking for the right words. "To me, most secrets are little better than lies. I'm not sure if it is fate or simple happenstance that has brought those of us in this room together, but I believe we are somehow caught up in a greater conspiracy. I don't know how I know this, but I'm sure of it. Therefore, it is time for us to stop keeping secrets from each other."

Brock and Rita exchanged glances but said nothing, waiting for Delno to continue.

"Nat will be traveling with me when I leave Orlean. He has helped me greatly with his knowledge of dragon lore, and in exchange for his help, I've agreed to allow him to accompany me and Geneva so that he can get a first hand opportunity to study dragons." At this point, he turned to the healer and said, "Show them, Nat."

While Rita and Brock watched, Nat removed a cord from his pocket and proceeded to tie his hair back in a ponytail, which revealed his pointed ears. "That explains how you know so much about the lore stored by the elves," Brock remarked. Rita just smiled and said, "There was an Elf who Brock introduced me to when I was very young. He was a healer and he traveled with his son who was half-human. I met them in Horne. I was injured very badly, and the father used his skills to save my life."

Nat smiled at her and responded, "I thought you looked familiar, too, but it's been such a long time, I wasn't sure. I actually saw very little of you then, and you have changed a little since we last met."

Since they were seated so close to one another in the sitting room, Rita was able to reach out and grasp Nat's hand without getting up. "You weren't much more than a boy then yourself, if I recall. I was quite taken with the both of you, once I was no longer delirious, that is."

The physician chuckled, "I had thought that perhaps you were taken with us *because* you were delirious."

They shared a laugh, and then Rita said, "Tell me, how is your father? I never got to thank him, and he was so very kind to me."

Nat smiled sadly and replied, "He was killed by Roracks in Horne over twenty years ago."

Rita shook her head, wanting to deny what the half-elf had said. She bit her lip lightly and than said, "Then I have one more reason to hate the beast-men. I am sorry for your loss, and the loss to the rest of the world. You're father was a great healer and a good man." A single tear trickled down her cheek.

"Well, I had suspected your identity for a while, but you have changed enough that I wasn't sure," Brock remarked, "and I figured that it was your business, and if you wanted to tell us you would. I had heard about your father, and I'm sorry. He was a friend, and I miss him."

Pearce had been silent up to this point, but he spoke up. "It would seem that all of you have a connection, except for Delno."

"Ah, but he is connected also," Brock observed. "His connection is through Geneva. Geneva's mother was the partner of one of the oldest and most respected Riders in the world, and we all knew him."

"Yes," Delno replied, "and I find it most interesting that we are being led to Horne and the Roracks, and it was the Roracks who killed Corolan in Horne. That's just too many coincidences for my liking."

Pearce said thoughtfully, "If all of this is some sort of plot to lure you to Horne, whether to kill you or to use you, can we be sure that the trouble in Horne is real?"

Delno slammed his fist on the heavily padded arm of the chair so hard that there was an audible crack from the wooden support underneath. "I wish I could accompany you to Horne!"

Brock held up his hand and said, "We've already discussed that: it's just not possible."

"I know," Delno replied, "that's what is so damned frustrating!" He slumped back hard in his chair before continuing. "I am the open tile in all of this. The one piece in the game that no one expected and no one can account for. That might give me some extra protection against any unknowns you may face when you get there." Then he sighed, "Unfortunately, you are right. Geneva would slow you down, and we saw today that, even though she is good, she is still at a disadvantage, since she is too young to breathe fire."

"Perhaps none of you should go," Pearce offered. "If you are being lured to Horne by lies, then shouldn't you stay away from there? If not, can't you at least wait until Geneva is older and can make the trip?"

Rita shook her head, "If Simcha had been the one who had brought the message, we could, but that isn't the case. I was in Trent, which is on the southern border of Ondar, east of Palamore, when the messenger arrived. He was not only calling for Dragon Riders, but for men and arms, as well. Simcha actually didn't arrive until after I had gotten the message and decided to go, although it was Simcha who suggested that we veer north and look for Brock. Since I would always prefer to not to travel alone with Simcha, I agreed to the detour."

"What was Simcha doing in Trent?" Brock asked. "He doesn't usually stray far from Llorn, which is north of Palamore."

"He said he was looking for Connor," she answered, "It seemed reasonable at the time."

Brock shook his head. "The last word we had on Connor was that he had been spotted well north of Trent. That's why I was up here looking for him, and Simcha knew that."

"Now that you say that, something else seems a bit strange," she responded, "He didn't appear at all surprised when he heard the news about the Roracks. In fact, he was somewhat annoyed that Trent was going to send troops and supplies. He tried to talk them out of doing so; said the Riders could handle the situation. He and the messenger from Horne got into a heated argument about it. At the time, I thought it was merely Simcha being his usual pompous self, but when I think about it now, it appears much more sinister."

"That would explain," Delno interjected, "why he was so adamant about not admitting that someone could be organizing the Roracks. He is in this up to his scheming neck."

Brock looked thoughtful for a moment; then said, "I don't want to believe it. Though he has always been a bit of an ass, Simcha was a good man, and a good Rider, once. However, all of the evidence we have thus far indicates that he is somehow mixed up in all of this. I don't think he is the mind behind it, though; he just isn't clever enough, but I'll wager he knows who is responsible."

"Well," Delno said, "Since the threat is real, you have no choice but to help the people of Horne. However, you must be doubly on your guard when you get there. The Roracks are a threat, but if one Rider can betray you, then others may as well."

"I don't like the idea of Riders mixed up with these creatures," Brock stated flatly, "nor do I understand it. These men are bonded to dragons, who are basically good, and dragons hate the Roracks; it's instinctive to them. How can they not only work with such creatures, but get their dragons to accept the alliance?"

"Well," Nat offered, "you three have gotten your dragons to go against their instincts without too much trouble."

The three Riders stared at him waiting for an explanation. He continued, "From everything I've read about them, dragons are solitary creatures. They won't tolerate another dragon within miles of them unless it's for mating. Yet, just outside the gates of this city are three dragons all nearly laying on top of each other contentedly."

"That's different," Rita said, "they are with us."

"It's not different," the physician replied. "They are not fighting with each other because the humans they are bonded to wish to congregate here: they simply have to get along, and there is no reason not to do so. Instincts aren't as strong as most people think. We train animals to do things that go against their instincts all the time. The horse is a perfect example. In the wild, they live in family groups led by a stallion. They instinctively run from danger and resist being caught or penned in. We not only keep them penned, we train them to work for us, or did you think a war horse instinctively runs into battle? In fact, the very act of allowing someone on his back goes against the deepest instincts of a horse, but he allows himself to be trained and ridden for social acceptance."

"But dragons aren't horses, they are much more intelligent," she responded.

"Exactly!" Nat exclaimed warming to his subject, "they are intelligent. The more intelligent a creature is, the easier it is for that creature to do something that goes against instinct. Humans suppress their instincts all the time for the sake of social acceptance. Dragons do the same. The idea of working with an instinctive enemy may be repugnant, but if that idea is introduced and reinforced over time, it will eventually become acceptable."

Everyone was thoughtful for a few moments, then Delno spoke, "Well, if one or more Riders are working with the Roracks, they haven't shown themselves yet, at least not by the time that messenger from Horne left for Trent, or he would have mentioned it. At this point, we don't even have any proof that Simcha has gone to join them. All we have is conjecture, although I do believe we are right."

"Yes," Brock responded, "conjecture and erratic behavior from Simcha aren't going to convince any other Riders that there is some conspiracy in the works. In the mean time, Rita and I have to travel into the jaws of the beast not knowing for sure who is friend and who is foe."

"At this point, the only people we can trust with any certainty are right here in this room," Delno observed. "You and Rita must be extremely careful from now on; just traveling to Horne is perilous. Simcha may be out there waiting for you. Be on your guard at all times."

"I wish you had killed him," Rita said coldly. "Then he would be out of this, and we would have one less enemy."

Nat shook his head and said, "We hadn't put this all together before now. If Delno had killed Simcha before, it would have been for simple vengeance, and he is too good a man to sink to such a level."

"Thank you, my friend," Delno responded. "However that may be, though, I feel that bird will come home to roost eventually." Then he turned to Brock and said, "When you two reach Horne, trust no one, and don't allow yourselves to be separated. Watch each other's backs. Make sure you scan anyone who is close enough to harm you." Then he turned to Nat and remarked, "That reminds me, though, the day that Brock arrived, you and Pearce were shielding your thoughts from being read. I know this because I tried to shield you and found you already protected. How is it that you both can do that?"

Nat smiled and said, "That is something that the elves teach all of their children. I decided early on that all of my apprentices should know the technique, also. All people can connect to the magic to some degree, even if they don't realize it, so anyone can learn to shield his thoughts even if he can't work any other magic."

Pearce spoke up, "I am still trying to put this all together. What still doesn't fall into place is Delno's connection. Obviously he is a Rider, and Geneva is the daughter of Corolan's dragon. But why was Corolan so important, and why his connection to Delno?"

"Well," Brock replied, "Corolan was the oldest Rider in the world. He was well respected by every other Rider. He would never have joined forces with the Roracks or even with any plot to overthrow the rightful ruler of any kingdom. If he got wind of some plot, he may have been killed to silence him, since he certainly wouldn't have willingly joined.

With Corolan standing against them, they would have a much tougher time swaying other Riders."

He stopped and slammed his fist down on his own thigh so hard that everyone else in the room winced. "Damn me for a fool; Corolan was also a holder of a Dragon Blade, and that blade was not recovered. It was because his blade and body weren't found that I held some small hope that he was still alive, even though Leera also felt her mother's passing. But his dragon confirmed his death, and Geneva has confirmed hers. Not finding the body is no great surprise: it pains me to think of it, but the Roracks usually eat their victims; the lucky ones are dead before the feasting starts. However, the Roracks wouldn't have use for a blade like that, and they would shun anything that was made by dragons or magic."

He turned to Delno and said, "You see, Corolan was originally from Palamore, but he had traveled to Horne as a caravan guard. The story of Corolan becoming a Rider begins during one of the many invasions the Roracks have made over the years. A group of Roracks attacked a village that his caravan was passing through, and the vanners were fighting along side the villagers. A dragon and Rider who were helping the ground troops had used all of their flame and were trying to retreat. For some reason, the dragon couldn't get out of arrow range fast enough, and she was pierced several times through one wing. It was enough to bring her down. Corolan saw her land, and, with his own quiver empty, he drew his sword and ran to their rescue. According to the tales, his attack was so fierce that a score of Roracks broke and ran. Then he stood his ground and covered the retreat of the dragon and Rider. As you might have guessed, that dragon was Geneva's grandmother, and she was pregnant. She laid her eggs that afternoon, and Corolan became bonded to Geneva's mother almost immediately after the egg was laid. The old female breathed a Dragon Blade onto the shell for Corolan's service to her."

"Well, I certainly didn't do anything that brave to earn my blade," Delno said.

Brock laughed out loud. Rita, thinking that he was mocking Delno demanded, "What is so funny?"

Brock held up both hands in mock surrender and said, "Peace, Woman, I'm not insulting the man. It's just that that was exactly what Corolan used to say about the deed that earned him his blade. He told me that he was so scared it was a wonder he didn't wet his trousers. Said that after almost three thousand years, he still hadn't figured out why he made what should have been a suicidal charge in the first place."

Rita relaxed and chuckled with everyone else. Brock continued, "Corolan was actually a small man, not too terribly much larger than Rita. He carried a blade that was similar to your saber, but a little lighter. I remember he went north twenty or so years ago to find a smith he had heard had the skill to remake the guard for the blade."

"That must have been Elom's father. When I took my blade to Elom, he told me that he had seen one like it. He said that a southern man had brought it in and called it a Dragon Blade. His father crafted a new guard for it, and the man was quite pleased. After the man retrieved the blade, Elom's father became so busy with work from the caravans that he had to expand his operation."

"That would explain why Geneva's mother went north," Brock said, "it was far away from everything she knew could be harmful to her eggs, and she was familiar with it. The rest was guided by fate, magic, and pure chance."

"Yes," Delno replied, "and, it is obvious that the two missing Dragon Blades are somehow linked to this. I think that it is more important than ever now that I go to Palamore and find out about that stolen Dragon Blade."

"Well, since we've decided that everything does fit together," Rita broke in, "now all we have to do is come up with a plan."

"What we need," Brock commented, "is a way to communicate with each other despite the distances involved. Unfortunately, the dragons need to be much closer to each other to use telepathy."

"I may have a solution," Delno said. Then he told them about the Dream State of the dragons. Both of the other Riders knew of it and had been taken there by their own dragons. "Good; I'll talk to Geneva and see if we can use that as a way of communicating. I don't think the other dragons will have a problem with it providing that we control our emotions and not disrupt their communion." They all agreed that was a good idea.

Nat said, "Since Orlean is as close as we are likely to get to a central location, with Pearce's approval we can use this place as a fall back house, and a safe place to leave messages for each other."

At Pearce's nod of approval, Delno said, "Good, I have the beginning of a plan."

# CHAPTER 39

LATER THAT NIGHT, lying in bed with Rita sleeping next to him, he thought about how much he had come to care for her in such a short time. He was completely enthralled by everything about her. It wasn't just the love making, though that was certainly pleasurable enough. It was everything; her beauty, though at first he had thought her just a bit on the plain side, her hair, her body, her mannerisms, the way her voice modulated with her emotion and enthusiasm on a subject, just everything. Even the way she slept was enchanting. She was laying half on top of him, as if she couldn't quite get close enough even with their skin pressed together like this. He knew he should sleep, he had a big day ahead of him tomorrow, but he was too content to lay there and feel Rita pressed against him, breathing peacefully.

"*You aren't contemplating a permanent situation here are you, Dear One?*" Geneva broke into his thoughts.

"*Contemplating it, but I know it isn't possible. Brock has told me that Dragon Riders tend not to marry, or form lasting bonds. Of course, that is because male Riders out number females by about six to one. Most male Riders have to take lovers who don't share their long life spans.*"

"*Well, I am mature enough to understand that you want the companionship of a female of your species, but I am still young enough to be quite jealous.*"

Delno nearly laughed out loud, and Rita wiggled even more tightly against him. "*Dear Heart, you have absolutely nothing to worry about. My love for you is on a different level and will not diminish because of my feelings for this woman.*"

"As I said, I understand intellectually, but emotionally, I am still very young."

"Look at it this way, Love; at least I have taken up with a woman who is a bonded Rider and will know better than to try and get between us."

"There is some truth to that. I am content with Fahwn's company, provided that she continues to give me space to hunt and eat by myself."

"There is something I need to ask you about, Love."

"I will answer what I can, Dear One."

Delno told her about his plan to use the Dream State to maintain communication with Brock and Rita once they separated. She said that she would do some research into the possibility and give him an answer in the morning. Then they said good night, and he settled down to sleep.

The next day they woke early and had breakfast at the garrison, but this morning he and Rita begged the pardon of the officers and men for not being able to practice with them. They needed to gather their gear and set out immediately on an errand that could take several days. Winston saw to it that they had enough supplies. The soldiers put so much in their packs they had to take nearly half of it out so as not to overburden the dragons. Then, with their packs and saddles ready, they met with Brock at the garrison gate.

"We should have everything we need for the journey," Delno told Brock. "Geneva has given me the image of Connor that Leera relayed to her, so I know who I am looking for. Rita has met the boy, so she will be a familiar face. I have concentrated on him some and have the direction, and I feel that he is close. We should be back soon."

"That's a pretty handy talent you have, my friend," the older Rider responded. "I'll have the arrangements made so that we can set out within two days of your return. That should give Fahwn enough rest and still get us to Horne in time to be of assistance."

"Speaking of assistance," Delno observed dryly, "Robbie wants to thank you for introducing him to Jennie. He says he never would have thought he could meet such a wonderful young woman in this backwater post. He seems quite taken with her."

"Yes, well, that," Brock said, a little flustered. "Look, Delno, it's a bad idea for a new Rider to get romantically involved, especially when his dragon is so young. I knew you were trying to put the girl off anyway, not wanting to take advantage of the situation, so I just pointed two young people at each other and let nature take its course." He smiled a bit sheepishly and added, "I thought I was doing you a favor."

Delno smiled and replied, "Well, no harm done, my friend, but in the future remember that I am a grown man and can handle my own love life."

Brock smiled back and, looking over Delno's shoulder he lowered his voice and said, "Speaking of which...."

"Are we all set?" Rita said as she walked up behind him.

"Ready when you are, Beautiful," he said.

"You lead, Handsome, I'll follow," she said, and they both laughed.

They grabbed their saddles and Tom and Jim grabbed up their packs. The boys were eager to help them since it afforded them another opportunity to get close to the dragons. It seemed that their familiarity with the Riders and their Partners had given the two lads, who were from two of the poorest families in the area, quite a bit of status with the other children in the community.

The dragons were waiting near the gates. There was a large gathering, mostly boys about the same ages as the two orderlies. Delno and Rita each saddled their own dragon but let the boys help with their packs. Delno looked at the other children and, on impulse, picked up Tim, the larger of the two boys, and put him up on Geneva's saddle. Rita shrugged and did the same, putting the other boy up on Fahwn. They let them sit there for a few moments while their friends got an eye full, then Rita smiled and said, "Ok, boys, you've impressed the crowd, but we have to go; time to climb down. The boys were nearly beside themselves as they got down. They thanked the Riders and sauntered past the other boys in the crowd.

As the boys walked away, Rita pulled him down and gave him a quick kiss. "That was a sweet thing you did for them, Handsome."

"It wasn't much," he replied, "but when you're that age, real bragging rights can be worth a lot."

Laughing, they mounted up. The dragons gathered themselves and launched into the sky. As always, Delno felt a surge of elation as they gained altitude. He also felt great pride in Geneva; she had grown visibly in just the last few days, and she was as large as Fahwn now. He could feel the powerful muscles beneath her hide working as she pumped her wings. Once they turned toward the direction his talent indicated, they spoke to each other.

"*You've grown again, Dear Heart; you're as big as Fahwn now, and she is full grown.*"

"Yes, the old female I have been speaking to in the Dream State believes that because our connection to each other and to the magic is so strong that I am maturing at a much accelerated rate. She thinks it might actually be possible that I will even be able to produce flame months ahead of what would be normal."

"We will see, Love, but I am not concerned. You have proven yourself fit to face whatever comes at us."

Geneva nearly glowed with pride at his words. Then she said, "Oh, yes, I have done some research concerning using the Dream State for communication. None of the wild dragons seemed too concerned, though one or two weren't sure they approved, and the old female said that as long as you keep your emotions under control so you don't cause a disturbance, there should be no problem."

"That is wonderful news, Geneva; we will take great pains not to abuse the privilege."

They flew for over three hours before Fahwn relayed that Rita wanted to take a break. Delno looked over at her and waved his assent. They angled their flight towards a clearing next to a large stream. When they landed, Rita quickly hopped down off of Fahwn and ran for the bushes next to the bank. Delno wasn't in dire need, but decided that he should take similar action.

Once they were both back in the clearing, and he had extended his senses as far as he was able, which was now about three miles, and determined that they had no unwanted company, they relaxed a bit. He used his talent to make sure they were still on course, and was rewarded with an increase in the feeling that they were going the right direction. His talent wasn't so precise that it gave him exact distance, but he was fairly sure that, at the speed they were traveling, even with having to stop early to allow Geneva to hunt, they would most likely find their quarry some time the next day.

They decided to have lunch before continuing. Rita pulled out a small bundle and said, "Brock sent this along; he said you would like it."

Delno opened the bundle: inside were a half a dozen biscuits and a small container of honey. Delno laughed out loud.

"Want to share the joke?" Rita asked.

Delno then told her all about Jennie. When he finished the tale, she smiled and said, "She sounds like a sweet girl; I hope she and Robbie get on well."

Some women he had known would have been jealous if told such a story. He was very pleased that Rita wasn't like that. He added that to the growing list of reasons he found her so enchanting.

She noticed that he was staring at her and asked with a smile, "What? Why are you looking at me like that?"

"Just thinking about how lovely you are," he responded.

He was lying on the soft grass. She reached out and took his hand and laid her head on his chest. They stayed that way for about a quarter of an hour before he said, "As much as I would love to stay here like this forever, if we don't get going, we will never complete our task."

She sighed and got up. They checked their saddles and within minutes they were airborne.

They flew for about three hours over forest before the sky turned almost black as a sudden storm came down out of the mountains. They landed in the first clearing they saw that was big enough to accommodate both dragons and were barely able to dismount and get their gear unstrapped before the first raindrops, nearly as big as small pebbles, began to pelt them. Geneva extended one wing slightly and Delno threw his gear under and grabbed Rita and pulled her, gear and all, under the improvised shelter. Fahwn moved along side Geneva and extended her own so that the overlapping wings kept them quite dry.

After nearly an hour, the rain showed no sign of letting up. Delno asked Geneva if she would be more comfortable if he and Rita set up the small tent they had brought so that she and Fahwn could fully retract their wings. Both dragons assured them that maintaining the shelter was no problem, so settled back and ate a cold supper of jerked beef and bread. Then they put out their bed rolls and tried to sleep. It wasn't as comfortable as a real bed, but they were warm and dry. Soon they were both sleeping.

Delno was aware that the light was red and that there was no rain. He sat up and realized he was in the Dream State. Rita was seated beside him and both dragons were there, though they didn't have their wings extended forming a shelter here. Rita was simply fascinated by the slowly swirling clouds in the sky and the circling dragons overhead.

Finally she looked directly at him and said, "This place is beautiful; I've only been here three times before now. I always seem to forget just how wonderful it is."

"Yes, I have been several times, but I am always amazed. You've only been here three times in over a century?" he asked.

"I think Fahwn doesn't bring me here because I tend to distract her, and she comes to talk with other dragons."

He noticed a dragon circling down as if to land, then he saw her color: it was Leera, and Brock was with her. Leera landed and Brock dismounted. "Well, it looks like this part of the plan will work," he observed as he joined them, "we can meet and communicate here."

"We just have to remember to keep our emotions under control," Delno replied, "The whole place is maintained by the females to relieve the stress from their loneliness. You can feel the undercurrent of emotion if you open yourself up to it. It's quite peaceful, actually. However, if we let our emotions get high and upset them, the dragons will eject us."

"We'll have to keep that in mind. The other problem is the time difference between our locations. Horne will be three hours behind you. By the time we settle into our beds, you will have been sleeping for at least that long."

"We'll have to work out a regular schedule of contact before we part company," Rita replied.

Geneva added, "I can monitor this place at other times and watch for Fahwn and Leera, and they can watch for me the same way."

"Well," Brock observed, "it isn't perfect, but it's certainly better than nothing, and it may be a lot more than our enemies have figured out." He looked at Delno and said, "It was a good idea. I wonder why no one has thought of it before."

They all shrugged, wondering the same thing. Then Delno said to Brock, "Hopefully, your part of the plan will work even better. What makes you so sure Connor will agree to stay in Orlean?"

"Well, he wasn't thrilled with Simcha's sword lessons and knows he is lacking in that respect. The soldiers at the garrison are some of the best I've met in a while, and not only have they agreed to teach him, they've offered payment if he will simply fly around a while each day and act like he's patrolling. It seems they've found that just the presence of a Rider in the air is enough to discourage all but the most hardened bandits."

The conversation died away and they all sat together for a while until Brock said, "Well, I'm going to get back. I still have a lot to do tomorrow, and this place makes me lazy; it's too pretty here." Saying that he rose and walked to Leera, though instead of mounting, the pair simply faded from view.

Delno and Rita stayed a while longer, content to just share the place with each other.

Delno woke first and was content to lay there with Geneva so close and Rita curled up on his left side with her head pillowed on his shoulder. He could think of no other place he would rather be than right there. It was Geneva who needed to move.

"I'm glad you are awake, Dear One; I need to go and hunt. I may have nearly reached my full size, and the need to eat almost constantly is tapering off quickly, but I didn't eat yesterday after a great deal of exertion, and this morning I must find food or we will not go far."

"No problem, Dear Heart; we need to wake up and start getting ready, also." Then he reached out with his magical senses and checked the area. When he had, he said, "I believe that you will find what you are looking for about a mile and half southeast of us."

"That's a neat trick," she said, "It eliminates the guess work and saves effort when looking for sustenance; I may just have to keep you around, Love." She stood on her hind legs, opened her wings, and launched herself skyward.

Rita grunted as if annoyed by Geneva's departure. "Time to get up, Beautiful," Delno told her.

"No, I'm not getting up. Leave me alone."

"We have to get ready to go. We have a task to accomplish," he responded.

"I'm not going. I'm staying right here, forever." She curled up in a ball and hid her head under the blanket.

"You can't stay right here," he said.

She mumbled something that sounded enough like "Why not?" that he answered.

"Because this river appears to be subject to annual floods and you are below the high water mark on the trees; by next spring, you will drown."

"Then wake me late next winter," she replied.

"All right," he said, "you can just lay there." Then, knowing she had not emptied her bladder, he added, "Just don't think about waterfalls."

She tried to squirm farther under the covers but it was no use. She sat up and glared at him. "I think I hate you," she said as she rose and stalked off into the bushes.

Smiling, he found a convenient place to do the same, then he went to the river to wash. While there, he caught several pan-sized fish with his hands like he had back in his first camp after leaving Larimar. This time, while it was still not what he would call 'child's play', it was easier than before.

As he caught the third fish, Rita, who had arrived in time to see him accomplish the feat, began clapping her hands. "Very good, Handsome! That's quite a trick; most people use a net." She was teasing him, but she was obviously impressed.

"I seem to have gained a lot from being bonded to Geneva. Apparently, because the magic flows so easily between us, we are both changing more and faster than is normal. At least, that's what that old female has been telling her."

Rita shrugged and bent to help him clean the fish at the side of the stream. When they finished, they took the gutted fish back and cooked them, spitted over an open fire.

As they were eating, Rita asked, "So which old female dragon has Geneva been talking to?"

"An older bonded dragon who has been teaching her a bit about dragons in the Dream State. Geneva said she is about two millennia old." He responded.

"Delno," she said, since she only used his given name when she was serious, he gave her his full attention. "There are very few old females around right now, at least among bonded dragons. Corolan and Geneva's mother were the oldest before they died. The oldest bonded dragon alive that I know of is Torin; her rider is Craig. They are about fourteen hundred years old, and they mostly keep to themselves, or study with the elves."

"That can't be," he replied. "Bonded dragons live about three thousand years or more; surely there are some left who are over fourteen hundred right now. Perhaps someone you don't know?"

She raised one eyebrow and scowled at him, "I may be young for a Rider, Sonny, but I'm still over a century old. I traveled extensively after I left Simcha's training: first with Brock, then on my own. There are only about a hundred Riders, and I have met them all. Corolan was the oldest. The next oldest was Warrick; his dragon was Hella, but they went north for her to mate about six years ago, and were never seen again."

"Only two elder dragons and Riders?"

"There were three others, but they've died," she answered.

"Died?" he asked. "How?"

She was thoughtful for a moment before answering. "One was killed in an accident while flying; his dragon was caught in a sudden crosswind and they crashed onto a rocky slope while flying a patrol in the mountains on the western edge of Horne. The second dragon was killed when a mating flight went badly and a wild female attacked her; her Rider couldn't bear the loss and took his own life. The third disappeared over the mountains of Horne, and it is assumed that the Roracks got them."

Delno was thoughtful for a few moments. "So, all of the oldest dragons dead, and the eldest and most respected Riders with them. Three of them definitely had a connection with Horne and possibly with the Roracks. And now I learn that there shouldn't be a two-thousand-year-old bonded dragon around for Geneva to talk to in the Dream State." He tossed what was left of his fish away for the small scavengers in the area to eat and rose up; his appetite was gone. "We need to finish our mission and get back to Orlean. I want to discuss this with our entire group present."

They arranged their equipment while waiting for Geneva to return from the hunt. She arrived and settled just as they finished everything they could do without her there. She had eaten lightly so that they could start traveling as soon as she was saddled and the packs were tied into place. Once they were airborne, Delno told Geneva about his conversation with Rita.

"I can certainly understand your concern, Dear One; it may well be that the old dragon is one of those who went missing, and that would mean that her Rider feels the need to hide. I will be much more careful about exchanging information from now on."

"I would prefer," he responded, "that you cease all contact with her until we can be sure of her intentions. I regret now that she knows of our plans to use the Dream State to communicate"

"Perhaps that would be best."

"Tell me, Love," he asked, "if we are using the Dream State to communicate with the others, can you and the other two dragons keep our conversation private?"

"Since many dragons hold private conversations each night, I don't think it will be a problem, but we may not be able to hide our presence, just our thoughts."

They flew on in silence until well past noon. Delno had Geneva set a pace that Fahwn, though fully mature, was having trouble keeping up with. Finally, three hours past noon, he called a brief halt. Once they had eaten lightly and rested for a short period, he was eager to push on again. He could feel they were close to their goal, and he wanted to get this task done so they could return to Orlean.

They flew until it was nearly dark and Fahwn was beginning to fall behind. Geneva was also tired, but she seemed to have reserves that the other dragon lacked. Geneva found a clearing, and the two dragons landed. As soon as the saddle was removed, she went off to hunt; she had used most of her reserves on the long flight. Even Fahwn went in search of food, though she went in a different direction from the younger dragon.

"You're pushing us very hard," Rita observed. "Fahwn isn't used to this kind of pace. Dragons are made for soaring, not hours of straight flight without rest. Neither dragon can keep this up two days in a row."

"They won't have to," he replied. "We're very close. We could have gotten there today if the light had held for another hour or so." Then he shrugged, "Just as well we stopped though; the dragons need to eat and rest before we get to our boy. He's apt to run, and I don't want to have to chase him if Geneva is worn out. She may be big and fast, but she isn't mature yet, so the pace is getting to her, too."

She noticed that he was distracted and said, "You're not completely here with me, are you?"

He looked at her and smiled, "I'm sorry, I'm still going over all that has happened in my head, trying to make sense of it."

"Any point in particular I can help you with?" She responded.

"There are so many points that focusing on one is difficult," he paused for a moment, then went on. "One thing that really has me wondering is why everyone seems to be deferring to me. I'm a novice Rider; Brock literally has centuries on me. Shouldn't he be the one to come up with the plans and make the decisions?"

"Let me tell you a bit about Brock, Handsome. He's a good instructor, and he's very wise—wise enough to know when he's outclassed." At Delno's puzzled look, she went on, "Brock was my teacher, and I traveled with him early on for almost two full years, and we've stayed in fairly close contact ever since. Even though he and I have never had an intimate relationship, you might say he is my first love." She paused and cocked her mouth to one side, thinking, and then corrected herself, "Ok, he's more like the big brother I've always looked up to, but anyway, I've learned a lot about the man over the years. He was Corolan's student, perhaps the best Corolan ever trained, but, whatever they were doing, he was always Corolan's lieutenant. Now that he's trained you, and you have shown that you're a natural leader, he is happy to let you lead."

"Natural leader, huh," he remarked, "The highest I ever got was lieutenant myself."

"Ah," she said, "but that was because of those ridiculous rules about being nobly born. All of the men at the garrison say that you would do much better in the south where men are promoted on merit. Every one of those men, even the Captain, would follow if you were leading. Face it, Handsome, you've found your niche. Now if you'll excuse me, I have private business over there," she pointed to the bushes.

Delno sat in silence while she walked away. When she returned, she said, "Why don't you relax and let it go for now, Handsome? You don't want to wear out your brain thinking."

He smiled at her and said, "All of my life, I've just wanted to be a normal person. I've never sought out fame or glory; in fact, I've tried to avoid it. I've never wanted to be a leader, but even as a child, the other boys would always seek my approval before we did anything. I realize now that I joined the army partly to get away from them. Later, in the army, I was quite content to work hard and fall into my bed exhausted at the end of the day, and let someone else lead, but they made me a corporal before the war even started; said I was a natural leader. Later, when the war was over, I got out. I said it was because I couldn't get promoted, but that wasn't all of it; I didn't want the responsibility of being in charge of other peoples' lives. When I got out as an officer, my friend tried to push me into politics. I was trying to find a way to escape that when I met Geneva's mother."

He paused for a long time, just sitting and staring into the darkness. She didn't know what to say to make him feel better, so she simply wrapped her arms around him and laid her head on his shoulder.

Finally, he said, "No matter how far or how fast I run from the responsibility of being a leader, Fate finds me and continues to force me to take charge. I guess it's time to stop running!" He paused and smiled at her, "Time to accept the tiles that I've been given and play the game to the best of my abilities."

She smiled back and said, "I can't think of anyone more able then you." She winked and then added, "You lead, Handsome, I'll follow."

# CHAPTER 40

ELNO WAS UP before the sun and had breakfast ready before he woke Rita. He was eager to get an early start. After they had eaten and stowed the gear in their packs, they woke the dragons. Once they were saddled up and mounted, Delno checked his direction again and made sure their target hadn't moved during the night. They rose above the trees just as the sun did also. The dragons held their position for several moments, just hovering, facing into the sunrise and watching as the light moved slowly outward from the horizon illuminating the tree tops. As the light touched a huge tree about three hundred yards directly in front of them, a flock of large birds took flight, the light gleaming off of their iridescent feathers. The Riders smiled to each other. The dragons roared their delight as they once again beat down hard on the air to gain altitude.

Once airborne, Delno and Geneva again set a swift pace flying toward the direction his talent pointed them. It was about an hour later when he asked Geneva to relay to Rita, through Fahwn, that they should be watchful since he felt they were very near. Rita signaled acknowledgement, and they both scanned the ground while the dragons opened their senses. They were soon rewarded for their efforts as Fahwn relayed that she had spotted their quarry and circled in for a landing with Geneva right behind her.

Geneva landed less then fifty feet away from a brownish gold dragon almost the color of honey. A dark-skinned young man with reddish hair was just climbing into her saddle. She was preparing to launch herself even as he tightened the straps around his thighs.

Delno yelled to him, "Connor, wait!"

Just before the dragon could launch, Fahwn buzzed her, looking like a large red blur. The gold dragon ducked quickly and lost her positioning for launch. Geneva jumped and pumped her wings resulting in a somewhat clumsy hop that covered about half the distance between them. Again Delno called out to the boy, but before he could tell the youngster that he was sent by Brock, flame erupted from the gold dragon's mouth. The flame came close enough to be uncomfortably hot, but passed harmlessly to Geneva's left. Geneva roared and tried to advance but wasn't quick enough.

The boy yelled, "I'm not going back!" and his dragon launched herself skyward.

At Delno's direction, Geneva was off the ground right behind them. She pumped hard, gaining altitude quickly. She was slightly larger than the gold dragon, and she was gaining fast. Again the gold dragon twisted her head and flamed. Geneva was below her to the right but she had flamed on the left side.

Geneva roared in anger and made ready to pounce. Delno said, "*Calm yourself, Dear Heart, we don't want to hurt them.*"

"*Tell that to them; she's the one trying to burn us to ashes.*"

"No, love," he replied, "*if she had actually wanted to burn us, we would have been dead on the ground; she's just trying to scare us off. Try to relay that we are friends and just want to talk.*"

Geneva calmed down, but she did get above the gold dragon while concentrating on trying to contact her. "*It's no good, Love; she has shut down and won't listen. They are determined not to let us catch them.*"

They were both flying at top speed and the gold dragon suddenly pulled up hard, pointing herself almost straight up. Geneva was ready for the maneuver and matched it. Unfortunately, they had forgotten about Fahwn. As they went into a stall and rolled to reverse their direction, Fahwn, whose speed had been unchecked since she hadn't joined them in the stall, passed between them at full speed. Geneva's talons came within inches of Fahwn's right wing, while Fahwn's talons came within inches of the boy's head.

"*A little less luck and they'd both be dead; maybe that will put some sense into that boy, and he'll land,*" Delno remarked.

"*I wouldn't count on it, Love,*" Geneva replied. "*Look!*"

Fahwn had turned quickly and caught up with the pair, but she came at them from underneath. Delno thought he could see Rita trying to shout at them, but doubted if they could hear. The gold dragon again turned to flame on the wrong side, however, Fahwn panicked and swerved almost directly into the blast.

"They nearly got crisped that time," Delno shouted both aloud and mentally. "This has got to end. Get above them, Love."

"*Delno.*" He knew Geneva was worried when she used his given name. "*What are you planning to do?*"

"*I plan to stop them before any of us get killed in this ridiculous game. Get me over them, Geneva.*"

She wasn't happy about it, but she quickly complied. Fortunately, both the boy and the dragon were so engrossed in watching Fahwn and Rita that they didn't notice Delno and Geneva approaching them. Delno unhooked his safety straps and Geneva hissed.

"*I know what you are doing; DON'T!*" Her words were nearly a scream inside his head.

"*Dear Heart, I need you to contact Fahwn; if this goes badly, one of you catch me.*"

Fahwn had gotten much closer to the gold dragon by then, and he could see Rita's face quite clearly. He smiled at her, and then, before Geneva could take it upon herself to slow down and thwart him, he launched himself out of the saddle and down toward the fleeing pair. Rita was so close that he actually hard her scream as he left his seat, but that was quickly drowned out by Geneva's roar.

The boy looked over his shoulder in the direction of the roar and stared wide-eyed as Delno plummeted towards him. Connor didn't have enough time to react. Delno got within reach and grabbed the boy's collar with his left hand and pulled himself forward. He quickly twisted his body so that he landed heavily on his butt on the hump behind the saddle. Then he slid down directly behind the youth and grabbed him in a bear hug, pinning the boy's arms to his sides.

Once he was sitting behind the lad, he said matter-of-factly in the boy's ear, "It's time to stop this nonsense and land before someone gets hurt, Son."

The boy hissed through clenched teeth, "I won't go back and work with Simcha, and you can't make me."

"Boy," he said, "do you honestly think I would go to all of this trouble just to take you back to that self-righteous ass? Your father needs your help and asked me to find you. Now get this dragon to land; I'm losing my patience."

As the gold dragon angled toward the clearing they had vacated only moments before, Delno relaxed his grip on the boy. When they landed, he and Connor hopped down. He was just about to introduce himself when Rita and Geneva both caught up with him. Rita was still wide-eyed and drained of color. She stood looking at him for a moment, than she swung her right hand around and hit him on the left shoulder with her fist.

"What the hell did you think you were doing up there?! You could have been killed. You're a great one to go on telling me and Brock to be careful and not take chances, and then you go and pull a damn fool stunt like that."

Delno looked at Geneva, who snorted loudly and said, "Don't look at me to help you out of this one; you're just lucky it was her who hit you and not me."

Fahwn had come up behind Rita; he looked at her and she said, "If you're looking here for support, you won't find it. You scared all of us nearly to death with that stunt."

Connor smiled at him and said, "For what it's worth, *I* was really impressed."

Delno turned back to Rita, her color was closer to normal now that she had vented her fear and anger. He moved closer and just stood looking at her until she finally relented. She shook her head and said, "Don't ever scare me like that again." Then she leaned into him and actually cried for several moments.

Rita, red-eyed, rounded on Connor, "What were you thinking? You know me, and you know how I feel about Simcha. Why didn't you stop when I told you to land?"

The boy merely shrugged his shoulders and looked at his feet.

"All right," Delno said softly, "it's over, let's get something to drink and discuss why we're here."

"So, my father wants me and Jenka to go to Orlean for martial arts study?" Connor asked when they had explained that they had come to take him back with them.

"Well, that's the cover we will use, and you *will* study; the men of the garrison there are very good, and they've agreed to teach you. However, you will also be housed with a friend we have there in case you are needed by either of us."

"Why do I have to be the one to stay in Orlean? You're the one with the immature dragon: how come you are going off adventuring and not staying and training at the garrison?"

"Partly because I will be looking for something. I may be able to use my talent to find it, like I found you."

"You said partly. That doesn't explain why I have to stay and spend my mornings on a practice pitch while you get to sleep in."

"Tell me, Connor, how many fights have you been in?" Before the boy could answer, Delno lowered his voice almost to a whisper; a dangerous whisper, "I'm not talking about boyhood scraps where your nursemaid pulls the two of you apart and makes you shake hands and say you're sorry. I mean real fights where the most likely outcome is that someone will end up lying face down in his own blood. Real fights, where there's three or four of them and you have to use every dirty trick in the book to make sure it's their entrails that are spilled out on the floor or the ground and not yours."

Connor looked Delno in the eyes and realized the man was serious, and backed away slightly.

"You see, boy," Delno continued, "I may be a new Rider, and Geneva may be young, but I was a blooded warrior before you were ever even a candidate for an egg."

Rita laid her hand on Connor's arm and said, "He's not just trying to scare you or impress you, Connor, he's telling you the truth. He was an officer in the army in Corice during two years of bloody fighting, and he's already proven himself against every man at the garrison, and against Simcha, though that last isn't really saying much."

Connor thought about it for a few moments and then said, "You said there was also work I could do there. What is it?"

Delno laughed a little and said, "Well, if nothing else got his attention, the chance to earn some coins did. The garrison is there to keep the bandits who operate in the area from preying on travelers. One thing they've found over the last couple of weeks is that just having dragons flying overhead makes most of the bandits look for greener pastures. What they want you to do is fly patrols. They don't even really care if you actually do patrol so long as it looks like you do. Of course, if you really want to earn your money, you can watch for any indications of bandit activity and report them to the garrison commander."

"All you have to do is practice your swordsmanship and fly maneuvers on Jenka and be ready should we need you," Rita said. "For that you get food, a nice soft bed, and some money in your pockets. Not a bad deal for you, if you ask me."

"All right, I'll do it," Connor replied.

'Good," Delno remarked, "We can get going right after lunch."

After what Connor had pulled earlier, Rita had been all for taking him back to Orlean bound and gagged, but Delno quickly relayed through their dragons, a good way to keep a conversation completely private even if it did require the inconvenience of relaying everything through two extra individuals, that he and Brock had agreed that it would be best if the boy went as a willing participant rather than a sulky, rebellious adolescent.

After lunch, they mounted up and headed back to Orlean. This time they took it a little easier; after the morning's exertions, they didn't want to push the dragons too hard. Delno called a halt after about four hours, and they landed and made camp for the night. The boy had his own tent, so sleeping arrangements weren't a problem, though Connor was a bit scandalized when he found out that Delno and Rita were sharing one tent rather than sleeping separately.

Delno was working on a carving and Connor was practicing the fingering of a tune on the flute that Delno had made so many weeks ago. Rita walked back to the fire and remarked, "There is something to be said for cooking over an open fire, watching the stars, and going to sleep listening to the crickets chirping, but I sure miss indoor plumbing."

Delno laughed and said, "Yes, all of the storytellers tell us tales of honor, glory and adventure, but they never mention having to dig latrines in the wilderness." Connor blushed.

As they sat, Rita began humming a tune. She had a very pretty voice, and soon Delno was more interested in the music than in his carving. Connor had laid the flute down when Rita had started humming, so he didn't interrupt her. Delno held his hand out and silently motioned to Connor for the instrument.

He put it to his lips and softly played along to her humming, picking up the tune easily. He played very softly so as not to disturb her, and harmonized with her. For a while she continued to hum, apparently unaware that she was even doing so.

Soon she began to sing softly:

> Hush now child, the night is warm,
> Daddy's safe, the sea is calm,
> Tomorrow's sun will bring no harm,
> Hush now chi-l-d and Sleeeeep.

Sleep my dar-lll-ing, Sleeeeep.
Now the moon is riding high,
The fish swim on the rising tide,
So Daddy's gone to-night,
Hush now chi-l-d and Sleeeeep.
Sleep my dar-lll-ing, Sleeeeep.

She stopped and looked around as he softly repeated the last bar on the flute. She hadn't even realized that she had been singing out loud. She blushed deeply.

"Please don't stop," Delno said, "You have a beautiful voice; it's pleasure to play along with you."

"Oh, it's just a silly tune from my childhood." She was near to tears.

Suddenly she got up and headed for the bushes. Connor scrunched up his face and looked at Delno and whispered "Again?" in an astonished voice.

Delno had the feeling that this time her departure had nothing to do with plumbing. He gave her a few moments to herself and then followed. She wasn't exactly hiding, but she had gone quite a ways into the darkness. Of course, with his magical ability to look for her life energy, he found her easily enough.

She was still crying softly when he reached her. He put his hand on her shoulder, and this time she pulled away angrily.

"We can't continue like this," she said.

He had a feeling he knew what she meant, but wanted her to talk it out, so he feigned ignorance. "Like what? We're taking the boy back, doing exactly what we have set out to do."

"Don't play the fool, Delno, I know you're not that thick." She stepped even farther away from him.

"Rita, we are just trying to take some happiness in each other's company while we can. Tomorrow may bring death to either one of us; aren't we entitled to something?"

"No," she answered. "We're Riders. I am preparing to go off to war, and you've got me singing lullabies from my childhood. I should keep my mind on the task at hand. What would Brock say?"

"The task at hand is to bring Connor back to his father. We are doing that. What ever else we do, providing that it doesn't interfere with our duties as Riders, is our business and no one else's, not even Brock's," he replied.

"You don't know anything about me, and you want some kind of commitment?" She demanded.

"I haven't asked for any more commitment than right now. I have no idea where our relationship might go, but I won't simply turn away from you because duty calls you elsewhere," he responded.

"I don't know for sure what you expect from a relationship, but I can guarantee that I can't give it to you," she nearly screamed at him.

"Rita, stop. Before you say anything else, I have to tell you. Brock told me your whole story; I know all of it."

She didn't need to say anything: the look of horror on her face was enough.

"I'm sorry. He didn't want to tell me, but he felt that I had some right to know since I had ended up in the middle between you and Simcha."

"Then you understand that I am not whole and can never be a real woman."

"Not a real woman? Rita, in the culture I come from, women are not defined by how many babies they can bear. To me, you are more real and whole than any woman I've ever met. You are exciting, alluring, and more importantly, you are all of that and intelligent enough to have a real conversation with. You're like having a lover and a best friend all wrapped up in one lovely, petite package. I would rather be with you than any woman I have ever met. I couldn't fantasize about a better woman than you."

She looked into his eyes, looking for any sign that he was simply saying what she wanted to hear and not speaking the truth. Then she said, "I don't know. I want to believe what you say, but. . . ."

"Rita, do you remember what I said about lying in Nat's sitting room?"

She nodded her head, but couldn't quite speak past the lump in her throat.

"Well, I meant everything I said," he continued, "I don't lie: that's plain fact. Not only do I find it abhorrent, I'm simply no good at it. I've never been able to lie successfully in my life, even as a child, my parents always caught me if I tried. I am just not made that way."

"Then you need to know this," she said. "When I awoke from the fever and found out that I would never have children, I wanted to die. My only hold on life was my connection to Fahwn. I don't want to have to deal with that again, ever. If you aren't absolutely sure of what you are saying, then, please walk away now."

As an answer, he wrapped his arms around her and pressed his lips to hers kissing her soundly. Then he picked her up and carried her all the way back to camp.

# CHAPTER 41

"WELL, WE'RE HOME, *Love*," Geneva said to him as she angled her flight towards the large field near the city gates. The remainder of the trip had been blissfully uneventful. Rita and Fahwn flew near, and Rita held up her fist to signal a job well done as they glided in for a landing.

Brock ran to meet them on the field. He, of course, had been alerted to their approach by Leera. When Connor dismounted, Brock picked him up off the ground in a bear hug. Then, still holding his son to him, he extended his arm and clasped hands with each of the two riders, thanking them for bringing his boy home.

Then Delno noticed a fifth dragon standing apart from the others. She was green and quite large. He turned to Brock and said, "I see we have another visitor."

Brock frowned, "Yes, more bad news, this time from Palamore, I'm afraid." Delno raised his eyebrow in inquiry, and Brock said, "Come, it's best we talk inside." He led the way back to the physician's house.

When they arrived, Missus Gentry met them at the door and said, "Mister Brock, sir, your friend hasn't returned yet, so I couldn't give him the message you left." She handed Brock a folded piece of paper. "Both of the healers are with patients. Make yourselves at home, and I'll fetch you some food and drink."

He smiled and said, "Thank you, Missus Gentry." He put the note in his pocket and said to Delno, "Our newest arrival needed his saddle repaired, and I sent him to Brandon. He had just left when Leera told me of your approach. Since he has only given me the barest bones of the message he carries, I think it best if we wait for him to return."

"Fine," Rita said, "I've been four days without a proper bath, and I itch all over. Since the news doesn't include enemies battering down our front door, I am going to take time to bathe." Then she smiled mischievously at Delno and said softly, "Want to wash my back, Handsome?"

Connor blushed and Brock rolled his eyes. Delno said, "We probably don't have much time before the other Rider. . . ." he gave Brock an inquiring look and Brock said, "Jason, his dragon is Gina." Delno continued, ". . . . before Jason returns." Then, at her pouting look, he quickly added, "So it's probably best if we share the bath so that Connor has time to bathe, also." She smiled and took his hand and led him up the narrow stairs.

"I'll be glad when you two get used to each other so that we can actually get some work done around here," Brock taunted good naturedly at their retreating backs.

Delno simply made a rude a gesture behind his back, and Brock laughed out loud. After being under Simcha's tutelage, Connor was shocked at the behavior of both grown men.

Since it was over an hour before Jason returned from the garrison, and the only activity that went on in the bathing room was bathing, they were all washed and dressed in clean clothing when they met in the sitting room. By this time, Nat and Pearce had joined them.

After introductions, Brock said, "So, Jason, you've given me enough information to pique my curiosity, but not enough to really understand what is going on. Why don't you start from the beginning and tell us all of it?"

Jason appeared to be no more than twenty and was tall and somewhat gangly, with long blond hair tied back in a ponytail. His face was long, and he had a rather large nose and blue eyes. He looked at the people around the room and was reluctant to speak. "I was told to give my message to you and the new Rider, if he was here."

"Told?" Brock asked, "Told by whom?" he demanded.

"The queen of Palamore herself, sir." The young man seemed a bit unsure of his position in this setting as he spoke.

"I know Lark, and she knows damn well that she has no right to give orders to Riders." Then he slid forward in his seat and said to Jason, "Look, lad, I know you've only been a rider for about ten years. . . ."

Jason straightened his back and said, "Twelve years, sir, Gina is mature enough that she's even mated this year." Then he added proudly, "She carries two eggs now."

Brock smiled at the young man, "That's good, that's very good; she comes from good stock." He turned to Delno and said, "Gina is Leera's daughter, Geneva's niece."

The boy sat up even straighter as Brock mentioned his dragon's lineage.

"However, lad, that doesn't change things here. Lark, the Queen of Palamore, has no right to order you about, and she can't expect you to keep us in the dark if she has asked you to deliver some kind of plea for help." Then he turned to Delno and said, "You see, the Dragon Riders have always shunned getting involved in local politics: even civil wars are normally ignored, provided that they are really sparked by internal conflict and not outside influences. We don't have a written code, but we have developed customs and guidelines over the years, and Riders are considered to be the equal of royalty."

"Well, sir, I just don't know anymore. There's been so much happening lately, it's hard to keep track. Seems that there won't be any independent forces left if things keep going the way they are now."

"All right then, you may as well give us your message. If you wait until we are alone, I will only tell the others gathered here. The only thing you will accomplish by waiting is wasting time."

Jason mulled it over for a moment, and then shrugged his shoulders before beginning, "Well, it seems it started when that Dragon Blade disappeared. The king was frantic, and the queen was furious. Apparently it has been a symbol of power in Palamore for over three centuries. With it gone, the queen, who is the one who actually rules the country, has been having trouble controlling the advisors. There are some of them who would like to see her gone because they know that without her they can control King Norton; he's not terribly bright, you see." The young man paused while he sipped his fruit punch.

"We already know all of this," Brock said. "How have things changed so much that Palamore suddenly requires our intervention?"

"Well," Jason replied, "Things were running as smoothly as they could under the circumstances. The queen didn't have quite enough authority to get rid of the advisors that she didn't like, but they couldn't consolidate their power enough to oppose her, either. The government was all locked up, kind of." He again paused to collect his thoughts. "Actually, the government was doing much better than before the blade went missing. Not much big was getting done, but the day to day stuff was still happening, so everyone but the politicians was pretty happy with the way of things. I'd dare say there are those in Palamore who would be just as happy if the blade was never recovered."

Jason took a break from his tale to eat a bit of sandwich and drink some more punch before continuing. "Well, like I said, everyone was gliding along, fat, dumb and happy, until that caravan returned from the north with tales of a new Rider who was on his way to Palamore. No one would have believed them, especially because they were saying that the new Rider's partner was the last daughter of Geneva, and they bore a new Dragon Blade. In Palamore everyone understands dragon lore more than in most other places since so many Riders have come from that royal line over the years."

"Great," Delno spoke out, "I asked those vanners to keep my presence quiet until I arrived. I thought they understood the need for discretion."

"Oh, it wasn't the vanners, sir," Jason may have been a Rider longer than Delno, but he recognized authority when he saw it. "It was that Northern man. Nice fellow, talks so fast you can't get word in edgewise, though. He said he was a friend of yours."

Delno slapped his forehead with his open palm, "Nassari!"

"Yes, sir," Jason replied with a smile, "that's his name."

Delno said, "I'll kill him. I'll strangle him, and then I'll feed his entrails to the vultures."

Jason was suddenly alarmed, "If he isn't a friend of yours, sir, we have big problems."

"Calm yourself, son, he's a friend," Delno responded. At the young Rider's perplexed look, he added, "I've know him since we were both children. We've been friends for over twenty years. He's a good man, but sometimes he lets his mouth run several minutes ahead of his brain."

"Yes, sir," Jason replied, "I've noticed that about him." Then he went on with his tale. "Well, anyway, within a couple of weeks, Nassari has the queen's ear and is sleeping on satin sheets at the palace. It looked like everything was going to return to normal at first. Of course, everyone assumed that, since Nassari is your friend, and he is the queen's newest advisor, you were coming to help the queen. That didn't sit too well with the other advisors."

Delno rolled his eyes and said, "Nassari may not actively seek to cause trouble, but he definitely has a habit of stirring the pot once it's brewing."

Jason nodded and went on, "Well, the advisors started talking about other Riders who were going to come in and take over everything. They seemed to think that there were Riders close by who want to oust the rightful rulers of Palamore."

"Who are these other Riders?" asked Brock.

"That's just it: no one has seen them yet, but the people believe they are there, somewhere in Llorn, and ready to fly in and take control. Things are pretty tense in Palamore right now, and the queen figures that you showing up would set people's minds to ease."

"Llorn," Brock said, "that certainly makes sense. First Simcha comes flying in from Llorn with his grandiose talk of the Riders being the rightful rulers of the world, and now we hear of Riders in Llorn poised to make a strike on the neighboring kingdom of Palamore. I wonder what has become of the rightful rulers of that little kingdom. Have they become puppets of these Riders, or are they even still alive?"

"Well, there's certainly one way to find out," Delno replied. He was about to add more when a knock on the door interrupted them.

They heard Missus Gentry open the door and greet the visitor. The man's voice coming from the entryway sounded familiar, but he was speaking too quietly to identify who he was. Nat got up to see who had arrived, and a moment later he came back in with Winston.

"Sorry to barge in, gentlemen," Winston began, then seeing Rita he added, "and lady, but something has come up which I believe may be of interest to you all."

Pearce stood and motioned the Captain to his seat while he went to the corner of the room and produced a folding chair from the small cubby there. Winston smiled and said "No, sir, I won't take your seat. I'll take the camp chair. I'm a soldier, so I'm used to it." Saying that, he took the chair from Pearce, unfolded it, and sat down. He then took a piece of paper out of his pocket, and looking at Delno, he said, "Officially, I shouldn't tell you about this, since it's an army communiqué, but I figure you're close enough to one of us, and I believe that it directly concerns you.

"The gist of the thing is this: Ondar has already sent men to Horne in response to a call for help against the beast-men. Now Palamore is calling for aid because they fear an impending invasion from Llorn. Palamore and Ondar have strong alliances; the royal families from each kingdom have intermarried often over the years. I've only got fifty soldiers at the garrison at any one time, and now I'm to leave twenty of them and my lieutenant behind and take the rest and march to Palamore where we'll meet up with men who have been pulled from other garrisons around the kingdom."

"Won't that leave the garrison terribly short handed?" Delno asked.

Winston said, "I'm worried about a couple of things. One is what's going to happen here with only twenty men to handle the patrols. This may look like a fair-sized town, but it's still just a poor agricultural community. The city maintains a guard, but they are more of a skeleton-crew than a real peacekeeping force. Orlean relies heavily on that garrison for protection."

Connor, who had remained silent and almost forgotten, spoke up. "I will be staying here and patrolling the countryside; that should free up your men some so the city proper isn't left unprotected." At Winston's look of uncertainty, he added, "I may be young, Captain, but I am a trained Rider, and while my own sword skills are somewhat lacking, as you have been told, my partner's flying skills *are* up to the task."

"Also," Delno added, "his youth won't be so apparent when he's several hundred feet off the ground. The bandits who are in the area will still be plenty impressed."

"Well then, that eases my mind considerably; I thank you," Winston replied to Connor. He then turned to Delno and said, "My other main concern is what is going on outside of Orlean. First, we are called to send help to fight the Roracks in the southwest, then we have to take men from our local garrisons to reinforce our neighbors to the east against those who are north of them. As a military man who is familiar with the concept of divide and conquer, I can't help but wonder if the two are related events designed to split our forces."

Everyone was silent for a moment until Nat said, "I've known you a long time, Winston; what else is bothering you?"

Winston took a moment trying to decide just how much to tell them, then shrugged his shoulders and said, "This communiqué," he held the note up for emphasis, "states that the original date my men and I were to leave was three days ago. The first message was sent so that it would get here in time to give us two days to prepare. This is a repeat message, since the original messenger disappeared and the message was never received."

After letting them think about it for a moment, he stated the obvious, "It's entirely possible that someone knows we are coming and will have an ambush ready for us along the way."

"I believe," Delno said, "that this news not only concerns us, it changes our situation considerably." He looked directly at Brock and the older rider nodded.

They quickly brought Winston up to date concerning what they had already found out. He was quite impressed by how much they had put together, and said, "So, it is obvious that Delno can't go off to Palamore alone on an immature dragon." He looked at Delno and added quickly, "No offense: Geneva is impressive, and she has already handled one mature dragon, but if she is alone and outnumbered. . . ."

Delno held up his hand and said, "No offense taken, my friend, you are absolutely right. Our plans to divide our own force must change to deal with the new threat."

Brock added, "I just wish we knew which threat is the greater. It could very well be that we are being drawn off to Palamore to keep us out of Horne for a reason. After all, no one has actually seen a hostile Rider in Palamore yet."

"Well," Rita interjected, "before I left Trent I had some news that four Riders were already planning to go to Horne. That is more than double the normal force of dragons there."

"I've heard of five that have definitely gone," Jason added, "With the three already there, that makes twelve: that's a lot of firepower by any standard."

"Provided all of them are on the same side," Nat replied.

Jason looked scandalized, "What's that supposed to mean?"

"It means," Brock answered, "that if Riders are working against us in Llorn, they may also be doing so in Horne. At this point, we must be careful; we can't be sure where someone's allegiance lies until we have met with them. It is possible that any of the Riders who have gone to Horne could be working against us." He didn't add that none of the original three Riders who stayed there could be considered trustworthy at this point, either.

Leera said to Brock, *"Delno wants to know, since we are wondering whom to trust, can we be sure of this young Rider? After all, he has been living in Palamore on the edge of Simcha's old territory."*

*"Relay this back to him: Jason is the rider of your daughter, and you would have told me if Gina was hiding anything. However, that does not mean absolute trust, but he has learned nothing here today that our enemies don't at least strongly suspect, if not outright know. For that matter, Connor, despite the fact that he is my son, was Simcha's student. We will remain watchful,*

*and if new information presents itself, we will be careful who listens when we talk of it."*

Delno smiled slightly and nodded as Geneva relayed Brock's words to him.

# CHAPTER 42

"**A**RE YOU SURE you wouldn't rather use a mule?" Sergeant Winslow, the Troop's chief teamster, asked Nat and Delno as they continued loading supplies on Nat's small wagon. He was looking at the pony Delno had originally purchased in Larimar. "That poor beast doesn't look big enough to keep up." The pony stood eleven hands tall.

"No, thank you, Sergeant. He may look too small for the job, but these northern mountain ponies are a tough breed. They've been bred for strength and endurance for thousands of years. I've a feeling that it won't be long before you start wishing that you had more like him instead of your mules." Delno replied.

Winston came over and said, "I do appreciate you Riders coming with us. I know that it will slow you down when you could just fly straight and not have to wait for us to catch up each day."

"Well," Delno responded, "Brock and I talked it over, and this serves two purposes: first, you're friends, and we can't just leave it to chance that you'll get through without a problem; second, if trouble comes, we may be able to take a prisoner or two and get some real information. Right now I'd trade half our supplies for some good intelligence reports."

Winston chuckled, "What commander wouldn't?" Then he observed, "At least we'll have the advantage of air surveillance."

"That's true: many was the time I could have used that in the war up north. If I'd had it, I'd have a lot more friends than I do now." He and

Winston exchanged knowing looks before he continued, "Of course, if our enemies have the same, it isn't as much of an advantage."

Winston shook his head and said, "I just don't understand how Riders could do such a thing. I've spent my whole life being taught that all Riders are like you and your group, and now I may have to fight those who aren't. It kind of sets my world at an odd angle, if you get my meaning."

"Well, Riders are men; they may live a long time, but they are men just the same." Delno replied.

Brock had overheard the conversation as he approached and added by way of greeting, "Which reminds me of something I want to make sure your men understand." The Captain gave him his full attention. "If your men have to fight dragons, they need to know that their arrows most likely won't penetrate the scales: they have to target the Rider; he is the weak part of the pair. Also, they really have to fight down their panic; facing a dragon is scary business. They need to be sure who they are shooting at, too; if I end up taking an arrow through the chest, I'd rather it be from an enemy's bow."

"Any advice about dealing with the dragon's fire?" Winston asked.

"Yes," Brock replied, "Don't. Find cover and stay out of the way when they breathe, and don't clump together in groups." Then he shook his head and added, "I wish I had more for you on that subject, but dragon fire is one thing that really sets the creatures apart from all others. It's a devastating weapon." Then he turned to the healer and asked, "Nat, do you have any of the glass that Delno gave you as a souvenir?"

The physician looked in his pack and pulled out several small pieces. Brock took one and handed it to Winston. "That," he said, "and the others like it, were made when Leera used her breath once on a sandy patch of ground."

Winston whistled as he examined the small dark fragment. Nat said, "Why don't you keep that one and show it to the men so they understand what they could be facing?" Delno noticed that the half-elf was now wearing two long, slender knives—each over a foot long—in a harness on his back; the curved blades were crossed with one handle showing above each shoulder. He was also carrying a bow case and quiver, and was leading Delno's horse; the horse's saddle was already stowed in the wagon.

"Expecting trouble?" Delno asked, pointing at the weapons.

"I hope not," the physician replied, "but it doesn't hurt to be prepared." He put the bow and arrows next to the seat and then walked to the rear and tied the horse to the wagon.

Sergeant Winslow came up and saluted Winston. "The men and equipment are ready to move out, Sir," he said.

"Very good, Sergeant," Winston replied, "We will leave as soon as the Riders are in the air.

Delno nodded to Brock, and they walked toward the dragons, who were waiting on the other side of the field so that they were far enough away that they didn't spook the animals when they took flight.

Brock went directly to Leera, and Jason was already mounted on Gina, but Delno signaled Rita to wait for a moment, and he walked over to her and hugged her tightly. "I just wanted to do that before we got airborne," he said with a smile.

She quickly kissed him and said, "You lead, Handsome," and smiled back.

They mounted, and Delno surveyed the scene before giving the signal to take off. Pearce and Connor waved as the four dragons gathered themselves and launched. Even from the other side of the field, the men could feel a difference in the air pressure as the four sets of giant wings simultaneously beat the air to gain altitude. The horses and mules all stirred. The only animal, including humans, that didn't seem to care was the little mountain pony hitched to Nat's wagon. As they had prearranged, the company of troopers waited until the Riders had flown far enough to start scouting the route ahead before Winston called for them to move out. The sun was just rising above the arm of the mountains that lay between Ondar and Palamore to the east.

Delno and Brock had talked privately with Connor after they had concluded the discussion with Winston and Jason and learned that Simcha hadn't discussed his plans with him, or tried to recruit him as he had with Rita. However, the boy was no fool; he had known that something was going on, because Simcha had regularly had meetings with other Riders with whom Connor was unfamiliar, always in the dead of night. On the few times that Connor had overheard any conversation at all, the other Riders had always seemed deferential to Simcha, except once. On that one occasion, Simcha had appeared intimidated, and he had been even more harsh during training afterward. It was because of the increasingly severe training regimen and what had precipitated it that Connor left. He had left partly to escape, but he was also looking for Brock, figuring that his father would want to know everything that had transpired in Llorn. After that conversation, it was decided that they would escort the troopers when they left two days later acting as scouts, and back them up should there be trouble along the way.

Their flight pattern wasn't complicated. Since the dragons could easily outrange the soldiers, they would basically fly in circles around them. The terrain was uneven and would soon give way to foothills that would become mountains a little farther on. There should be plenty of good updrafts for the dragons to use for gliding, so conserving their strength shouldn't be a problem since dragons could soar for hours without fatigue. Brock and Jason would stay fairly close together since they knew the territory, and because Brock, Rita, and Delno weren't one-hundred-percent certain that Jason could be trusted. While the first two Riders maintained that pattern Rita and Delno would fly back and forth across their scouting grid to catch anything the first two might miss. This would allow them to scan about three to four leagues ahead and several miles to either side while still being able to watch behind the company. Even if the enemy were expecting them, they most likely wouldn't expect four dragons, since the original plan was for Brock and Rita to go to Horne. Hopefully, if anyone ducked out of sight before Brock and Jason could spot them, then they might be back out in the open when either Rita or Delno flew over ten minutes later. Also, the dragons' ability to see heat as well as visible light would help to find anyone who might be hiding along the route.

Winston halted the company shortly after noon. They had traveled about six hours and had put around ten leagues between themselves and Orlean. They were making good time for a large group traveling with wagons, but they wouldn't be able to keep up such a pace. Even with only Nat's small wagon, and the two larger ones belonging to the soldiers, they were still heavily laden. Winston had pushed them hard this morning to make a good start, but they would have to move more slowly from now on to conserve the beasts of burden. The pony was, of course, holding up fine.

Brock and Jason landed first while Delno and Rita finished their part of the patrol. Once all four Riders were on the ground, they joined Winston, Nat, and Sergeants Smith and Winslow. Lunch consisted mainly of some packed sandwiches and the fresh fruit they had brought, since the fresh food had to be eaten first.

"You've made good headway this morning," Brock remarked.

"Yes," Winston replied, "but we can't maintain such a pace. It might seem slow to those on dragon-back, but about one league an hour is the best we'll be able to manage if we want to conserve the draft animals, and we won't be able to travel for more than about eight hours a day."

Brock looked at Delno who shrugged and said, "Be glad we don't have a larger force, or it would be even slower. Winston is getting all he can out of man and beast. If we were only traveling with light cavalry, we could do better, but the orders were to bring two wagonloads of other supplies, and that slows us down considerably."

The Riders and the soldiers studied their maps after they had eaten. Delno put his finger on the map and said, "There: if I were planning an ambush, that's the place, in that pass. It's narrow, and the canyon walls are high. Your men would have to shoot almost straight up to return arrow fire, which puts them at a disadvantage when aiming, and they run the danger of the arrows not hitting anything and coming back down at them."

"You're right, of course," Winston replied, "but there's no way to go around. It's the only pass within thirty leagues either way. If we don't go through there, we'll lose seven or eight days in travel time."

"And if you do go through there," Rita replied, "you'll be sitting ducks."

"Not if we can help it." Delno said. "I would take the extra time to go around if it weren't for the dragons. The problem for anyone trying to ambush the Troop at that point is that where the canyon narrows down, so does the ridge on either side. There's no room to get away from the dragons and there isn't much for cover. If we get ambushed at that point with four dragons in the air, it's they who will be sitting ducks."

"Four dragons?" Jason responded, "but Geneva still can't breathe fire yet."

"Leave that to me," Delno replied. "I'm hoping that no attack will come, but if it does, while you, Rita, and Brock are doing what must be done, I will use the diversion to try and take a prisoner or two."

Everyone nodded and Delno turned to Winston, "How many hours do you think you will travel this afternoon?"

"I had planned on calling a halt well before dark. If we are attacked in the open after we make camp, I want to be sure we've had enough time to prepare what fortifications we can before nightfall." Then he thought for a moment and said, "We'll push on for another four hours, get as much as we can out of the beasts today, and then go easier after that. I want to put as much distance behind as we are able while morale is still high."

The Riders all nodded and Winston ordered his sergeants to have the men ready to move in ten minutes.

As they were walking to their dragons, Jason stopped him. "I know that you and Brock don't completely trust me," he said. Delno started to respond but Jason held up his hand to stop him. "I understand the reason; in your place I'd feel the same. I just want you to know, for what its worth, that I am loyal to our cause. I won't let you down."

Delno put his hand on the young Rider's shoulder and shook it gently and said, "Thank you, Jason."

The rest of the afternoon was uneventful. They saw no one while in the air, and camp was set up by the time they all landed. They erected their own shelters, and then Delno and Nat took out their instruments and entertained everyone until full darkness fell before they retired to their tents. This time, though they both desperately wanted to be together, Rita and Delno slept in separate tents. Since, even on the ground, the Riders were still the weakest part of the pairs, Brock had insisted that all of the Riders sleep separately as a precaution against assassins; with only one to a tent they could only get one Rider at a time. Delno laid down on his bedroll and fell asleep almost immediately.

# CHAPTER 43

THE NEXT DAY passed uneventfully except that the mountains continued to loom larger with each passing hour. They were moving more slowly, as Winston had told them would happen. Still, they expected to be at the pass in two days time. At noon, the company called a halt.

While flying was exhilarating at first, it soon became monotonous flying in circles, and the Riders were glad to get back on the ground at meal times. They talked more about the possibility that they would face one or more dragons in the pass. Delno and, surprisingly, Sergeant Winslow, both felt sure that it wouldn't happen. Delno didn't feel the opposing Dragon Riders would show themselves for such a small unit as theirs, especially since it would pit them against other dragons. After getting a close hand look at the dragons accompanying them, Winslow was certain that the pass was just too narrow for the animals to maneuver.

"I'm curious about one thing," Rita said. "Why are we so certain that there will be an ambush in the first place?"

Winston drew a breath and responded, "They have the information. Since they know our position and troop strength, not ambushing us would be foolish unless they don't care if we get there or not."

"But, why would they care so much?" she asked. "Not to give insult, but you are only a small force."

Winston smiled and said, "You've sparred against these men and you've done well for yourselves, but you have the advantage of having magically enhanced strength and reflexes, not to mention a century or more of training. Most common soldiers with little or no training wouldn't. Each of the men in my command was hand-picked for his job. The first qualification was fighting ability, and then I chose them for their secondary skills. Sergeant Winslow is not only a fine animal handler, but he can put an arrow or javelin through a moving target at over fifty feet while mounted and riding at a full gallop. Sergeant Smith is not only a weapons master, but a superb mountaineer and a technical genius when it comes to finding a way through enemy fortifications. Each and every man in my company is an elite soldier. Together, they are a fighting force to be reckoned with."

Rita nodded her head and said, "Well, I guess that explains why they would be so anxious to stop you."

By an hour after noon, they were back on the road. They traveled for another five hours before the animals showed any sign of fatigue and they made camp. Delno remarked to Winston, "Another day and half should see us at the pass."

"Aye," he replied, "and then we should see some action. How do you want to handle this?"

"I have a couple of thoughts, but I'd like to sleep on it tonight and discuss it tomorrow."

Delno was carrying three books; he sat down and opened the largest one and started reading. Rita walked up and stood over him, "Hi, Handsome, what are you doing?"

"Reading."

"And here I thought you just looked at the pictures," she retorted. "I meant, what are you reading about?"

He looked at her and smiled. Then taking her hand in his he said, "It's a book on anatomy and physiology that Nat loaned me. I am studying so that I can learn to be a better healer."

"I thought you were pretty good already." Then looking down and noticing the other two books on plants and herbs sitting beside him, she added, "Planning on taking up the whole profession?"

"I've always believed that a man should broaden his horizons; specialization is for honey bees."

They talked for a while and then, reluctantly, went to their own tents to sleep. Almost everyone except the soldiers assigned to guard duty went to bed as soon as it was fully dark.

"DELNO, WAKE UP!" Geneva's contact was a shout in his mind. He came awake and grabbed his sword.

"*What is it, Dear Heart?*"

"*There are several creatures sneaking through the camp; two of them appear to be moving in your direction. They are trying to be stealthy, and they are also carrying weapons.*"

"*Alert the other Riders, and be ready,*" he said.

"*The other Riders are already moving; you were sleeping heavily,*" she admonished.

He quickly crawled out of his small tent and scanned the area. He noticed that his night vision had improved considerably. While it wasn't like he had a full moon to give him light, it was certainly better then normal.

He reached out to Geneva. "*Where are they, Love?*"

"*Twenty yards due north of you and moving fast; I'm coming.*"

He was about to tell her to stay back, but he didn't have time. She had been right about the speed of the creatures; they were almost on top of him. They moved with a curious loping gate, swinging their arms as they ran; almost like they were trying to run on all fours even though they were upright on their legs. That was all the time he had for curiosity; the closest one, though still nearly three yards distant, leaped at him.

Time seemed to have slowed down, and he was able to focus on details. The creature, for it had a face similar to but unlike a human, struck out with a strange-looking blade. The blade was about two feet long and curved, and it widened at the business end. The point was somewhat blunted and there was a gut-hook just behind it: it was also nearly three quarters of an inch thick at its widest point.

The jump covered the distance so fast that Delno barely had time to get his blades up to block. Though time appeared to be slowed, it didn't help him react faster; his blades were moving to block just as slowly as the other was moving to strike. He realized that the effect was an illusion caused by the surge in adrenalin and widened his focus to compensate. As his field of focus broadened, time resumed something approaching normal. The creature made a vicious cut, but Delno got his saber up and used his *main gauche* to stab into its lower belly. Then he used the momentum of the creature's weight to throw it up and over himself while pulling his large dagger out in a slashing motion. The attacker, more like a huge bipedal cat than a man, fell heavily on its side.

He didn't have time to ponder who or what it was; he just barely ducked in time to avoid being decapitated by the second beast. This time, the man-thing pulled the blade up and back trying to catch him in the neck with the gut-hook. He blocked that with his sword and the two blades locked briefly. The cat-man pulled hard and nearly disarmed him, but the dragon blade seemed alive in his hand, and he was able to hold on and twist it free. As he did so, his attacker aimed a vicious kick at his left side. He put his *main gauche* in position and let the cat-man impale his own leg on the big knife. The beast didn't make a sound; it just pulled its leg free by twisting to the side. It landed awkwardly but quickly got its balance and began to circle looking for an opening.

Delno realized that the first creature had also risen and, even though he could clearly see about two feet of gut hanging out of the large gash he had opened in its middle, it was up and moving. It launched itself at him; the heavy blade came around before he could get his blade up to block and hit him in the left hip. Fortunately, he had been practicing and the energy shield he had managed to get into place, though weak, did prevent the vicious cut from opening a huge wound, though the impact still hurt—a lot. He stabbed out with his *main gauche*, but the cat-man was quick enough to avoid the blade this time.

The second beast hadn't been idle. It had circled around behind him and was just launching itself in an attack when there was a deafening roar and Geneva leaped first, as Jason, who has just arrived also, yelled, "Behind you!"

Geneva landed heavily on the cat-man. She had put her front feet as close together as she could, one above the other, and as her claws sunk in and came out of the creatures back, she gripped and pulled her feet apart, ripping the thing in half. This time it didn't get up. The first cat-man turned to help its comrade and lunged at Geneva. Geneva twisted her head and ducked under a sword cut that would have cloven a man in two and closed her powerful jaws around the creature's torso. She bit down hard, and the creature struggled for a second and then went totally slack. She spit it out as if it tasted foul.

There was a gout of flame on the other side of the camp, and Geneva said, "Gina has just finished off the last of them. There were two others; they attacked Rita. The other Dragon Riders were ignored."

"Interesting," he replied, "Any idea what these things are? They obviously aren't men, and even though I have never seen a Rorack, I am guessing these aren't of that species, either."

"The only thing I know about them so far is that they taste foul, and having the beast in my mouth has left my tongue strangely numb."

Once they were all assembled in the center of camp, and the guard had been doubled around the perimeter (the men had had to make room for the dragons because they absolutely refused to leave their partner's sides). Nat, with Delno's help, began examining the bodies. There were only three, since one had been reduced to little more than ash by Gina. Those remaining were badly mauled, but Nat had insisted that even the parts of the one Geneva had rent asunder be brought into the light to be examined.

They were indeed feline in appearance. They were covered in brown fur everywhere except on their palms and the pads of their feet. The curious gait came from their legs being more like a cat's. At first, they appeared to have their knees bent the wrong way, but that was because the feet were greatly elongated and the actual knees were much higher up near the hips, like a four-legged animal. The strong thigh muscles and overall shape of the leg explained why the creatures could jump so far. Their arms were fairly man-like, but they had retractable claws in their fingers. Though their ears were set on the side of their heads, they were up higher than a man's ears and they were pointed. Nat couldn't be sure now that they were dead because the pupils had totally relaxed, but he guessed that they had elongated pupils, also. They certainly had the mouth configuration. The upper lip was split up to the nose, and they had pointed canines. The jaws were slightly protruding so that they would be able to use the teeth effectively as weapons. The rest of the dentition was also similar to a feline and obviously made for a meat diet.

"This is quite interesting," Nat remarked. He pulled something out of the mouth of the creature he was examining and held it up in the light. It was a leaf of some kind.

"What is it?" Winston asked.

"I can't be completely certain because it's been chewed, but if it is what I think, it explains much."

He took the leaf closer to the fire and examined it more closely. He washed it off carefully and finally, to the amazement of all, he put it in his own mouth. He quickly spit it out and rinsed his mouth with water.

Then he said, "Yes, that explains it." At the confused looks around him, he said, "Oh, I'm sorry, I tend to get lost in my own thoughts and forget to explain myself. This leaf, and I have found evidence of it in the mouths of all of the creatures, is an anesthetic. It can be crushed and used topically to relieve local pain. However, if chewed, it causes a system-wide deadening of pain and gives the user a great deal of endurance and a sense of invulnerability. It isn't widely used for two reasons. One; it tends to make the user ignore wounds that should incapacitate him; it makes him hard to kill, but more prone to suicidal headlong charges."

Brock said, "That would explain why both Rita and I had to hack and stab that creature we killed so many times. I was beginning to think that if we cut it to pieces the pieces would get up and attack us again."

Delno added, "I gutted the first one that attacked me, and it just got up and came back for more."

Winston looked at the healer and said, "You said there were two reasons the herb isn't more widely used."

"Oh, yes," Nat replied, "it's rare in these parts, especially in leaf form like this. The leaves lose a lot of their effectiveness if dried. It is grown in the extreme south of Horne and then processed, so that the extract, which still isn't as effective as the fresh whole leaves, can be kept for later use. In its processed form, it's hideously expensive. I keep a small amount, but I use it only sparingly." He paused, looking at the creatures, lost in his thoughts for a moment. Then he said, "These creatures had enough fresh leaf in their mouths and stomachs to kill a human being; it's a wonder they could even function."

"Even so," Jason asked, "how did they expect to complete their mission and get out of camp?"

"Obviously, they didn't expect to get out," Delno said. "They had to expect to be killed by the dragons once they had finished murdering me and Rita. It was a suicide mission."

"If it was a suicide mission," Winston replied, "then whoever sent those creatures will most likely be watching to see if they succeeded." He turned to Delno and said, "If they see Geneva and Fahwn in the air, then they will know that they failed."

# CHAPTER 44

THE PASS LOOMED ahead of them. The sun was low on the horizon, so the canyon was completely dark and forbidding. The Troop had halted about two hundred yards shy of the mouth of the passage. Leera and Gina spiraled down and landed about fifty yards from the front of the column. The Riders quickly dismounted and joined the two officers sitting on horseback. There were no other dragons in evidence.

The officers dismounted, and Brock spoke to the lieutenant, "I hope you know what you are doing, Delno."

"Well, if not, I won't have long to regret it," he said, using a little gallows humor to relieve his own tension.

"I'd feel a lot better if you were in the air on Geneva rather than getting ready to climb that damn pass and scout around on foot," Brock replied.

"We've already discussed this, my friend," Delno responded. "They expect that Rita and I are dead, so we have to keep our dragons out of sight. We need to scout the pass from the top and can't do it from the air because they will be watching for that. Even in Corice, where almost everyone is a mountaineer, I am considered better than most when it comes to climbing. Also, I have been involved in quite a few battles in terrain just like this. I'm the logical choice to go."

"I know all of that," Brock retorted, "and I agree in principle, but that doesn't mean I have to like it."

Delno slapped the smaller man on the shoulder affectionately and said, "None of us like it, Brock. Did you spot anyone watching us as you flew up?"

"Aye, I saw two on the left ridge and Jason spotted two on the right. I don't think there are any more; there just isn't enough cover up there.

Delno turned and nodded to Winston before turning to Sergeant Winslow and "ordering" him to have the men take a quick break and then make camp for the night.

The men, including Delno and Sergeant Smith, headed pell-mell for the rocks as if they hadn't had a chance to relieve themselves all day. After a few moments, the men began to return to the wagons, while the two dragons took off to scout the pass ahead.

By the time all of the confusion had settled down and the dragons were more than two hundred feet off the ground, Sergeant Smith and Delno had reached a small trail that led some ways up the toward the top of the canyon wall. They knew perfectly well that the men waiting in ambush would expect the dragons to scout the canyon and conceal themselves when Brock and Jason flew overhead. However, not doing so would probably alert them to the fact that the Troop knew about the ambush. The whole disorganized scene of men running off to relieve themselves then returning by ones and twos while the dragons were taking to the air was just to hide the fact that two of them didn't return to the camp site.

Delno stopped the sergeant before he could put his foot on the trail and said quietly, "Before we take another step, there is one thing I need to know."

The sergeant asked, "What's that?"

"What the devil is your first name? I've never heard anyone refer to you as anything other than Sergeant Smith."

The man both laughed and said, "It's Ambrose."

Delno said, "Ambrose?"

"Now you know why I don't go by my first name, and why I can fight so damn well." After a slight pause, he added with a smile, "My friends call me Smitty."

"Well, Smitty, let's go see what we can see."

They took the path as far as it went, which was about three quarters of the way up and half way along the pass, but on the outside of the ridge. After that, they had to climb for real. Smitty was impressed with Delno's climbing skills. Even though Delno frequently stopped to wait for the man, he was hard pressed to keep up. Delno was careful to keep track of where they were and where the hand and foot holds could be found, since they would have to climb back down in the dark, and Smitty didn't have the advantage of his enhanced night vision. Fortunately, Delno had also brought rope which he'd carried, even on horseback, coiled around his waist; it was now looped over his shoulder.

There was about an hour of daylight left when they reached the ridge. They found a rock outcropping, about the only place to hide on the ridge, and hunkered down there, since they would need to wait for darkness because cover on the ridge was so sparse.

Delno spoke to Geneva, who was hiding along with Fahwn and Rita about three miles back from the rest of the company. "Tell Rita that I am on the ridge."

"She says to be careful; she doesn't like this, and neither do I, for that matter."

"I know, Dear Heart, but we need to know what to expect before we place the other men in danger. Did Brock see anything?"

"No, but Leera did. There are about thirty men on each side of the canyon. They tried to hide their presence by huddling under tarps the color of the ground. Leera could see their heat and reported them to Brock. He flew a little lower and could just make out the edges of the camouflage."

He was thoughtful for a moment and then asked, "What kind of weaponry do they have?"

"Dear One," she sounded annoyed, "you know that heat vision doesn't work that way. All she could see was the heat of their bodies. That's why she couldn't get a more accurate count. The weapons are the same temperature as the surrounding objects and aren't distinguishable from them."

"Yes, I'm sorry, Love, you've explained this to me before; I was just hoping that she might have seen something else."

"Be thankful it was late afternoon and the ground had cooled, or you might not have any information at all."

He sat silently waiting for darkness. When the sun finally set and night fell, he and Smitty went in search of their enemies. They crept from their hiding place and someone off to their right said, "Whew, it's good to be out from under that damned cover."

He and the sergeant both froze. They weren't more than ten yards from the man who had spoken. Someone else said in whisper, "Quiet, you idiot, sound carries off of these rocks, and that canyon acts just like a megaphone; if the men in the camp don't hear you, the dragons will!"

Delno and Smitty continued to lay perfectly still, waiting for the men to move away. After half an hour, two more men arrived. These two relieved the first pair on watch. The voice that had originally whispered for quiet said, "You'll be relieved at dawn; if you see anything, one of you hightail it to the main camp and let us know, but keep it quiet."

Another voice answered in an annoyed whisper, "You don't have to tell us our job; we know what we're doing."

Two of the men walked away, but the two who remained sat down to watch the pass.

Delno realized that they would either have to sneak away right under the men's noses, or deal with them. If they dealt with them, the fact that he and Smitty had been there would be obvious when their relief showed up at dawn. He silently signaled Smitty to crawl away. They were nearly a hundred feet from the guards before they stood and moved more quickly towards the ambush point.

They reached the center of the canyon, and Delno could see the enemy camp. Many of the men were sleeping on the open ground. He signaled Smitty to wait while he lay down and inched forward on his belly. There was a slight gully that ran almost to the center of the camp. It wasn't much, but if he stayed low and moved slowly, he could get quite a ways without being seen. As he got close, he found that several men were filling one gallon jars with oil from larger vessels. Once a jar was full, they stuffed a rag in the opening and then set it down and repeated the process. He slid forward several more feet until he could see the edge of the canyon. The men were stacking the filled jars at the precipice. He had seen enough; he began backing up in the direction he had come.

Once he had rejoined Smitty, they began stealthily heading back to the point where they could climb to the trail. They avoided the sentries and made their way down the rocks. It was hard going, and often Delno had to actually take Smitty's foot and place it in a hole in the rock, so the man could find the footholds, but they eventually reached the path and trotted back to camp.

"Yes, light the rags and drop them over the edge on us," Winston replied to the information that Delno and Smitty had brought back. "Especially since the road through the canyon is just gravel covered with tar. The oil itself will splash and burn some men, and those who aren't hit directly will be burned when the oil lights the tarred surface."

"The thing I don't understand is; how do they expect to deal with the dragons?" Jason asked. "They know we're here, and they have to know that we won't sit idly by and watch our comrades get burned alive."

"I've a feeling that they have something they think will be effective against the dragons." Delno replied.

"We still have the advantage of surprise on our side," Brock replied. "They think we have only two dragons; they are *assuming* that Rita and Delno are dead."

"So, Handsome, what's the plan then?" Rita asked.

"The only one that makes sense," he answered.

# CHAPTER 45

ALL FOUR RIDERS were mounted on their dragons. The sun would be up soon: already they could see the light on the horizon. Delno carried his bow and a large quiver of arrows; he'd had more arrows made before leaving Orlean, but he'd hoped they wouldn't be needed. The dragons crouched and spread their wings, ready to take off. Winston signaled them that the men were ready, and Delno gave the signal to take flight.

The plan was quite simple; because of the devastating ambush the enemy had devised, Delno and Winston had decided that they simply would not enter the canyon, but would engage on their own terms and in their own time. They would attack the ridges just before dawn's light. The dragons would make their first pass using their heat vision to aim. After that, there should be enough fire on the ridge to see quite clearly.

Delno was certain that the enemy had something to fight against the dragons with, probably some magic user, so he would stay aloft and watch for anyone gathering power, while using his bow to cover the other dragons.

As a final fall back plan, the troopers had spent the night entrenching themselves in case any of the enemy got off the ridge and attacked the camp.

The dragons got the altitude they needed, and Brock signaled that they were ready. None of them liked the idea of flaming the enemy this way, but they had been left with no other choice: the enemy had chosen the rules of engagement, and the Riders were simply playing by them.

Brock, since he and Leera were more experienced, took the left ridge himself, and Jason took the right; Rita would fly in after Jason had made his first pass, so that the two dragons wouldn't get in each other's way. Delno watched as Brock and Jason began their run. The dragons angled their flight so they would pass over the largest number of heat signatures they could, and then they swooped down to about twenty feet off the deck. Flame erupted from their mouths as they passed over. The first men were caught mostly unaware and they died quickly, but as the dragons got farther along, many men, alerted by the dying screams of their comrades, tried to get out of the way; most were unsuccessful.

Then Delno noticed a powerful energy source on the left ridge. He had Geneva angle towards it while he nocked an arrow. There was fire everywhere, and some of the containers of oil began to explode from the intense heat. The mage on the ground was momentarily distracted while he moved to a safer place; Delno followed and began taking aim as the man began conjuring. Instinct told him to put a shield in front of the mage, so he held his fire while he did so. Energy shot out from the mage and hit the shield. The shield stopped whatever the mage was throwing at Brock, but that alerted the man to the presence of another magic user, and he began to look around. Delno was so close now that he could feel the heat of the fire. Brock had done well at the terrible task. Nearly every other man on the ridge was dead or dying and most of the oil that they had was now pouring all over their own position, increasing the amount of flame in the area.

On the other ridge, Jason hadn't done quite so well, but he'd still done a lot of damage. A few men were standing unharmed, and much of the oil had not been set ablaze. Just when the men still alive and unhurt on the right hand ridge thought they had gotten off lightly, Rita and Fahwn made their pass. The men scrambled for what cover they could find as the dragon spewed death at them. As Fahwn finished and began to pull up, more oil casks began to explode.

Delno could actually see the magic user's face now, and he watched as the man became enraged and began raising energy while following Fahwn's flight path. Delno drew the bow and fired. The arrow hit him right in the chest and went completely through. He crumpled and the energy he had been gathering went awry, hitting the last cask of oil, which exploded engulfing his body in flames. Delno looked to the opposite ridge and saw only fire. The battle was over.

He called a halt just as Brock got into position to make another pass.

"*Leera wants to know why we are not attacking again,*" Geneva relayed.

"*Because there is nothing left to attack. I'm not even sure there is anyone left alive to interrogate.*"

As if to punctuate his words, another cask of oil exploded on the right ridge.

Fahwn relayed that she and Gina had each found and captured a survivor; they were the sentries on the right ridge. Their dawn relief had never gotten the chance to change places with them. They were the only men from the enemy camp left alive.

The stench of burning oil and flesh was making Delno nauseous. He said to Geneva, "*Let's find some cleaner air, Dear Heart. Head back to camp.*"

Geneva said nothing as she complied.

Winston came running up as they landed. The fires on the ridge were clearly visible. The Captain saw the look in Delno's eyes, the same look that was reflected in the eyes of the other three riders, and said, "It is done then." It wasn't a question.

One of the men who had accompanied his commander said, "But, they haven't been gone more than half an hour!"

Sergeant Smith rounded on him and snapped at the man, "Close your yap and secure those prisoners."

The two prisoners presented no problem: they were still in shock, partly from being snatched up by dragons and flown down off the ridge, but mostly from the horror they had just witnessed.

# CHAPTER 46

PALAMORE WAS THE name of both the country and the capital city. The city itself was huge: bigger than Larimar by at least half. The streets were crowded with all manner of people, including soldiers. Delno wondered that the city guard could keep order with so many people about. Of course, the soldiers weren't on leave, or even pass. The country was at a state of declared war and all of the soldiers were busy with preparations for such.

It had only taken four more days to reach the city once they had gotten through the pass. The four Riders had decided that they would send word of their presence, but would bivouac with the Troop until summoned to the palace, which was at the heart of the city. Technically, they shouldn't have to do so, but it was a courteous gesture.

They soon found out that it was also prudent. Two other Riders had shown up earlier in the week and declared that they, and the entire group from Orlean, had been destroyed at the pass, and the pass to Ondar was now held by men from Llorn. Apparently, they had neglected to check on their men, and didn't know that the only two survivors of the troops that had been sent to ambush the Ondarians were now *guests* of the very people they were supposed to have killed, and both men were being quite forthcoming about everything they knew concerning the preparations for war in Llorn; unfortunately, what they knew wasn't much. However, the two Dragon Riders, both younger men who had trained under Simcha, informed the rightful rulers of Palamore that Simcha was now regent of the entire area, and that they should prepare to either be ruled or destroyed by dragon fire.

If Delno, Geneva, and their companions had simply flown to the palace, they might have gotten arrows through the chests before they could have been identified.

Brock was nearly beside himself with anger at Simcha, but Delno had expected as much. Simcha was most likely working with, or for, the person, or persons, responsible for the trouble in Horne. What they didn't know, and needed to know quite badly, was how many other Riders had joined the plot. Also, it would be nice to know the number and strength of any magic users they had working with them. They would have to have at least one powerful mage working nearby; most likely in Llorn. After all, those cat-men hadn't evolved on their own in the last few years.

Delno was interrupted in his musings by a messenger from the palace. The presence of the Riders was requested at once. He put on his best shirt and pants and joined the others in front of the large command tent Winston had been given when he'd arrived, just after the Captain had received his letter of promotion and been placed in command of four full companies of men.

Colonel Winston Eriksson grasped Delno's arm and said, "We may not see each other again before this is over, so, good luck to you, my friend." Then he turned to the other Riders and said, "My men and I owe you our lives; good luck and good fortune to you all."

Because the Palace was in the middle of the city, and the courtyard there was adequate to hold at least two dragons comfortably with room for the others on the walls, and since they felt it would be foolish to be away from the dragons, they had decided to fly to the meeting. As they mounted up and took off, all of the men of Ondar, but especially those from Orlean, cheered them. It was only about a mile and half to the palace, so the flight was quite short. Delno had Jason land first since he was well known here. As Gina flew up onto the wall to make way for the next dragon, Brock had Leera land, since he was also familiar with the palace and its inhabitants. Rita was next, and Delno couldn't help but notice how stunning she looked in her red tunic and black pants sitting astride the neck of the red dragon.

Once Fahwn was perched on the wall with the others, he and Geneva landed. It was an impressive show of dragon power with the leader landing last, and the locals were suitably awed by the spectacle. It also served another function: as the last to land, Geneva was the only dragon on the ground, with the others perched on the palace walls. This put her in a protective ring of dragons who could breathe fire if any hostile dragons showed up while they were here.

As Delno joined the others, a group of five people came out to meet them. At their lead was a tall, beautiful woman who he guessed was in her mid-forties; Delno thought it safe to assume she was the queen. He shouldn't have been surprised, but walking right behind her and to her left was Nassari. There were two soldiers for each member of the other party. The three soldiers in the lead stopped out of reach of swords, but close enough to use the spears they were carrying. The queen looked annoyed at the soldiers and simply elbowed her way through them and walked right up to Brock.

She took both of his hands in hers and said, "It's good to see you, my old friend. It's been far too long since you were last here."

Brock smiled and said, "Events of the world have conspired to keep me away. Even now my stay here will be brief, I'm afraid."

"So it would seem," she replied.

Brock turned to the rest of the Riders, "This is my former student, Rita. You already know Jason, since you sent him to find me." He allowed just the barest hint of annoyance into his voice when he said that, but Delno noticed the Queen raised one eyebrow almost imperceptibly in acknowledgement of the rebuke. "And this," he went on as if no subtle communication had occurred between them, "is the leader of our group, Delno Okonan of Corice."

Then he turned to the group and said, "This is Carol Lark Moreland Glenmore, Queen of Palamore."

Brock had told Delno to watch very closely while interacting with these people because the slightest shift in facial expression would speak louder than their words. If that were the case, the shocked look on the Queen's face when Brock introduced him as their leader was like shouting. She quickly got herself under control and said, "Most people just call me Lark."

They were quickly hustled into the palace and escorted to a room where they would have privacy for their meeting. Nassari managed to place himself at Delno's side. He whispered to him, "See me when this meeting is over; I have a letter for you from your mother." The Queen cast a subtle look their way and Nassari quickly resumed the place assigned to him.

The guards left the room, and they sat quietly while several servants poured drinks for everyone. Then the servants left the pitchers on the table, and closed the doors behind them as they left.

The Queen was interested in all of the events that had led up to them coming to Palamore. Delno was just glad that she didn't want to hear the story of him bonding with Geneva. Once they had told her their story, she sat back for a few minutes and simply digested the information.

Finally she said, "Things have not gone so well here in the capital city. The betrayal of Simcha and those Riders who follow him has the whole advisory staff in an uproar. Some have already called for a no-confidence vote in the council."

At Delno's look of confusion, Brock added, "In Palamore the throne is passed on through lineage, but the council of advisors has the right to a no-confidence vote that would force the king and queen to pass the throne on to their successors."

Lark sighed heavily; for a member of the Palamore royal line, it was the equivalent of weeping uncontrollably. She said, "I might even be tempted to step down, except that there is no clear successor. Stepping down would put the succession up to another vote of the council. With everything else that is going on right now, the country would be thrown into anarchy and our enemies would simply walk in and take over. By the time those fools wake up and realize what they are doing to themselves, it will be too late."

Delno was about to ask how many advisors were still loyal, but he was interrupted by the sound of dragons roaring and bells pealing out a warning. The Riders expressions went blank for a few seconds and then Delno announced, "There are dragons and Riders flying in." To the Queen he said, "I would like to talk with them; make sure your men don't precipitate any aggression." To Brock and the other Riders he said, "I guess it's time to earn our keep; let's get into the air."

Delno had gotten used to being obeyed, so he didn't wait for anyone to confirm his orders; he simply got up and strode toward the door of the chamber. The Queen was unused to taking orders from anyone, but his abrupt departure left little else for her to do.

As he walked back to the courtyard, he contacted Geneva. "*How many are there, Love?*"

"*Three, and the harsh Rider is not with them. The others in our group and myself have all taken flight; we will land one at a time and collect you so that the ones in the air can provide cover.*"

*"I would much prefer to get their riders on the ground,"* he replied. *"It is just too easy for this to get out of control if we are all mounted and ready for a fight."*

*"They do not appear to be interested in landing,"* she responded. *"They are confused at finding us here, but they are ready for a fight; they have filled their flame bladders already."*

"Damn," he looked at Brock walking beside him, "Geneva says the newcomers have already prepared their flame."

"Leera relayed the same message to me," he replied. "How do you want to handle this?"

"I'd prefer to talk with them before we all start killing each other."

"I hope they are agreeable to that," Brock answered.

Delno lengthened his stride. The other two men did the same, and Rita had to almost trot to keep up.

Once in the courtyard, Geneva was the last to land. The others circled in a pattern that prevented the newcomers from getting close enough to be a threat. Delno deliberately took his time, double checking his saddle and the security straps as if this were just another scouting patrol, and he had all the time in the world.

"What is he doing?" one of the Queen's advisors asked.

"Making them wait, obviously." The reply had come from Nassari, who had also followed them to the courtyard. "Those other Riders have shown up here like they are in charge. They expect us to hop-to-it and attend to what they have to say. Delno is deliberately taking his time to show them that *he* is the one in charge here." Nassari was obviously impressed with his friend.

The Queen said nothing but allowed just the barest trace of a smile to show on her lips.

Delno finished checking his equipment and then untied his Dragon Blade from where it was secured on the saddle. He fastened it to his belt and then drew the blade and checked it also. The soldiers in and around the central courtyard took immediate notice. Someone whistled appreciatively. Delno then put the blade back in the scabbard and mounted Geneva with slow deliberate movements.

Though the other three dragons wouldn't let the newcomers close enough to be dangerous, Delno had relayed to them through Geneva to let the hostile Riders watch the show.

"Sure you don't want to go to the privy before we leave? Perhaps you could take a little nap so that you will be fresh for the negotiations?" she asked sarcastically.

"You know perfectly well why I took so long to mount up."

"Yes, you explained it to me. I just hope it doesn't have the opposite effect from what you were looking for." She pushed off, and the palace quickly fell away behind them. As she leveled off, she continued her thought, "We are facing three fully mature dragons, and I have no flame. I don't like being the weak link in the chain."

He reached in front of the saddle and patted her neck, "You aren't, Love, you definitely aren't."

"They are already trying to contact me, Dear One. Should I answer?"

"No," he responded. "We will answer in our own time. Tell Brock to back off a bit; he's supposed to protect us, but I don't want it to look like he's protecting us."

After surveying his Riders and adjusting their positions relative to himself, he told Geneva to tell the leader of the other Riders to land.

"Besides calling you several unkind names, he has refused to land. He says that we are trespassing, and if we do not leave immediately, they will attack us." Geneva sounded nervous.

"Tell him that if he wishes to talk, he is to land in the field to the south. If he wishes to attack, he should shut up and do so." Then he added, "Once you have relayed that message, refuse to relay any further communication. If he wants to talk to me, he will do it on the ground."

The other Rider's face turned bright pink as his dragon relayed the message. He stared into Delno's eyes as their dragons circled. After several moments, the other Rider looked at the field Delno had indicated as a landing place. Delno knew he had scored a point even before the man gave the signal to fly there.

Once over the field, the other Rider's dragon tried to relay another message, but Delno had Geneva block her out. He then signaled that the newcomers were to land first. Again, they circled while the other Rider tried to get Delno's party to land. Again, Delno won the contest, as the man and his companions spiraled down to the field.

Delno landed next, over Brock's objections. The leader of the other Riders started to walk toward him. At a signal from Delno, Geneva bellowed a warning and the man stopped and waited. Delno deliberately kept them waiting while the rest of his group landed and dismounted, one at a time.

Then, with the other riders standing about forty yards away, Delno and his group advanced until they were half way between the dragons on either side; only then did he signal for the newcomers to advance. Without hesitating, the other three Riders obeyed.

Delno said to Brock and Rita, through the dragons, "Good, we've established who is in charge here." They all nodded agreement. Rita was smiling brightly. Knowing her attitude toward anything that Simcha might have his hand in, Delno had Geneva relay to her, "We haven't won any real victories yet. Please remain discreet." Her lips puffed as she pouted, but she nodded.

As the other Riders got close, their leader said, "Simcha, the Regent of this territory, has demanded. . . ."

Delno cut him off, "Simcha is in no position to demand anything. It is you who are trespassing on the sovereign soil of Palamore. If Simcha wishes to refute that, he should show his cowardly face and do so. If you throw your tiles with his, you are likely to find the stakes of the game to be more than you bargained for."

None of the three seemed to understand why this was going so badly for them. They were all young. Brock had told him that none of them had been riders for more than two decades.

Delno continued, "You thought us destroyed between Palamore and Orlean, yet here we are. You also thought your little ambush had destroyed the soldiers we escorted, but if you fly back to that pass, you'll find the ridges that overlook that canyon blackened and those of your force not completely turned to ash are food for the vultures and crows. I do not take to any cause lightly, and I don't abandon my friends. As Simcha found out in Orlean, I am extremely hard to kill and full of surprises."

All three of the men looked as if they had been gut-punched. Finally, the leader spoke again. "There were over sixty men at that canyon," he said.

"Yes," Delno replied before he could add more, "over sixty men. They didn't die gloriously, or with honor; they simply burned alive. Many of them perished before they even had a chance to know what killed them; those who were missed by the dragon fire burned when the oil they had planned to pour down on our troops exploded from the heat. The mage you sent to deal with the dragons died just as quickly as the rest. It only took us about a quarter of an hour to secure the pass."

The three young Riders were stricken; one looked like he might actually be sick. Delno added, "That's the reality of the war you have started, boy. Those men died the same way they had planned for our troops to die, horribly, by fire!"

The young Riders looked confused. Delno was about to add more when the dragons again started roaring. At Geneva's direction, he looked to the east and could see two more dragons flying towards them. They were a ways off still, but they would not be long getting there.

"Now we'll see who is the coward," the young leader scoffed. "Simcha will put paid to your account, upstart."

Both groups turned and ran back to their dragons. Geneva did that same hopping-flying move as before and landed right in front of Delno, so he was the first one off the ground. Brock was second, but two of the newcomers took off together. Brock and Delno circled over Gina and Fahwn protectively while their Riders mounted.

As Fahwn was gaining altitude, the young leader of the original three hostiles dove at her, obviously intent on attacking. They were less then thirty feet from their target and moving fast. Suddenly the attacking dragon's head was whipped back and her whole body flipped forward, breaking her neck and crushing her rider. As the dragon fell, her flame bladder ruptured and a gout of flame shot out under pressure; however, once the pressure was low enough for the air to get inside it, the bladder exploded and blew the rider and saddle off and nearly decapitated the beast.

They had run into the transparent but solid shield that Delno had put up to protect Rita and Fahwn. He had made the shield especially strong because he had expected the pair to use flame instead of trying to use the beast's talons. Rita, realizing what had happened, looked over and blew him a kiss.

"Tell her to be careful," he told Geneva.

"She says you should take your own advice. She also says that you had best keep your arse in that saddle, or she will personally beat you to within an inch of your life."

"Does she think she can do that with you protecting me, Love?"

"I'll hold you down so she can, Love," Geneva replied.

One of the other young Riders charged directly at him. This time the dragon was obviously trying to get above him to use flame. Geneva beat down furiously with her wings and gained altitude. The other dragon followed. The newcomer was quite fast, and she knew how to fly well.

Geneva was just barely staying ahead of her attacker. Delno began to reach out with his magical senses to find a good power source. What he found was that the attacker was trying to do the same to him as he had done a few moments earlier. He warned Geneva, but had her fly as close to the invisible barrier as possible. Just when the other Rider thought he had fooled them, Geneva slowed and turned toward the other dragon. She then turned almost on her side and reached out with her front talons and raked the other dragon's wing badly. The wounded dragon was able to stay aloft, but there was a hole ripped in her right wing starting just behind the leading edge and ending more than halfway back, and she was bleeding. She wouldn't be able to do much more than land. Delno returned his attention to the rest of the dragons.

The last of the original three newcomers had just flown between Brock and Jason. Leera, being more maneuverable, had avoided any injury, but Gina had been hit on the wing and dropped. The attacker immediately turned his whole attention to catching Brock. Leera had other ideas. She was smaller than her foes, and they mistook that to be a disadvantage. They soon discovered their mistake. Leera was capable of flying circles around the larger dragon. With their whole attention focused on catching Leera and Brock, they had also overlooked one other small fact. Gina wasn't hurt that badly; she was flying a little more slowly because of the pain in her wing, but she was still airborne and dangerous. Leera turned back the way she had come, and her attacker followed. Leera flew about twenty feet under Gina and the newcomers didn't notice what they were flying into until it was too late; then they did the worst thing they could have done. They tried to slow down to avoid Gina's flame. If they had maintained their speed, they might have gotten scorched and lived. However, because they slowed down, they were caught in the blast long enough that the dragon's left wing membrane was burned away almost completely. The dragon and rider spiraled down several hundred feet. As if to remove any doubt about their fate, the stored gas exploded when the flame bladder ruptured as they hit the ground.

Delno told Jason to return to the palace and ordered Rita and Brock to cover his retreat. Gina was hurt, and he didn't want to lose one of his own. Jason relayed that they would be fine, but Geneva bellowed, and Gina complied whether her Rider wanted to or not.

The other two Riders were now close enough that Delno could clearly see Simcha's face. The man was enraged by the scene; clearly, he had thought the battle would go differently. Delno had Geneva relay to Simcha that he wanted to land and talk. Simcha pulled a Dragon Blade from a scabbard strapped to his back. They now knew the whereabouts of the blade that had been stolen from Palamore.

Geneva said, "He says that he has the Dragon Blade that is the symbol of the rulers of this kingdom. He also says that we are trespassing, and therefore our lives are forfeit."

"Relay this to him. Saying it is one thing; making it happen will be something else entirely."

Delno kept his senses completely open so when the other Rider, this one older than the first three, began to draw energy, he was aware of it. He reached out himself and pushed the man the way he had pushed Brock on the practice ground. While the action didn't unseat the Rider, it distracted him while Brock tried to move in. The other Rider wasn't to be taken so easily, though. He avoided Leera's flame and rounded on his attacker.

Simcha had not been idle while Delno was distracted. He charged from above, and Janna tried to flame them. There was no time to avoid the flame, but Delno was able to get a shield up. The flame broke on the shield and curled around them slightly. Geneva pumped her wings harder and gained speed and altitude; having been burned once, she wasn't about to allow her antagonist to get another chance.

Rita and Fahwn made a reckless dive at Simcha trying to score a hit on Janna's wings, but the pair avoided the attack easily, and Janna turned at the last second and nearly got Fahwn instead.

Delno quickly ordered Rita and Fahwn to help Brock and stay out from between him and Simcha. They reluctantly withdrew as Simcha taunted them. Rita almost turned, but Geneva bellowed and Fahwn obeyed. Ever since the Riders had made Delno the leader, Geneva's orders were obeyed by the other dragons.

Simcha appeared disappointed at her withdrawal and began to chase the pair, unwilling to give up a chance to strike out at Rita. It was almost his downfall. As he and Janna turned to chase Rita and Fahwn, Delno and Geneva attacked from above. Janna realized that they were being attacked a second too late. As Janna tried to roll away, both dragons struck out with both front feet and their legs became entangled. Neither of the dragons could use her wings effectively, and they both went into a spin together.

Janna brought her head around as Delno pulled his blade. He had intended to slash at her as she tried to bite Geneva, but then he realized that he was her intended target. She tried to bite him and he shoved the point of his saber into the roof of her mouth. She screamed as the blade bit painfully into her palate. He twisted and wrenched the blade around, feeling it grate against the bone. She screamed again and pulled her head back safely out of reach of his saber.

Geneva used the distraction to get her hind feet up and into her opponent's belly. She knew she would only have one shot at this since the ground was so close. She raked her claws down as she dug her left front claws into the underside flight muscles. Then she pushed off with all of the strength she had in her back legs. She gasped in pain as Janna's claws ripped a two-foot-long gash in her right wing.

Both dragons were able to arrest their fall, but they were only about a hundred and fifty feet off the ground. Since Geneva had severed the muscles on the underside, Janna could not stroke down on that side. The gash that Geneva had torn in her belly was bleeding profusely. She began to glide toward the field below.

Delno could see the injury to Geneva's wing and was able to heal it while remaining in the air. He looked for Brock and Rita and saw that they had done a good bit of damage to the other rider and were forcing him down several hundred yards away.

Delno had Geneva land a little more than fifty yards from Janna. Simcha was dismounted and was desperately trying to heal Janna. Delno could tell that he had closed the gaping hole in her belly, but he was unable to heal the internal damage. He closed enough distance that he could be heard if he shouted, but he still stayed far enough back to be out of range of Janna's flame.

"You can still live through this, Simcha," he called out.

Simcha rounded on him. "I'll kill you for all you've done to me," he yelled as he began stalking forward. "I'll kill you for what you have done to this world."

"I haven't done this to you, Simcha," he responded. "All that has happened is because of your machinations. These things are the direct consequences of your own actions. I am merely the vehicle through which those consequences operate."

"Do you think you are innocent in all of this?" Simcha asked.

"No," Delno replied, "not innocent, just caught up in events that you have precipitated."

Simcha continued to walk forward, blade drawn. "For over seven hundred years I've watched the moral decline of this civilization. I've watched as the rightful rulers have been turned into little more than puppets by parliamentary councils. I've watched the Riders decline from being the guiding force of the world to being little more than parasites who have to attend parties to sing for their suppers."

"Simcha, the Riders are still a guiding force," Delno responded, "but times change, and we must change with them. People have the right to choose how they live."

"What would you know, pup?" Simcha demanded as he advanced another step. "You're as caught up in the moral decline as the rest of these common-born bastards. You talk of honor and what's right, but you're no better than any of the rest of them, you and that little alley cat of yours."

"What is between Rita and me is none of your business. The fact that you are so concerned makes me wonder just what your real motivations are. Do you honestly think that she would be the least bit attracted to you after what you did to her? Those scars will never heal, Simcha; she will never forget, or forgive."

"She'll never get the chance to, either; you've seen to that. Do you think that I'm the whole force behind this? Have you forgotten about what is happening in Horne? There is a storm coming, a firestorm, and it is going to sweep the land clean of all of the debauchery that is so rampant now."

"You can still walk away from this path. I can heal Janna as I've done before, if you will surrender. . . ." Delno didn't get the chance to complete his thought.

"Surrender," Simcha sneered; he was less then ten feet away. "NEVER!" he shouted and, raising the stolen Dragon Blade above his head, he charged.

Delno waited until the last possible second and then simply sidestepped and swung his own blade with all of his strength. Simcha's head left his shoulders so quickly that his body actually took another step before it fell. Janna screamed and tried to lunge at Delno, but Geneva was too quick for the wounded dragon; she jumped and landed on Janna's back, breaking her spine just behind the flame bladder. The older dragon grunted and lay very still, breathing shallowly for a few moments, and then she died.

Fahwn landed and Rita dismounted. She walked over and looked at Simcha's body for several moments. She turned to Delno and said, "I thought I would be happy to see him dead." She paused for a moment, and then added, "I'm not. His death doesn't change anything, and it brings me no comfort, and the death of another dragon," she looked at Janna's body, "even one who has tried to kill us, is not a cause for celebration."

"Part of the reason I started this whole adventure was because I thought that losing a dragon was a tragedy. Geneva's brother had already died before he got a chance to live; her mother wanted to die because she had lost her Rider, and Geneva's egg was stuck inside her body. I remember that I thought that the loss of three dragons was too much tragedy for the world to bear." He looked deep into her eyes and said, "Now I have caused the deaths of three dragons, and I have a feeling the world will not be the same again."

# CHAPTER 47

JANNA AND THE other dragons were just too big to bury, so Rita, Brock, and Delno put Simcha's body on top of hers and the remains of the others with them, and burned them all together. Their dragons had brought all the dead wood they could find in the area, and then Leera and Fahwn used their flame to set the pyre ablaze. They stood silently and watched it burn for a long time.

Later, back at the Palace, they discussed the war with Llorn. The death of Simcha and the surrender of the two remaining Riders wasn't the end of it. There was still a large force on the march toward them. According to the two Riders, they had been set to march three days before and were less than two days out. They thought they were coming to consolidate Simcha's victory.

It was decided that Delno, Rita, and Brock would accompany the army to meet the men of Llorn. Hopefully, when the force from Llorn found themselves out numbered, and also facing three dragons with no dragons of their own for support, they would be willing to talk rather than fight. Jason and Gina, although healed and able to come along, would stay and watch the prisoners as well as act as backup should anything get past Palamore's main force.

The only possible problem was the mage who traveled with the army of Llorn. According to the two Riders, the mage was rather full of himself and thought that he was more than a match for any Rider. They might have trouble with him.

"That reminds me," Delno said, "I am supposed to find Jhren and seek his help. That was my original reason for coming to Palamore."

The Queen looked at him and said, "Jhren? He disappeared the same time the Dragon Blade did. We had assumed that he was involved in getting it out of the palace. Why would you need to see him?"

"Because he was a friend of Corolan, and Geneva's mother told me I should find him and ask him to instruct me in the use of magic," he replied.

"Well," she remarked, "since Simcha had the blade, and he had little love of mages, and even less of Jhren, I think it's a fair bet that the man is dead. Now, if you will all excuse me, I must retire; this has been a very long day."

The King, Norton, had finally put in an appearance. He had been watching one of the serving girls and not paying attention to anything else. He barely noticed when the Queen rose to leave. Delno wasn't impressed with the man. He seemed removed from all that had transpired, but Delno suspected that he was more simple-minded than aloof.

Brock got up and excused himself a few minutes later. He left for his room, but Delno noticed that the direction to Brock's room was the same direction that the Queen had taken.

By that point, the assembly had broken down into little more than a cocktail party, so Delno decided that he would plead fatigue also. He looked for Rita, who had gone to look for food about a quarter hour before. He found her at a buffet table being chatted up by several men; one of them was Nassari.

Rita was delighted to see Delno and immediately took both of his hands in hers and kissed him lightly. While their faces were so close together, she whispered, "The men of this kingdom are absolutely lecherous, and that friend of yours is the worst of them."

"Don't worry, Beautiful," he whispered, "I'll save you. Come to my room."

She raised one eyebrow and looked at him. Then she shrugged and said, "You lead, Handsome, I'll follow."

The men were quite disappointed, though Nassari did wink at him. Then Delno remembered, "Nassari, you still have a letter for me?"

"Oh, yes," Nassari responded, "it's in my room. Since it's in the same direction you are going, and you are taking the reason I was staying here away with you," he indicated Rita, "I may as well walk along and fetch it."

Nassari's room was actually only two doors down the hall from his own. He retrieved the letter and gave it to Delno, who thanked him and moved on quickly before Nassari could get him caught up in a conversation. He had missed his friend, but so much had happened, he just wanted to go to his room and hold Rita while they rested.

Once inside the room, he put the letter down to take off his shirt, and then became totally engrossed in watching Rita peel off her clothing layer by layer. When she was naked, he almost wished there had been more layers; it had been fun to watch.

It wasn't until he woke up about an hour before dawn that he remembered the letter. He got out of bed and called up enough energy to light a candle. "Nice trick, Handsome. I knew you were a handy guy to have around," Rita said.

"I'm sorry," he replied, "I didn't mean to wake you. We have to leave in a few hours, but you still have time to rest a bit, if you like."

"No, when I'm finished with the call of nature I'm going to take a bath. I was hoping I could get you to wash my back."

The palace was well accoutered, so each main guest room had its own bathing room and toilet. Rita headed into theirs and he said, "I'll be in as soon as I've read the letter from my mother."

"I would never get between a boy and his mother," she said as she disappeared through the door.

He opened the letter and read:

My dearest son Delno,

I am not sure why I am writing this letter, but there are things that I have come to feel that you should know, especially now that you have gone away south. It is interesting that this letter will find you in Palamore, since that is where my father's family is originally from. I know that I have told you that I am an orphan, but that is not entirely true. My mother died while giving me life, but my father was still alive when I settled in Larimar.

He couldn't raise me alone, so he left me with his kin. They were vanners, and I was raised in a wagon on the caravan trails. I saw my father several times a year, and my life was actually pretty good, though the work was hard. I loved my father, and I loved my foster parents, but I wanted so much more for my children than the life of a vanner. When

I met your father in Larimar the year I came of age, I married him. He has been good husband and you boys couldn't ask for a better father.

I feel though, that you have more of your grandfather in you than you have of anyone else. Even your good looks come from my father's side of the family. You look so much like your grandfather, though your height, I believe, comes from my mother's side.

My son, I've always told you that my maiden name was Warden, but warden simply means guardian. I took the name to distance myself from that life; my original maiden name, the name of my father, was Moreland. The last time I saw your grandfather, you were three. He even came in and looked in on you. He was so proud of you. He wanted to get to know you, but he had to leave. He didn't know when he would return, and I haven't seen him since.

You bear his grandfather's name. You should look for him when you reach Palamore. Delno, I know this will be hard for you to believe, but it is the truth. Your grandfather is a Dragon Rider; his name is Corolan Delno Moreland.

Delno, I should have told you all of this long ago, but I thought that none of it would ever have bearing on your life. Son, you've never been able to lie to me, and I know there is something you aren't telling me about your reasons for leaving. I feel that you are heading south and will somehow find yourself a part of what I left behind.

There is so much more I would like to tell you about your grandfather, but time is short. Your father will be home any minute, and your friend Nassari must leave with the letter anyway. Perhaps you will return to me soon, my dearest son, and we can actually talk about this.

Your loving mother,

Laura Moreland Okonan

Delno sat dumbstruck for a long time, then he re-read the letter several times. The information just didn't change. Rita called him from the other room, and he went to her. He had her read the letter while he washed her back. When she finished, she, too, was dumbstruck for several moments.

Brock was nowhere to be found this early in the morning. Delno had a funny feeling that actually finding the man too soon might cause some problems, so they went looking for food instead. They were just finishing up with breakfast when Brock came in looking for them. Delno didn't ask where he'd been. He did, however, hand Brock the letter.

The Queen came in and sat down while Brock was reading Laura's correspondence. He arched one eyebrow and glanced in the Queen's direction, and Delno nodded. Brock handed it to the Queen, and she read it. Then her eyes went wide, and she read it again. Finally, she looked at Delno and all she said was, "Welcome home, Cousin."

It had taken a day for the army to march to the field and set up. Brock had traveled with the soldiers and was to act as air support. The plan was simple. Brock would make an impressive display when the advancing forces came out of the pass, and then, if necessary, take out the mage who traveled with the army. Brock wasn't as good magically as some, but he felt he and Leera were up to the task.

Delno and Rita had flown straight to Llorn that same morning, leaving well before dawn, so they would arrive close to first light. They figured that since the entire army of Llorn was now on the move to Palamore, they should stop in and see who was still guarding the kingdom. Also, according to the two Riders still held prisoner in Palamore, who were quite cooperative now that Simcha was dead, Jhren was indeed alive and being held in a cell at a local garrison's jailhouse. They were unclear as to Jhren's part, if any, in the theft of the Dragon Blade. The man was kept drugged to keep him from using his magic to escape. It was thought to be from Jhren's notes that Orson, the mage traveling with the army, had been able to make the cat-men. He wanted Jhren alive so that he could learn more from the man once the campaign was over.

The route that had taken the army of Llorn, just over two thousand men, almost six days to march had only taken Fahwn and Geneva a little over three hours to fly. It wouldn't have taken that long if they had pushed harder, but Delno figured that conserving the strength of the dragons was wise, especially since, if all went well, they would have a passenger on the return trip.

Rather than make a pass to scout the city and risk alerting any soldiers left behind of their presence, they opted to fly straight in using the directions the prisoners had given them. The building was a very long rectangle. Since there was no courtyard, and only one entrance, they landed in front of the massive wooden doors. At first, no one took notice of them. Then a guard realized they weren't part of Simcha's group and raised the alarm. Delno banged hard on the jailhouse doors with the hilt of his *main gauche* and demanded entry. The two guards inside stuck their spears through the peek holes in each door trying to skewer him.

He simply stepped back and said aloud, "Geneva, they seem to be having trouble finding the key."

"Here," she replied, "use mine." She crouched low and drove her talons through the three-inch-thick, iron-bound oak and pulled both doors out of the portal. The two guards inside tripped as they tried to scramble backwards out of the way and fell flat on their backs. Delno stepped across the threshold and glanced down at the guards lying there rigid with fear. He leaned a little closer, and said, "She's a bit like a cat, attracted to movement; I would stay very still if I were you." The two guards shifted only their eyes to glance at each other.

"*Like a cat? Attracted to movement? I resent that.*"

"Sorry, Love," he said. "*It worked, though; they are almost afraid to breathe, much less get up and give me trouble.*"

"*You owe me for that one, Love,*" she responded. "*When this is over and we have time, you are going to take that wonderful brush you bought back in Corice, and we will find a nice river.*"

"*Of course, Dear Heart; we will do just that.*"

"*Besides,*" she added, "*if you can scrub* **her** *back, there's no reason you can't scrub mine.*"

"*And you say you aren't cat-like,*" he retorted.

Geneva growled at his last statement. Since the guards couldn't hear the exchange between Dragon and Rider, they thought she was growling at them. One of them wet himself.

Delno quickly looked around and found a large ring with about a dozen keys on it hanging from a hook on the wall. He grabbed the keys and proceeded down the long hallway, unlocking doors as he went. The first couple of cells were empty, and the next two held men, but not Jhren. The men looked hopeful and asked him to free them. Delno knew that just because the local government was totalitarian didn't mean that everyone being held in a cell was a political prisoner. Ordinarily, he wouldn't like the idea of letting criminals go free, but he was in a hurry, and they might make a bit of a distraction. He simply left the doors open and got out of their way. "Mind the dragon," he called as they headed for the exit. One of them actually laughed out loud at what he thought was Delno's joke, until they all almost ran into Geneva.

Geneva was beginning to find the whole thing somewhat amusing. The prisoners came running up the hall and several squealed like school girls when they saw her. They stood there as still as the two guards who were lying on the floor. Finally, she said to the prisoners, "Well, leave if you are going."

One of the braver men slid along the wall sideways, then inched past her through the portal where the huge doors had been. The others saw that he made it out alive and did the same. One actually stopped long enough to bow slightly and say, "Thank you, ma'am," before disappearing into the early dawn light outside.

Delno opened another door and found an old man lying on a filthy cot. He could barely recognize the man from the description he had. It was Jhren, but he was in sorry shape. He had obviously been starved as well as drugged. He was nearly Delno's height, but probably didn't weigh much over eight or nine stone, and he was as filthy as his surroundings.

One of the other prisoners had followed Delno to Jhren's cell. Delno handed the man the key ring and said, "Unlock the other doors, and then get out of here."

He didn't wait to see if the man had obeyed. He walked to Jhren and knelt down beside him. He put his hand on the old man's forehead and said, "Jhren, can you hear me?" The old man's eyelids fluttered. "I've come take you out of here."

Jhren opened his eyes and looked, but Delno wasn't sure if he could actually focus. The man reached up and grabbed him feebly. Then he smiled and said in a weak voice, "Come to save my life again, huh, Corolan." Then the old mage pulled himself against Delno's chest and began to weep softly.

Delno cradled him for a moment and then said, "Geneva and I are taking you home, old friend." At this point, if the old man wanted to believe he was Corolan, it would hurt nothing to humor him, and it might save time that would otherwise have to be spent explaining.

As he picked up Jhren to leave, Geneva shouted both aloud and in his mind, "Fahwn says that company is coming; time to go, Delno."

He strode quickly out of the cell and down the hall. He could hear shouts coming from outside the jail as he reached the entryway. Geneva pulled her head back out of the portal and turned to face the owners of the voices outside. With Geneva otherwise occupied, one of the guards regained some of his lost courage. He rolled over and wrapped his hand around his spear haft as he started to rise. Delno simply kicked him in the face while he was still on his hands and knees. The sound of the man's jaw breaking was audible even over the din from the street. Then the light outside suddenly got much brighter and men began screaming.

Geneva stuck her head back inside the portal and said, "It really is time to go, Love."

He walked through the portal expecting to see the burned corpses of the men who had been killed. There were no bodies to be seen. As he looked toward the sound of running feet, he saw the last of the guards who had answered the alarm just disappearing around the corner farther up the street. The walls of the stone buildings were blackened about three feet above the height of a man.

"You said you didn't want to kill anyone unless we had to," Rita remarked.

He smiled and began mounting up. The task was a bit more difficult with the semi-conscious man in his arms, but he managed it. The guards had apparently realized they weren't on fire and regrouped. They came around the corner, cautiously this time, with bows. Delno gave the order and the dragons launched themselves into the crisp mountain air. The soldiers fired arrows at them but the missiles merely impacted harmlessly on the shield that Delno maintained until they were out of range.

As the army of Llorn came through the pass, they found themselves facing nearly four thousand troops of the combined forces of Palamore and Ondar. They quickly spread out and formed ranks. Brock made one pass, flaming the grass just out of bow range as a show of force. The men of Llorn waited nervously for their own air support, but, of course, it never came.

At four hours past dawn, a group of a dozen men from the Palamore side advanced under a white flag of parlay. They stopped halfway between the two opposing armies, and Brock landed on the field with them. He, however, remained mounted. They didn't have long to wait before an equal number of men and officers, and one man dressed in robes, came across the field to meet them, also under white a flag.

The man in the robes drew himself up haughtily and said, "We have come to discuss your terms."

The spokesman for the Palamore army said, "Our terms are simple, your entire army will vacate Palamore as quickly as humanly possible; if you do not, your forces will be destroyed."

The man laughed and said, "By this Rider? Or perhaps the youngster who is with him? You forget that we have riders of our own, and you have no mage who is capable of standing up to my skills."

Brock spoke up. "Are you referring to Simcha and the four young Riders he duped into following him? I'm afraid, my overconfident friend, that you are waiting for a wind that will never blow. Simcha and two of his Riders are dead; the other two are, and will remain, *guests* of the kingdom of Palamore."

"You lie," the man hissed.

"Do I?" Brock said as he drew the Dragon Blade. "Do you recognize this?" The mage's eyes went wide, but before he could say anything, Brock went on, "This blade that Simcha so coveted as a symbol of his power was taken from his hand shortly after his head was taken from his shoulders."

The men who had accompanied the mage onto the field stared in shocked disbelief. Some of them looked skyward, hoping against the evidence of their own eyes that Simcha would appear and prove this a lie.

"Don't look to the sky for help," Brock exclaimed. As he did so, two dragons, a red and a bronze rose behind him, though the bronze was without a Rider. "The only dragons you will see there carry no salvation for you, only death if you persist in this course. Your only deliverance lies back on the road by which you came."

The mage sneered, "You are forgetting me, Rider. I am a match for any three of you."

A dry, almost cackling laugh came from the back rank of the Palamore entourage. Then a high-pitched man's voice said, "You always did like to play in front of an audience, Orson. Perhaps this time, though, you should have hightailed your arrogant little arse out of here."

Orson stared wide-eyed as the front rank parted and Jhren, leaning heavily on Delno's arm, stepped forward. The old man's eyes were clear and, though still weak of body, it was obvious that he was quite strong of spirit.

"How did you get here?" Orson asked incredulously.

Jhren laughed at the confused look on his former apprentice's face and said, "Let me introduce you to someone. This young man is Delno," he pointed to the man lending him support, "Corolan's grandson. I met him a few hours ago when he and his dragon opened that jail you put me in like it was made of paper instead of stone. You got so cocky and sure of yourself concerning Dragon Riders you forgot that they fly, huh?" He laughed again, then added to the other men from Llorn, "There is one final condition if you all want to leave safely; my former apprentice stays. It seems I still have a few things to teach him."

Orson sneered at the old mage and said, "I bested you once old man; I can do it again. Do not try me. You may find that I am more than you can handle."

Jhren nodded, "Yes, you bested me. But only because I let my guard down, and you drugged me before I could do anything to stop you. Then you kidnapped me and stole the Dragon Blade. This time though, you will find that I am not drugged, and I will not let my guard down."

Delno could see the magical energy swirling around both of the mages and motioned the others to move back. He stayed by Jhren, lending the old man support. Suddenly, both mages gestured towards each other with their hands while speaking arcane words. The energy force was tremendous and all of the men at the center of the field except Delno and the two mages were knocked to the ground. Delno was saved only because he was so close to Jhren that he was within the area shielded by the old wizard. Leera and Brock were even caught up in the maelstrom of power, though it didn't affect them nearly as badly because of Leera's size and natural resistance to magic.

The energy being expended was tremendous, and Delno was sure that Jhren, in his weakened condition, was beginning to falter. He drew his *main gauche* and threw it at Orson. Orson saw the blade at the last second and diverted enough energy to deflect it. Brock noticed the diversion of the mage's attention, and flame erupted from Leera's mouth. Orson was engulfed. He screamed, but managed to extend the shield he had place before he was consumed. He was blistered and his robes were smoldering, but still he continued his attack on Jhren, though it was greatly diminished, and the old man was now holding his own. Delno reached out with the magic and pushed Orson. That small distraction was the last straw; Orson buckled under Jhren's powerful attack and was crushed. He collapsed to the ground with blood trickling from his nose and mouth; he wasn't breathing.

Jhren straightened himself and said sadly, "Lesson learned."

The commanding officer from Llorn retrieved Delno's *main gauche* and brought it to him. He bowed as he handed the blade over, hilt first. Then he straightened and said, "It will take an hour or more for our men to get organized and start the march back to Llorn." Delno nodded, and then turned and helped Jhren from the field.

# CHAPTER 48

"SO TELL ME, Handsome," Rita asked, "Why did the Queen give the Dragon Blade to Brock? Here they've spent two years looking all over the world for it, and then when they get it back, she gives it away?"

"Well, the blade was a symbol of power. It's a mark that connects the bearer with the position of King or Queen."

"That's what I'm talking about." She sat up and he couldn't help but appreciate how nice she looked with the light satin sheet barely clinging to her breasts. "She gets the damn thing back, and then gives it away?"

He smiled and said, "I'm trying to explain, if you will let me finish." She pouted prettily and he continued, "Why don't you sit just like that while I collect my thoughts and explain it to you?"

She gave him sardonic look and then hit him in the belly with a pillow. The movement caused the sheet to slip down to her waist.

"That's even better," he said.

"You know, people say that women are more attractive with their clothes on, and only immature men prefer them naked."

"What can I say, I'm just a big kid at heart," he responded. "Besides, I think that is just a vicious lie started by prudish ugly women and fostered by impotent men."

"The sword?" she prompted with mock annoyance.

"Oh, yes, that," he responded. "Well, the sword was the symbol of the royal house. When it was still here, the factions in power fought over control of it. Since the King is the rightful heir, and he held the sword, he held the power. Unfortunately, while he's basically a good man, he is an idiot and easily manipulated by his advisors. With the sword gone, the Queen was able to consolidate her power base. She is still opposed by about half of the advisors, but neither side can actually gain full control. With neither side having a power advantage, and Norton having no heir, the monarchy will be placed up for vote when either of the current rulers dies or retires."

"But wouldn't the sword help consolidate a victory for her?" she asked.

"No, not really. You see, she is an heir to my family's line, but that line is actually too far removed from the original rulers. Norton is from the original line." As she opened her mouth to ask a question, he held up his hand, "Don't ask me to explain the lines of succession unless you want to be all week. I've been studying them since we sent the soldiers from Llorn packing three days ago, and I'm still somewhat confused. What it boils down to, though, is this. Norton has no sons or daughters, but he has the right to name his own heir. That heir will have his power, but not his lineage. Unless that heir holds some powerful symbol, such as the Dragon Blade, he or she will have somewhat less authority than Norton himself."

"I don't understand why he doesn't have an heir," she responded. "From what I've seen and been told, he is one of the most lecherous men in the kingdom."

"Well, and this stays strictly between you and me, that is because the Queen has been feeding him an herbal tonic that doesn't stop his amorous tendencies but renders him totally sterile."

The look of disbelief on her face was quite clear.

"Oh, it's true," he said. "Nat discussed it with me. It seems the Queen's physician borrowed some herbs from him to make the formula, not knowing Nat's prowess on the subject."

"She's poisoning him?" Rita was astounded.

"No, she's not poisoning him; the formula is actually good for him. If he hadn't been taking it all these years, he would have burned himself out, the way he carouses. The only negative side effect is sterility."

"But why keep him sterile? If she bore him an heir, wouldn't she be able to govern the child and raise him to be a good king?"

"Possibly, if they didn't produce another idiot. The adage 'like father – like son' is what the Queen is afraid of. You see, where you come from, promiscuity is the accepted norm, but the people take pains to avoid inbreeding. Here, promiscuity is less acceptable, but inbreeding has been regularly practiced to keep the 'royal lines' as 'pure' as possible. According to Brock, the Queen believes that Norton's low intelligence is the result of that inbreeding. In her line, the line my family comes from, inbreeding is much less common. Still, an heir from the two of them would be little more than a toss of the dice as to the child's competency, so the Queen is unwilling to risk the future of the country to such chance. That is why she has been taking the same herbal formula with her husband every morning for years; it has the same drawback, or in this case, advantage, for both sexes."

Rita shook her head as if it hurt. "So why doesn't the Queen just conceive with another man? And don't tell me she hasn't been lying with Brock since he arrived."

"Oh, I believe that she and Brock have been having an affair for years. It's probably the only thing that has kept her sane living here with an idiot husband and a bunch of scheming advisors. As to your question though, she can't have a child now; she's well past the age: she's sixty-three. As to why she didn't do so before, that's actually pretty simple. Before an Heir of the Blood can be confirmed, he or she has to be proven by a dragon." At her puzzled look, he added, "You do realize that dragons can smell your lineage, don't you?"

There was a knock on the door, and once Rita had thrown on Delno's shirt, they opened it, and Brock walked in. He apologized and started to leave, but they asked him to stay. He poured himself a glass of wine and sat in a chair near the bed. Delno then brought him up to speed on their conversation.

"Brock had mentioned it to me, but I didn't realize it was literally true," she replied.

"And here I thought you were really paying attention to my lessons," Brock teased.

"Oh, yes, it's true; that's why Geneva's mother smelled me so carefully and then pronounced me a Rider after she had heard my mother's name. She knew I was Corolan's grandson, and that her daughter was fated to be my Partner."

"I'd forgotten about that part of the story," she said.

"I hadn't," Brock spoke up, "I suspected when I saw your face—you really do look like him—and once I heard that part of the story, I was almost certain. I didn't tell you because at the time there was no point, and I wanted to make sure you had enough training before you found out so you wouldn't get cocky."

Delno smiled at Brock, and then turned to Rita, "Don't feel bad, Beautiful, I'd almost forgotten it, too, until I read my mother's letter. So, anyway, according to tradition, the heir would have to be smelled by a dragon and confirmed as the King's offspring. Since lineage is so important to dragons, no dragon would lie about such a thing. That option just wasn't open to the Queen, and she wants to do what is right for the country, even though it has meant not having children of her own. Lark knows where her duty lies, and she really is a good queen."

"So, why don't the King and Queen just abdicate in favor of a more parliamentary government?" she asked.

"These things take time, my dear. From what I have been able to gather from bits and pieces I've picked up here and there," he looked at Brock and the older Rider nodded, "it was Corolan himself who started subtly manipulating the politics of this and other countries over two thousand years ago to get to the point we are now."

"Corolan? But why? I thought Dragon Riders were not supposed to get directly involved in such things?" she asked.

"Don't misinterpret that; Corolan never directly got involved," Brock said. "He simply made suggestions here and there. He would spend time with the children of royalty and earn their trust, and then be around to advise them occasionally once they had reached adulthood and taken power. People resist change, so what he did was very subtle. He would make suggestions that would take several generations before the actual change he was looking for took place. To the people involved, it seemed like nothing more than a natural progression."

"I still don't understand why he didn't just let the political system evolve on its own, though," she responded.

"I'll let Brock answer that question; he knows the story, and I'm just learning the whole tale." Delno replied.

Brock took over the narration. "Corolan, as you know, was the oldest Rider alive. He was alive when all of the kingdoms and large cities we have now were nothing more than dozens of city-states. Those city-states were ruled by families, houses that controlled them. Then came the Clan Wars. The city-states fought horrendous blood feuds over the slightest provocation. The world hadn't seen war on that scale in a long time. The houses were bankrupting themselves, and people were being slaughtered wholesale. Finally, with the aid of a few Dragon Riders, Corolan among them, two houses were able to take control and declare themselves kings. It looked as if the world would then settle down and have a chance to recover. However, a son from each of the two houses was captured, and their minds were wiped clean and their memories replaced so that they could infiltrate their own families and assassinate the rulers. The two houses were devastated, and, eventually, with the help of Corolan and the other Riders, they managed to relocate to the north. Otherwise, they may have been destroyed completely."

Rita nodded and said, "I remember this lesson: The Exiled Kings."

Brock nodded, "The exiled kings wanted nothing further to do with magic; even the Riders who helped them weren't welcome, but Corolan never gave up on them. He went back as often as he could and checked on how the Northern Kingdoms were doing, and that is what brings us to the last part of the saga of Corolan. He was over three thousand years old, and figured that he wouldn't live many more years than the normal life span of a human being, so he married a young woman he had fallen in love with."

Delno said, "I've got a feeling you are about to tip my world on its side again, my friend."

"Oh, yes," Brock replied, "Your grandmother was a daughter of the royal house of Corice, a direct descendant of one of The Exiled Kings. You are part of Corolan's grand scheme to bring the world under parliamentary rule to prevent something like the Clan Wars from ever happening again. He had hoped that by marrying your grandmother, he could bring Corice into a more active role in Southern politics. Unfortunately, your grandmother died in childbirth and Corolan, partly due to the need for a wet nurse, left your mother with one of his cousins whose wife had just had a baby, but he also figured that no one would look for a child of the royal house of Corice among the vanners. Just when he was beginning to make new connections in the north again and was preparing to present you and your mother to the King up there, everything went sour in Horne, and he ended up dying in the south, instead."

All three companions were silent for several minutes. Finally, Rita asked, "So what does all of this mean for us?" meaning all three of them.

"I don't know," Brock answered.

Delno said, "It means that for now we stick to the original plan. We stay here for a while and recuperate while I train and Geneva matures. Then we settle accounts in Horne, which, I'm still certain, is where all of this trouble has come from in the first place."

He let them digest that for a few moments before he added, "If we survive all of that, then we can decide what we will do about Corolan's grand scheme and his plans to bring home The Exiled Kings."

They considered that for a few moments, and then Rita said, "Well then, since the plans are made, and our survival is not certain, I think it is time for Brock to return to his room, and you to take decisive action right now."

The three friends laughed and Brock got up and walked to the door. As he left, Delno said, "We'll see you at breakfast, my friend." Brock smiled at them as he closed the door.

# About the Author

J.D. **HALLOWELL** has been, among other things, an automotive mechanic, a bouncer, a soldier, a dog trainer, a cowboy, a jeweler, a tow truck driver, a stereo installer, a battery salesman, an after-school program counselor, a psychiatric technician, an EMT, a phlebotomist, a paralegal, a medical coder, a photogra-pher, a self-defense instructor, and a massage therapist. He lives and writes on the Space Coast of Florida.

*A Portrait of the Author with Indie the Wonder Dog and a Hawk*

CPSIA information can be obtained at www.ICGtesting.com
Printed in the USA
LVOW07s0255111115

462015LV00001B/55/P